Praise for Stephen Leather's
bestselling thrillers

'The sheer impetus of his storytelling is damned hard to resist . . . A writer at the top of his game' *Sunday Express*

'As tough as British thriller writers get' *Irish Independent*

'Explores complex contemporary issues while keeping the action fast and bloody' *Economist* on *Dead Men*

'Exciting stuff with plenty of heart-palpitating action gingered up by mystery and intrigue . . . Leather is an intelligent thriller writer' *Daily Mail* on *The Tunnel Rats*

'As high-tech and as world-class as the thriller genre gets' *Express on Sunday* on *The Bombmaker*

'A whirlwind of action, suspense and vivid excitement' *Irish Times* on *The Birthday Girl*

'An ingenious plot, plenty of action and solid, believable characters, wrapped up in taut, snappy prose that grabs your attention by the throat . . . A top-notch thriller which whips the reader along at breakneck speed' *Yorkshire Post* on *The Long Shot*

'A gripping story sped along by admirable uncluttered prose' *Daily Telegraph* on *The Foreigner* (previously *The Chinaman*)

STEPHEN LEATHER

The Foreigner

previously published as

The Chinaman

HODDER

First published in Great Britain in 1992 as
The Chinaman by Hodder & Stoughton
An Hachette UK company

2

This paperback edition published 2017

A CIP catalogue record for this title is available from the British Library

ISBN 978 1 473 66209 4

Typeset in Plantin Light

Printed and bound by Berryville Graphics, USA

Hodder & Stoughton policy is to use papers that are natural, renewable
and recyclable products and made from wood grown in sustainable forests.
The logging and manufacturing processes are expected to conform to the
environmental regulations of the country of origin.

Hodder & Stoughton Ltd
Carmelite House
50 Victoria Embankment
London EC4Y ODZ

www.hodder.co.uk

For Nuala

They made an odd couple as they walked together through the store, the girl and the old woman. The girl was beautiful, quite, quite beautiful. Her sleek black hair hung dead straight down to the middle of her back and it rippled like an oily tide as she wandered through the racks of dresses and blouses. She was tall and slim and wore tight green cord trousers and cowboy boots and a brown leather bomber jacket with the collar turned up. She moved like a model, smoothly and controlled, as if used to being watched. The men that followed her with their eyes had no way of knowing where she came from other than that she was Oriental. She could have been Thai or Chinese or Korean but whatever she was, she was beautiful and that was all they cared about. Her cheekbones were high and well defined and her skin was the colour of milky tea and her eyes were wide and oval and she had a mouth that seemed to be in a perpetual pout. Every now and then something would catch her eye and she would take a dress or a blouse off its rack and hold it up and then shrug, not satisfied, before replacing it. Her hands were long and elegant and the nails were carefully painted with deep red varnish.

By the girl's side walked a gnarled old woman, a head shorter and an age older. Her face was wrinkled and pockmarked like chamois leather that had been left for too long in the sun. Her hair was grey and dull and cropped close to her head and her eyes were blank and uninterested in what was going on around her. When the girl asked her opinion on an item of clothing she would barely look at it before shaking her head and then she'd drop her gaze and concentrate on the floor. She wore a thick cloth coat and a faded scarf and she kept her hands thrust deep into her pockets despite the warmth of the store.

It was a Saturday in January and the weather outside was bitterly cold, piles of dirty slush squashed up against the kerb and wisps of white vapour feathering from the mouths of passers-by. The girl looked over the top of a rack of imitation fur coats topped with a sign that promised thirty per cent off, and through the streaked window. She shivered and didn't know why. She'd lived in London for as long as she could remember, and unlike her mother she was well used to the British climate. It was as if someone had walked over her grave, or the grave of her ancestors.

She took one of the coats and held it against herself. A middle-aged man in a fawn trench coat waiting outside the changing rooms with a carrier bag full of packages looked at her and smiled and nodded his approval. She ignored him and studied the coat. The old woman snorted and walked off. The girl looked at the price tag but even with the sale discount she realised she couldn't afford it.

She looked through the large glass window again at the bustling crowds fighting to get into the department store across the road. She wanted to join them and go hunting for bargains but she could see that the old woman was tired and impatient to go home and they had an hour's travelling ahead of them. She put the coat back on the rack.

A large black and red motorcycle threaded its way

through the traffic and parked on the double yellow lines in front of the main entrance to the store. It was brand new and gleaming apart from the tyres which were crusted with ice. On the back carrier box was the name of a courier firm. She watched the rider dismount like a cowboy getting off a horse. He was dressed in black leather with a white wrap-around helmet and a tinted visor. There was a walkie-talkie in a leather case hanging from a belt around his waist and a black receiver clipped to his left shoulder. The rider switched on his hazard warning lights and the amber flashing was reflected on the wet road. He looked up and down the pavement as if checking for traffic wardens and then turned his back on the bike and crossed the road towards the boutique. He stepped to one side to let a trio of giggling school-girls leave the shop and then came in. As he passed the girl he looked at her, up and down, and she turned to watch him go, his leathers squeaking with every step. The rider was empty handed so the girl assumed he was there to collect something, but he continued to move through the shoppers, passed the pay counter and then he pushed open the doors at the other side of the shop and went out into the street.

The girl frowned and turned back to the window. The bike's lights were still flashing. Her frown deepened and at that moment the twenty-five pounds of Semtex explosive in the back carrier box exploded in a flash of blinding white light, blowing in the window and striking her with thousands of glass daggers. At the last moment she tried to turn towards her mother, to shield her, but they died together in the hail of glass.

★　★　★

The Press Association news desk received the call as the first ambulance arrived at the department store, blue light flashing and siren whining. The reporter who took the call later told the police that the voice was Irish and had given a codeword that the police identified as genuine; the tip-off was not a hoax. The voice was that of a man, he couldn't tell if he was young or old, and the caller said that a bomb had just gone off in Knightsbridge and that the Provisional Irish Republican Army claimed responsibility for it. The reporter hadn't recorded the call, he was new on the job and no one had told him that he was supposed to. The line went dead and he took his notebook over to the news editor who told him to check with the police that there had indeed been an explosion and three minutes later the story went out over the wires as a flash – IRA BOMB EXPLODES OUTSIDE LONDON STORE – AT LEAST FIVE DEAD.

By the time it appeared on the screen of the news editor of the *Sunday World* he'd already had a phone call from a member of the public keen to earn a tip-off fee. He'd assigned two reporters to start phoning the police and their Sinn Fein contacts and was trying to track down their Belfast stringers.

It was 5.30 p.m., the crossing over point when the day shift began to drift off to the pub and the night reporters were arriving. The picture desk had sent two freelances and a staffer to the scene, but Knightsbridge was at least half an hour's drive away from the paper's Docklands offices.

More information was trickling over the wires on PA and Reuters and the death toll kept climbing with each snatch of copy.

'Jesus, now they're saying twelve dead,' said Jon Simpson, the news editor. Behind him stood the chief sub and the editor, reading over his shoulder.

'Splash?' said the chief sub, knowing the answer would be yes. The front page lead at the afternoon conference had been a sixties pop star's drug problem.

'We'll have to pull our fingers out if we're going to make the first edition,' said the editor. 'We'll take the whole of page one, two and three, let me see the pics first. Hold the MP story until next week and hack back the food safety feature. Hang on, no, drop it altogether. And we'll save the splash until next week as well, it's exclusive.' The chief sub scurried back to his terminal to redraw his page plans, shouting to the picture editor to send over everything he had.

'You've got two hours until the first edition, Jon. Get everybody on it.' The editor wandered over to the picture desk while Simpson picked up the phone.

'Where's Woody?' Simpson yelled at his deputy who was busy scrolling through the PA wire.

'Where do you think?' he shouted back, raising his eyebrows.

'Drunken pig,' said Simpson and rang the King's Head, a short stagger away from the office.

As the phone trilled behind the bar, Ian Wood was downing his second double Bells and trying to look down the front of the barmaid's blouse. She saw what he was up to and flicked her towel at him and laughed. 'Don't let Sandy catch you doing that,' she scolded and he grinned.

'Your husband's too good a guv'nor to go slapping the customers around,' he said, finishing his whisky.

'Another?' she said as she picked up the phone. She

listened and then mouthed silently 'Are you in?'

'Who's asking?' he mouthed back.

'The office,' she replied, and he realised they looked like a couple of goldfish gasping for breath. He nodded and took the phone off her. She picked his glass up and refilled it.

'Woody, are you on for a double shift?' asked Simpson.

Woody looked at the double measure of whisky in his glass and licked his lips but hesitated for only a second before he told Simpson he'd do it. Woody was a freelance and he needed the money. If he'd been staff he'd have told the news editor where to get off, but it had been a long time since anyone had given Ian Wood a staff job.

'What's up?' he asked.

'IRA bomb. A big one. Knightsbridge.'

'Christ. How many dead?'

'They're saying twelve now, no make that thirteen, but they're still counting. Get out there and get the colour. Link up with the monkeys while you're there, they'll need their captions written.' Woody heard Simpson call out for the names of the photographers. 'Dave Wilkins is the staffer, find him,' he said.

'I'm on my way,' said Woody and hung up.

He took the glass off the bar and swallowed it down in one.

'You off, Woody?' said the barmaid, surprised.

'Duty calls, darling,' he said. 'Can you cash me a cheque?'

'Fifty?' she asked.

'Fifty is magic. You're a life-saver. If ever that husband of yours . . .'

She waved him away and counted out the notes as Woody handed over the cheque.

'See you later,' he said, and walked down the dimly lit corridor and out of the pub door into the street. He turned right and walked the short distance to The Highway and hailed a cab heading towards the City.

The driver looked over his shoulder when Woody told him where he wanted to go. 'We'll never get near the place, mate,' he said. 'There's a bomb gone off.'

'Yeah I know,' said Woody. 'I'm a reporter.'

'OK,' said the cabbie and sped off down the road. 'Which paper d'yer work for then?'

'*Sunday World*,' replied Woody.

'Yeah?' said the cabbie. 'What happened? Page Three girl killed was she?' His deep-throated laughter echoed around the cab.

They hit unmoving traffic long before they reached Knightsbridge and though the cabbie tried to find a way through the side-streets they were soon helplessly locked in.

'Best I can do,' said the driver apologetically, his professional pride wounded.

'No sweat,' said Woody, getting out. He handed a ten-pound note through the window. 'I'll walk from here. Call it a tenner and give me a receipt, please.'

'Clamping down on expenses, are they?'

'Yeah, tell me about it.'

The cabbie signed a receipt and handed it to Woody. Then as an afterthought he ripped off a few blank receipts from his pad. 'Here,' he said, 'fill these in yourself.'

'You're a prince,' said Woody, and put them gratefully into his raincoat pocket.

He began to jog slowly towards the sound of sirens, his feet slapping on the wet pavement and his raincoat flapping behind him. Despite the cold he soon worked up a sweat. Ian Wood was not a fit man. He was slightly overweight but that wasn't the problem, he was out of condition because he never took any exercise, hadn't since his schooldays.

The police had cordoned off the area around the store and a burly sergeant blocked his way when he tried to duck under the barrier. He fished out his yellow plastic Metropolitan Police Press card and after the copper had scrutinised it he was waved through.

It was a scene from hell. Wrecked cars were strewn across the road, still smoking and hissing. There was an assortment of emergency vehicles, all with their doors open, radios crackling and lights flashing. There were two fire engines though their hoses were still in place, unused. There had obviously been a number of small fires burning but the firemen had used extinguishers to put them out. There were half a dozen ambulances, and as Woody walked towards the police top brass one of them pulled away and its siren kicked into life. Something squelched under Woody's shoe and he looked down. He was standing on a hand. It was a small girl's hand, the skin white and unlined, the nails bitten to the quick. The hand was attached to a forearm but that was all, it ended in a ragged, bloody mess at the point where there should have been an elbow. Woody's stomach heaved and he pulled his foot away with a jerk, a look of horror on his face.

He backed away and bumped into a policeman wearing dark-blue overalls, black Wellington boots and thick, black rubber gloves that covered most of his arms. The policeman picked up the dismembered arm and dropped it into a plastic bag he was carrying. As he straightened up, Woody saw that the man's face was covered with a white surgical mask and then he saw the blonde wavy hair and realised it wasn't a man at all, but a woman in her twenties. There were tears streaming down her face. She turned away from him, walked a few steps and bent down again. This time she picked up a shoe with a shattered bone sticking out of a green sock. Woody shuddered. There were dozens of policemen dressed in the same overalls and following the girl's grisly example. Woody realised with a jolt why the body count hadn't been finalised. It was at least an hour since the bomb had gone off and they were still picking up the pieces. Ambulancemen were ferrying bodies on stretchers at the run, some of the victims moaning or screaming, others still, their faces covered with blankets. The policemen in their blood-spotted overalls worked at a slower pace, knowing that it was more important to be thorough than fast. They were not in the business of saving lives, simply collecting evidence.

Woody looked around, surveying the damage. All the windows of the store had been blown in, as had those in the shops opposite, and the stonework was pitted and blackened. Lying half on and half off the pavement was the twisted frame of a motorcycle, the back a mass of scorched and melted metal. It was being examined by two middle-aged men in white overalls.

Shocked shoppers and staff were still filing out of the store, urged on by uniformed constables in yellow reflective jackets, as an inspector shouted through a megaphone that there could be another bomb in the vicinity and would the crowds please keep back. Woody knew that he was just saying that to keep the ghouls away. Two bombs would have meant double the risk for the bombers planting the devices, and the IRA never bothered using two devices against civilian targets, only against the security forces in Northern Ireland. Besides, if there was any chance of a second device they'd keep the ambulancemen back while the Bomb Disposal Squad gave the place a thorough going over.

There were a handful of sniffer dogs and their handlers checking the street, and Woody could see more dogs inside the store, noses down and tails wagging, happy to be working. One of the dogs in the street, a long-haired Retriever, lunged forward and seized something in its jaws. Its handler yelled and kicked its flanks and the dog dropped whatever it had been holding. It was an arm. The handler yanked his dog away, cursing. The dog cowered, all the time keeping its eyes on the prize.

Woody went over to the Chief Superintendent and two inspectors who were surrounded by a pack of reporters and photographers. He recognised many of the faces and he knew that all the tabloids and heavies would be represented. If not, some news editor would be getting his backside soundly kicked. The older hacks were taking shorthand notes in small notebooks while the younger ones thrust mini tape-recorders in front of the police. Behind the pack were two television crews trying in vain to get a clear shot. He heard the click-whirr of a motor-drive and he turned to see Dave Wilkins aiming his Nikon at a torso lying in the gutter.

'They won't use it,' Woody told him. 'Too gory.'

'So?' said the photographer.

Woody listened to the Chief Superintendent explaining

what he thought had happened. A bomb in the back of a motorcycle, no warning, the streets crowded and the stores packed. No idea yet how many had been killed. Fifteen at least. Yes, almost certainly linked to the recent wave of London bombings, four so far. Correction, five including this one. Yes, the IRA had claimed responsibility.

'And that, gentlemen,' he said with the wave of a gloved hand, 'is all that I can tell you right now. Would you please all move back behind the barriers and let my men get on with their work. We'll be having a full press conference at the Yard later tonight.' He politely pushed his way through the journalists, and they moved aside to let him go, knowing that the officer had said all he was going to say. There was no point in antagonising him. Besides, they all had their own police contacts who would be a hell of a lot more forthcoming.

Woody went over to the shops facing the department store, noting down the names on the signs. His feet crunched on broken glass and he stepped to one side to let two ambulancemen with a stretcher out of a boutique. They were carrying a girl, her leather jacket and green cords shredded and ripped and dripping with blood. He knew she was a girl because of her long black hair. There was nothing left of her face, just strips of flesh hanging off white bone. Woody felt his stomach heave again. He'd been at accident scenes before, far too many to remember, but he'd never seen such carnage. The area reeked of death, of blood and burning and scorched meat. He fought to keep his emotions under control, knowing that he had work to do. It was harder for the reporters he thought bitterly. The monkeys had it easy. They looked at everything through the camera lens and that insulated them from the reality of it. But reporters had to be there and experience it before they could write about it, they had to open themselves to the horror, the grief and the pain. Sometimes it was almost too much to bear. Almost.

He stood by one of the ambulances and got some snatched quotes from a couple of harassed stretcher-bearers and then he followed a woman in a fur coat that he'd seen leaving the store, ducked under the barrier and caught up with her. Her eyewitness account was harrowing and she had no qualms about giving her name and address. Her eyes were glassy and Woody knew she was in a state of shock and he held her arm gently as he spoke to her and then gestured over at Wilkins, standing to one side so that he could get a head-and-shoulders shot of her.

'Got all you want?' Woody asked the photographer.

'Yeah,' said Wilkins. 'I'll head back and leave the free-lancers to get the rest. You coming?'

'No, I'll ring the story in, it'll save time. I'll see you back there.'

Woody half-heartedly looked for a call box, but knew that he stood little chance in Knightsbridge. He walked to a small Italian bistro and went inside.

'Can I use the phone?' he asked a waiter. The waiter began to protest in fractured English so Woody took out his wallet and gave him ten pounds. The protests evaporated and he was soon through to the office and dictating to a copytaker straight from his notebook. Twenty-five paragraphs, and he knew it was good stuff. When he'd finished he asked the copytaker to transfer him to the news desk and he checked that everything was OK with Simpson.

'Got it here, Woody,' he said. 'Great read.'

'OK, I'm going back to see what else I can get. I'll call

you.' He hung up before Simpson could order him back to base. On the way out he got a receipt from the waiter.

There was a pub down the road and Woody gratefully walked up to the bar and ordered a double Bells. It was only when the whisky slopped around the tumbler that he realised how badly his hands were shaking.

The intercom buzzed, catching them all by surprise, even though they were waiting for him. There were three of them in the flat, drinking tea and watching television. They were casually dressed – baggy pullovers, faded jeans and grubby training shoes – and looked like sociology students stuck with nothing to do between lectures. One of the men was smoking and on the floor beside his easy chair was a circular crystal ashtray overflowing with cigarette butts. He leant over and stubbed out the one in his hand, pushed himself up and walked into the hall. On the wall by the door was a telephone with a small black and white television screen; he pressed a square plastic button and it flickered into life.

'Welcome back,' he said to the figure waiting down below and pressed a second button, the one that opened the entrance door four floors below. As he waited for him to come up in the lift he went back into the lounge. 'It's him,' he said, but they knew it would be because no one else knew they were there and if they did they wouldn't be coming in through the front door but through the window with stun grenades and machine guns.

There was an American comedy show on the television and canned laughter filled the room. Through the floor-to-ceiling sliding windows at the end of the lounge the man saw a tug struggle along the Thames, hauling an ungainly barge behind it.

He went back into the hall and opened the door as the lift jolted to a halt. The man who stepped out of the lift was in his early twenties, wearing grey flannel trousers and a blue blazer over a white polo neck sweater. He had dark-brown curly hair and black eyes and was grinning widely. 'Did you see it?' he asked eagerly, before the other man even had a chance to close the door. He punched the air with his fist. 'Did you bloody well see it?'

'Calm down, O'Reilly,' said the man who'd let him in.

O'Reilly turned towards him, his cheeks flaring red. 'Calm down?' he said. 'Christ, man, you should have been there. You should have seen me. It was fan-bloody-tastic.' He turned back to look at the television set. 'Has it been on yet? How many did we get?'

'Fifteen so far,' said the man sitting on the leather Chesterfield directly opposite the pseudo-antique video cabinet on which the television stood. 'You did well, O'Reilly.' He was the oldest of the group but even he had barely turned thirty. Although he had the broadest Irish accent he had Nordic blond hair and piercing blue eyes and fair skin. His name was also far removed from his Irish origins but Denis Fisher was Belfast-born and he'd killed many times for the Cause. 'What about the helmet and the leathers?' he asked O'Reilly.

'In the boot of the car. Just like you said. It was so easy.'

'Not easy,' said Fisher. 'Well planned.'

'Whatever,' said O'Reilly. 'I deserve a drink.' He went into the white-and-blue-tiled kitchen and opened the fridge. 'Anyone else want anything?' he called, but they all declined. O'Reilly took out a cold can of Carlsberg and opened it as he walked back into the lounge. He pulled one of the wooden chairs out from under the oval dining-table and sat astride it, resting his forearms on its back.

'What next?' he asked, grinning.

'Yes,' said the man who'd opened the door and who was now sitting on a flowery print sofa by a tall wooden book-case. His name was McCormick. 'What do we do next?'

Fisher smiled. 'You're so bloody impatient,' he laughed. He turned to look at the occupant of the chair by the window, the one they called The Bombmaker. 'That depends on what MacDermott here comes up with.' The Bombmaker grinned.

The comedy show was interrupted for a news flash and a sombre man with movie-star looks reported that sixteen people had died in a bomb explosion and that the Provisional IRA had claimed responsibility. They then cut to a reporter in a white raincoat standing under a street-lamp in Knightsbridge, who said that police now believed that the bomb had been in the back carrier of a motor-cycle and that it had been detonated by a timing device.

O'Reilly punched the air again, and The Bombmaker's grin widened.

The police car drove slowly down Clapham Road. Constable Simon Edgington's left hand was aching from the constant gear changing and he cursed the bumper-to-bumper traffic under his breath. It wasn't even worth switching the siren on because there wasn't enough room for the cars and buses to pull to the side.

'It's getting worse,' he groaned.

'Sorry?' said his partner, a blonde WPC called Susan Griffin who had joined the Met on the graduate entry scheme. One of the high-flyers, a sergeant had told

Edgington, closely followed by a warning not to try anything on because she'd reported the last constable whose hand had accidentally slipped on to her thigh during a hasty gear change.

'The traffic,' he said. 'We're going to be all night at this rate.'

She looked down at the sheaf of papers on her black clipboard. 'This is the last one,' she said. 'Chinese or something. God, I don't think I can pronounce their names. Noog-yen Guan Fong and Noog-yen Goy Trin. Does that sound right?' The names on the sheet were written as Nguyen Xuan Phoung and Nguyen Kieu Trinh.

He laughed. 'Sounds like a disease,' he said.

She gave him a frosty look. 'It's not really a laughing matter is it, Simon?'

Edgington flushed. Griffin was a year younger than him but she acted as if she already had her sergeant's stripes. But his embarrassment came from the fact that he knew she was right, it wasn't the sort of thing to joke about. He wanted to tell her that he was just nervous, that he was trying to relieve the tension that was knotting up his stomach, and that he'd never thought when he signed up three years earlier that he'd have to knock on the doors of complete strangers and tell them that their nearest and dearest had been scattered all over Knightsbridge by a terrorist bomb. He wanted to explain but knew he'd sound like a wimp so he concentrated on driving.

They'd been given three addresses, all south of the river. The first had been a middle-aged couple in Lambeth, a schoolteacher and his wife. Their teenage son had been in the passenger seat of an old Mini that had been fifty feet or so from the motorcycle when the bomb had gone off. Several pieces of wire that had been wrapped around the explosive had burst through the windscreen and torn his face and throat apart. The couple had already seen a report of the bombing on the evening news and before Griffin had spoken the wife's legs had given way and her husband had had to help her to a chair in their cramped kitchen. Edgington had been quite happy to let his partner do the talking, he didn't think that he could have kept his voice steady. He'd joined the police to catch criminals, not to act as some kind of messenger of death. And she'd done it so bloody well, sat them both down, made them cups of sweet tea, phoned their daughter and arranged for her to come round and look after them. She'd sat with them on the sofa until the girl came and then left them to their grief. All the time Edgington had stood by the kitchen door, feeling useless, but Griffin hadn't mentioned it when they got back into the car.

The next call had been at a small flat in Stockwell. No relatives this time, but a boyfriend who burst into tears and hugged the WPC when she told him what had happened. They were going to get married, he'd sobbed. She was pregnant, he said. She held him until the tears stopped and sat him down and asked him if there was anyone she could call, a friend or a relative. Did she suffer, he asked. No, she lied. The sergeant had told them that the girl had died screaming on the pavement with both her legs blown off. 'No, she didn't suffer,' she said without hesitation.

He wiped his eyes with the back of his hand and she gave him a handkerchief while Edgington telephoned the boy's mother. She said she'd be around in fifteen minutes and Edgington and Griffin decided that he'd be OK on

17

his own until then. They left him hunched over a mug of tea which he clasped tightly between his hands.

'It's coming up on the left,' she said.

The traffic crept along and eventually they reached the turning.

'Number 62,' she said before he asked.

He drove slowly, counting off the numbers. 'Are you sure?' he asked.

She checked the computer print-out on the clipboard and nodded. 'That's what it says here.'

He stopped the car and they both looked at number 62. It was a Chinese take-away, with a huge window on which were printed gold and black Chinese letters and above it a sign that said 'Double Happiness Take-Away'. Through the window they could see two customers waiting in front of a chest-high counter.

'That's it,' she said, opening her car door. Edgington caught up with her as she reached the entrance and followed her in.

Behind the counter was an old Oriental man shouting through a serving hatch in a language neither of them could understand. He turned and placed two white plastic carrier bags full of cartons of Chinese food in front of one of the customers and took his money. There was a loud scream from the kitchen and the man stuck his head back through the hatch and shouted and waved his arm.

He came back to the counter and smiled up at Edgington and Griffin.

'What I get you?' he asked. He was a small man, his shoulders barely above the counter. His face was wrinkled but the skin wasn't slack, his cheekbones were clearly defined and there were no loose folds under the chin. It

18

was hard to tell exactly how old he was, he could have been in his forties and had a rough life, or he could have been a well-preserved sixty-year-old. Griffin noticed how sad his eyes were. They were eyes that had seen a lot of suffering, she decided.

'Are you Mr Noog-yen?' she said, and he nodded quickly but corrected her pronunciation, saying his name as 'Newyen'. The single customer left at the counter stood openly watching and listening to the conversation. Edgington stared at him until the man's gaze faltered and he studied the menu pinned to the wall.

'Is there somewhere we can talk?' Griffin asked the old man.

'I very busy,' he replied. 'No staff. You come back later, maybe?' There was a thud from the hatch and he went over and picked up another carrier bag. He handed it to the customer. 'Come again,' he said.

'I'm afraid we have bad news for you,' said Griffin. She looked at the clipboard again. God, she thought, how do you pronounce these names? 'Mr Nguyen, do you know a Xuan Phoung or Kieu Trinh?' Both names started with Nguyen so she'd guessed that that was the family name and that everything that came after it were their given names.

The man frowned. Another customer came in and stood behind Edgington. Griffin tried pronouncing the names again but still nothing registered so she showed him the computer print-out and pointed to the two names.

He nodded, his eyes wary. 'My wife,' he said. 'And my daughter.'

'I'm afraid there has been an accident,' said the WPC. 'Is there somewhere we can talk?'

The man waved his hands impatiently. 'What has happened?' he insisted.

'Mr Nguyen, please, it would be much better for you if we could sit down somewhere.'

'No staff,' he said. 'My wife not in kitchen, so much work to do. What has happened?' He spoke each word carefully, as if stringing a sentence together was an effort, and he had a vaguely American accent. But he seemed to have no trouble in understanding what she was saying.

'Mr Nguyen, your wife and daughter are dead. I'm very sorry.'

He looked stunned. His mouth dropped and his hands slid off the counter and down to his sides. He started to say something and then stopped and shook his head. Edgington turned to the customer and found himself apologising, but for the life of him he didn't know why. He felt his cheeks redden.

'Do you understand, Mr Nguyen?' asked Griffin.

'What happened?' said the old man.

'Is there somewhere we can talk?' she asked again. She didn't want to explain about the bomb while she was standing in a Chinese take-away.

'We can go back of shop,' he said. He shouted through the hatch and as he opened a white-painted door a balding Oriental with sleeves rolled up around his elbows and a grease-stained apron came barrelling out. He ignored Nguyen and glared at the customer. 'What you want?' he barked.

Nguyen led them down a tiled hallway, up a flight of wooden stairs and through a beaded curtain. Beyond was a small room with heavy brocade wallpaper and a faded red patterned carpet. The furniture was dark rosewood, a square table with carved feet and four straight-backed chairs with no cushions. On one wall was a small red and gold shrine in front of which a joss stick was smouldering, filling the air with sickly sweet perfume.

In a corner by a small window was a semi-circular table on which stood a group of framed photographs of Nguyen with an old woman and a young girl. Edgington walked over to the table and studied the pictures as Griffin sat down with the old man. Most of the pictures were of the girl, she was obviously the focus of the family. In the most recent photographs she looked to be in her mid-teens and she was absolutely gorgeous, long black hair and flawless features. She could have been a model. There were pictures of her in a school uniform and even in those she looked sexy. The old woman was obviously her mother, but there was little or no physical resemblance. The girl was tall and straight and the woman was small and stooped. The girl's skin was smooth and fresh and the woman's dark and wrinkled. The girl had eyes that were bright and sparkling while the woman's appeared lifeless. As he studied the photographs he heard Griffin explaining about the bomb. Edgington did the calculations in his head – if she'd had the child when she was twenty she'd be under forty, and even if she'd given birth at thirty the woman couldn't be much older than forty-eight and yet she looked much older. In one of the photographs, the biggest of the collection, the girl was sitting in a chair, her parents behind her. Nguyen was smiling proudly and had a protective hand on her shoulder. They looked more like her grandparents. Something else struck him. There were no pictures of her as a baby or a toddler. In none of the photographs was she any younger than seven or eight. Curious.

'Please,' said the old man behind him and Edgington turned round to see him holding out his hands. 'Please, the picture.'

Edgington took over the big framed photograph and handed it to him. He didn't speak, he didn't know what to say.

The old man cradled the frame in his arms and then hugged it to his chest. There were no tears and he made no sound, but the intensity of his grief was painful to watch.

'Who did this to my family?' he asked eventually.

'The IRA,' said Edgington. They were the first words he'd spoken in the room and his voice sounded thick with emotion. He cleared his throat and Griffin looked up, surprised that he'd spoken. 'The IRA have claimed responsibility,' he said.

'IRA,' said Nguyen, saying each letter slowly as if hearing them for the first time. 'What is IRA?'

Edgington looked at Griffin and she raised her eyebrows. Was he serious? He sat down next to the old man.

'Terrorists,' he said quietly.

'What do they want, these terrorists?'

Edgington was stumped for an answer and he looked helplessly at Griffin. She shook her head, knowing that what the old man needed was sympathy and a sedative, not a political discussion. The man turned to her. 'What do they want?' he asked her.

'They want British troops out of Ireland,' she said reluctantly.

'How does killing my family do that?' he asked.

She shrugged. 'Is there someone I can get to come and take care of you?' she asked. 'Do any of your family live nearby?'

'I have no family,' he said quietly. 'Now I have no family. I am alone. These IRA, will you catch them?'

'Yes,' she said, looking him in the eye.

'And will they be punished?'

'Yes,' she repeated. Lying was coming easily to her today.

'Good,' said the old man. He nodded as if satisfied.

The second edition was coming off the presses when Woody finally got back to the office. He slumped in his chair still wearing his raincoat. He'd spilled something down the front of it and when he dropped his head on his chest he could smell whisky. 'What a waste,' he mumbled.

The reporter at the desk next to his leant round a potted plant and said: 'Simpson is after your arse, Woody.' There was more than a hint of sadistic pleasure in his voice as he passed on the bad news. Like Woody he was a freelance and each time a freelance was shafted there was more work to go round for everyone else.

'Thanks,' said Woody, determined not to show how worried he was. He needed the work, God he needed the work, and he'd been banned from most of the London papers over the last twelve months or so. He was finding it harder and harder to get through a shift without drinking, and that didn't go down well in the new high-tech world of modern newspapers. In the old days, the days when reporters looked like reporters and they worked on typewriters that sounded like typewriters, then the Street was full of characters – men and women who could take their drink and whose work was better for it, and who would be fondly forgiven if they were found late in the evening, flat on their backs under their desks. The news editors then would call for the office car and have them sent home. If they were really badly behaved then perhaps a just punishment would be handed out, a nasty door-stepping job in the pouring rain or a night-time road accident in the middle of nowhere, character-building rather than malicious. Not these days. These days most of the journalists seemed to be straight out of university with weak chins, earnest eyes and stockbroker voices. Few of them could even manage shorthand, Woody thought bitterly, and it was a common sight in the newsroom to see them plugged into tape-recorders transcribing their tapes and breathing through their mouths. Woody remembered the purgatory he'd gone through to get his own spidery shorthand up to the required one hundred words per minute, and the rest of the shit he'd had to go through before he got to Fleet Street. Now the papers were all staffed by kids, kids who if you managed to drag them bodily into a bar would drink nothing stronger than bubbly water. Ian Wood was forty-two years old but at that moment he felt he was going on eighty.

'Woody!' screamed a voice from the far end of the room. 'Where the hell have you been?'

The question was rhetorical, Woody realised, because it was swiftly followed by a torrent of abuse. He heaved himself out of the chair and ambled over to the source of the noise, hoping that if he got close it'd cut down the decibels and reduce the embarrassment factor. Simpson was sitting back in his reclining chair with his expensively shod feet on the desk. The news editor spent twice as much on a pair of shoes as the paper paid its freelances for an eight-hour shift. They were well polished and gleamed under the overhead fluorescent lights and Woody looked down involuntarily at his own soaking wet, brown Hush Puppies. Woody began to explain but Simpson cut him off and told him that he should have been back hours ago and that he was to get the hell out of the building and not to bother coming back, that he'd got pissed on the job once too often and that there would be no more shifts for him on the paper. Woody could feel that he was being watched by everyone in the newsroom, and he could tell without looking around that more than half the voyeurs were grinning and enjoying his discomfort. His face reddened. He knew there was nothing he could do, he'd have to wait until Simpson had calmed down, maybe some time after Hell had frozen over, but he couldn't face the walk to the door, not with everyone staring at him. He opened his mouth to speak but Simpson waved him away and turned his back on him.

Woody stood there swaying for a few seconds and then with every ounce of control he could muster he slowly walked across the newsroom, his head held high and his eyes fixed on the purple door that led to the stairs and the street and the pub. There was only one thing he wanted, other than a double Bells, and that was to get out of the room with what little dignity he had left intact. He almost made it. He didn't notice the overflowing wastepaper bin and he crashed over it and sprawled against the door. He pushed the door but it wouldn't budge so he pushed harder and then he saw the sign that said 'Pull' and cruel laughter billowed around him as he eventually staggered out into the corridor.

He headed for the sanctuary of the King's Head but realised that there would be other reporters there, probably knocking back Perrier with the way his luck was going, so instead he walked to the Coach and Horses. They wouldn't cash cheques for him there, not since the bank had bounced one, but at least he wouldn't be laughed at.

It started to rain so he put up the collar of his coat and hunched his shoulders and he stuck close to the wall until he reached the pub. It was fairly busy with closing time fast approaching, but Woody knew that the landlord paid little attention to the licensing laws and that it would be many hours before the last customer left. He took off his coat and shook it before hanging it up by the fruit machine.

'Evening, Woody,' said the barman, a teenager whose name Woody couldn't remember. 'Usual?'

Woody nodded and the barman poured a double Bells. A woman sitting on a stool looked at the Bells bottle and then up at Woody. She shuddered. 'You should try a real whisky,' she said. She was sitting next to a man in a brown leather jacket and they both had glasses of amber fluid in front of them. Woody reached for his glass and toasted them.

'This will do me fine,' he said, and drained it in one.

'Now I'll have one of whatever they're having, and one each for them, too,' Woody said, mentally calculating how much he had in his wallet. They were drinking a ten-year-old malt the name of which Woody didn't recognise but it was smooth and mellow and warmed his chest. He fell into amiable conversation with the couple, talking about the weather, about Docklands, about the Government, anything but what he'd seen that evening.

They asked him what he did and he told them he was a journalist. Her name was Maggie and his was Ross, he sold fax machines and she worked for an insurance company.

As the level of whisky in the bottle dropped Woody began opening himself up to them, about how unhappy he was in his job and his plans for a new life in Los Angeles. An old pal of his had gone out to LA a couple of years ago and had set up an agency specialising in showbiz features and oddball stories for the tabloids, and he'd been pestering Woody to go out and join him.

'You know, I think I will go,' Woody said, and they nodded in agreement and Maggie bought a round. Some time later the man slapped Woody on the back and said he had to go. He kissed Maggie on the cheek, a brotherly peck Woody noticed, and left. Woody was surprised as he'd assumed they were married or lovers, but Maggie laughed and said no, just friends. He slid on to the stool vacated by Ross, even though he generally preferred to stand while drinking. He was quite taken by Maggie. She had shoulder-length red hair and grey eyes, and the freckles of a teenager even though she must have been in her early thirties. She spoke with a faint Scottish burr and laughed a lot and told jokes dirtier than even Woody thought was proper.

'Are you serious about LA?' she asked, and Woody said he was. She told him that she had a friend living there, and that if he did go she'd put him in touch. She asked for his telephone number and he gave it to her. Eventually she said she had to go. Woody offered to walk her home but she thanked him and said no, she only lived around the corner. Woody shrugged and said goodbye, wondering how she'd react to a brotherly peck on the cheek from him but deciding against it. After she went he finished his whisky and left the pub in search of a black cab. Ten minutes later he was back for his raincoat. It wasn't his night.

Sergeant Fletcher's heart sank when he saw The China-man walking slowly up to his desk. He kept his eyes down on his paperwork and wished with all his heart that he'd go away. Nguyen Ngoc Minh coughed quietly. Sergeant Fletcher ignored him. Nguyen coughed again, louder this time. The policeman knew he could put it off no longer. He looked up and feigned surprise.

'Mr Nguyen,' he said. 'How can I help you?' His fingers tensed around his ballpoint pen.

'Sergeant Fletcher. Is there news about the bomb?' said Nguyen slowly. He stood in front of the desk, his head bowed and his fingers clasped together below his stomach. He was wearing the same clothes he'd worn on his four previous visits to the police station, brown woollen trousers, a blue and green work shirt and a thick quilted coat with a hood. His dark-brown boots were scuffed and worn and if Sergeant Fletcher hadn't known better he might have assumed that the man was a down-and-out looking for a warm cell for the night.

The policeman shook his head slowly. 'I am afraid not, Mr Nguyen. But we are doing everything we can, believe me.'

The look in The Chinaman's eyes suggested that he did not believe the sergeant, but he smiled nevertheless, his face wrinkling into deep crevices. It was an ingratiating smile, an eager-to-please look that for some reason made the sergeant immediately feel guilty.

'Do you know who exploded the bomb?' Nguyen asked.

'As it says in the papers, the IRA has claimed responsibility.'

'And do they know who in the IRA is responsible?'

'No, Mr Nguyen, they do not.' Sergeant Fletcher fought to keep himself from snapping at The Chinaman, but it was hard, bloody hard, because every time he came and stood in front of the desk he asked the same questions with the same inane grin on his face. He realised that the man must be devastated, losing his wife and his daughter, and God knows Fletcher wanted to help, but there was nothing he could do. Nothing.

'How long will it be, Sergeant Fletcher?' Nguyen asked quietly.

The policeman shook his head sadly. 'I wish I knew,' he said.

'The lady policeman who came to see me last week said that the men would be caught.'

'I am sure they will be.'

'She said that they will be punished.'

The silly cow. Fletcher wished she'd kept her mouth shut and not raised The Chinaman's hopes. He made a mental note to find out who she was and give her a piece of his mind.

'I am sure that when they are caught they will be punished, Mr Nguyen,' agreed Sergeant Fletcher.

Nguyen began wringing his hands as if washing them. 'When will that be, Sergeant Fletcher?' The smiled widened, the lips stretched tight across his yellowing teeth.

It was a nervous smile, Fletcher realised. The policeman put his palms down on the desk. 'I do not know. I simply do not know.'

'I know you and your men are doing their best. I know they want to catch the men who killed my family. But I wonder . . .' He left the sentence unfinished, his eyes fixed on Fletcher's face.

'Yes?' said the sergeant.

'I wonder if there were any other policemen on the

case. How do you say, specialists? Policemen who hunt the IRA. The terrorists.'

Fletcher suddenly felt the sky open and the sun beam down. He saw a way of getting The Chinaman off his back once and for all.

'There are such policemen, Mr Nguyen. They are called the Anti-Terrorist Branch.'

'Where do I find the Anti-Terrorist Branch?'

Fletcher found himself grinning. 'Mr Nguyen, stay right where you are. I'll go and write down their address and telephone number for you.'

Elliott Jephcott drove the white Rover off the main road and into the small cobbled mews. He switched off the radio and looked at his watch. It had just turned 8.30 a.m. and he didn't have to be in court until 11.00 a.m. He had plenty of time. He checked his hair in the driving mirror and then reached into the glove compartment for his breath-freshener aerosol and gave his mouth two minty squirts. He put the aerosol back and as he did he saw that a streetsweeper was watching him while he attacked the cobbles with a long-handled brush. Jephcott blushed like a schoolboy caught with a dirty magazine and was immediately angry with himself. A High Court Judge feeling guilty under the scrutiny of a roadsweeper in a filthy donkey jacket? Ridiculous, he thought. He locked the car and walked to the door of Erica's cottage. It opened just as he was reaching for the brass knocker.

'I heard the car,' she said. She looked ravishing, her blonde hair carefully arranged so that she gave the impression that she'd just got out of bed. She moved to the side to let him in and he smelt her perfume. It was the one he'd bought her last month and he was pleased that she'd worn it for him. She was wearing a purple blouse with a high collar and pockets over each breast, and a purple, green and pink flower-patterned skirt that reached halfway down her calves, and around her waist was a purple leather belt. On her left wrist was a thick gold bracelet and around her left ankle was a thin gold chain. He'd bought her the jewellery, too. And the Alfa Romeo outside. That had been a twenty-first birthday present. She was worth it, God she was worth it.

She closed the door and stood behind him, helping him to remove his jacket. She took it and put it on a hanger before putting it away in a cupboard by the front door.

'What time do you have to go?' she asked. He knew that she wasn't nagging, not the way his wife did when she asked the same question, she just wanted to know how much time they had together so that she could plan accordingly. He turned and smiled and slipped his arm around her waist.

'Not long enough,' he said and kissed her.

She opened her lips as their mouths met and he felt her soft tongue and heard her moan. She took him by the hand and led him upstairs. 'Let's not waste any of it,' she said.

Outside in the mews, the roadsweeper worked carefully, pushing the litter and dust into small, neat piles before using his shovel to scoop it into the plastic bag on his cart. He whistled quietly as he worked, his breath forming white clouds in the cold morning air. The collar of his donkey jacket was turned up and he was wearing thick, woollen gloves. On his head was a blue bobble hat that had seen better days. He stood up and surveyed the area he'd cleaned and nodded to himself. He clipped the

31

shovel to the side of his cart and moved it further down the mews, stopping next to the Rover. Out of the corner of his eye he saw the upstairs curtains being closed.

He began to sweep around the car, slowly and conscientiously, still whistling. He moved between the cart and the car and knelt down to unclip the shovel. As he did he took a metal box, about the size of a box of chocolates, from the rear of the cart and in a smooth motion slipped it up under the wheel-arch of the driver's side of the Rover. There were two large magnets on the box and they latched on to the metal of the car through the underseal and its coating of mud. There was a small chrome switch on one side of the box and he clicked it on as he pulled his hand away.

Inside the box were two batteries, a black plastic alarm clock with a digital display, a small aluminium tube, a tangle of different coloured wires and five pounds of pale-brown Semtex explosive in which was embedded a detonator. As the roadsweeper unclipped his shovel and carefully swept up a cigarette packet and a pile of dust, the clock began ticking off the seconds. The man was in no hurry. The clock was set for five minutes, but even when the time was up the bomb would not explode. The clock merely completed the circuit for the second switch, a mercury tilt-switch which acted as a motion sensor. The design prevented the device going off accidentally. It was one of The Bombmaker's favourite bombs, and one of the simplest. There were no booby traps because it was a small bomb and if it was discovered the bomb disposal experts would dump it into an armoured chest and take it away rather than try to deal with it on the spot.

The streetsweeper left the mews just as the five minutes were up. He left his cart a quarter of a mile away, along with the hat, the donkey jacket and the gloves. Fisher had planned everything down to the last detail. O'Reilly kept on walking until he saw a black cab. He hailed it and took it to Victoria Station where he waited for half an hour before catching another cab back to Wapping.

The front door of the mews cottage in Chelsea opened at the same time as the cab turned into Wapping High Street.

Erica's hair still looked as if she had just got out of bed, but this time her lipstick had gone and as Jephcott kissed her he smelt her sex rather than her perfume. Her classy clothes had gone, too, and in their place she wore a white silk dressing-gown. Something else that he'd bought for her.

'Tomorrow?' she breathed, her body tight against his.

'No, my love, I'm afraid not,' Jephcott replied. 'I'll call you.' Over her shoulder he looked at his watch. Plenty of time. He kissed her again and then pulled himself away. She closed the door behind him with a final goodbye, and he adjusted his tie as he went to the car. He unlocked the door to the Rover and got in. He looked at himself in the driving mirror and smoothed down his hair before using the breath-freshener again. The Rover started first time and as he edged it forward the bomb went off, blasting through the wheel-arch and taking off both of his legs in a burst of fire and exploding metal.

Detective Chief Inspector Richard Bromley was filling his briar pipe from a weathered leather pouch when the phone on his desk rang.

'It's the front desk, sir. He's here again.'

Bromley groaned. 'Tell him I'm busy.'

'I've done that, sir. He says he'll wait.'

'Tell him I'll call him when there's any news.'

'I've done that, sir.'

Bromley groaned again. He'd had the same conversation more than a dozen times over the past three weeks but he always hoped that it would end differently, that Nguyen Ngoc Minh would just give up and go home. It had started with phone calls to the general enquiry office, but somewhere along the line somebody had told him that Bromley was handling the case. Nguyen began telephoning him twice a day, once at nine o'clock prompt and again at five o'clock, asking for Detective Chief Inspector Bromley, always polite and deferential. When he first spoke to Nguyen, Bromley felt sorry for him and when he asked how the investigation was going he did his best to sound optimistic. That was his mistake, he realised, he should never have raised the man's hopes. Nguyen explained what had happened to his wife and daughter, quietly and seemingly without emotion, and he told Bromley that the men responsible must be caught. Bromley had agreed and said that they were doing everything they could. Nguyen had thanked him and asked that Bromley call him when the men had been caught. He'd said 'apprehended' but had pronounced each syllable separately as if reading the word for the first time. Five seconds after replacing the receiver, the inspector had forgotten all about the man with the strange name and the awkward English. Until the next day when he rang again. He was just as polite, always calling him 'Detective Chief Inspector Bromley' and never raising his voice. He simply repeated the questions once more. Was there any news? Did they know who had set off the bomb? Were the police about to catch the men? When? He listened to Bromley's replies, which were less

34

optimistic this time, told him how important it was that the men were found, thanked him, and rang off. He rang again the following day. And the day after. Bromley stopped taking his calls and forgot about him.

Three days after the last call he was told that there was someone waiting for him at reception. It wasn't unusual for people to arrive at New Scotland Yard with information that might be useful for the Anti-Terrorist Branch, but he was surprised that the man had asked for him by name because most of his informers wouldn't have wanted to have been seen within a mile of the building. It was Nguyen. Bromley told the man on reception to send the old man away, but he had simply sat down on one of the hard grey sofas and waited. He'd waited until the main offices had closed and then he'd left, only to return the following day. He'd maintained his vigil for more than a week, never making a fuss or doing anything that would justify ejecting him from the premises. He just waited. Bromley had been impressed by the man's stubbornness, but he was also hugely irritated by it. Several times he'd had to walk through reception while he was there and he'd glanced at the slightly built Oriental sitting with his hands in his lap, head lowered like a monk at prayer. Once he'd looked up as Bromley passed and he'd bitten down hard on the stem of his pipe and quickly averted his eyes, but too late to keep the guilt from his face. The old man had called out his name but Bromley didn't look back as he headed for the sanctuary of the lift.

Bromley tamped down the tobacco with his thumb. It wasn't that he was afraid of talking to Nguyen, it was just that there was nothing to tell him. There had been six bombs in all, a total of thirty-two people dead, and the

IRA had claimed responsibility for each explosion and assassination. The bombs had been of different types, though Semtex was always used. They were pretty sure it was the work of one IRA active service unit and that they were based in London for most of the time, but other than that, nothing. They were no closer now than they were when the bombing campaign had started ten weeks earlier. Bromley had told Nguyen that during one of the first telephone calls. Maybe what the old man needed was counselling, or a psychiatrist. Bromley held the phone between his shoulder and his ear while he lit the pipe and puffed it until the tobacco glowed. The pipe, and the tobacco, had been a birthday present from Chris, his fifteen-year-old son, paid for from the money he'd saved working on his paper round.

'She was only sixteen,' Nguyen had said of his daughter. Bromley wondered how he would feel if Chris had been killed. His stomach went cold at the thought of it and he heard himself tell the man on the desk that he'd come down and speak to Nguyen.

'You'll come down, sir?' repeated the man, not believing what he'd heard. Bromley hung up without replying.

Nguyen was standing by the reception desk and he stepped forward to meet Bromley as the lift doors opened.

'Detective Chief Inspector Bromley, it is good of you to see me,' he said slowly and bowed his head. No mention of the countless times that the policeman had refused to even acknowledge his existence. Bromley felt a rush of guilt. He asked the man behind the desk if there was an interview room free and he was told there was. Bromley took Nguyen through a pair of double white doors and along a corridor to a small square room containing a table and two orange plastic seats. He motioned Nguyen to the seat nearest the door but the old man waited until Bromley was seated before he sat down. Bromley drew on his pipe and studied him through a cloud of smoke.

Nguyen was smiling earnestly like an eager-to-please servant. His clothes were clean but scruffy, as if they'd been slept in, and his hair was lank and uncombed. The hands clasped on the table were wrinkled but the nails were neatly clipped. After twenty years as a policeman Bromley had acquired the knack of summing people up at a glance but he had no idea where to start with Nguyen. Maybe it was because he was Oriental. Certain points were obvious. Nguyen was not a rich man, but he had the look of a man who was used to hard work and respons-ibility. There was suffering too, but you didn't have to be Sherlock Holmes to work that out, Bromley knew. His English was reasonably good, though he had to make an effort to choose his words carefully, and there was some-thing vaguely American about his accent. He seemed honest and straightforward and he looked Bromley in the eye as he waited for him to speak.

Bromley took the stem of the pipe from his mouth and ran his left hand through his short-cropped beard. 'Mr Nguyen, you must realise that we are doing everything we can to find the people who killed your wife and daughter. Everything that can be done, is being done, you must believe me when I tell you that. There is no point in you coming here every day. If there is something to tell you, we will telephone you or we will write to you. Do you understand?'

The old man nodded twice, and his smile widened. Several of his back teeth were missing, and one of his canines was badly chipped. 'I understand, Detective Chief Inspector Bromley,' he said slowly.

Bromley continued with the speech he'd rehearsed in his mind while travelling down in the lift. 'The men are members of the IRA, we think they are living in London, probably moving from place to place, perhaps living in bedsitters or cheap boarding houses. They will be using false names and they will be experts at blending into the background. What I am trying to say to you, Mr Nguyen, is that it will be very difficult to find them. Do you understand?'

Nguyen nodded again.

'In fact, it might well be that we never find them. That is a possibility that you must come to terms with. Sometimes the IRA will mount a bombing campaign and then the political climate changes and the bombing stops. If that were to happen, we might never catch the men. But at least the killing will stop. Do you understand?'

Nguyen nodded. 'No,' he said quietly. 'That cannot be so.'

'It is so,' said Bromley.

'It is not something I can accept, Detective Chief Inspector Bromley,' the old man said, still smiling as if he was afraid to offend the policeman. 'You must catch these men.'

'If it is possible, we will, Mr Nguyen. That I can promise. But if it is impossible . . .' He shrugged and put his pipe back into his mouth.

'These men in London. They are doing this because they are told to, yes?'

'We believe they are members of the IRA, yes.'

'But this IRA is not a secret organisation. You know who is in it, you know where they are.'

'Yes,' said Bromley doubtfully, not sure where the man was heading.

'Then why cannot you arrest someone else who you know is in the IRA and make them tell you who is doing the killing?'

Bromley smiled ruefully, knowing that there were a good many men in the Royal Ulster Constabulary and even his own squad who would be more than happy to do just that, to pick them up off the streets and take them to an underground cell and attach electrodes to their private parts and squeeze every bit of information out of them. And there were others who'd welcome a shoot-to-kill policy, official or unofficial, so that they could blow them away without bothering about the niceties of evidence and procedure and witnesses.

'That is not how we do things in this country,' said Bromley.

'What I do not understand is why the Government allows this IRA to be,' said Nguyen.

'To be what?' said Bromley, frowning.

'To exist, to be,' Nguyen said. 'Why does the Government not arrest everybody who is in the IRA. Lock them up. Then there will be no more killing. And perhaps then you find who murdered my family.'

Bromley held his hands up in surrender. 'Life is not so simple, Mr Nguyen. It is a question of politics, not policing. You should speak to your MP.'

'MP?' said Nguyen, his brow creased.

'Member of Parliament,' explained the policeman. 'Perhaps he can help you.'

Bromley got to his feet. 'Mr Nguyen, there is nothing else I can tell you, I am afraid. I don't want to offend you, but you must not keep coming here. I am very sorry about what happened to your family, but your coming here is not helping. It makes it more difficult for us. Do you understand?'

Nguyen pushed back his chair slowly and stood in front of Bromley, still smiling. 'I understand, Detective Chief Inspector Bromley. And I thank you for talking to me.' He held out his hand and Bromley shook it. The small, wrinkled hand was surprisingly strong, as if there were steel rods under the old skin. Nguyen turned and walked out, leaving Bromley alone with his pipe.

Tempers were flaring on the football pitch. It wasn't that there was anything at stake other than the game itself, it was just that the army team hated to lose and they were two goals down with less than ten minutes to go before half-time. Their opponents, the local police team, had the edge when it came to skill and finesse but the army boys had the aggression. The referee looked at his watch and missed the sharp elbow jab in the ribs that sent the police sweeper sprawling but he heard the cop swear and he blew hard on his whistle. The crowd jeered as the referee fumbled in the pocket of his shorts for his notebook.

There were two groups of supporters, one on each side of the pitch. The police supporters, mainly loyal girlfriends and bored wives, stood with their backs to Woolwich Common, facing Stadium Road. The army supporters, mostly soldiers with nothing else to do on a Saturday morning, were ranged along the other side. O'Reilly was standing with the police wives as he studied the referee through the lens of his Pentax. The man's cheeks were flushed red as he spluttered at the policeman who was waving his arms and protesting his innocence. He moved the lens to the left and the Queen Elizabeth Military Hospital came into focus and then he saw the road sign. Shrapnel Close. He smiled at the irony of it.

The referee blew his whistle to restart the game as O'Reilly walked slowly along the sideline, stopping every now and again to take photographs. Over his shoulder was a black camera bag. Close to the corner flag was a stack of sports bags and towels and two polythene bags full of quartered oranges. The crowd roared as a big, beefy, army striker sent the ball ripping into the net, and as his team-mates rushed to congratulate him O'Reilly dropped his camera bag down among the sports bags. He walked back to the line and took more photographs before checking his watch. Three minutes to go. A red Renault drove down Repository Road and into Stadium Road and came to a halt at the junction with Shrapnel Close. O'Reilly knew that he'd attract attention to himself if he walked behind the goalmouth while the game was on, so he stayed where he was until the referee's whistle blasted out and brought the first half to a close. The players ran across the pitch to where the bags were as O'Reilly walked over to the car. McCormick opened the passenger door for him and he got in. They both looked over at the footballers, clustered around the now-opened polythene bags and helping themselves to pieces of orange.

'Now?' said McCormick, licking his lips nervously.

'No, Fisher said we wait until we're on Shooters Hill Road,' replied O'Reilly.

'Let's go then.' McCormick put the car in gear and drove to the main junction and indicated before he turned. He pulled the car to the side some fifty yards down the road. O'Reilly nodded and opened the glove compartment and took out a small walkie-talkie. It was an Icom IC2 transceiver, a hand-held model. There was another in the camera bag, though it had been modified. The Bombmaker had attached a relay switch to the loudspeaker circuit which was connected to a second circuit, containing a 1.5 volt battery and a gunpowder detonator. The detonator was embedded in twenty-five pounds of Semtex explosive, around which was wrapped a cluster of three-inch nails. There was no timing device because the bomb would be detonated at a safe distance by the transceiver in O'Reilly's hand. And there were no booby traps because they weren't sure when he'd be able to put the bag down.

O'Reilly saw the avaricious look in McCormick's eye, the pleading of a dog begging for a bone. He handed it over. McCormick handled it reverently like a holy icon.

'Are you sure?' he asked.

'Go for it,' said O'Reilly.

McCormick switched the control switch to 'send' and held the transceiver to his mouth. 'Bang,' he said, and they saw the flash of light followed quickly by the thud of the explosion and felt the tremor through the car seats.

'Come on, let's go,' said O'Reilly.

They were driving along the A102 heading for the Blackwall Tunnel by the time the first white-coated doctor reached the blood-soaked pitch.

Sir John Brownlow was getting irritable, so Ellen brewed him a fresh cup of coffee and placed it on the desk in front of him. He smiled his thanks and she could read his discomfort in his eyes. Ellen Howard had been the MP's personal assistant for almost three years and she'd reached the stage where she could pretty much judge what he was thinking by the look on his face. Today he was wearing his professional, caring mask but she could tell that he was far from happy. He hated the regular constituency surgeries where the punters queued up to present him with their problems and to ask him to put their lives in order. The ones at the local party office weren't so bad because they were mainly an opportunity of pressing the flesh with the party faithful, it was when he had to go out and about that he suffered. Ellen knew what the problem was, though she would never dare tell the MP to his face. It was that Sir John simply did not care about the man in the street, and he sympathised even less with their trials and tribulations. But he was all too well aware of how narrow his majority had been at the last election, and he had resigned himself to the fact that being seen helping his constituents with their problems was a vote-catcher. Holding the surgery in a local citizens advice centre eased some of the pain as it meant he could usually pass them on to someone else. Teflon Time, he called it. The trick was to make sure that nothing stuck and that the punters went away thinking that their MP had done his best and was worth supporting.

The middle-aged woman sitting opposite him in a thick tweed coat and a fake fur hat had bought her council house by mortgaging herself to the hilt. Her son had helped out with the payments until they'd had a row and he'd left home. Now the building society was threatening to evict her. If she sold the house would Sir John be able to get her into another council house? The MP smiled benignly and told her that there were people at the centre who would help her negotiate with the building society and have the payments frozen or reduced. He motioned at Ellen and introduced her to the woman and then stood up to shake her hand, patting her on the back as he ushered her to the door. Ellen took her down the corridor into another room and left her with one of the advisers there. Teflon Time strikes again, she thought. There were half a dozen people sitting on a line of chairs in the corridor outside the office commandeered by the MP. There was an old couple, a young man in jeans and a motorcycle jacket who looked like he might be troublesome, two housewives, and a Chinese man in a blue duffel coat. He was muttering something, reading from a small piece of paper in his hands and repeating something to himself over and over again. As she walked past him it sounded as if he said 'elected representative'.

'Next please,' she said, and the old man stood up and helped his wife to her feet. Sir John greeted them with his hand outstretched and a caring smile on his face.

Ellen sat behind her own desk, to the left of Sir John's and at right angles to it, and watched and learned. She had hopes of one day following him into the House of Commons. Her degree was in political science and she'd been chairman of her university's student union, but what she needed now was hard, political experience. Sir John Brownlow was providing that, even if it meant that she had to tolerate the occasional wandering hand on her buttocks or suggestive remark, but so far she'd been able to fend off his passes without offending him. Besides, he'd stopped being quite so chauvinistic once she'd become a good friend and confidante of his wife and taken his two teenage daughters to the cinema a few times. Ellen knew what she wanted, and how she wanted to get it, and what she didn't want was to

44

get her ticket to the House by lying on her back with the Honourable Member between her legs.

He spent half an hour with the old couple, and then Ellen took them out and called for whoever was next. The Oriental man looked around, saw that everyone was looking at him, and got to his feet. 'I think it is my turn,' he said quietly.

She asked his name and then he followed her into the office. Sir John was already in position to shake hands and Ellen saw his jaw tighten when he saw Nguyen, but only for a second. Then the teeth flashed and the eyes crinkled into the face that smiled down from the posters at election time. Sir John was nothing if not professional.

'Mr Nguyen,' she said by way of introduction. The MP shook the man's hand firmly and he waited until Nguyen was seated before going back behind the desk.

'How can I help you, Mr Nguyen?' he said, steepling his well-manicured hands under his square chin.

In a low, quiet voice, Nguyen told him what had happened to his wife and daughter, about the bomb, and the conversations he had had with the police and the Anti-Terrorist Branch. 'My family died more than three months ago,' he said. 'And still the men responsible have not been caught.'

Sir John nodded understandingly. 'But what is it that you want me to do?'

'I wrote to you many times, Sir John. Many times.'

The MP gave Ellen a sideways look and she nodded quickly. Yes, she remembered his letters now. Carefully handwritten, every word in capital letters. She had drafted sympathetic replies promising nothing and Sir John had signed them without reading them.

'I asked you to help bring the men to justice,' Nguyen

45

continued. 'Detective Chief Inspector Bromley said that the capture of the men was a political matter.'

'Detective Chief Inspector Bromley?'

'He is a policeman who catches terrorists. But he told me that he could not force the men in the IRA to tell him who killed my family.'

'That is probably true, I am afraid,' said Sir John. 'There are many people who probably feel that the police and the army should have stronger powers, but we are, when all is said and done, a democracy. We cannot torture people or imprison them simply because they do not give us the information we seek.' He looked concerned, but to Ellen he sounded pompous and uncaring.

'But could not the Government change the law so that such things could be done? So that the police could force others in the IRA to tell what they know?'

'In theory yes, but it would not happen. I am afraid you must allow the police to do their job, Mr Nguyen. I am sure that they are doing their best.'

Nguyen smiled nervously. 'What I would like, Sir John, is for you to change the law.'

Sir John snorted. 'Come, come, Mr Nguyen. What makes you think I can do that?'

'Because you are my . . .' The old man seemed to stumble on the words before finishing the sentence. 'My elected representative.' He seemed to take pride in the fact that he had remembered the words. 'You are my MP. I wish you to change the law so that the killers of my family can be brought to justice.'

'You have a strange idea of the powers of an MP, Mr Nguyen. I cannot change laws just because you think justice has not been done.'

46

Nguyen hung his head and said something quietly.

'I'm sorry?' said Sir John, leaning forward to listen.

Nguyen looked up. There were tears in his eyes and Ellen's heart went out to him.

'What am I to do?' he asked the MP. 'My family is dead. What am I to do?'

Sir John leant back in his chair and folded his arms across his chest. Ellen recognised his defensive position. There was nothing he or anyone else could do. The IRA was an insurmountable problem. Even if they were to catch the men behind the latest series of bombings, it would not stop, another active service unit would come to life. The killings would never stop, not until the British pulled out of Northern Ireland. And there was little like-lihood of that happening.

'How long have you been in this country, Mr Nguyen?' Sir John asked.

'I have been a British citizen since 1982. Very long time.' He reached into his duffel coat pocket and took out a passport, the old type, dark-blue with the gold crest on the front. He held it out to the MP but he seemed reluc-tant to take it and kept his arms folded. Nguyen put it back in his pocket.

'From Hong Kong?' Sir John asked. Ellen realised then why he was so defensive. He had been one of the most outspoken critics of the Government's offer of passports to the colony's middle classes.

'Do you not have family back in Hong Kong? Can you not go back there?'

The old man looked surprised. 'Hong Kong? Why I go back there?'

Sir John appeared equally confused. 'That's where

47

you came from,' he said. 'Surely you still have family there?'

'I not Hong Kong Chinese,' Nguyen explained. 'I am Vietnamese. From Vietnam.'

Realisation dawned on the MP's face and he sighed audibly. He was, Ellen knew, even more vehemently against Vietnamese boat people being offered sanctuary in Britain. God, the number of times she'd listened to him address meetings on the difference between political and economic refugees and how Britain couldn't offer homes to everyone in the world who wanted a better standard of living.

'North or south?' asked Sir John.

Nguyen smiled. 'Today there is no north or south. Only Vietnam.'

'When you escaped,' the MP pressed. 'Where were you from then?'

Nguyen shrugged. 'Both,' he said. 'North and south.'

'And why did you come to England?'

'Because I could not live in Vietnam. Because the Communists persecuted me and my family. I helped the Americans in the war. When the Americans go they put me in prison. So we escaped. To Britain.'

'Why Britain?'

'Because here we can be free.'

The MP nodded. 'But do you not see, Mr Nguyen? The reason that you can be free in this country and not your own is because we have laws for everybody here. Nobody is above the law. But equally nobody is denied its protection. That is what makes democracy work. That is why you wanted to come here in the first place, to be free. You cannot now ask for the laws to be changed, to take away the rights of others.'

48

'Even if they have killed my family?'

'You must allow the police to do their job. You must have faith in our system, Mr Nguyen.' He put his hands on the desk top and pushed himself up. Nguyen tilted his head up and for the first time it gave him a more confident, vaguely arrogant look. Then he stood up and he became once more the stooped old man, alone in the world. Sir John patted him on the back as he guided him through the doorway and into the corridor and then he slipped back into the office.

'Christ, Ellen, these people. They come over here, we give them homes, we give them money, and still they want more. If they don't like this country the way it is, why don't they just get the hell out and go back to where they came from?'

'He's still in shock, poor man,' said Ellen. 'His whole family was wiped out. Think how he must feel.'

'That was four months ago, Ellen. And there have been what, two or three bombs since then. And how many other victims? Yet you don't hear their relatives demanding that we pull in IRA members off the street and pull out their fingernails.'

'He wasn't actually saying that, Sir John. He was . . .'

The MP snorted angrily. 'Bullshit! That's exactly what he wanted. And can you imagine what the Press would do if they even thought we were considering something like that? They'd scream "Big Brother" and "Violation of Human Rights" and you know they would. Remember Gibraltar? They don't think about the people whose lives were saved when the SAS stopped the car bomb from being detonated. All they remember is the IRA being shot while they were on the ground. Remember the uproar over the *Belgrano*?'

Ellen didn't argue. She knew full well that there was no point in taking sides against her boss. She was there to learn from him, not to antagonise him. She smiled and brushed a loose strand of hair off her face. 'I'll get the next one in for you,' she said sweetly while wondering how such a racist could ever get elected. There was so much she still had to learn, she realised.

Jon Simpson took the call from the uniformed security guard at reception. 'There's a chap down here wants to speak to a reporter,' he said gruffly.

'What about?' asked Simpson.

'Dunno,' said the guard.

'Do me a favour and ask him, will you?' sighed Simpson. The security guards weren't paid for brain power, just for bulk, but there were times when Simpson wished they were a mite brighter. There was a pause before the guard's laconic voice returned.

'Says it's about the bombs.'

Simpson felt the hairs on the back of his neck stand up. The IRA bombing campaign had been going on for more than four months and the police seemed to be no nearer catching the bombers. Maybe the punter downstairs held the key, it was amazing the number of times that they came to the paper rather than going straight to the police. Or perhaps it wasn't so surprising – the paper paid handsomely for information. The news editor looked around the newsroom to see who was free and his eyes settled on Woody who was reading the *Daily Star* and picking his teeth with a plastic paper-clip. It had taken Woody weeks of plaintive phone calls before Simpson had allowed him to start shifting again and only after he'd promised not to drink on the job. Not to excess, anyway. Expecting Woody not to drink at all was asking the impossible. And he was a bloody good journalist.

'Woody!' he yelled.

Woody's head jerked up and he came over immediately, pen and notebook in hand. He was still at the eager-to-please stage. 'There's a punter downstairs. Something about the bombs. See what he's got, will you?'

Woody nodded and headed for the lift. The man waiting downstairs was Oriental, wearing a blue duffel coat with black toggles, faded jeans and dirty training shoes. He was carrying a plastic carrier bag and was wiping his nose with a grubby handkerchief. He snorted into it and then shoved it into his coat pocket before stretching his arm out to shake hands. Woody pretended not to notice the gesture and herded the old man towards a group of low-backed sofas in the far corner of the reception area. Carrier bags were always a bad sign, he thought, as he watched the man settle into a sofa next to a large, spreading tree with weeping leaves. Punters who arrived at newspaper offices with carrier bags often produced strange things from them. During his twenty years as a journalist Woody had just about seen everything. There were the paranoids who thought they were being followed and who would produce lists of numbers of cars that were pursuing them, or taxis, or descriptions of people who had appeared in their dreams, or lists of MPs who were in fact aliens operating from a base on the far side of the moon. There were the punters who felt they'd had a raw deal from one of the big international companies and had photocopies of correspondence going back ten years to prove it. There were the nutters who claimed to have written Oscar-winning film scripts only to have their ideas stolen by a famous Hollywood director, and they'd open their plastic bags to show their own versions. Sometimes they were written in crayon. Not a good sign.

'How can I help you?' asked Woody, his heart heavy.

'My name is Nguyen Ngoc Minh,' the man said, and Woody scribbled in his notebook, just a random motion because he didn't reckon there was going to be a story in this and he didn't want to go through the hassle of asking the guy to spell his name.

The old man thrust his hand into the carrier bag and took out a colour photograph and handed it to Woody. It was a family portrait of the man, an old woman and a pretty young girl. Woody raised his eyebrows inquisitively.

'My wife,' said Nguyen. 'My wife and my daughter. They were killed this year.'

'I'm sorry to hear that,' said Woody, his pen scratching on the notebook. He wasn't using shorthand, he just wanted to be seen to be doing something so that he didn't have to look the man in the eye. The brown eyes were like magnets that threatened to pull him into the old man's soul and several times Woody had found himself having to drag himself back. They were sorrowful eyes, those of a dog that had been kicked many times but which still hoped one day to have its loyalty rewarded.

'They were killed by IRA bombers in January,' continued Nguyen. He delved into the bag once more and pulled out a sheaf of newspaper cuttings and spread them out on the low table in front of Woody. Among them he saw the *Sunday World* front-page story on the Knightsbridge bombing and the pictures they'd used inside. Strapped along the bottom was a list of the reporters and photographers who'd worked on the story. The intro and a good deal of the copy was Woody's but his name wasn't there, Simpson had insisted that it stay off. Another punishment.

'I remember,' he said.

'There have been many bombs since,' said Nguyen, and he pointed to the various cuttings. The judge blown up outside the house of his mistress, the bomb at Bank Tube station, the police van that had been hit in Fulham, the Woolwich football bombing. Good stories, thought Woody. He waited for the old man to continue.

Nguyen told him about the visit by the police, of their promise that the men would be caught. He told him about what he'd later been told at the police station, and by the Anti-Terrorist Branch and finally of his conversation with his MP, Sir John Brownlow. 'They all tell me the same thing,' he said. 'They tell me to wait. To let the police do their job.'

Woody nodded, not sure what to say. He'd stopped writing in the notebook and studied the cuttings while the old man talked.

'I want to do something,' Nguyen said. 'I want to offer money for the names of the men who did the bombs. A reward.'

Woody looked up. 'I don't think the newspaper would be prepared to offer a reward,' he said. Too true, he thought. A right bloody can of worms that would open up. It was OK to offer money for the return of a stolen baby, or to pay some amateur model for details of her affair with a trendy businessman or a minor pop star, but he could imagine the response to a request for a reward in the hunt for IRA killers. Put the paper right in the firing line, that would.

Nguyen waved his hands and shook his head.

'No, no, you not understand,' he said. 'Reward not from newspaper. From me. I have money.' He picked up the carrier bag by the bottom and tipped the rest of its contents on the table. It was money, bundles and bundles of it, neatly sorted into five-, ten- and twenty-pound notes, each stack held together with thick rubber bands. Woody ran his hands through the pile and picked up one of the bundles and flicked the notes. They looked real enough.

Nguyen read his thoughts. 'They are real,' he said. 'There is eleven thousand pounds here. It is all the money I have.'

Woody saw the guard staring at the money open-mouthed and so he began to scoop it back into the plastic bag. The old man helped him.

'You shouldn't be carrying so much cash around with you,' whispered Woody. 'Why isn't this in the bank?'

Nguyen shrugged. 'I not trust bank. Many people have money in bank when Americans leave Vietnam. They would not give money back. They steal. I take care of my own money. This all I have. I want paper to use it as reward. Can do?'

Woody pushed the bag across the table. 'I'm sorry, no. My paper wouldn't do that sort of thing. And I don't think that any newspaper would.'

The old man looked pained by what he'd been told and Woody felt as if he'd just slapped him across the face. He stood up and waited until Nguyen did the same, the bag of money held tightly in his left hand. He offered the right hand to Woody and this time he took it and shook it. He felt intensely sorry for the old man, sorry for what he'd been through and sorry that there was nothing that could be done for him. He heard himself say: 'Look, why

54

don't you give me your phone number and if I can think of anything I'll call you?'

Nguyen smiled gratefully and told Woody the number, repeating it slowly and checking as he wrote it down. Woody didn't know why but he had a sudden urge to help the old man, to make some sort of gesture to show that he really did care and wasn't just making polite noises. He wrote down his home number on another sheet of paper and ripped it from the notebook. 'Take this,' he said. 'Call me if . . .' He didn't know how to finish the sentence, because he knew there was nothing tangible he could offer. Nguyen bowed his head and thanked Woody and then left. Woody watched him walk down the road, a small man in a duffel coat with eleven thousand pounds in a plastic bag. 'And I thought I'd seen everything,' he said to himself.

O'Reilly walked up the steps to the main entrance of the police station and turned round so that he could push open the door with his shoulder. He was using both hands to carry a large cardboard box. The box was new and the lettering on it said that it contained a Japanese video recorder. A housewife with a crying child in a pushchair held the door open for him and he smiled boyishly at her.

He took the box over to the enquiries desk and placed it in front of an overweight uniformed constable who looked at him with bored eyes.

'How can I help you, sir?' the policeman asked unenthusiastically.

'I found this in my back garden this morning,' said O'Reilly, nodding at the box. 'It's a video recorder.'

'You surprise me,' said the policeman. He opened the

flaps at the top of the box and looked inside. He saw a black video recorder, still in its polythene wrapping. There was a blank guarantee card and an instruction booklet.

'You've no idea where it came from?' the officer asked, and O'Reilly shook his head.

'It looks new,' said O'Reilly. 'I thought of keeping it but my wife said no, it might belong to someone, and besides, you know, there might be a reward or something. So she said take it to the police, you know, and so here I am.' O'Reilly smiled like an idiot. He was wearing horn-rimmed glasses with thick lenses, a flat cap and a sheepskin jacket. That was all the disguise he needed because even if they ever connected the delivery of the video recorder with the explosion, all the guy would remember would be the hat and the glasses. People's memories were generally lousy when it came to describing faces, even with the latest computerised photofit systems.

'Very public-spirited of you, sir,' said the policeman. 'Now, can you give me your name and address?'

O'Reilly gave him a false name and an address in nearby Battersea and explained again how he'd found the video recorder while the policeman carefully wrote it all down.

'Right, sir, that's all. We'll be in touch if it isn't claimed,' he said, and O'Reilly thanked him and left. He passed the housewife outside, kneeling by her child and wiping its face with a paper handkerchief. She looked up at him and smiled and he winked at her. 'Lovely kid,' he said.

The policeman lifted the box, grunting as he did so, and carried it out of the office and down a white-tiled corridor to a windowless storage room. He found a space for it on one of the grey metal shelves, next to a set of fly-fishing tackle and a bundle of umbrellas. The room was full of abandoned or forgotten belongings, all waiting to be taken to one of the city's lost property storage centres. The policeman walked back to the reception desk and forgot all about the video recorder and the man who'd delivered it.

The bomb was similar in design to the one they'd used outside the Knightsbridge department store. The Bombmaker had stripped out most of the workings of the video recorder and replaced it with twenty pounds of Semtex explosive. There were no nuts and bolts in this bomb because the aim was to demolish a building rather than mutilate crowds of people but it used a similar detonator and timer. There were two anti-handling devices, though, just in case it didn't go off for any reason. Any attempt to open the casing would set it off, and it was also primed to explode if it was connected to the mains, just in case any light-fingered copper decided to pop it into his car and take it home. The Bombmaker did not have a very high opinion of the police, be they in Belfast or London.

O'Reilly delivered the bomb at four o'clock and it was set to explode an hour later, just as the shifts were changing at the station. He was back in the Wapping flat well before the timer clicked on and completed the circuit which detonated the bomb in a flash of light. The force of the explosion blew out the front and the back walls of the police station and the two floors above it collapsed down, trapping and killing dozens of men and women in an avalanche of masonry and timber and choking dust.

Woody was reading the morning papers when the tele-phone rang. As usual he'd started going through the tabloids first, and on the desk in front of him he'd opened the *Sun* and the *Daily Mirror*. Both had used pictures of the after-math of the police-station bombing. The *Sun* had the better photographs but the *Mirror* had the edge when it came to eye-witness accounts. He reached for *Today* as he answered the phone.

'Mr Wood?' asked a voice that Woody didn't recognise.

'Yes?'

'It is Nguyen Ngoc Minh. I came to your office three days ago.'

'I remember,' said Woody. The Chinaman. He flicked through *Today*. Same pictures as the *Sun*, more or less. Plus a line drawing of the inside of a booby-trapped bomb, a Blue Peter do-it-yourself guide for amateurs to follow. And here's one I exploded earlier, thought Woody with a wry smile. 'How can I help you?'

'You have seen the newspapers today?'

'The bombing?'

'These people must be stopped, Mr Wood.' Woody was only half listening to the man, he had a sickening feeling that he knew where the conversation was heading. Would the paper offer the reward? Would the paper put pressure on the police? The army? The Government? Woody didn't want to be rude to the old man but he wasn't prepared to be used as the paper's agony aunt. Not on a freelance's pay, anyway. He thought of giving The Chinaman the phone number for *Today*. He began turning the pages looking for the number.

'Mr Wood?'

'Yes?'

'You said that you would help me.'

'Well . . .' said Woody, about to back-pedal while he hunted frantically for *Today*'s telephone number.

'I want to speak to somebody at the IRA. Do you know anybody that would talk to me?'

Woody stopped turning the pages of the newspaper.

'What are you thinking of doing?' he asked suspiciously, scenting a possible story.

'I want to talk to somebody in the IRA, that is all.'

'I don't think they'll help you, I really don't. And it might backfire.'

'Backfire? I do not understand.'

'They are dangerous men, if they thought you were a threat to them, or even just a nuisance, there's a good chance they'd hurt you.'

'All I want to do is to talk to them.'

Woody sighed. 'OK, for a start you don't want to talk to the IRA. You'd be better off trying Sinn Fein, that's the political wing of the organisation. The Sinn Fein spokesmen are well-known.'

'Could you give me some names, and tell me where I might find them?'

Woody looked at the photographs of smashed brick-work, broken glass and misshapen metal. What the hell, he thought. Why not?

'I'll have to call you back, give me your number.'

'I gave you before.'

'I know, but I'm using a different notebook now.'

Nguyen read out the figures slowly, and Woody promised to ring him back later in the day. He was about to go over to the cuttings library but had second thoughts and instead decided to call one of the paper's Belfast stringers. Might as well get it from the horse's mouth. For a change the stringer, Pat Quigley, was helpful, sober and in his office, a hell of an unusual combination and Woody took full advantage of it. He gave Woody three names, potted biographies, where they lived, and contact phone numbers, and told him a foul joke involving two nuns and a bar of soap from which Woody deduced that the man wasn't a Catholic.

When Woody called The Chinaman back the phone was answered with a guttural 'Double Happiness Take-Away'.

'This is Ian Wood,' he said, suddenly realising he couldn't remember The Chinaman's name. He had just written 'Chinaman' in his notebook.

'Double Happiness Take-Away,' the voice repeated.

Woody cursed under his breath, then he heard another voice and the sound of the phone being transferred.

'Mr Wood?' said Nguyen.

'I have the information you wanted,' Woody said. He read the notes from his notebook, spelling out the names and repeating the numbers several times until he was sure The Chinaman had got them down correctly.

'Thank you, Mr Wood. I not bother you again.' The phone went dead before Woody had the chance to ask The Chinaman for his name. There could be a story in this somewhere. 'Heartbroken Father Pleads With IRA Killers'. 'Bomb Mission Of Tragic Dad'. That sort of thing. Good Sunday-paper stuff. Woody was about to ring back when there was a shout from the far end of the office.

'Woody! Call for you. What extension are you on?'

'4553,' he yelled back, and waited until the call was put through.

'Woody?' said a girl's voice, soft and with a Scottish burr.

'Yeah, speaking,' he answered, groping for a pen.

'It's Maggie.' Maggie? His mind raced, frantically trying

to put a face to the name and the voice. 'How are you?' she asked.

'Me? I'm fine, fine.' He closed his eyes and began banging the palm of his hand against his forehead as if trying to jolt his memory.

'You do remember?' she asked, sounding hurt.

'Of course I do.' He began flicking through the images in his head, searching for a Maggie.

'The Coach and Horses,' she prompted.

Maggie! The girl with red hair and grey eyes and the earthy sense of humour. He remembered how much he'd enjoyed being with her, though for the life of him he couldn't recall what they'd talked about, other than the fact that she'd told him a couple of fairly risqué jokes. Would she appreciate the one about the nuns and the soap? Probably not.

'Of course I remember, how are you?' He tried to recall the name of her partner. Todd? Rob? Ross? It bobbed away on the outer fringes of his memory, just out of reach. Most of that evening was a blank, though he vaguely remembered putting away the best part of a bottle of a very civilised malt whisky. Had he kissed her? He couldn't remember. There was something else as well, something sad, very, very sad. Woody's eyes glanced at the photographs in the *Sun* and it all flooded back as if a dam had burst. It had been the day of the big bombing in Knightsbridge. He'd locked away the sickening images of that day, the pictures that had been too horrific to use in the paper, the twisted bodies, the severed limbs, the blood, the Retriever with its jaws clamped on its gory prize. He didn't want to think about that day, but Maggie had been part of it and recalling her brought everything back into focus. He breathed deeply, trying to clear his head.

'I'm fine, too. Isn't it a lovely day?'

'Is it? We've no way of knowing, here. All the blinds are down so that we can use the terminals.' That's what management claimed, but Woody reckoned it was just to stop them looking out of the windows and daydreaming.

'Well, take it from me, the sun is shining and the birds are singing. I was wondering if you fancied going out for a drink again one day this week.'

'Sure, that'd be great. What about tomorrow night?'

She agreed, and they arranged to meet at the same pub.

'Woody, are you OK?' she asked. 'You sound a bit distant.'

'Yeah, somebody walked over my grave, that's all. Nothing to worry about. I'll be fine by tomorrow.'

When she'd gone Woody put his head in his hands and closed his eyes, but he couldn't block out the images of death and destruction. He needed a drink. Badly.

The function room had been booked in the name of the Belfast Overseas Investors Club but the dozen men sitting at the long mahogany table had little interest in investment. The man standing at the head of the table in a green tweed jacket and black woollen trousers could have passed as a mildly eccentric provincial stockbroker with his greying hair and slightly flushed cheeks. He was in his fifties and looked like a rugby player gone to seed, which is exactly what Liam Hennessy was. But after playing for his country he'd gone on to become a political adviser to Sinn Fein. Married with two children, Liam Hennessy was one of the most powerful men in the Republican movement.

The eleven listening to him were all high-ranking

Provisional IRA officials and they had all been called to the hotel in Belfast at short notice. On the table in front of them were jugs of iced water and upturned glasses, but none had been touched. Each man also had a notepad in a red leather folder and a ballpoint pen.

Hennessy stood with his arms folded across his chest and spoke in a soft Irish brogue. He first thanked them for coming, though a summons from Liam Hennessy was not something that any of them could ignore. The group met regularly, always in different venues and under different names so that the security forces wouldn't be able to eaves-drop, usually to discuss financing or strategy or matters of discipline, but today's gathering was special. They had all seen the television reports of the south London police-station bombing and the pictures of ambulancemen and firemen hauling the rubble away with their bare hands, and they had heard that the IRA had claimed responsibility.

To Hennessy's left was a large flat-screen television on a matte black stand, and underneath it was a video recorder. He took a videocassette off the table and slotted it into the recorder. The screen flickered and then there were shots of the Kensington bombing recorded from the BBC news. It was followed by a report of the Woolwich bombing, the explosion in Bank Tube station and the crop of car bombs that had killed or injured judges, police and army officers. Then the screen dissolved into black and white static and Hennessy bent down and switched the machine off.

'This must stop,' said Hennessy quietly. He was not a man who needed to raise his voice or bang his fist on the table to make his anger felt. 'Never in the history of the Cause have we been closer to getting a political solution.

Look at South Africa. The Government there is now talking to the ANC and that would have been unthinkable a few years ago. The ANC's acts of terrorism go way beyond anything the IRA has ever done. With the Americans withdrawing their troops from Europe and the opening up of Eastern Europe, this Government is finding it harder and harder to justify its armed presence in Northern Ireland. This Government is getting tired, politically and economically, and it is through the ballot-box and by lobbying in Westminster that this war will be won.'

There were grumblings from several of the men at the table and Hennessy held up his hand to silence them. 'I am not saying that we give up the struggle, nor that we release the pressure here. What I am saying is that it does us no good at all to take the conflict to the mainland. We have tried in the past and the backlash, both political and from the public, has done us more harm than good. That is why what is happening in England now is so detrimental to our cause.'

A few of the men nodded in agreement, but Hennessy could see that others were still not convinced.

'We cannot succeed in our political struggle by using violence in English cities. It must stop. Which brings us to our second problem. Who in God's name is behind this bombing campaign?' He looked at the men around the table but was met with a wall of shaking heads. Over the previous four months Hennessy or one of his associates from the upper echelons of Sinn Fein had met with all of the top IRA organisers in Belfast and in Dublin in an attempt to identify the team behind the bombings. When they'd first been told that the terror campaign was an unsanctioned one they had been astonished – most had assumed that it had been ordered on a 'need to know' basis. It was inconceivable, they thought, that a campaign of such ferocity and technical sophistication could be masterminded from outside the organisation. The bombs were all variations of IRA designs and explosives, and whenever the bombers claimed responsibility they always gave the current identifying codeword, but as far as Hennessy could determine they were most definitely not acting under IRA authority. Unless one of the men around the table had been lying.

He studied their faces, most of them in their fifties and sixties, hard men whose eyes looked back at him levelly. Most of them had killed, and the few who hadn't had arranged or ordered assassinations, yet to the outsider they would have looked no more sinister than a group of pigeon fanciers gathered to discuss their annual show.

'After an extensive investigation, we have come to the conclusion that we are dealing with a rogue group, a group that we are sure must have been within the organisation until recently, who are now operating on their own,' said Hennessy. He saw one or two frowns. 'The fact that they know the codewords, even after they are changed, suggests that they still have connections, and high level connections at that. And the type of explosive devices would indicate that they are IRA trained. It could even be that they passed through one of the Libyan training schools.'

One of the older members of the group, white-haired and with rosy cheeks from years on the hills around his farm, cracked his knuckles under the table to catch Hennessy's attention. 'If what you say is true, Liam, then it should not be too hard to pin these people down.'

Hennessy nodded. 'In theory that's so, Patrick. But it

will require a hell of a lot of legwork. We are going to have to speak to everyone within the organisation who has bomb-making skills, to find out where they are and if they have been out of the country. Or if they have instructed anyone else. And it cannot be one man, so we'll also be looking for any other IRA members who are unaccounted for. In short, gentlemen, we will have to interview every single member of the organisation.'

Patrick Sewell leant back in his chair and cracked his knuckles again. 'That could cause some resentment, Liam, especially when many of our younger people are actually in favour of what has been happening. The bombing campaign has its supporters, you know. And it wasn't all that many years ago that you yourself weren't averse to taking the struggle over the water.'

Hennessy leant forward and placed his hands flat on the highly polished table. 'I'm all too well aware that there are hotheads within the movement who would prefer to see us blowing up police stations in London, but they must learn to understand that there is a time for violence and a time for negotiation,' he said.

Sewell grinned. 'And if they don't agree?'

'Then, Patrick, you are free to blow their fucking kneecaps off, sure enough.'

Hennessy grinned and so did Sewell and the group burst into deep-throated laughter. The two men were best of friends and they went back a long way. A hell of a long way. They both had a powdery dry sense of humour and took great pleasure in winding each other up.

Hennessy waited for the laughter to die away before continuing. 'There is a second line of enquiry which we must pursue,' he said. 'Whoever is behind the bombing campaign appears to have a ready source of explosives and bomb-making equipment. I want every single stockpile of arms checked, both here and on the mainland. And I don't mean that we just check that they are there, I mean every item must be verified. Verified and then re-hidden. It could be that they have access to more than one of our stockpiles and have taken a small amount from each place. You see what I mean? A few pounds of Semtex from here, a detonator there, a transmitter from somewhere else. Hoping that we wouldn't notice.'

A thin, angular man with tinted glasses and slicked-back greying hair caught Hennessy's eye with a wave of his hand. His name was Hugh McGrath, and his main job within the organisation was to liaise with the Libyans, providers of much of the organisation's money and equipment.

'Liam, you can't be serious. The whole point of these stockpiles is that they remain untouched until we need them. Disturbing them unnecessarily risks drawing attention to them,' he said.

Hennessy took his hands off the table and stood upright. He could understand his concern, McGrath had personally supervised the importation of much of the IRA's ordnance and was all too well aware of what it had cost, in terms of hard cash and lives lost.

'We'll be careful, Hugh. We'll be damned careful. But I think that a thorough examination of all our stockpiles will give us our best indication of who is behind the bombing campaign. I agree it's a risk, but it is a calculated one. It's a risk we must take, right enough.'

'If you say so,' said McGrath, but Hennessy could tell from his tone that he wasn't convinced. He made a mental note to massage his ego after the meeting.

'What I need from you all is a full list of all your ordnance stocks. And I mean every single one, authorised and non-authorised. I know that we all like to have a little something tucked away for a rainy day, but the list must be comprehensive. And alongside the contents of each stockpile I want the names of all the people who know its location.'

There were a few heavy sighs from his audience.

'A list like that will be a very dangerous thing, Liam. In the wrong hands it could be fatal,' said Sewell.

'I know that. There will be only one copy, and I will have it. I will arrange for the stockpiles to be checked, and I will arrange for different teams to do the checking. Only I will know all the locations. And the men I get to visit the stockpiles will not be told why. If all goes to plan I will eventually know which have been tampered with, and then by cross-referencing the names I should be able to identify the common links. Now, if you don't object, I suggest we compile the list as best we can. Any omissions can be made good later, but only directly to me.'

The men reached for their pens as Hennessy sat down again. He waited until the men had finished writing. It took several minutes until the last man replaced his ball-point pen on the table. Hennessy asked for the written sheets to be passed to him and he placed them in a neat pile and then carefully folded it three ways and slipped the sheets into his inside pocket. He then asked them to tear off the top half dozen sheets from the pads and he gathered them together and screwed them up before dropping them into a wastepaper basket. He used a silver cigarette lighter to set the papers alight. He realised it

68

looked a bit theatrical, but at least it proved that he was serious about secrecy.

At the end of the room was a table covered with a starched white linen cloth, and on it were bottles of spirits and a selection of mixers, an ice bucket and a row of crystal glasses. Hennessy personally poured drinks for the men in the room, never once having to ask what they wanted. They stood in two groups, drinking and talking, mainly about horse-racing and football, there being an unwritten rule that business was discussed only at the table. Hennessy was the first to leave, shaking them all by the hand as he went.

Outside the room he was joined by his two bodyguards, Jim Kavanagh and Christy Murphy, big-shouldered men with watchful eyes. Even here, on home territory, they were constantly alert. Kavanagh led the way, six paces ahead of Hennessy, while Murphy walked one pace behind, covering his back. Kavanagh pressed the button for the lift, checked it when it arrived, and then he and Murphy stood to one side to allow Hennessy in. They then stood together between the door and their boss. The three men moved smoothly as if their actions were well choreo-graphed, and in a way they were because they had been together for more than a decade and had been through the actions many thousands of times. Murphy and Kavanagh knew without looking where Hennessy was and in which direction he was moving, where the danger points were and where they had to stand to get in between their boss and any attackers. Twice they had saved Hennessy's life, and both bore their scars with pride – Murphy's left shoulder was a mass of tangled scar tissue where a soft-nosed bullet had ripped away a chunk of flesh but thankfully had missed the bone, and Kavanagh's legs still bore the burn marks of a badly placed car bomb that had exploded as he was about to pick up his boss.

Hennessy's car, a black Jaguar, was waiting outside the hotel with his regular driver, a small, intense man called Jimmy McMahon, at the wheel. Hennessy stood patiently while his bodyguards checked the pavements and then the three men quickly moved to the car.

They drove through the Belfast traffic, and McMahon's skilful touch on the wheel had them back at Hennessy's office in Donegall Square within five minutes. Only when Hennessy was safely behind his desk did Murphy and Kavanagh relax. They sat on two large, green sofas in the legal firm's reception area until they were needed again. Hennessy's secretary, a buxom redhead, put cups of coffee down in front of them before knocking twice on Hennessy's door and entering before he had the chance to respond. Like Murphy and Kavanagh, she knew her boss well. He was sitting in a high-backed leather chair, his eyes closed in thought. In front of him on his well-ordered desk was a file of outgoing letters awaiting his signature. Hennessy opened his eyes and smiled.

'I'm getting to them, Beth.'

She raised her eyebrows. 'We'll miss the post, Liam, sure enough we will,' she admonished like a schoolteacher scolding a naughty pupil. She was a good fifteen years younger than Hennessy, but she knew there were times when the lawyer needed a good push to get things done. And she always used his first name, unless there were clients around.

Hennessy sighed and took a gold fountain pen from his inside pocket.

'You're a hard taskmaster, Beth, that you are.' She stood in front of the desk, her arms folded across her ample bosom, as Hennessy scanned each letter and signed his name. When he'd finished she scooped them up with a flourish and rewarded him with a smile. She was hellish pretty, thought Hennessy, as he did at least a dozen times a day. If he was younger, and single, and if she wasn't the proud mother of twins, and if he hadn't been married to a woman who made his heart ache. God, there were so many 'ifs' that it was laughable. He smiled and her lime-green eyes twinkled as if reading his thoughts.

'Anything else?' he asked, replacing the top on his pen.

'Mr Armytage would like you to call him about his case, and you have a four o'clock appointment with Mr Kershaw. And there's a man trying to get hold of you.'

'A man?'

'A foreigner. Calling from London.' She saw Hennessy smile and she held up her hand. 'No, I don't mean he was a foreigner just because he was phoning from England. He sounded foreign, Oriental. Chinese, maybe.'

'And what did he want, this Chinaman?'

'He wouldn't say. Said he had to speak to you. If he calls again, do you want to speak to him?'

'I don't see why not. Right, can you get me Tom Armytage's file? He must be getting nervous about tomorrow.'

Beth nodded and left his office. Hennessy watched her hips swing as she went, then caught sight of his wife's smiling face in the brass frame on the right-hand corner of his desk, her arms around their two teenage children. Hennessy grinned at the picture. 'I was only looking, darling Mary, only looking. You know that.'

The phone on the desk rang, making him jump. It was Beth, telling him that The Chinaman was calling again.

'Put him on,' said Hennessy, his curiosity aroused.

Nguyen introduced himself and explained what he wanted, speaking softly and slowly, sometimes so quietly that Hennessy had to ask him to repeat himself. When Hennessy finally realised what the caller was requesting he was stunned, unable to believe that the man could be so naïve.

'What on earth makes you think that I know the men who killed your wife and daughter?'

Nguyen was insistent. Polite but insistent. There was a rustle of paper on the line as if he was reading something. 'Because you are a political adviser to Sinn Fein, the political wing of the IRA.' The phrase came out so confidently and smoothly that the contrast with his earlier carefully controlled speech and ungainly vocabulary convinced Hennessy that The Chinaman had indeed read it, from a newspaper cutting perhaps.

'I do offer advice to politicians, that is true. But I condemn, as do they, violent acts against innocent members of the public, both in England and here in Northern Ireland.' Hennessy realised he had shifted into the standard speech he gave journalists or visiting MPs, the words slipping off his tongue as easily as The Chinaman's when he was reading from the cutting. 'You have the wrong man.'

'If that is so, Mr Hennessy, could you tell me who in the IRA would tell me?'

Hennessy marvelled at the man's stupidity. 'Offhand, I can think of no one who would be in a position to help you. And I would add that the sort of men you are talking

72

about are not the sort who would take kindly to being approached with such accusations.' Hennessy kept the threat veiled, aware as always of the possibility that the security forces had his lines tapped. 'I suggest that you speak to the police, I am sure they are doing their best to identify the men responsible. But I can assure you that I do not know.'

Nguyen fell silent for a while. Hennessy was just about to hang up when he spoke again. 'I am afraid I do not believe you, Mr Hennessy. You are their adviser. You know who they are.'

Hennessy snorted angrily. 'I have already explained, I advise politicians, not terrorists. There is a world of difference.'

'I think that IRA politics and IRA terrorism are different ends of the same snake,' said Nguyen. 'It does not matter which end you seize, you still have the snake.'

This, thought Hennessy, was like talking to a fortune cookie. 'Using your analogy, I would suggest that it makes a great deal of difference which end you attack,' he replied. 'One end will fight back.' Hennessy felt pleased at the turn of phrase. It had given him the same sort of buzz that he got in court demolishing his opponent's legal arguments.

Nguyen was not deterred. 'I have chosen, Mr Hennessy. You will tell me who is responsible.'

Hennessy's temper flared. 'You are wasting my time. Goodbye.' He cut the connection and then buzzed Beth on the intercom.

'Yes Liam?'

'If The Chinaman rings again just tell him I'm unavailable. I don't want to speak to him again. Ever.'

* * *

Nguyen knelt down in front of the red-painted wooden shrine and lit a stick of incense with an old Zippo lighter. He snapped the top of the metal lighter back in place and then held it with both palms pressed together. He rubbed his hands slowly, caressing the smooth metal. The sweet-smelling smoke curled upwards, drifting in the air, and he breathed it in. He opened his hands and looked at the lighter. On one side there was an insignia etched into the metal. There was a short-handled dagger, superimposed on a badge the shape of the blade of a spear, and across the dagger were three bolts of lightning. Above the badge was a banner containing the word 'Airborne'. Nguyen had had the lighter for many years, but it had never let him down. His wife had carried it out of Vietnam and had proudly presented it to him when they were reunited in a refugee camp in Hong Kong. She had never let him down, either.

He slipped the lighter back in his pocket and sat back on his heels, his eyes closed and his hands together in prayer as he emptied his mind of everything save his wife and three dead daughters. When his first two daughters had died he had been powerless to help and by the time he was in a position to do anything the men responsible were hundreds of miles away. He'd thirsted for revenge then, he'd wanted to tear the men apart with his bare hands, but there was nothing he could do. It had been a long time since the two young girls had suffered, all those years ago in the South China Sea. He remembered how he'd had to watch. How they'd screamed and begged him to help, and how something inside him had died. The urge for revenge had never died, in fact if anything it was stronger now than it had ever been, though it was tempered by the knowledge that he had done everything he could. But this time he would not allow the deaths of Xuan Phoung and Kieu Trinh to pass unresolved into memories. He would not allow the men responsible to escape unpunished. He swore to himself he would not. On the souls of his family he swore it. He didn't move for almost an hour and when he opened his eyes again they were moist, though no tears rolled down his cheeks. He slowly stood up, his joints clicking and cracking as he stretched his legs. He had decided what he was going to do, but he knew there would be a thousand details that he still had to work out, so he took a pencil and one of his daughter's unused exercise-books from a drawer in the kitchen and sat down at the dining-table and began writing.

It was dark, so dark that the man could see the car's headlights from more than a mile away, carving tunnels of light through the blackness. He lay down in the grass and waited for it to pass. It was two o'clock in the morning so cars were few and far between along the road connecting the A4008 with the A409 near Bushey Heath, just south-west of the M1. The man was lying face down on farmland, his nose close to the dew-damp soil, listening to the engine noise grow louder and then fade away. He got to his feet, picked up the spade and the metal detector by his side and walked towards a small brook that cut through the fields. He had memorised the location and if he was unlucky enough to be caught he'd say that he was just a treasure hunter out looking for buried coins, but getting caught was the last thing on his mind. He heard the trickling water before he reached the bank of the brook, and turned left and followed its meandering path to a small copse. He pushed his way through waist-high bushes until he came to the base of a towering beech tree. One of its roots, as thick as a man's thigh, crawled along the peaty ground for six feet or so before plunging into the earth, and it was midway along its length where the man began to dig. He was well-built and used to physical exercise, and though he was breathing heavily after half an hour he had dug a hole four feet deep and three feet across. He began to take more care then, and before long the spade clunked into something that sounded vaguely metallic. He bent down and pulled up a long thin package, wrapped in polythene. He laid it on the ground next to the tree and unwrapped it. Under the polythene was a sack, tied at one end with a piece of wire. He undid it and pulled the sack down.

Inside were three Armalite rifles and two handguns, along with several boxes of cartridges. There was a plastic-wrapped package labelled Semtex and a polythene bag containing detonators. The man slowly counted them. His eyes were used to the darkness and he could see enough to identify the contents. He had already memorised the list he'd been shown, the list of what the cache should contain, and he mentally crossed them off one at a time. Eventually, satisfied that nothing was missing, he packed up the munitions and put them back in the hole. He replaced the soil and then stamped up and down to flatten the earth before kneeling down and gently smoothing it over. He walked some distance away from the beech tree and gathered twigs and small branches and placed them haphazardly over the freshly dug soil. It would fool most casual observers and in a day or so it would have blended in perfectly with its surroundings. There was little chance of it being discovered. That's why the hiding place had been chosen in the first place.

Nguyen came out of Charing Cross Tube station and walked to the Strand. He found the shop he wanted and stood looking through the window. It was packed with camping equipment, everything from compasses to water-bottles, a huge range of knives, racks of anoraks, sleeping-bags, dehydrated food in silver-foil packets, first-aid kits, crossbows and a range of martial arts equipment. It was all so different during the war, Nguyen thought. So very different. Equipment then was what you could beg or borrow, or take from a fallen comrade or steal from an enemy. And to think that now you could simply walk into a shop and buy it. If they had been able to get hold of equipment like this thirty years ago, then perhaps none of this would have happened and he and his family would be together in a free Vietnam. He shook his head, trying to disperse the thoughts, knowing that there was no point in dwelling on the past.

He walked into the shop and looked through the racks. A young man tried on an army-type pullover with rein-forced patches on the shoulders and elbows as his blonde girlfriend looked on admiringly. A skinhead in a shiny green bomber jacket weighed a small throwing knife in his hand and then ran a finger along the blade. A father and son examined a two-man tent as an elderly shop assis-tant rolled it out along the floor for them. Nobody gave Nguyen a second look.

He picked a camouflage jacket from a rack and looked at it. It was made of nylon and he heard it rustle even as he held it up. Useless, he thought. You'd hear it hundreds of yards away. And the fasteners were made from the Velcro material that made a ripping noise every time you used it. It was for show, like the knife the skinhead was testing. Pretty to look at, but useless in the field. Just by looking at it Nguyen could tell that the knife had no weight, it would bounce off any live target. He took down another jacket, similar colour scheme of dark and light greens, reminiscent of the tiger-striped fatigues he used to wear in the jungle, made from a soft cotton material that probably wasn't waterproof but which looked warm. He tried it on and the sleeves were about six inches too long, even over his jacket. He looked at the label. Medium it said. European medium, obviously, because Nguyen was not small for a Vietnamese.

'Can I help you, sir?' said a young assistant.

Nguyen held up his arms. 'Small size?' he asked, and the youngster smiled and helped him get it off. He flicked through the racks and pulled out a smaller size, pressed it up against Nguyen's shoulders, nodded, and asked him to try it on. It fitted.

'Trousers. Same style,' said Nguyen, and the youngster found a pair of trousers made from the same soft material.

'Anything else, sir?' he said, and Nguyen nodded enthusiastically.

'Oh yes, yes,' he said. 'Many things.'

He picked up a pair of binoculars, powerful and covered with thick, green rubber, and asked the assistant if it was OK to try them. The boy said yes, but went with him to the door and waited while Nguyen scanned up and down the crowded street.

'I will take these,' said Nguyen, handing them to the

78

boy. He walked back into the shop. So many things to buy. 'Bottles,' he said.

'Bottles?' queried the boy.

'Water-bottles,' said Nguyen, pointing to a canteen, khaki-coloured with a green strap. It looked big enough to hold a quart. 'Two of those. No, three.'

The boy piled up the purchases by a cash register, sensing that the customer was going to be here for some time. On the wall behind the cash register were a number of replica guns and rifles, dull metal and polished wood. They looked so real, Nguyen marvelled. How could such things be on sale in England? he wondered. Some of the guns he recognised, a Colt .45, a Ruger .22, an M9 9-millimetre semi-automatic. Suddenly he stopped, his heart pounding. It couldn't be, could it? His eyes widened and he walked over to stand in front of an AK-47, a Kalashnikov automatic rifle, perfect in every detail with even its curved ammunition magazine in place. He reached up to touch it, to remind himself how it felt. At the last moment, just before his fingers touched the cold metal, he pulled back his hand and shook his head to clear away the memories.

'Compass,' he said, and the assistant took him over to a glass-topped counter. On a shelf underneath were a selection of compasses and map-reading equipment. Nguyen pointed at several and the boy took them out for him to examine. Nguyen chose one. 'Knife,' he said.

There were so many knives, more than he had ever seen in any one place. There were penknives with all sorts of gadgets attached – nail files, spanners, scissors, bottle-openers. There were throwing knives, useless ones like the skinhead had been playing with, but also serious, properly balanced heavy knives that could kill from twenty yards in the right hands. Nguyen held a pair of the heavy knives, feeling their balance and knowing they were perfect.

'Can try?' he asked the assistant.

'Try?'

Nguyen showed him the knives. 'Can I throw?'

'Here?' said the boy. 'No, no. God, no.' He looked confused.

'Never mind,' said Nguyen, putting them on top of the camouflage trousers. There was a big selection of survival knives, big sharp blades, serrated on one side, with hollow handles containing a small compass, a short length of fishing line and a few cheap fishing hooks. Nguyen snorted as he looked at them. Joke knives, not what he was looking for. He was looking for a strong blade, one that he could sharpen until it would cut paper like a razor, with a groove in the blade so that the blood could flow out as it was thrust into a body. No groove and the suction effect would make withdrawing the knife that much harder. The tip of the knife had to be angled, too, so that it could ease the ribs apart and allow the killing thrust to the heart. And the handle had to be heavy enough and sturdy enough so that the blade was kept steady as it was used. A knife was important, your life could so easily depend on it. The choice of scabbard was vital too, the action had to be smooth and silent when the blade was withdrawn and the straps had to be strong and hard-wearing. Nguyen spent a lot of time examining the knives in stock before deciding. The one he eventually selected was expensive, one of the most expensive in the shop, but it was the best. He also took a small Swiss army knife, for its tools rather than its blades.

What else? He looked up and down the shop. There

was so much he could use. A tent. A sleeping-bag. A small stove. A lightweight blanket made from foil. A folding axe. A rucksack. A first-aid kit. Nguyen was tempted, but at the same time a part of him knew that equipment was often a trap. It slowed you down, you spent more time and effort carrying it and looking after it than you did fighting. He remembered how he used to go into the jungle in fatigues and sandals, with a water-bottle, a few pounds of cooked rice in a cloth tube tied around his waist and nothing else but his rifle and ammunition. He and his comrades travelled light and covered ground quickly and silently. How they laughed at the ungainly Americans, sweating like pigs under the weight of their huge ruck-sacks. You could hear them coming for miles as they hacked and tripped their way through the undergrowth. So many were killed before they even had a chance to open their precious backpacks, but they never learned.

'Anything else?' asked the assistant, jarring Nguyen's thoughts.

He walked over to a rack of walking boots but decided against buying a pair. The ones he had back at his house would be better because they wouldn't need breaking in. 'I want a small rucksack,' he said. The assistant showed him a big, blue nylon backpack on an aluminium frame with padded straps and Nguyen said it was too big and that the colour was wrong. 'Too bright,' he said. He pointed to a small dark-green rucksack, the sort that children might use to carry their school-books. It had no frame and when Nguyen tried it on it lay flat against his back. He adjusted the straps and walked up and down the shop. It felt comfort-able and made next to no noise. He removed it and handed it to the assistant. 'This one is good,' said Nguyen.

81

The assistant placed all Nguyen's purchases in a large plastic carrier bag, totalling them up on the cash register as he did. Nguyen paid in cash. As he waited for his change he looked wistfully at the AK-47 replica. So many memories, he thought.

On the way to the Tube station he walked past a photographer's shop with shelves full of cameras and lenses. He went in and asked if they sold flash-bulbs.

'Flash-bulbs?' said the man behind the counter. 'Don't get much call for those these days. They all have built in flashes now.' He frowned and rubbed his chin. 'I've got some somewhere, I saw them a couple of weeks ago. What sort of camera are they for?'

Nguyen shrugged. 'Any sort. But not the square ones, the ones they use in the little cameras. I want the single bulbs.'

'Yeah, I know the sort you mean. Hang on, let me check out back.' He disappeared through a door and Nguyen heard boxes being moved and drawers opening and closing.

'You're in luck,' he called. 'How many do you want?'

'A dozen,' Nguyen shouted back.

The man returned with two packets and handed them to Nguyen. 'I can't guarantee they'll still work, mind,' he said. 'They're old stock and I don't know how long they've been there.'

Nguyen examined them carefully and then nodded. 'They will be perfect,' he said. He paid in cash, put the packets into his carrier bag and left the shop.

'We need more explosive,' The Bombmaker said. Fisher ran his fingers through his hair and sighed. He stretched his legs out and lay back in the leather sofa.

82

'How much do we have left?' he asked.

'A couple of kilos, no more. We've plenty of detonators, though.'

Fisher smiled. 'Fat lot of good they'll be to us without the stuff that goes bang,' he said. 'I'll get us more, don't you worry.'

McCormick came into the lounge from the kitchen and put down four mugs of coffee on the table by the side of the sofa. O'Reilly got up from his easy chair and took one of them. He walked over to the french windows and looked over the Thames as he drank.

'Isn't it about time we moved?' asked McCormick.

'Why move?' said Fisher.

'In case they track us down. We've been here for months, sure enough. Normal procedure is to keep moving, never stay in one place for too long.'

Fisher shook his head. 'No, that's exactly what they'd expect us to do. They'll be checking all the small hotels and bed and breakfast places. A group like us moving around will stick out like a sore thumb. And after the Knightsbridge bombing every landlady in Britain is on the lookout for Irishmen. How long do you think it would take until we were rumbled?'

'I suppose you're right,' said McCormick reluctantly. 'It's just . . .'

'Look,' interrupted Fisher, 'we've had this flat rented for almost a year. It's on a long-term lease, paid direct from a dummy company bank account. As far as the landlord is concerned, it's rented to a stockbroking firm who use it for visiting executives from the States. This place is perfect.'

O'Reilly tapped on the window. 'And if the SAS knock

on the front door, we can leg it over the balcony and down the Thames,' he said.

'If the SAS find out we're here, we won't be going anywhere,' said McCormick. 'Bastards.'

'Nobody is going to find out where we are,' said Fisher. 'Nobody. So long as we stay right where we are. Our more immediate problem is to get hold of some more Semtex.'

O'Reilly turned away from the window, sipping his coffee. He took the mug from his lips and smiled. 'You want me to get it?'

Fisher nodded. 'Tonight. I'll come with you.'

'I can do it.'

'I know. But this one is hard to find. You'll need me there.'

McCormick coughed. He took a handkerchief from the back pocket of his jeans and sneezed into it. 'I'm going down with a cold,' he said, but nobody registered any sympathy. He inspected the contents of the handkerchief and put it back into his pocket. 'And when we've got the stuff, then what?' he asked.

Fisher's eyes sparkled and he looked over at The Bombmaker. 'Something big,' he said. 'Something very, very big.'

Nguyen took the Tube back to Clapham and stored his purchases in the shed at the back of the yard behind his shop. It was a big metal garage but the main door had long ago been boarded up and now it contained three big chest freezers full of frozen meat and vegetables, sacks of rice and bottles of soy sauce. There was also a long wooden bench and racks of tools along one wall. Nguyen placed his carrier bag on the bench, padlocked the door and then went through the shop to his van which was parked outside. He drove to a large do-it-yourself store in south London and spent more than an hour filling a large trolley. He bought sections of plastic drain-pipe, insulation tape, three large bags of fertilizer, a soldering iron and several packs of solder, and other tools that he knew he'd need which he didn't already have in his shed. He paid in cash, and on the way back he stopped at a large filling station. He filled the tank and bought two large plastic bottles of antifreeze, three cans of Shell motor oil and half a dozen cans of white spray paint to match the colour of his van, and a can of black paint.

Pham was washing bean sprouts in the kitchen sink and he grunted a greeting as Nguyen walked by. Pham had agreed to buy the restaurant and had already paid Nguyen in cash. The bank had agreed to transfer the mortgage on the property to him and after a long but good-hearted argument over the value of the kitchen equipment and the food in the fridges Nguyen had agreed to accept thirty thousand pounds. Nguyen didn't ask where Pham had got the money from, but he had relatives in Manchester who had probably helped out. He was planning to switch to Vietnamese cooking, though Nguyen doubted that it would be a success, so far away from the West End. He and his wife had decided when they first moved to London that they were more likely to make money if they kept to a Chinese menu, even though they personally found the cuisine bland and boring. Still, it was up to Pham now. Nguyen had promised to be out by the end of the week but he knew that Pham was keen for him to go as soon as possible so that he could move into the flat upstairs.

After putting the rest of his purchases away in the garage, Nguyen sat at his table and crossed off the list everything he'd already bought. There were three items left: two kinds of acid and glycerine. He knew how to make the acid he needed from other quite innocuous and easily available materials. It was messy, but possible, but there was no need because this was England not Vietnam and here there were firms where you could buy chemicals, no questions asked. He took a well-thumbed copy of Yellow Pages and looked up Chemical Manufacturers and Suppliers. After three calls he had found one firm who would supply him with concentrated acids (for etchings, he'd said) and he arranged to collect a gallon of glycerine from another firm. Nguyen thought it prudent not to buy all three from the same supplier.

Fisher stopped the car and switched off the engine and the lights, allowing the darkness to envelop them like a shroud. He and O'Reilly waited until their eyes became used to the blackness, listening to the clicking noises from the engine as it cooled. They were parked at the end of a lonely lane not far from Bexley station, half and hour's drive south-east of central London. Both men were dressed in dark pullovers, jeans and black shoes, outfits that wouldn't stick out at night but which didn't obviously mark them out as burglars. If they were unlucky enough to come across the police then they'd just pretend they were a couple of queers looking for a bit of privacy. That had been Fisher's idea, and O'Reilly hadn't been exactly bowled over by it.

'Look, I promise not to kiss you,' Fisher had joked.

O'Reilly had laughed nervously.

'Not on the mouth, anyway . . .' O'Reilly had winced and Fisher knew he'd hit a nerve so he let the joke drop. He mentally filed O'Reilly's over-reaction for future reference, a possible weak point. Fisher did that with everybody he came into contact with, memorising their strengths and weaknesses and the buttons that had to be pressed to get the desired responses.

'Are you right?' he asked O'Reilly.

O'Reilly nodded. They got out of the car and Fisher led the way, climbing silently over a stone wall and walking across the dew-laden grass. O'Reilly's foot knocked against something hard that crunched and rolled, and then he heard a rustling noise behind him, something small scampering through the grass and making snuffling sounds. Hedgehogs, he realised. There were dozens of them, rolling into tight, spiked balls whenever they sensed the two men.

They reached another wall, this one taller than the first, and they had to scramble over. It surrounded a graveyard, close-clipped grass and gravelled paths, the gravestones a mixture of old stone crosses, chipped and weather-worn, and new, clean-cut marble. To their left was a grey stone church with a steeple. In the distance a vixen barked, and her call sparked off a cacophony of howls from dogs in the nearby housing estate. The two men dropped down into a crouch, their backs against the wall, while Fisher got his bearings.

He pointed towards a white concrete angel with spreading wings. 'This way,' he said, and took O'Reilly along the grass verge, past the angel and between two waist-high tombs, the sort vampires might lie in to sleep away the daylight hours, safe from sunlight. They walked through the drooping branches of a willow and then Fisher headed over to five tombstones lined up in front of the boundary wall like a stud poker hand. He kicked the one in the centre.

'There it is,' he said. 'Help me get it up.'

They knelt down together, scraping away the soil to slip their hands underneath the stone and then they pushed it up, grunting with the strain until it came off the ground with a wet, slurping sound. They stood the stone upright and then leant it against the wall. The smell of damp, stale earth filled O'Reilly's nostrils and made him want to gag. Fisher scraped away the soil like a dog looking for a bone. Less than a foot down his fingers touched plastic and he pulled up a polythene-covered parcel which he handed to O'Reilly. There were two other bundles, one of which was obviously a rifle, but Fisher ignored them. All they needed this time was Semtex. They unwrapped the parcel and took out half the packages of explosive, six in all. They took three apiece, rewrapped the rest and put them back in the shallow hole before pushing the damp soil back and replacing the gravestone. They checked the surroundings to make sure that they were still alone in the graveyard, and then they left as silently as they'd arrived.

Nguyen drove his Renault van down the alley behind the shop, the early morning sun glinting off the bonnet. He'd already opened the two wooden gates that led to the shop's back yard where they usually unpacked deliveries and transferred the food into the freezers in the garage. He parked the van and switched off the engine. He had put on a pair of old overalls after he'd bathed that morning, and he pulled on a pair of plastic gloves. The van was white, three years old and mechanically sound. It had always been parked outside because the garage was used for storage, so it was rusting a little, and it had taken a few knocks from other cars. The name of the restaurant and the telephone number had been drawn in black paint on both sides. Nguyen had painted each letter himself, slowly and carefully, it had taken him hours, but it was the work of minutes to spray over them with a can of white spray paint. He sprayed the paint thinly so that it wouldn't run and he waited thirty minutes before giving it a second coat, and then a third to make sure that the lettering was completely covered.

While the third coat dried he transferred the tool box, bottles and bags from the garage, methodically crossing the contents off the list in his exercise-book so that he was sure he hadn't forgotten anything. It was all there, the acids, the bags of fertilizer, the bottles of antifreeze and cans of oil. He'd forgotten nothing. When he'd finished he used a screwdriver to prise the lid off the can of black paint and, resting a brand new artist's brush against a piece of garden cane, painted on a new set of letters and numbers. As he worked he suddenly felt as if he was being watched and he turned and looked at the upstairs window. A curtain twitched. It could have been Pham wondering what he was up to, or it could have been the wind. Nguyen stared up at the window but saw nothing so he returned to the painting.

When the final letter was in place he stood back and admired his handiwork. It was good. Almost as good as before, even though it had taken him about half as long. 'Green Landscape Gardeners' it said, along with a London telephone number he'd taken from the Yellow Pages. The white paintwork around the lettering looked whiter than the rest of the van, but driving through the city streets

89

would soon fix that up. The hairs on the back of his neck stood on end and he whirled around, but this time the curtains weren't moving and there was still no one there.

He went into the house through the back door and up the stairs. His suitcase was already packed. He picked it up and was on the way to the door when he had a sudden urge to kneel and pray before the shrine. He got down on his knees and used his Zippo to light a stick of incense. He closed his eyes and breathed in the perfume and tried to empty his mind, to steel himself for the trials to come.

The incense filled his lungs. It was the same rich scent that always reminded him of his parents' farm, the room where he'd been born so many years ago. When was it? Could it really have been so long ago? Could it really have been 1943? Where had the years gone, how had they slipped by so easily? He could still picture every inch of the small family farm, close to the Gulf of Tonkin in North Vietnam.

Nguyen shuddered and opened his eyes. They were moist and he wiped them with the back of his hand. It was time to go.

He carried the bag downstairs, not bothering to say goodbye to Pham. He put the case in the back of the van, locked the doors and drove the van out of the yard. He headed north, towards Stranraer in Scotland and the ferry to Northern Ireland. Before he left London he stopped at a garden centre and loaded up the van with bags of peat and more fertilizer, a selection of bedding plants, and a spade and a fork.

It was a long, tiring drive to Stranraer, but Nguyen knew there was no real alternative. He needed the equipment and supplies in the van, so flying was out of the question. He had thought he'd be able to take a ferry from Liverpool direct to Belfast, but he'd discovered that the route had been cancelled some months earlier. The only car ferries now operating seemed to be from Stranraer to Larne in County Antrim, north of Belfast, or from Holyhead in Anglesey across to Dun Laoghaire, near Dublin in the South. Either route would mean hours behind the wheel, but he had reservations about driving through Southern Ireland and across the border. Better, he thought, to go direct to Northern Ireland and not worry about Customs or passports. He drove through the night and slept in the van during the morning before catching the ferry.

When he arrived at Larne he saw two men in a Ford Granada being taken to one side and their car searched by four men in bottle-green uniforms while a Labrador retriever sniffed around and wagged its tail, but he wasn't even given a second look. He knew why, it was nothing more than racism working in his favour. He was Oriental and the fighting in Ireland was between Caucasians.

He drove the van from the ferry terminal south to Belfast city centre. It was late evening and he had to find somewhere to stay. He stopped at a filling station and filled up with petrol and then bought a street map. He asked the teenage girl if she knew where there were any guest-houses but he couldn't understand her when she replied. He asked again and this time she spoke more slowly, as if he were a child, but the accent was so strange he couldn't follow what she was saying. He smiled and paid for the petrol and the map and left, none the wiser. He was starting to realise that he was, after all, in a different country.

There were other reminders. The police wore green uniforms and drove around in heavily fortified blue-grey Land-Rovers with metal screens protecting the sides. And there were soldiers everywhere wearing camouflage uniforms and helmets and carrying automatic rifles at the ready, barrels aimed at the ground. The army used green Land-Rovers, open at the top so that the men in the back were exposed but able to react quickly. It made good sense, Nguyen thought.

He drove by what he thought was a prison until he saw a sign that said it was a police station. He was so surprised that he stopped to look at it. He had never in his life seen such a thing, not even in Saigon. Thick metal mesh fences surrounded the building which had what appeared to be a gun turret on one corner. The top of the fence was a tangle of barbed wire and all the windows were firmly shuttered. It was a fortress. He had been considering asking a policeman to suggest a place to stay, but from the look of it the police in Northern Ireland were not geared up for handling general enquiries from the public. They were in a state of siege.

There were posts at each corner of the building, and on the top were surveillance cameras covering all the approaches.

There was a metallic rap against the passenger window of the van and Nguyen jumped. An unsmiling face under a peaked cap glared at him. He knocked on the door again with the barrel of his handgun. Nguyen leant over and wound down the window.

'Can I be of help to you, sir?' the policeman asked. Another officer appeared on the driver's side of the van. In the rear-view mirror he saw two more.

Nguyen smiled and waved the map at them. 'I need somewhere to stay tonight. Do you know anywhere?'

The officer was already relaxing. He slid his gun back into his holster.

'Give me the map,' he said. Nguyen switched on the small reading light and the policeman jabbed a finger in the bottom left-hand corner. 'See this road here, Wellington Park?'

Nguyen nodded.

'There are a few places there, quite cheap.' He handed the map back to Nguyen. 'You'd best be on your way. And in future don't hang around in front of police stations in a van. We're a touch sensitive about that sort of thing. Understand?'

'I am sorry,' said Nguyen. 'Thank you for your help.'

The policemen grouped together and watched him go, four stout figures in dark-green bullet-proof jackets.

Nguyen followed the map until he reached Wellington Park. He drove slowly down the road, looking left and right. He soon saw a guest-house but it had a sign in the window saying 'No Vacancies'. Further down the road there was another house with a sign saying 'Vacancies' and Nguyen stopped the van in front of it.

It was dark now and the van appeared yellow under the streetlights. Nguyen pressed the doorbell and waited. The front door was wooden with two vertical strips of dimpled, frosted glass. Through the glass he saw a light come on and a figure ripple towards him. The door opened to reveal an overweight elderly woman with close-cropped grey hair and horn-rimmed spectacles. She was wearing a blue and white diamond-patterned dress and a plain white apron and was drying her hands on a red tea-towel.

'Do you have a room?' Nguyen asked her.

She looked him up and down and then scrutinised the van over his shoulder, screwing up her eyes to read the lettering.

'How long would you be wanting it for?' she asked.

Nguyen had difficulty understanding her accent but she spoke slowly enough for him to get the drift.

'Two nights, that is all. A room with a bath.'

The old woman sucked her teeth and shook her head. 'No baths in the rooms, but I do have one with a shower and a toilet. And a small wash-basin. It's right at the top of the house, very cosy.'

Nguyen said he'd take it and the woman seemed doubtful, but then he pulled his wallet from his jacket and offered to pay her cash, in advance, and she smiled and ushered him inside. On the way up the stairs she introduced herself as Mrs McAllister as the notes disappeared behind the apron. He told her his name and she tried to repeat it, but gave up. The room was small with a single bed, an old wooden wardrobe, a dressing-table with an oval mirror, and a bedside table with a brass lamp with a pink lampshade. There was an ornate crucifix above the bed and to the left of the dressing-table was a black-framed photograph of John F. Kennedy. The ceiling sloped down to a window overlooking the street. Opposite the window was a door leading to a tiny bathroom with a tiled floor, a shower cubicle, a wash-basin with a cylindrical gas heater on the wall above it, and a low toilet with a black plastic seat. It was perfect.

The two pirates stood by the bar, tapping their feet to the driving beat of a pop song that Woody only vaguely recognised as they sipped orange juice from tall glasses. One of the pirates was middle-aged with a greying beard and a black patch over one eye, the other was younger with curly blond hair and flushed cheeks, but they wore matching outfits, baggy white shirts, red scarves around their necks, tight black breeches, white socks and shiny black shoes with big brassy buckles.

'Pirates?' said Maggie as she followed Woody to the bar.

'Yeah, they're with the pirate ships,' said Woody, squeezing in between two stockbroker types and trying to catch the attention of the young barmaid.

'They would be,' said Maggie, still mystified.

Woody pointed over her head, towards the large windows at the far end of the bar. 'Pirate ships,' he explained. 'They're a tourist attraction. A sort of cross between Madame Tussaud's and the Cutty Sark. Those guys are sort of tour guides, cross their palms with silver and they'll take you below decks and tell you blood-curdling tales of life on the salty sea.' The barmaid finally saw his plaintive look and came over. She gave him a beaming smile which faded a little when she saw that he was with a girl. Woody tended to attract barmaids, but was never sure why. He was still good-looking, he knew that, though he had allowed himself to go a bit recently. It was his eyes, an old girlfriend had told him. 'Your eyes make me go weak at the knees, they're hot. Really hot,' she'd said. Woody reckoned it wasn't anything to do with his looks, though. He thought it had more to do with the way he made them laugh. Sometimes he laughed them into bed before they realised what was happening. Woody winked at the barmaid, ordered drinks and carried them over to an empty table, close by the window so that Maggie could look at the sailing ships.

'They're not real, are they?' she asked, sitting down.

'I don't think so, they were built to pull in the punters to Tobacco Dock.'

He raised his glass to her and she smiled. He was glad he'd taken her to Henry's Bar in Tobacco Dock because at least they could sit in comfort. Standing at the bar was essential when you were with the lads, but Maggie demanded a higher standard of comfort. No, that wasn't right, she didn't demand it. She deserved it.

'What are you thinking?' she asked.

'Just thinking how pretty you look,' he said.

'Why thank you kind sir,' she laughed. 'You look exhausted.'

'Yeah, I'm not sleeping well. It's the heat.'

She frowned. 'It's not that hot at the moment,' she said.

Woody laughed. 'No, it's my place. I've a bedsit in a house with about a dozen others, and mine is right next to the only bathroom. The landlord has fitted a hot-water tank as big as a Saturn rocket and my room is always in the high eighties. I have to have the window open even in winter.'

Maggie smiled and shook her head. 'Why don't you move, you daft sod?'

Woody shrugged. 'It's cheap.'

'You're not short of money, are you?'

Woody was immediately embarrassed because the answer was yes, he was bloody short of money. Always was. And always would be unless he got a staff job. The shifts weren't coming as often as they used to, he was overdrawn at the bank, yet he still had to stand his round at the pub while he brown-nosed his way back into the good books of the guys on the news desk. 'No, it's convenient, that's all.' Sure, if you fancied an hour on the bus to get into work.

'So is LA still an option?' she asked.

'Sure. Sure it is.'

They drank and sat for a while looking at each other in silence. Woody spoke first.

'Now it's my turn to ask what you're thinking about.'

Maggie pulled a face. 'I was actually wondering why you didn't get a better job, why you waste your time on a comic like the *Sunday World*.'

He sighed deeply, and explained that he didn't even have a job with the *Sunday World*, that he was only a freelance, dependent on shifts, and that even that didn't pay particularly well, not since the print and journalists unions had been broken along with the dockers and the miners and any other groups that had once been able to withhold their labour. She listened patiently and then reached over and touched his shoulder, a friendly nudge that showed she understood. Maybe even cared. She asked him why he couldn't get a staff job. At first he didn't want to tell her, but she pressed, pointing out that he was obviously bright, she'd begun reading his stuff and she could tell that it was good, so what had happened? She wormed it out of him eventually, his time on one of the broadsheets, the investigation into high-level corruption within a north of England police force, the drive home along the motorway, the blue flashing light in his rear mirror, the two surly traffic cops and the discovery of two hundred grams of cocaine under the passenger seat of his office car.

'They framed you?' she asked, wide-eyed.

'Yeah. I managed to avoid being sent down, but I lost the job and for a few years I couldn't get any sort of work. The papers didn't trust me, partly because of the drug thing, but I know for a fact that the cops were putting the word around, too. I stuck with it, though, went to work in the West Country for a while, and then some of the nationals began taking my copy again and now at least I've got my foot in the door. I'm lucky to have that, I guess.'

'Jesus, Woody, that's terrible. That's appalling.'

'That's life, Maggie.'

She forced a smile. 'I suppose the *Sunday World* isn't that bad,' she said sympathetically. 'Do they let you travel much?'

'Oh sure, we get around. There are always lots of freebies to be had.'

'And do you get political stuff to do?'

'Sure. That's one of the good things about working on a Sunday paper. They have small staffs so there isn't too much specialisation. I mean, I have to do a lot of showbiz crap and weird stuff, but we get to help out with the big ones too.'

'What are you working on at the moment?' she asked.

Woody coughed.

'Pardon?' she asked.

Woody looked shamefaced. 'Vampire cats,' he said. Maggie collapsed into hysterics.

The man approaching the churchyard was short but powerfully built and even in the dark it was obvious he was not a man to get into a fight with, not by choice anyway. He was wearing a brown leather jacket, scuffed and cracked with age, and dark-brown corduroy trousers. He carried a small sack, tied at the end with a short length of rope, and in one of the pockets of his jacket there was a flashlight and half a dozen metal snares. He'd done a fair bit of poaching in his youth, but he wasn't looking for rabbits, the snares were just cover in case he was discovered. In the back pocket of his trousers was a short-handled knife with a wicked blade which he was quite prepared to use if anyone saw through the poacher's disguise.

Somewhere in the dark he heard a hedgehog snuffle then squeal and he stopped and listened but heard nothing other than the night sounds of the English countryside and an airliner rumbling high overhead, red and green lights flashing.

He swung easily over the wall and landed silently in freshly dug soil. He was standing within inches of a new grave, a gaping black rectangular hole that seemed bottomless. He breathed a sigh of relief, if he'd vaulted the wall just a couple of feet to the right he'd have pitched headlong into it and broken a leg, or worse. The luck of the Irish, he thought with a smile. He stepped off the mound of earth and used the sack to smooth away his footprints before moving on. He skirted around the church and headed for the five tombstones.

He knelt down and lifted the stone that covered the stockpile, pushing hard with his legs. He carefully leant it against the wall and then stood still, counting off sixty seconds in his head as he listened for anything out of the ordinary, because there was no way a poacher would be able to explain what he was doing lifting a gravestone, especially a gravestone that concealed IRA explosives. Still nothing, even the hedgehogs had fallen silent.

He dug into the earth with his hands and pulled out three polythene-covered packages, working quickly but carefully. If he was surprised to see half of the Semtex explosive missing, his face showed no sign of it. He rewrapped the parcels, replaced the soil and dropped the stone back over the hiding place. He brushed the dirt from his hands, checked that the surrounding area was clean and then walked down the gravel path and out of the churchyard.

Beth McKinstry was on the telephone when Nguyen walked into the office. He stood in front of her desk and waited. He was wearing his only suit, a grey one that was starting to go shiny at the elbows. He had on a white shirt and a blue V-necked pullover with three white skiers across the front. He was holding a white carrier bag in both hands, clasping it to his chest like a baby. Murphy was sitting on the sofa reading a magazine and massaging his aching shoulder. He'd looked up when Nguyen entered, but immediately dismissed him as any sort of potential threat and carried on reading.

Beth watched Nguyen as she talked, frowning slightly. He smiled and nodded at her and she looked down. She didn't look up again until she'd finished the call. As she replaced the phone Kavanagh came out of Hennessy's office and quietly closed the door behind him. He barely glanced at Nguyen before sitting down next to Murphy.

'Yes?' said Beth.

'Please, I would like to speak with Mr Liam Hennessy.'

'And your name is?' she said.

'Nguyen Ngoc Minh,' he answered.

'Can I tell him what it is about?' She couldn't even attempt to repeat his name.

'It is very difficult to explain,' he told her.

She reached for the intercom button but stopped halfway. 'Are you the man who phoned last week?' she asked.

'I phoned many times,' said Nguyen.

Beth took her hand away from the intercom. 'I'm afraid Mr Hennessy is very busy. He won't be able to see you.'

'I must see him,' Nguyen repeated.

'He's busy!' insisted Beth, raising her voice. Her cheeks flushed red.

Murphy and Kavanagh glanced up. The secretary was good-natured to a fault and rarely lost her temper. Nguyen said nothing, he just smiled.

'If you leave your number I'll call you to arrange an appointment once I have spoken with Mr Hennessy,' she said.

Still Nguyen said nothing.

'You must go!' she said. Murphy and Kavanagh got to their feet and walked over to Nguyen.

'Best you do as the lady says,' said Murphy quietly.

Nguyen looked at Murphy and the Irishman could see there was no trace of fear in his eyes. 'I must see him,' he said quietly.

Kavanagh put his hand on Nguyen's shoulder. 'What's the crack?' he asked Beth.

'He's been ringing up at all hours asking to see Liam. He won't take no for an answer.'

'Yez heard the lady, Mr Hennessy doesn't want to see yez,' said Kavanagh, gripping Nguyen's shoulder and pulling him away from the desk. For a second Nguyen was off balance and he clutched the carrier bag tightly as if afraid that it might fall.

'What have you got there?' said Murphy, for the first time regarding the man as a possible threat. It wasn't likely that the Loyalists would use a Chinaman to attack Hennessy, he thought, but these days you never could tell. He reached for the bag.

'My shopping,' said Nguyen.

'Let's see,' said Kavanagh. 'Let's see what yez got there.' At first it looked as if Nguyen would resist, but then the tension in his wiry body eased and he handed the bag to Kavanagh. Kavanagh opened it. It contained two bottles of lemonade, a loaf of bread, a can of Heinz baked beans and a brown paper bag full of new potatoes. Seeing that he was satisfied with the inspection, Nguyen held out his hands for the bag, but Kavanagh kept it away from him.

'Pat him down,' he said to Murphy. Murphy moved behind Nguyen and ran his hands expertly up and down his body, checking everywhere that a weapon could be concealed. There was a Swiss Army knife in one of the side pockets of the suit, but other than that there was nothing remotely suspicious – a small roll of Sellotape, a box of matches, some string, a set of keys, a pack of cigarettes and a wallet. The normal sort of pocket junk that anyone might have on them. 'He's OK,' he said to Kavanagh, who handed back the carrier bag.

'Go,' he said. 'Before we make yez go.'

Nguyen shook his head. Kavanagh and Murphy roughly seized an arm each and were preparing to frog-march him out, when the door to Hennessy's office opened. Hennessy's face creased into a puzzled frown when he saw what was going on.

'It's the man who's been phoning,' said Beth, before he could speak.

'Ah . . . The Chinaman,' said Hennessy, walking across to Beth's desk. 'You're a long way from home.'

Nguyen held the carrier bag tightly to his chest. 'You would not talk to me on the telephone,' he said.

'Out,' said Murphy, but Hennessy held up his hand.

'No, if he's come all this way I might as well talk to him, boys.'

'Yer man's got a knife,' said Kavanagh.

'A knife?'

'A Swiss Army knife.'

'Well take it off him. Look at him, for God's sake. How much damage can he do with two strapping fellows like yourselves around? Jesus, Mary and Joseph, let the man be.'

Kavanagh took the knife from Nguyen and Murphy took the carrier bag.

'You can pick them up on your way out,' said Beth as Hennessy led Nguyen into his private office. He waved him to a hard-backed leather seat in front of his desk while he closed the door behind them.

Nguyen sat with his hands folded in his lap while Hennessy sat down behind the desk and leant forward, his arms folded across the wide blotter which took up most of its surface. 'Let me tell you right from the start, you are wasting your time.' Hennessy said each word clearly and slowly as if addressing a particularly thick-skulled juror because he wasn't sure how good The Chinaman's command of English was. 'I realise you are upset and angry, and I understand how you must want revenge for what has happened to your family, but there is nothing I can do to help you. And you must know that it is very dangerous for you to be in Belfast asking about such things.' He pressed the tips of his fingers against his temples as if trying to suppress a headache and studied Nguyen. 'It is very dangerous,' he repeated.

Nguyen nodded thoughtfully. 'I do understand. But if you do not know who the men are, you can surely find out. I want you to find out for me.'

Hennessy shook his head, amazed at the man's audacity, or stupidity. Nguyen took the pack of cigarettes and the matches from his pocket.

'Can I smoke?' he asked Hennessy. Hennessy nodded and Nguyen held out the pack to him, offering him one. The lawyer refused and watched as Nguyen lit a cigarette and inhaled deeply. Hennessy noticed how steady The Chinaman's hands were, as steady as the unblinking brown eyes that seemed to look through his skull as easily as they penetrated the wreathes of smoke.

'You will change your mind,' said Nguyen, and it was a statement, not a question.

'No,' said Hennessy.

Nguyen smiled, and it was the smile of a man who has the sure and certain knowledge that he is right. He stood up and bowed once to Hennessy and then left the office. Murphy and Kavanagh were waiting for him outside, and they gave him his carrier bag and the penknife. He thanked them politely and turned to Beth and thanked her as well.

'Can I use your toilet?' he asked, and she told him there was one in the corridor outside. She pointed at the large sheet of glass at the entrance to the reception and through it he saw the door with 'Gentlemen' on it. He thanked them all again and left the office, closing the door quietly behind him. The washroom was small with whitewashed walls and a black tiled floor. There was a wash-basin, a urinal and a toilet in a cubicle. There was a mirror screwed to the wall above the basin and by the door was a paper-towel dispenser and below it a large steel wastepaper bin.

Nguyen entered the cubicle, shut the door and locked it. There was a black plastic lid on the toilet and he closed it and then sat down, placing the carrier bag gently on the floor. He took one of the bottles out and held it between his knees. It contained the antifreeze. He took out the second bottle, the one containing concentrated sulphuric acid. He used the Sellotape to bind the bottles together, wrapping it round and round until he was certain they were secure. He took out the length of string and tied it around the necks of the bottles, making quite sure there was no way it could slip. Individually the bottles of liquid were inert, but together they were very dangerous. He put the bottles on the floor and draped the string over his left leg. He took the box of matches out of his pocket and slid the string through it. He pulled the string to check that it was safely tied and then put his hands under the bottoms of the bottles and stood up slowly. The cistern was high up on the wall and Nguyen stood on the toilet seat to attach the string to the lever which operated the flushing system. When he was sure it was secure he care-fully removed his hands. The bottles turned slowly in the air above the tiled floor. He unscrewed the caps from the bottles and slipped them into his pocket. Then he pulled the filter off the cigarette and stuck the frayed end into the matchbox so that the burning tip was about three-quarters of an inch beyond the match heads. Nguyen stepped down, picked up the carrier bag and left the cubicle. He used the penknife to slide the lock closed so that it showed 'Engaged'.

As he left the toilet he smiled a goodbye to Beth. There was no rush, it would take at least two minutes for the cigarette to burn down far enough to set the matches alight. He walked slowly down the stairs and into Donegall Square. Overhead a helicopter hovered high in the air like a bird of prey searching for a victim.

The intercom on Beth's desk buzzed and Hennessy's voice summoned her into the office. From their sofas, Kavanagh and Murphy watched her hips swing as she walked to the door.

'I would,' said Murphy, whispering because he knew what a tongue-lashing he'd get if she heard him.

'Who wouldn't?' replied Kavanagh. 'But her old man'd focking kill ye.'

Hennessy was standing by his window watching Nguyen walk down the road, swinging his carrier bag full of shopping.

'I'm sorry, Liam,' she said, before he could speak. 'He caught me by surprise. Next time I won't let him disturb you.'

'That's all right, Beth. Just tell Murphy and Kavanagh to take care of it if he turns up again.' Nguyen stepped off the pavement, crossed the road and disappeared into a side street. Hennessy turned his back on the window. 'I think that man is going to be trouble,' he said.

'Don't be silly, Liam,' she said as if admonishing a child. 'What can a man like him do?'

The sound of the explosion made them both flinch, Beth putting her hands to her face and Hennessy ducking away from the window. Through the open door they saw

Kavanagh and Murphy dive to the ground. 'Keep down!' Murphy yelled at them.

'What's going on?' Hennessy shouted. They didn't answer. They were as confused as he was.

Beth was already on the floor, crouched by the side of the door. Hennessy went over to her and put his arms around her.

Murphy and Kavanagh were crawling over the carpet to check out the corridor. Kavanagh nudged open the door. The corridor was empty, then a pale-faced young man in a three-piece suit nervously appeared from an office further along.

'Mother of God, what happened?' said the young man.

Kavanagh got to his feet. Smoke was billowing out of the Gents, acrid-smelling and burning as he inhaled. He coughed and his eyes watered as he gingerly pushed open the door to the toilet. Fumes billowed out and the sprinklers in the corridor hissed into life and he ducked back into the office. In the distance he heard a police siren, and then another. He told Murphy to guard the door while he went back to Hennessy's office and helped him and Beth to their feet.

Beth flopped on to a chair and Hennessy went over to his drinks cabinet and poured two Irish whiskeys. He didn't offer one to Kavanagh, who was teetotal. Beth gulped hers down and Hennessy followed her example.

Before long, half a dozen green-uniformed RUC officers in bullet-proof vests came tearing down the corridor. A bull-necked sergeant ordered them to stay where they were and left a constable to keep an eye on them. The area round the toilet was cordoned off and then two men in dark-blue overalls carrying big black cases went in. The phone on Beth's desk rang, startling them all, and she asked the constable if it was OK to answer it. He nodded, his face blank. The men in the RUC had no love for Hennessy and his associates and Hennessy knew that the constable would probably have preferred them all to have been plastered over the walls by the explosion rather than sitting at the desk and drinking whiskey. While Beth was talking on the phone a CID officer in a sheepskin jacket arrived. He flashed his card to Hennessy and introduced himself as Inspector Greig. Behind him stood a young plain-clothes sergeant, a tall, gangly youth with a small, toothbrush moustache. He had the same couldn't-give-a-shit look as the uniformed constable.

'It seems as if you've had a wee bit of bother, Mr Hennessy,' said Greig. 'Unless it was one of your own boys being a tad careless.'

Hennessy shrugged. 'These things happen,' he said. 'Can I offer you a whiskey, Inspector?'

Greig refused, as Hennessy knew he would. 'I suppose it's a waste of time asking if you have any idea who might have done this?' said Greig, smiling through tight lips.

Kavanagh laughed sharply but Hennessy threw him a withering look. It was bad enough having the RUC in the office, but if they antagonised them they'd end up being hauled in for questioning and Hennessy didn't want the inconvenience or the publicity.

'Anyway, you'd better take care in future, Mr Hennessy.'

'What do you mean?'

'It looks to have been more of a warning than anything else. According to our forensic boys it was a home-made device, in fact device is hardly the right word. They reckon it was a couple of bottles of chemicals that did the damage.'

Murphy remembered the bottles in The Chinaman's carrier bag but said nothing.

'An accident?' said Hennessy.

Greig smiled thinly again. 'I hardly think they tied themselves to the toilet cistern,' he said. 'No, it was a simple chemical bomb, the sort we used to make as kids. Sulphuric acid and ethylene glycol. Antifreeze to you and me. Tie a bottle of each together and drop on to a hard surface. Bang! Did you never do that when you were a kid, Mr Hennessy? Great crack.' He could see by the look on the lawyer's face that the answer was no. Greig shrugged. 'I suppose we went to different schools, eh? Anyway, it would make a big enough explosion to wreck the room, and you wouldn't be laughing if you were in there, but it never stood a chance of damaging the building. It wasn't what you'd call a serious bomb, if you get my drift. Which makes me think that perhaps it was a warning. I don't suppose there's any point in asking if you've got any enemies, is there Mr Hennessy?' Greig was enjoying the Sinn Fein adviser's obvious discomfort.

'I'll certainly keep you informed if anyone comes to mind, Inspector,' Hennessy replied.

'I won't hold my breath.'

'Probably best,' said Hennessy.

'Can I show you out, Inspector?' asked Beth, sensing that underneath the banter her boss was beginning to lose his temper.

Greig hesitated as if loath to let Hennessy off the hook, but then he nodded and followed her out of the office. His sergeant looked hard at Murphy and Kavanagh as he went out, but the two men returned his gaze with easy smiles. They were long past the stage of fearing the police, the army, or anyone else who tried to impose their authority. Greig went into the toilet to speak to the forensic team again. The sergeant turned to speak to Beth but she closed the door firmly in his face.

Hennessy watched her from the door of his office and, satisfied that she wasn't in shock, gently closed the door. Kavanagh and Murphy tensed, fearing the sharp edge of Hennessy's tongue a thousand times more than hard looks from under-age detectives, but his anger wasn't directed at them.

'I want that Chinaman found,' he said with barely suppressed fury. 'I want him found and brought to me.'

The phone rang and Hennessy picked it up.

'Liam, it's him!' said Beth. She knew that Hennessy had said he wouldn't take any more calls from him, but she was smart enough to know that the situation was now different.

'Put him on please, Beth. Are you OK?'

'I'm fine, Liam. Really.' The line clicked and Hennessy waited for The Chinaman to speak.

'Mr Hennessy?' said Nguyen, not sure if he had been put through.

'What do you want?' said Hennessy.

'Mr Hennessy, you know what I want. I telephoned to see if you had changed your mind.'

'Why would I have changed your mind?' said Hennessy quietly.

'You know why,' said Nguyen.

Hennessy took a deep breath. 'I think that perhaps it would be a good idea if we spoke about this again. It might be we can come to an arrangement. Come back and we'll talk.'

Nguyen laughed without humour. 'I think not,' he said.

'You will not see me again, Mr Hennessy. But you will be hearing from me.'

'It will take a lot more than a loud noise in my toilet to change my mind.'

'So be it,' said Nguyen, and hung up.

'The bastard,' spat Hennessy. 'Who the hell does he think he is, threatening me like that?' He slammed down the phone and glared at the two men by his desk.

'Get his description to the boys,' he said. 'I want him found.'

'It might be an idea if yez left Belfast for a few days, just in case,' suggested Kavanagh.

'Are you telling me that you can't protect me in my own city?' said Hennessy.

'I'm not saying that, but it would be easier if we went down to yez farm. That's all.'

'No,' said Hennessy. 'He is not driving me out of my own city, he's not going to make me run like a scared dog. Just put the word out.'

He waved them away impatiently and flopped down into his chair. He took a mouthful of whiskey, and then another. He knew he shouldn't have lost his temper, but the bombing had shaken him badly. It made him acutely aware of his own mortality, that his own threescore years and ten wasn't all that far away, and the fact that a vindictive Chinaman with a bottle of antifreeze could steal away the years he had left made him very angry. And afraid. The supercilious detective had said it had been a warning. Very well, he would regard it as just that.

Nguyen didn't drive straight back to the guest-house. Once he'd collected his van from the car park off

Gloucester Street he headed north along Victoria Street and then cut westwards across the city along Divis Street, past grim blocks of flats, to where it turned into Falls Road. It wasn't that he was worried about being followed, because he knew he was long gone from Donegall Square before the bottles crashed on to the floor. It wasn't that he enjoyed driving, either. He'd always found sitting behind the steering wheel stressful and he'd been looking forward to the day when his daughter would pass her driving test so that she could do all the restaurant deliveries for him. He drove around to get a feel of the city and its people, and at the back of his mind lurked the thought that by understanding the people of Belfast he might be able to understand why the IRA had killed his family. The city centre was prosperous, shiny fronted shops and clean pavements. The cars in the streets were mainly new and well cared for and there were few signs of a city in the throes of sectarian violence. 'Belfast Says No' said a banner Nguyen had seen hanging under the green dome of City Hall in Donegall Square, but he didn't know what the city was saying 'no' to. There was a strong police and army presence, with some streets sealed off with metal railings manned by armed policemen and turnstiles to allow pedestrians through one at a time, but there was no air of tension, none that Nguyen could detect, anyway. He had a large-scale map of Belfast and its surroundings spread over the passenger seat, and as he stopped at a red traffic light he scanned it, trying to pronounce the strange names: Knocknagoney, Ballyhackamore, Cregagh, Skegoneill, Ligoniel, Ballynafeigh.

A horn sounded and he realised the light had turned

green. He missed first gear and went into third by mistake and the van stalled. The horn blared out again and it was joined by others until he got the engine started again and pulled away jerkily.

He drove along the Falls Road, the Royal Victoria Hospital on his left, and the city changed character. It took on a brooding, menacing air. He saw burnt-out cars down side roads, rusting hulks that had obviously been there for months, like the skeletons of long-dead animals. There were children everywhere, in push-chairs, playing football on the pavements, walking with their parents, standing on street corners, loitering outside pubs, children with worn clothes and unkempt hair and runny noses. He drove by red-brick houses that had been gutted and never repaired, derelict wrecks like rotting stumps in a mouthful of bad teeth. There were splashes of colour among the drab greyness – extravagant murals on the gable ends of the terraces, paintings of masked men with machine guns, elaborate crosses, memorials to hunger strikers who had died in prison, and the tricolour, the Irish flag. There were slogans too, many of which Nguyen didn't understand, but there were some he could read: 'Support The Provisionals', 'Troops Out', 'Ireland for the Irish'. He drove by a pub, windows protected with thick wire mesh. There were two men standing either side of a black wooden door with their hands in their pockets and they scrutinised the van with hostile eyes. Lookouts, Nguyen decided. He would have to be more careful where he showed himself. The city centre had lulled him into a false sense of security. Out here, in the Catholic working-class areas, he could feel the mistrust in the air like the cloying damp of a morning mist. The men saw that Nguyen was Oriental and immediately lost interest in him.

The road curved gently and on his right Nguyen saw a huge graveyard which stretched as far as he could see, and then another cemetery on his left as he followed Glen Road and then turned left at a roundabout and headed south-east on Kennedy Way through the district shown on the map as Andersonstown. He slowed down to look at two depressing rows of flats, precast greying concrete with dirty windows and badly painted frames. The muddy verge of trampled grass that surrounded the blocks was littered with empty crisp packets, tattered pages of abandoned tabloid newspapers, stale fish and chip wrappers and broken bottles, the flotsam and jetsam of inner city life. Nguyen was unable to understand why the people who lived there did not take better care of their surroundings. How could they tolerate such squalor, he thought. Living in poverty was one thing, but that was no excuse for behaving like animals. He shook his head sadly.

He drove towards a place called Malone and the surroundings improved, the depressing neglect giving way to well-kept gardens and freshly painted houses, and then he indicated left on to Malone Road, heading back to the city centre. Just before he reached the city's Botanic Gardens he turned left into Wellington Park, musing over what he had seen. The people who lived in the depressed areas had little to lose, he realised. If his enemy came from the rubbish-strewn slums and the neglected high-rise monstrosities, then surely prison would hold no fear for them. Children reared there would be tough, uncaring, loyal to their own and aggressive against intruders. Their poverty would bind them like iron chains. He wouldn't be taking on one man, he would be going against the whole of the IRA. He switched off the engine and stared out with unseeing eyes. It had to be done, whatever the cost. He had no choice. He owed it to his wife, and to his daughters.

Liam Hennessy stood in his garden and looked up at the rocky outcrop they called Napoleon's Nose. Not that it looked like a nose, or any other part of Napoleon's anatomy. Jackie, his red setter, loped out of the house and over the lawn towards him. He bent down and ruffled her ears and let her lick his hands.

He walked around the lawn with his dog, checking the trees and plants. He was a keen gardener but his law practice and political activities left him little time to attend to the half acre or so that surrounded his four-bedroomed red-brick house in Antrim Road. He employed part-time a retired gardener who had formerly helped to tend the city's Botanic Gardens, but he insisted on checking his progress every morning. He knelt down and examined a heather-covered rockery and Jackie ran up and licked his cheek with her sloppy tongue. He pushed her away and laughed.

'She wants a walk,' said his wife. He turned and straightened up, brushing his knees.

'You could creep up on the devil himself, Mary,' he laughed. She handed him a mug of tea.

'Your dog wants a walk,' she repeated. Mary Hennessy looked a good deal less than her forty-six years, tall and slim with dark brown, lightly curled hair in a pageboy cut. Hennessy looked at her appreciatively as he took the mug. She didn't look like a woman who had two teenage children. Her skin was smooth and lightly tanned and the few wrinkles she had made her look all the more beautiful.

She still turned the heads of men half her age and she knew it. There were times when he was so afraid of losing her that his stomach churned.

'Our dog,' he corrected.

She nodded at the setter as it sat at his feet looking up at him with undisguised love. 'Just look at her,' she said.

'I can remember when there was a look not unlike that in your own fair eyes,' he teased, and she laughed. The phone rang and she ran across the lawn to the house. She runs, for God's sake, thought Hennessy, she runs like an excited child and she laughs out loud. He tried to remember when he'd last laughed out loud. He couldn't recall exactly when it was but it was after hearing Ian Paisley being interviewed on television and it wasn't a gentle, lilting laugh like Mary's, it was sarcastic and biting.

'Jackie,' he said, 'I am getting old.'

The red setter looked up at him and woofed as if agreeing and he reached down and patted her on the head.

'There's no time for a walk, old girl. The car will be here any moment, sure enough.'

Jim Kavanagh and Christy Murphy were at Hennessy's side all day and most of the evening, but during the night they went home to sleep and their places were taken by two men from a pool of about a dozen trusted volunteers who stayed outside his house in whatever car they were using. Jimmy McMahon took the black Jaguar to his own house in north Belfast and brought Kavanagh and Murphy with him first thing in the morning. Hennessy looked at his watch. They were late.

Mary appeared at the back door and waved to him. 'It's Christy,' she shouted.

Jackie's ears pricked up and she romped towards her

in the mistaken belief that she was being called in for some titbit. Hennessy walked after her, cursing under his breath and taking care not to spill his tea. The Jaguar had only just come out of the garage after a very expensive service and he hoped it hadn't been in an accident.

Mary handed the phone to him. Murphy sounded short of breath. 'The bastards tried to kill us,' he said.

'What are you talking about?' asked Hennessy.

'The bastards tried to blow us up.'

'Calm down, Christy,' Hennessy soothed. 'Just tell me what happened.'

He heard Murphy take a deep breath before speaking. 'We went to get the Jaguar out of Jimmy's garage. He got into the driving seat and was just about to start up the sodding thing when we saw it. Holy Mary, mother of God, if we hadn't spotted it we'd all have been . . .'

'What happened?' interrupted Hennessy impatiently.

'They used a flash-bulb and a couple of wires.'

'A flash-bulb?'

'A flash-bulb, and it had been covered in some sort of red powder. It was a home-made detonator, as soon as the ignition key was turned it would have exploded the petrol in the tank.'

'OK, Christy. Where are you now?'

'We're all in Jimmy's house.'

There was a muttering in the background and the sound of a bottle clinking against a glass. The boys were having a wee snort to calm their nerves, and Hennessy didn't blame them. They'd had two narrow escapes in as many days.

'Listen, this is what you do. Have you removed it?'

'Sure enough, we pulled it out of the tank, but it's still connected.'

'Leave it just as it is. Call Willie O'Hara and get him to look at it, he knows what he's doing. And get him to check out the whole car, from top to bottom. As soon as he's given it the all clear, you and Jim come on over. And Christy?'

'Yeah?'

'Take it easy.'

He replaced the receiver. The mug of tea was still in his left hand, untouched. He sipped it, a deep frown on his forehead.

'Something wrong?' asked his wife.

He nodded. 'Somebody has just tried to blow up the car.'

Mary's eyes widened and her mouth opened. He hadn't told her about the explosion at the office because he hadn't wanted to worry her, but he took her into the kitchen and sat her down at the pine breakfast table and told her that there had been two attempts on his life, albeit half-hearted ones.

There was a scratching noise at the door and Hennessy walked over to let in the dog. She scuttled beneath the table and Hennessy realised then how vulnerable he was. He went down the hall, opened the front door and waved over the two men sitting in a blue Ford Escort to the left of the driveway. He told them to be extra careful and sent one of them to stand guard by the back door until Murphy and Kavanagh arrived.

He returned to the kitchen and flashed his wife a smile as he sat down.

'Who do you think is behind this? The Ulster Defence Association?'

Hennessy shrugged and looked down at his mug of

tea. A brownish scum was beginning to form on the surface and he poked it with his finger.

'There was some clever dick inspector at the office who said it might be a warning.'

'A warning?'

Hennessy looked up and was pleased to see the concern in her eyes. 'The bomb in the office wasn't really a bomb, it was a home-made affair that was limited in terms of the damage it could do. And from the sound of it the job they tried to do on the car today was pretty amateurish, too. I mean, they must be pretty stupid not to realise that the first thing we do every morning is to check out the car.'

'But why would anyone want to warn you, Liam? The UDA don't normally bother issuing warnings, do they?'

She was right, of course. In recent years there had been an unspoken agreement between the various political groupings not to assassinate the top echelons, an understanding that the leaders had to be able to talk with their opposite numbers without the constant fear of a shotgun blast through the letterbox or a pistol to the back of the neck. The Brighton bombing had shown that no one was safe, not even the Prime Minister, and the whole world had seen a President take a bullet from a lone gunman. The Paisleys and the Adamses and the Hennessys wouldn't last a week if they ever declared open season on each other, but as it was they could move fairly safely through the city. They still kept their bodyguards and trusted the opposition about as much as they trusted the British Government, but the bad old days when a bodyguard had to take a bullet in the shoulder to protect Hennessy were long gone. But if the truce was now over, there'd be no warning, they'd just cut him down with a hail of bullets as he got out of his car. They wouldn't mess around with do-it-yourself bombs. No, this couldn't be political. But if it wasn't political, what was it?

He stood up and put his hand gently under Mary's chin, tilting her head upwards. 'There was a man came round to the office yesterday, a Chinaman. His wife and daughter were killed in one of the London bombings. He thinks I'm responsible.'

'He came all the way to Belfast to see you?'

'He wants me to tell him who's behind the bombing campaign. I sent him packing and a few minutes later our toilet exploded. Now this.'

She shook her head away from his hand. 'Why haven't you told the police this?'

'We're not sure it's him. And anyway, it's the sort of thing we can handle ourselves.'

'Liam!' she said angrily. 'You're playing with our lives here!'

'If it is him we'll soon stop him, don't worry. He's Chinese, he won't be difficult to spot in Belfast.'

'I hope you're right,' she said. The look of concern had gone now, and it had been replaced by something else, something that seemed to Hennessy to be uncomfortably like contempt. It was a look that his wife was giving him more and more often these days, he thought with a heavy heart. He couldn't seem to do anything right. He decided not to try to win her around, knowing that he was sure to fail.

'I'll be in the study until Jim and Christy get here,' he said as he walked out of the kitchen. Jackie rushed out from under the table, her claws clicking against the tiles, and loyally followed him out.

He went into his study and closed the door. Jackie went to her wicker basket by the side of the french window which led on to the small patio and she settled into it with a deep and mournful sigh as if offering sympathy for the rough treatment he was getting from Mary. He knew that she would prefer him to take a tougher line with the Protestant extremists, and on more than one occasion she'd urged him to mount an all-out offensive against the UDA. It was so strange, he thought, the way that he himself had mellowed over the years and she had become more and more committed to an armed struggle. The more he tried to persuade her that the only solution was a negotiated one, the more she seemed to turn away from him, physically and emotionally. But he knew that he was right, that his way was the only way forward. Anything else would only end in bloodshed. Knowing that he was right didn't make him feel any better.

There was a safe set into the wall behind a framed hunting print over a cast-iron fireplace; Hennessy opened it and took out a brown A4 manila envelope. He flicked the open end with a thumbnail as he walked over to the desk. Inside was a sheaf of papers, each a report on an individual arms cache. There were fifteen in all, and he was expecting a further six by nightfall. He spread the sheets out on the desk and examined them. Three of the caches had been interfered with. In all, fifteen kilograms of Semtex had been taken, along with a dozen detonators, two mercury tilt switches, two handguns and a small amount of ammunition. Everything else necessary for the construction of bombs – wires, timing devices, transmitters – could be bought from High Street stores. Hennessy was sure that the maverick IRA team had been stealing from the organisation's munition dumps and he was equally certain that they were being helped by somebody inside the organisation. The trouble was that there was no pattern, no connection between the three dumps. They were the responsibility of three different IRA cells. He grunted and gathered up the papers. Jackie lifted her head and watched him put the sheets back into the envelope.

'Maybe the remaining inspections will supply the answer,' he said to her and she chuffed in agreement.

Hennessy heard a car arrive outside and footsteps crunching on the gravelled drive before the doorbell rang. He waited to see if Mary would answer it, but he wasn't surprised when she didn't. He went and opened the door to let in Kavanagh and Murphy and a small sharp-faced man with a straggly moustache and grey, watery eyes, Willie O'Hara. Jimmy McMahon stayed outside in the Jaguar, reluctant to let it out of his sight. Willie was wearing his normal baggy grey suit, the trousers held up by a greasy brown belt, and he was carrying a paper bag. Hennessy took the three men into the study. 'Was the car clear?' he asked O'Hara.

'Other than this?' answered the little man, holding up the bag. 'Yeah, this was all, but it would've been more than enough.' He reached in his hand and took out a coil of black wire and held it out to Hennessy. 'Crude, but it would've done the job.'

There were two pieces of wire, each about ten-foot long, and both had been soldered to the flash-bulb.

Hennessy pointed to the red powder which covered the flash-bulb. 'What's this?' he asked.

O'Hara's eyes shone. 'Ground up match-heads,' he said. 'Mainly potassium chlorate. Just to add an extra kick.

Probably wouldn't have been necessary, but it's a nice touch.'

'How does it work?'

'Whoever it was had prised open the fuel cap and left the flash-bulb dangling just inside the tank, in the fumes above the petrol. You turn the key and up she goes.'

'Guaranteed?'

O'Hara frowned, wondering what Hennessy was getting at. 'Pretty certain. I mean, it's not the sort of gadget we'd use because there's always an outside chance that the bulb might fall into the petrol in which case it wouldn't ignite it. And it's also pretty easy to spot.'

'A warning?'

O'Hara nodded eagerly. 'Yeah, that's exactly what I was thinking. Is somebody giving you trouble?'

'I've an idea who it might be, yes. Willie, thanks for your help.' Hennessy shook him by the hand and showed him out, telling Jimmy to drive O'Hara wherever he wanted to go.

Back in the study he sat behind his desk and told Kavanagh and Murphy to make themselves comfortable. He offered them tea or coffee but they declined. He didn't offer them anything stronger because even under stress Kavanagh didn't touch alcohol and he could already smell whiskey on Murphy's breath and they'd all need clear heads.

'I'm coming round to thinking that maybe you were right about what you said yesterday, Jim,' Hennessy said to Kavanagh.

'About going to the farm?'

Hennessy nodded. 'I think it's best. The weekend's coming up, and I can just as easily run things from there, for a short time at least. Mary and I will go tonight, Jimmy and Christy can come with us and we'll take another couple of lads with us just to be on the safe side.'

'Ye want me to stay here?' asked Kavanagh.

'I want you to organise a search for this Chinaman. He shouldn't be that hard to find, not in Belfast. There can't be that many Chinese here, and this one's a stranger, from London. He's got to be staying somewhere.'

'No problem,' said Kavanagh.

'And I'm bringing Sean Morrison back.'

Both Kavanagh and Murphy smiled. They knew Morrison well and had worked together on many occasions.

'He's still in New York?' asked Murphy. Morrison had left Belfast more than two years earlier.

'Yeah, he's liaising with the various Noraid groups in North America.' Morrison had told Hennessy he wanted to get out of Belfast for a while and his request had come at a time when fund-raising in the United States had been going through a rough patch. Morrison had made a difference, not the least because his broad Belfast accent and typical Irish good looks went down so well with the Americans. He looked just like they expected an IRA activist should, tall, broad-shouldered, with curly black hair and piercing blue eyes. He spoke well and with conviction about the aims of the organisation and the Noraid groups had used him to full advantage. Morrison had also been a great help in arranging for forged passports and visas for IRA members who wanted to get in and out of the United States without being identified, and had recently begun to form links with arms suppliers. He had been a godsend. But right now Hennessy needed someone he could trust, and he trusted Morrison with his life.

He told Kavanagh to start the hunt for The Chinaman right away, and asked Murphy to step up security arrangements around the house. He waited until he was alone before picking up the phone and calling New York.

Morrison answered on the third ring, his voice thick with sleep.

'Good morning, Sean. What time is it in the Big Apple?'

Morrison groaned. 'Almost five o'clock,' he said. 'What's wrong, Liam?'

'I need you back here, Sean.'

'When?'

'Today.'

Morrison groaned again. 'You don't ask much, do you?' He didn't ask why because he knew the security forces weren't averse to tapping Hennessy's phone, legally or otherwise.

'I'd like you to come straight here, to my house,' Hennessy continued. 'I'll explain everything when you arrive. How long do you think it'll take you?'

'Ten hours or so, Liam, a lot depends on the timing of the direct flights.' His voice was clearer now. 'I'll call you if there are any problems.'

Hennessy thanked him and replaced the receiver. He picked up the wires and flash-bulb that Willie had left on his desk and toyed with them, deep in thought.

Nguyen drove the Renault to a Chinese take-away and bought six portions of plain boiled rice, three of roast pork and three of roast chicken. He told the Hong Kong Chinese behind the counter that he didn't want any sauce or anything, just meat. The food came in the same foil containers with white cardboard lids that he'd used in his

125

own shop in Clapham. He asked for a carrier bag, put the food in the back of the van and then drove to a pub in the countryside to buy ice. The landlord of the first place he tried said he didn't have enough for his own use, never mind to sell to someone who wasn't even a regular. The man behind the bar at the second pub was more sympathetic to Nguyen's story of a wife with an arthritic leg which the doctor said would be helped if she lay with it in an ice bath. He sold him three carrier bags full of ice-cubes shovelled from a large clanking ice-machine for a nominal sum and Nguyen drove back to the guest-house as quickly as he dared. He parked the van, put the packs of ice and one of the bags of fertilizer into two holdalls and carried them inside. Mrs McAllister was dusting the hall and she smiled when she saw him. 'Lovely day, isn't it?' she said.

He smiled, nodded and slipped by her. He put the fertilizer on the bathroom floor, dropped the ice into the bottom of the shower and listened at the door until he heard the landlady go into the kitchen. He slipped downstairs and refilled the holdalls. He carried them back up the stairs, walking softly on the balls of his feet close to the wall so that he made the minimum of noise. The less he saw of the landlady and the other guests, the better.

He entered his room and slid back the brass bolt before placing the bag on the bedcover and unzipping it. He unpacked the bag carefully, first removing the two glass bottles of concentrated acids, which he took one at a time into the bathroom and put on the floor by the shower.

He tore open the plastic bags and tipped most of the ice into the shower and then fetched a box of salt and sprinkled it over the cubes before pushing the bottles of acid into the freezing mixture.

While it cooled he emptied the holdall on to the bed. There was the bottle of glycerine, a can of motor oil, several boxes of matches, a tube of glue, a jumble of plastic piping, plastic-coated wire, a box of baking soda, a pair of washing-up gloves, a thermometer, a Pyrex measuring jug, two large Pyrex saucepans and a Teflon-covered stirrer. He took what he needed into the bathroom and switched on the light so that the ventilator would start working. The acid fumes would be painful if he inhaled them.

Nguyen had worked with explosives a lot during the war. Whenever possible the Vietcong had bought explosives or used equipment captured from the Americans, but supplies weren't always easy to get and they were quite capable of manufacturing their own blasting gelatine, TNT, plastic or nitroglycerine. Most of the raw materials for explosives could be bought quite legally, though in the later years of the war there were restrictions on the sale of electric timing devices. Not that it mattered, though, because clockwork alarm clocks were just as good.

It took almost half an hour before Nguyen had completed the complex and dangerous series of chemical reactions that left him with an oily white substance forming a milky layer at the bottom of the measuring jug.

Nguyen settled back on the cold floor and sighed. His jaw ached and he realised he must have been grinding his teeth with the tension. He was starting to get a headache, a piercing pain behind his eyes that could be a result of the stress or more likely the effect of the fumes. He got to his feet, his knees cracking as he straightened up and walked unsteadily into the bedroom. He opened the window wide and then sat on the edge of the bed, breathing deeply to clear his head.

When he felt a little better he took the bag of fertilizer into the bathroom and tore it open. He spread out one of the empty plastic bags that had contained the ice and scooped handfuls of fertilizer on to it. it was important to get the ratio of motor oil, nitroglycerine and fertilizer right. He added the oil to the fertilizer first, kneading it like dough until it had been absorbed and then carefully poured out the nitroglycerine a little at a time, placing it back in the shower between pourings. The nitroglycerine could be used as an explosive on its own but it was dangerously unstable and would explode if knocked or dropped or if it got too hot. Once it had been mixed with the fertilizer and oil it would be quite inert until detonated but would be almost as effective.

Nguyen worked slowly and methodically and it took him the best part of an hour until all the nitroglycerine had been worked into the mixture and he had a dark-brown gooey paste on the plastic bag. He stripped off the gloves and laid them on the floor and went back into the bedroom. The headache was worse. He looked at his watch. It was six o'clock. He had plenty of time, so he lay down on the bed and rested.

He woke with a start two hours later when the landlady knocked on the door. 'Would you care for a cup of tea, Mr Minh?' she called.

Nguyen thanked her but said no and she went back down the stairs. He sat up and rubbed his eyes. The curtains were blowing into the room and the sky was darkening outside. He slid off the bed and turned on the light. There was a lamp on the dressing-table and he put it on the floor, under the window, and pulled out its plug from the mains. He spread a newspaper on the shiny wooden

128

surface and then took the soldering iron, solder, flash-bulbs and wire and put them on the newspaper. He plugged in the iron and while he waited for it to heat up he used the Swiss Army knife to cut twelve sections of wire, each about eighteen inches long, and then stripped a short section of plastic from the end of each piece. He soldered a wire to the bottom of each of the flash-bulbs, and another to the side. He used a battery to test one, touching the ends of the wires to the two terminals. It burst into white light and hissed as it melted. He tossed it on to the bed.

In Vietnam they'd had a plentiful supply of blasting caps, but they were hard to get hold of in peacetime. Not that it mattered, because the home-made explosive was sensitive enough to be detonated by a flash-bulb. Nguyen had decided he would make extra sure. He opened two boxes of matches and emptied them on to the newspaper. He stripped off the red heads until he had a pile of several dozen and then he crushed them with the blade of his knife, one at a time. Occasionally one would burst into flames as he worked and he'd use the blade to extinguish the fire. When he'd finished he had a neat pile of red powder. He smeared glue over the bulbs and then rolled them in the powder until they were completely covered. He left them to dry on the newspaper while he prepared the plastic piping. It was the sort used as drainpipes in cheap housing. He'd cut each piece with a hacksaw so that they were about a foot long. He sealed up one end of each pipe with strips of insulation tape and then took them into the bathroom. He put his gloves back on and half filled each pipe with the explosive mixture, then went back for six of the detonators. He held the wires in his left hand as he carefully eased the sticky mixture around the detonators, two for each pipe, and pressed it down. When he'd filled all three he sealed the ends closed with tape with just the wires protruding. They looked childish and inelegant, but Nguyen knew how deadly and effective they were. Properly planted in a road, they could destroy a car and leave a crater more than six feet across. All that was needed to set them off was to pass an electric current through the wires.

He wrapped them in newspaper and put them into the holdall. He placed the tools on top and zipped up the bag. Everything else he put into a black rubbish bag. He tied the top and lifted it, but realised immediately the thin plastic was in danger of tearing, so he slid it inside a second bag, and then a third, before twisting the open ends together and fastening them with tape.

It was almost ten o'clock. He lay down on the bed and looked for a while at the picture of the former American president. He closed his eyes, knowing that his internal alarm clock would wake him at dawn, but sleep eluded him at first. The face of the man who had first committed the US military to suppressing the Communists in the North floated in front of him and brought with it a flood of memories. He tried to push them away but they were persistent and eventually he surrendered to them.

Nguyen's father was a fanatical Communist but also appreciated the value of money and when Nguyen was nine years old he sent him to live with a cousin in Hanoi, almost 250 miles to the north of their village. The cousin ran a small garage in a back street and there Nguyen learnt how to service cars and each week he sent back half of his meagre wages to his father. In the evenings he went to a night school run by a local Catholic priest where he was taught to read and write and to question the Communist views he had picked up from his father.

He turned eleven on the day that Vietnam won its battle for independence and the French pulled out and he was in the street cheering with his friends when Ho Chi Minh returned to Hanoi. There was no peace, not even when the last French soldier left Vietnam. The struggle then became a struggle between North and South. Nguyen was eighteen when the first American soldier died in Vietnam, working in an armaments factory which manufactured grenade launchers. The factory was in a ramshackle hut in a Hanoi suburb containing little more than rows of metal tables, a brick forge with bellows powered by a bicycle and a lathe run by a rusting Citroën engine that had been fixed to a heavy wooden frame. He spent four years in the factory during which time he married Xuan Phoung and she bore him two children, both girls. They were three good years, the work he did seemed distant from the fighting going on in the south and though the hours were long and the work hard they lived in a small flat in a pretty part of Hanoi and there were occasional supplies of fresh vegetables sent up from his father's farm.

It all changed in 1967 by which time US bombs were regularly falling on Hanoi. Nguyen was drafted into the North Vietnamese Army. There were no arguments, and it didn't matter that he had a young wife and two babies. It would have been earlier if he hadn't been helping the war effort in Hanoi, but now they said his skills were needed down south. After two weeks basic training Nguyen was sent into action as a sapper. Before he left Hanoi he arranged for his family to leave Hanoi and stay at his father's farm. It was a lot closer to the fighting than Hanoi, but he knew that the bombing could only get worse and that in the city there would be no one to take care of them.

Nguyen and his fellow sappers were taken to within twenty miles of Saigon, to an area the Americans called The Iron Triangle, where they spent six months helping to build and equip a network of tunnels that housed hundreds of NVA and Vietcong soldiers. Deep underground were hospitals, training schools, supply stores and munitions factories. For weeks on end he never saw the sunlight. Nguyen was then put to work manufacturing home-made mines from captured US 105-millimetre howitzer shells of which the NVA had an abundant supply. The cash-rich Americans were notoriously careless with their equipment and there were crates upon crates of the shells for Nguyen and his team to work on.

One day when he was supervising a new batch of the mines a VC officer came to watch and began talking to him. The officer had been a mechanic many years before and it turned out that he'd originally worked in a garage in Hanoi not far from where Nguyen learnt his trade. The man complimented Nguyen on his work and after watching for a while longer he went away. The following day Nguyen was called to his commanding officer and told that he was being transferred to a Vietcong guerrilla unit. He'd asked what sort of unit and the officer had shrugged and said that it didn't matter. Nguyen didn't press it because he knew there was no point. He wasn't surprised when he was told that he was ordered to report to the VC officer who'd been watching him earlier. That was when Nguyen had been taught to fight. And to kill.

Nguyen was told that he'd be working in a team of three, setting booby traps on trails used by the American forces. He was given a black uniform to replace his grey NVA fatigues, but he was told he was to keep his AK-47 rifle. And that was that. Nguyen spent almost a year living in fear, creeping out of the tunnels at night, planting mines, setting trip wires and doing everything possible to terrorise the Americans. He became expert at moving silently through the jungle and quickly learned to camouflage himself so effectively that he was almost invisible from a few feet away, even during daylight.

Nguyen himself gave little thought to the politics involved: he was happy to fight for his country and, besides, if he had ever expressed any reservations about what he was doing he would have more than likely been shot in the back of the head. But that all changed one night in the summer of 1968 while he was in temporary attachment to a VC training camp close to Chap Le. The camp was only thirty miles away from Dong Hoi and Nguyen was hoping to be granted leave so that he could visit his family on his father's farm, when word reached him that his father had died. When he officially applied for leave it was refused, with no explanation. He went anyway, borrowing a battered Vespa scooter and driving through the night. When he arrived at the farm he was greeted by his tearful wife and children, and he learnt the full story.

A truckload of Vietcong soldiers had arrived at the farm three days earlier and demanded that they provide them with food and supplies. They helped themselves to rice from the storage sheds and half a dozen chickens. One of them untethered a bleating goat and began pulling it towards the truck. Xuan Phoung had protested that she needed the milk for her children, but one of the soldiers pushed her away and when she tried to take the goat back hit her in the stomach with the butt of his rifle. Nguyen's father went to pick her up and the soldier turned on him, hitting him on the head. The soldiers dragged him to the truck, along with the goat, and drove off. They took him to a nearby hamlet and tied him to a stake and called out all the villagers to watch. They accused him of being a bad Communist and of conspiring against the National Liberation Front and then they slowly disembowelled him as the crowd cheered.

The old man was still dying as Xuan Phoung arrived on foot at the village, and she cut him down and cradled his head in her lap. The VC had left by then and one of the braver villagers helped bury him. No funeral, because that would antagonise the Vietcong and there would be more killings.

Xuan Phoung took Nguyen to the unmarked grave and stood with him in silence as tears ran down his cheeks. He made his mind up then, as he stood by the wet soil, and later that night he took his wife and two children, precariously balanced on the scooter as they headed south. As they got closer to the area controlled by the South Vietnamese forces he took them into the jungle, travelling by night and hiding from all patrols, US, NVA and VC, until he reached a South Vietnamese camp near Hue, on the banks of the Perfume River.

There he gave himself up to the ARVN, the Army of South Vietnam, and applied to join Chieu Hoi, the 'Appeal to Return' programme. He'd read about Chieu Hoi in the jungle after a low-flying helicopter had thrown out handfuls of propaganda leaflets. The VCs kept them and used them for lighting fires and as toilet paper.

His wife and children were resettled in a safe village south of Saigon while Nguyen was sent to a rehabilitation camp. He wasn't there long. He'd never had any great love for Communism and the ARVN realised how useful Nguyen would be. When he crossed over he hadn't thought that he'd be fighting for the South, he'd had some vague hope that they'd simply allow him to go back to what he enjoyed doing, working in a garage somewhere and spending the nights with his wife and daughters. He was wrong. The ARVN didn't threaten to put a bullet in his head, but they didn't have to. The South was infiltrated with VC soldiers and agents and if Nguyen and his family weren't kept in a safe village they'd be killed within weeks. Their survival depended on the goodwill of the Government of South Vietnam. And the price exacted for that goodwill was for Nguyen to serve them in the best way he could.

Once he'd satisfied them that he wasn't a VC agent he was sent to the Recondo School, run by the 5th Special Forces Group at one end of Nha Trang airfield, near Saigon. The Recondo School was where the US army trained the men who made up the Long Range Reconnaissance Patrols – or Lurps to the men who served in them. The Lurps operated in six-man teams deep in enemy territory as the eyes and ears of the army, and often as its assassins.

It soon became obvious to the instructors that there was nothing Nguyen could learn from them. Within two days he was teaching them about VC booby traps and camouflage techniques and then the top brass got to hear about his talents and inside a month he found himself seconded to a Lurp unit on the edge of the Iron Triangle.

Time and time again, Nguyen was sent into enemy territory, along the same trails that he'd travelled when he was a VC. He knew many of the hiding places and the supply dumps and the secret trails, and he had a sixth sense for spotting the VC trip-wires and traps.

Nguyen was allowed regular visits to his wife and daughters, and as he drew regular US army pay, life was good fighting for the Americans, until it became obvious that the NVA were going to overrun the South. Nguyen began to worry about what would happen if the Americans pulled out, but he was always assured that he would be taken care of and that his family would be given sanctuary in the United States. He'd believed them.

Nguyen tossed fitfully on the bed, sweat beading on his forehead. His breath came in ragged gasps as he relived in his mind what had happened to his wife and his three daughters, how they'd died and how he'd been powerless to help.

Mary Hennessy was sitting alone in the lounge watching television when the doorbell rang. She got to her feet and smoothed down her dress before going into the hall, but Murphy had got to the front door ahead of her. There were four suitcases by the door, mainly clothes that she wanted to take with her to the farm. Liam had said they were only going for the weekend, but she could see that he was holding something back, and realised that he'd been badly shocked by the two bombing attempts and that they'd probably end up staying on the farm until it had been sorted out.

It was ten o'clock already, but Liam had said he was waiting to see someone before they left and it was a desire to see who the mysterious visitor was rather than a sense of politeness that had taken her to the hall. He was hidden by the door, all she could see was a sleeved arm shaking hands with Murphy, but then she heard his spoken greeting and she gasped, her hand flying involuntarily up to her mouth. The door opened wider and he stepped inside. Morrison was holding a blue holdall in his left hand and he bent down to put it on the floor by her suitcases and it was only as he straightened up that he saw her. He smiled and his eyes widened.

'Mary,' he said, in a voice that could have meant a hundred things. He seemed unsure how he should greet her, stepping forward as if to kiss her on the cheek but then holding himself back and offering her his hand instead. Was that because Murphy was watching them, or because he knew Liam was nearby, or was it something else? It had been two years since she had seen Sean Morrison and she couldn't read him as easily as she used to. His hand felt strong and dry and she pressed her fingers into his palm, holding him a little longer than was necessary. He squeezed her gently and he seemed reluctant to take his hand away. That's what she told herself, anyway. She was immediately glad that she'd worn her blue silk dress which showed her figure off, especially around her waist. She wanted to look good for him. He looked wonderful, his hair was longer than when she'd last seen him but otherwise he hadn't changed: smiling blue eyes, his mouth which always seemed ready to break into a grin, and a body that could have belonged to a dancer.

'It's good to see you again, Sean,' she said. 'How's New York?'

'Hectic,' he said. 'A lot different to Belfast, I can tell you.'

'You're here to see Liam?'

He nodded. 'Yeah, is he in the study?'

She wanted to keep him in the hall, to talk with him and find out why he was back, but she knew that she'd already spent too long looking at him, any longer and Murphy would suspect there was something going on. Mary smiled to herself. He'd be wrong, of course. There was nothing going on between her and Sean. There hadn't been for two years, but she could tell from his touch that the electricity was still there between them.

'He's waiting for you,' she said. 'Perhaps I'll see you later.' She held his gaze for a couple of seconds and then turned and went back into the lounge. She poured herself a brandy and held the balloon glass between both hands and breathed in its rich bouquet. 'Welcome back, Sean Morrison,' she said quietly to herself, smiling.

In the study, Morrison shook Hennessy's hand and sank down into one of the chairs in front of the desk. 'The boys seem nervous,' said Morrison, and Hennessy explained briefly what had happened, the phone calls from London, the visit from The Chinaman, the explosion in his office and the attempt to blow up the car. Morrison listened without comment, but when Hennessy had finished he was frowning, not sure what was wanted from him.

'You've brought me back to deal with this Chinaman?' he asked.

Hennessy shook his head. 'No, no, we'll take care of him. No, Sean, I need your help to stop this bombing campaign on the mainland.' He told Morrison about his fears of a rogue IRA unit, and the missing ordnance.

'That explains a lot,' said Morrison. 'At first the bomb-ings were good news in the States, donations poured in,

138

but some of the recent stuff has produced a real back-lash. The Tube bombing especially. The Irish Americans are keen to support us, but massacres like that . . . I've got to tell you, Liam, I'm bloody pleased to hear you hadn't sanctioned it. How can I help?'

Hennessy spoke to Morrison for another quarter of an hour and then the younger man left for the airport to catch the last shuttle to Heathrow.

Mary Hennessy looked up when her husband entered the lounge and tried to hide her disappointment when she saw that he was alone.

'It's been a long time since Sean Morrison was in Belfast,' she said. Hennessy went over to the drinks cabinet and poured himself a double measure of whiskey.

'I need his help,' he said.

'With The Chinaman?'

Hennessy swirled the whiskey in his glass and shook his head. 'Something else. I need someone I can trust, somebody without an axe to grind, and he's been away for almost two years now. He's, how can I put it, untainted. Yes, that's the word I'm looking for. Untainted.'

'So he'll be coming to the farm with us?' she asked.

'No, I need him to go to London.' He saw from her face that she didn't understand and he smiled down at her. 'I need his help to get to the bottom of the bombings. Despite everything that's happened, that's the more important issue at the moment.'

Mary's eyes narrowed. 'You've got a plan?'

'Something like that.' He finished his drink and put the empty glass down on the cabinet. 'Are you all packed?'

She said she was, and they went together to the car where Jimmy McMahon opened the door for them and put the luggage in the boot. They sat together in the back while Murphy slid into the front seat. Jackie squeezed under Hennessy's legs and woofed quietly to herself. A red Ford Sierra with three young men waited at the entrance to the drive, its engine running. Four other heavily built men got into a dark-brown Range Rover and followed the Jaguar out into the road. They drove in convoy, the Sierra first, then the Jaguar, and the Range Rover bringing up the rear, down the Antrim Road, through the city centre and on to the A1, the main road south.

Nguyen was jolted awake by a distant siren. He lay for a while on his back staring up at the ceiling and trying to calm his breathing. He was soaking wet, drenched with sweat as he always was when he came out of the nightmare. The visions were always the same: the small boat drifting in the South China Sea. His daughters screaming for help. The helplessness. The anger.

He focused on what he had to do, driving all other thoughts from his troubled mind and gradually his breathing steadied. He sat up slowly and looked around the room as if seeing it for the first time. He checked his watch. It was six o'clock in the morning. Time to go.

The ice in the shower had melted away and Nguyen stepped in and washed himself all over. He didn't use any soap or shampoo because he didn't want any lingering smell of perfume. He towelled himself dry and put on a pair of loose jeans, a faded grey sweatshirt and an old pair of black sneakers before packing the rest of his stuff in his suitcase. He checked the room carefully to make sure he'd forgotten nothing and then he looped the holdall and its deadly contents around his neck and carried the case and the black plastic bag of rubbish down the stairs. He took out his key and left it and a ten-pound note by the telephone and then slipped the catch on the front door and gently eased it closed behind him. He took the rubbish bag down the side of the house and put it in the bin. The case he put in the back of the van, the holdall he slid under the passenger seat. The van started first time and he drove slowly down Wellington Park and turned left into Lisburn Road, the A1. On the seat next to him lay several large-scale maps that he'd bought from a newsagent in the city centre. Ian Wood had told him that Hennessy had a farm between a town called Castlewellan and a place called Haltown in County Down, about forty miles south of Belfast. He hadn't been able to say exactly where, but Nguyen didn't expect to have any problem finding it. The van identified him as a landscape gardener, he'd just drive around claiming to have mislaid Hennessy's address and eventually he'd find someone to point out the right farm.

Sean Morrison had booked into the Strand Palace Hotel late on Friday night so he waited until Saturday morning before calling the offices of the Anti-Terrorist Branch and asking for Detective Chief Inspector Bromley. He wasn't surprised to be told that he wasn't in, because it was Saturday, after all. He asked the duty officer if Bromley was at home or away on holiday and was told that he'd be in the office on Monday.

'Can you get a message to him for me?' Morrison asked.

The duty officer was crisp and efficient, not the least because of Morrison's Irish accent, and he confirmed that he could pass on a message to Bromley.

'Tell him Sean Morrison wants to speak to him.'

'Can you give me your number, please, sir?' asked the officer. Nice try, thought Morrison. Either the guy was naïve in the extreme or he had a very dry sense of humour.

'Just tell him Sean Morrison needs to talk to him urgently. I'll call back at noon. Tell him to either be in the office or to have you give me a number where I can reach him. Got that?'

'Yes, sir.' Morrison cut the line.

Morrison's next phone call was to Liam Hennessy but a woman's voice answered. 'Mary?' he asked.

'Sean? Where are you?'

'London,' he said. He wasn't sure what to say to her. Two years was a long time.

'Do you want to speak to Liam?' she asked, and he realised from the edge to her voice that her husband was in the room with her. He immediately felt relieved, as if Hennessy's presence solved the problem of which way the conversation would go.

'Yes,' he said.

Morrison heard the phone being handed over and then he heard Hennessy's voice. 'Everything OK?' said Hennessy.

'Everything is fine. I was just calling to let you know where I am. I've booked into the Strand Palace . . .' Hennessy interrupted him, telling him to wait while he got a pen and paper. 'OK, go ahead,' he said.

'I'm at the Strand Palace Hotel,' said Morrison, and he dictated the number to Hennessy, who repeated it back to him before hanging up.

Jim Kavanagh had press-ganged a dozen IRA men to help him with the search for The Chinaman, most of them teenagers, but their lack of experience didn't matter because most of their enquiries were done over the phone. They'd moved into Hennessy's office in Donegall Square, the air still acrid from the explosion. Kavanagh divided them into six pairs and distributed copies of the city's Yellow Pages and tourist guides he'd obtained from the Tourist Information Centre in the High Street. The Chinaman had arrived from London, which meant that, unless he had friends or relatives in the city, he'd have to have booked into a hotel or guest-house. He distributed the telephone numbers of all the places where a visitor might stay among the teams, one member to make the phone calls, the other to keep a record. There were more than enough telephones to go round. He hoped they'd be lucky because if not the next stage would be to visit every Chinese family in Belfast and that could take a hell of a long time.

Kavanagh made himself a cup of coffee and settled down on the sofa in the reception area. He was preparing himself for a long wait when a gangly red-haired youth burst into the room, breathing heavily.

'I think we've got it!' he said.

His partner, a head shorter with shoulder-length brown hair, came running after him waving a notebook. 'A guest-house in Wellington Park. The landlady is a Mrs McAllister, she says there was an Oriental man staying with her for two nights.'

'Is he still there?' asked Kavanagh, getting to his feet.

'She said he left this morning.'

'Damn his eyes!' cursed Kavanagh. He called over two men, bigger and harder than the teenage helpers, Roy O'Donnell and Tommy O'Donoghue. He went with them to collect his car and they drove to Wellington Park.

Mrs McAllister showed them into her lounge, a fussy room with a statue of the Virgin Mary in one corner, dozens of small crystal animals on the mantelpiece and lace squares on the backs of the easy chairs. She was a Catholic, a good Catholic, and whereas she didn't have much sympathy for the IRA she knew better than to obstruct them. Kavanagh asked her to describe her former guest and she did her best but found it difficult: not very tall, black hair, brown eyes, rough skin. She was able to give a better description of his clothes and Kavanagh knew she was talking about the same man that he'd seen in Hennessy's office.

'How did he get here?' he asked.

'He had a van, a white van. It was some sort of delivery van, I think, with writing on the side.'

'Can ye remember what it said?'

She shook her head. 'I'm sorry, son, I can't.'

'Not to worry, Mrs McAllister. Can ye show me his room?'

She took him upstairs leaving O'Donnell and O'Donoghue sitting uncomfortably in the lounge. 'You keep a very tidy house, Mrs McAllister,' soothed Kavanagh as she led him to the bedroom door. She waited outside while Kavanagh checked the room. There was nothing under the bed or in the cupboard drawers. He went into the bathroom but it too was spotless and smelt strongly of pine.

'Yez'll have already tidied up the room, then?' he asked the landlady.

'Aye, son. I dusted and ran the Hoover over the carpet this morning. He was very clean, though, you'd have hardly known the room had been slept in. Except for the bathroom, there was a funny smell in there. Like vinegar or something. I had to spray air freshener around.'

'Vinegar?'

'Something like that, a terrible bitter smell.'

Kavanagh looked around the gleaming bathroom, not sure what he expected to find.

'I don't suppose he left anything behind, did he Mrs McAllister?'

'No, nothing. He even made the bed before he left. He went early this morning, before I was up. He'd paid the bill in advance, even left me a tip.' She was burning with curiosity but knew it was pointless to ask what it was he'd done. If they wanted her to know they'd have told her.

'And ye've no idea where he went? He didn't ask for directions or anything?'

The landlady shook her head. 'I barely spoke to him.'

Kavanagh tut-tutted to himself, not sure what to do next. The van was a possibility, but a white delivery van with writing on the side wasn't much to go on. Still, it would probably have English plates which would make it a bit easier to find. 'OK, Mrs McAllister, thanks for your help. I'm sorry we disturbed yez.'

They went back downstairs. O'Donnell and O'Donoghue were already waiting in the hall, expectant looks on their faces. Mrs McAllister opened the door for them and watched them go down the path. She suddenly remembered something and called after Kavanagh. 'Oh, son! You might want to check the dustbin round the back. When I was emptying the Hoover I saw he'd left some rubbish there, in a black bag.'

Kavanagh's hopes soared and he practically ran down the path to where two dustbins were standing. The first one he looked in contained nothing but kitchen refuse, but in the second, under a layer of carpet fluff and dust, he found a black plastic bag, knotted at the top and sealed with insulation tape. He pulled it out, ignoring the cloud of dust that billowed over his trousers. He opened the bag and looked inside and frowned.

O'Donnell appeared at his shoulder. 'Anything?' he said.

'I think so,' said Kavanagh. 'I want O'Hara to see this.'

Kavanagh put the bag into the boot of the car and the three men drove to O'Hara's house, a two-up, two-down terrace in Springfield Road. He was in the kitchen eating bacon and eggs when they were shown in by his wife. His sharp eyes fixed on the bag by Kavanagh's side.

'What have ye got there, Jim?' he asked, wiping a piece of bread across the plate and popping it into his mouth.

'I'm hoping yer'll tell me, Willie. When yez finished your breakfast, that is.'

O'Hara took the hint, putting his knife and fork together on the remains of his meal. His wife took the plate and put it in the oven to keep warm and then left the room, knowing that it was IRA business and that the men would want to be left alone. O'Hara wiped his greasy hands on his grey trousers and cleared the rest of the table, a stainless steel cruet set, a bottle of Heinz ketchup and the morning paper.

Kavanagh lifted the bag on to the table and O'Hara gingerly opened it. He took the contents out one at a time: the empty bag of fertilizer, the Pyrex pans, the measuring jug, sections of piping, a burnt-out flash-bulb, empty bottles, empty matchboxes, pieces of cut wire. He inspected each item closely before eagerly moving on to the next one like a schoolboy going through his presents at Christmas, hoping that each one would be better than the last. When the black bag was finally empty and all its contents lined up beside it, O'Hara looked at Kavanagh, a wicked grin on his weaselly face.

'This is from the wee bugger that tried to blow up Liam's car, isn't it?' he asked.

Kavanagh wasn't impressed by the small man's insight – the flash-bulb was obviously the same type that they'd found in the Jaguar's petrol tank. 'He left it behind when he checked out of a guest-house this morning. What do yez make of it?'

O'Hara waved his hand at the ragbag collection of items. 'This is trouble, right enough,' he said. 'Big trouble.'

Morrison checked his watch for the hundredth time and called the Anti-Terrorist Branch. This time Bromley was there. 'I'm sorry to drag you in on a Saturday,' said Morrison.

'I'm always happy to speak to public-spirited citizens, Mr Morrison,' said Bromley with more than a hint of sarcasm. 'The last FBI report that passed over my desk had you alive and well and living in New York. What brings you back to these fair shores?'

'I need to see you,' answered Morrison.

'Not thinking of changing sides and working alongside the forces of law and order, are we?'

'Let's just say that I want to make you an offer you won't be able to refuse.'

'In what context?' asked Bromley, suddenly serious.

'Not over the phone. I have to meet you.'

Bromley snorted. 'In a dark alley, I suppose. Come off it, Morrison, why the hell should I put myself at risk?

Haven't you been reading the papers in New York? The IRA has declared open season on us here. If you want to speak to me you can come here.'

'And how long do you think I'd last if I was seen going into your office, Bromley? I'm not after a bullet in my mouth.'

'I suppose that's a Mexican stand-off, then,' said Bromley.

'Not necessarily. You can choose the venue, so long as you go alone. Somewhere with lots of people where you'll feel safe and where I can blend into a crowd. Somewhere noisy so I know we won't be recorded.'

'When?'

'This afternoon.'

Bromley considered the offer for a few seconds. 'I can't today. It'll have to be tomorrow. In Trafalgar Square. Be close to Nelson's column at four o'clock.'

'Make sure you come alone,' said Morrison. 'Don't put me under any pressure. I'm not wanted for anything, and I won't be carrying. I just want to talk.'

'So you said.'

'One other thing – I don't know what you look like. How will I recognise you?'

'Don't worry, Mr Morrison. I've seen enough photographs of you, I'll introduce myself.'

'That's maybe so, but don't creep up on me. I startle easily.'

'Understood. Until four tomorrow, then.'

Morrison hung up. Nothing to do now but wait. He switched on the television and rang down to room service to order a club sandwich and coffee.

★　★　★

Hennessy was walking across Three Acre Pasture with Jackie at his heels when he heard the shrill whistle, two piercing blasts that made the dog jump. He shaded his eyes with his hands and saw Murphy standing by the kitchen door waving his arm high above his head. When Murphy realised he'd caught his attention, he made a miming action with his hand, holding it clenched to his ear. The phone.

It took him a brisk five minutes to get back to the farmhouse, by which time Murphy had gone back inside the cool, oak-beamed kitchen. He held the receiver out to Hennessy, who was slightly out of breath. It was Kavanagh. He described the visit to the guest-house and what they'd found in the dustbin.

'And what did O'Hara say?' Hennessy asked.

'Nitroglycerine,' said Kavanagh. 'The Chinaman made nitroglycerine in the bathroom. Willie reckons he mixed it with weedkiller and packed it into plastic pipes and is planning to use flash-bulb detonators, the sort of thing he stuck in the petrol tank of the Jag.'

'How much damage could they do?'

'Judging by the stuff he left behind, Willie says he could have made three or four devices, each big enough to blow up a car. It's hard to say because a lot depends on the purity of the nitro he made, but Willie says the guy seems to know what he's doing.'

Hennessy felt a cold chill run up his spine because the sort of bombs Kavanagh was talking about didn't sound like warnings. It looked as if The Chinaman was raising the stakes. 'What are your plans now, Jim?' he asked.

'I reckon the van's the best bet. The landlady said he's driving a white delivery van with black writing on the

149

side. I'll have our lads scour the city. It shouldn't be too hard to find, a Chinaman in a white van with English plates. We'll get him, Liam. Don't ye worry.' Kavanagh tried to sound as optimistic as possible because he could sense how worried his boss was.

'OK, keep at it, Jim. And let me know as soon as you get anything.'

'Will do,' said Kavanagh.

Mary came into the kitchen as he replaced the receiver and asked him if he wanted a coffee. He declined and said he'd prefer something a little stronger. She sniffed, a noise that was loaded with disapproval. She was wearing tight Levi jeans, cowboy boots and a floppy pink pullover that he'd last seen their daughter wearing. He took a bottle of whiskey down from the Welsh dresser and poured himself a double measure.

'I'm driving down to the village to get some bread,' said Mary. 'Do you want anything?'

He sat down in an old rocking chair and rocked backwards and forwards, nursing the whiskey. 'I'm fine,' he said.

She turned to look at him, standing with her hands on her hips. 'I don't think you should be moping like this, Liam.'

'I'm not moping, I'm thinking. And you're acting like my mother.'

'And you, Liam Hennessy, are behaving like my grandfather. Now pull yourself together and stop feeling sorry for yourself.' She turned on her heels and banged the kitchen door behind her. He heard the car start up and drive off and wondered what it was that was upsetting her so much.

When he first met Mary all those years ago her temper and unpredictability were among her attractions. She was stimulating, she was fun, and there was never a dull moment with her. She'd quietened down after the birth of their children but now that they were at university she seemed to be behaving more and more like she did when she was in her early twenties. Some days she was so gentle and loving that she took his breath away and yet on others she was so cold that he felt sure she was about to leave him. Sexually, too, she had him in a state of constant confusion. When they'd first married they seemed to spend all their time in bed, and it was hardly surprising that they'd had two children so quickly. He'd wanted more children but she'd said that two was enough though even then sex had been good and regular, albeit more calculated and careful. It had been when the children were in their teens, at school, that she had seemed to withdraw from him. She even went through a period when she'd slept in one of the spare bedrooms, claiming that she was having trouble getting to sleep. When he did approach her she would be friendly but insistent: she didn't want to be touched. Eventually she moved back into the main bedroom. He never found out why, but even when she slept in his bed she only occasionally allowed him to make love to her and when she did it was usually quick and unenthusiastic.

Sometimes, though, she would be totally different, she'd wait until he'd switched off the light and climbed into the bed and then she'd reach for him and it would be like it was in the old days, she'd hang on to him tight, biting his shoulder, making him lie on his back as she rode him on top. Those were the worst nights, because she'd close her eyes as she gasped and groaned and he knew deep inside that she was thinking about someone else, that he was being used, but while it was happening he didn't care because her lovemaking was so energetic and sensual that he wanted to die. Only afterwards, when she flopped down on to the sheets and rolled away from him to curl up with her own thoughts, only then did the revulsion set in. He would lie awake with tears in his eyes, filled with self-loathing, and promise himself that next time she reached for him in the dark he'd refuse her and tell her that he wanted her to make love to him, not to use him as part of whatever fantasy she was enjoying. But he never did refuse her.

Hennessy was genuinely confused by the way she acted in bed, because in every other respect she was a perfect wife and mother. She ran the house like a dream, their children were good-looking, intelligent and well-balanced, she took an interest in his work and his politics, she laughed at his jokes, she entertained their friends, she seemed to thrive in his company. Everyone who knew them said they were the perfect couple, and when they were with friends of their own age he took a particular pride in her apparent youth and vitality. She was stunning, and while her women friends had put on weight and had their hair permed and started to dress like their mothers, she had kept her figure, so much so that she would still go without a bra if the dress warranted it. Over the years Hennessy had tried to talk himself into accepting his wife as she was, to convince himself that the lack of sex was a small price to pay to have her in his life. Sometimes he believed it. He rocked himself backwards and forwards in the chair. The motion was reassuring and he closed his eyes.

★　★　★

The drive from Belfast to the B8 between Castlewellan and Haltown took a little over ninety minutes, but it took another three hours for Nguyen to locate Hennessy's farm. The two towns were about ten miles apart and there were many farms nestled among the patchwork of fields and hills. Eventually a bearded giant of a man in a tractor sent him in the general direction, to the north of the B8, away from the border, and some time later he came across a postman in a battered old van who pointed at a collection of weathered stone buildings and modern barns.

Nguyen spent some time examining his large-scale map of the area. He circled the spot where the farm was. To the east was the Tollymore Forest Park, and to the south-east was a rocky ridge called the Mourne Mountains. Due south was a place called Warrenpoint, which rang a bell in Nguyen's subconscious. He couldn't remember exactly what it was, but he knew something bad had happened there in the past, an explosion or a massacre. The name had cropped up in a news programme on television, he was sure of that much. He'd regularly watched television news with his daughter as a way of helping her to improve her English.

There was a wooded hill a mile or so behind the farm and according to the map he'd be able to get close to it if he took the road to the village of Rathfriland. He started the van and drove to within half a mile of the hill. He parked in a layby, slung the binoculars around his neck, took his compass from the glove compartment, pocketed the map and walked briskly up the hill, following a stony track that zig-zagged through the lush grass. The track was obviously used by a shepherd to round up his flock. There were dog droppings in several places and boot-prints of a man who walked with a stick and all around were sheep and young lambs.

He reached the top of the hill and lay down in the grass, surveying the farmland and its buildings far below through the powerful binoculars. The farmhouse was an L-shaped building, stone with a steep, grey slate roof. Nguyen was looking at it from the rear, he could see the back door leading off the kitchen. The main part of the house was two-storeys high but the shorter section of the L was one-storey and seemed to be made up of outbuildings, the windows streaked with dirt. There was a square tarmac courtyard in the angle of the L where there were several cars parked: a Range Rover, a Jaguar, two Land-Rovers and a Ford Sierra. Nguyen recognised the Jaguar and smiled. He hadn't expected Hennessy to be there. It was an added bonus. Bordering the courtyard, directly opposite the outbuildings, was another single-storey building and behind it was a grass paddock. In the paddock two horses stood nose to nose. At right angles to the stables was a two-storey cottage built in the same solid style as the main house which Nguyen guessed was the farm manager's home.

In front of the cottage was what looked to be a vegetable garden, with tidy rows of cabbages and other green vegetables, and beyond it a small orchard of mature fruit trees. A gravel driveway led from the courtyard, between the farmhouse and the stables, and curved around the front. The fourth side of the courtyard was bordered by two open-sided barns, one full of bales of hay, the other stacked high with sacks at one end, the rest of the space being used as a shelter for farm equipment. Behind the barns were three gleaming white towering silos, like rockets awaiting lift-off.

The driveway led to a single-track road which wound between the fields, linking up with several farms before disappearing to the north where, according to the map, it linked up with the B7. There were passing places every few hundred yards and hedgerows both sides. The fields were mainly devoted to the raising of cattle and sheep but there were crops, too; several of the patchwork squares were yellow with rape-seed and there were green plants growing in a field behind the barns that could have been potatoes or turnips. The area undulated like a down quilt that had been thrown untidily on to a bed and the places that were steep or inaccessible had been left wooded.

Nguyen laid the map on the grass and took his bearings with the compass. With a pencil he drew several routes to Hennessy's farm, from the B180, the B8, the B25 and the B7, following the contours through woodland wherever possible or alongside hedgerows and ditches where there was no tree cover. There was a stream trickling through Hennessy's land, too small to be shown on the map, and with great care Nguyen traced its route as a thin pencil line. He also carefully drew a sketch map of the farm buildings, showing their positions relative to each other, and made a sketch drawing of the farmhouse, including the drainpipes. The soil-pipe was next to the middle of five upstairs windows and the glass was frosted and there was a circular ventilator fan in the right-hand corner so Nguyen marked it as the bathroom. In the distance a twin-rotor helicopter, a Chinook, flew close to the ground, heading towards border country. He waited until it had passed out of sight before walking back down the hill.

His first priority now was to find somewhere to hide

the van, because he'd soon be spotted if he kept driving around in the vicinity of the farm. There were very few vehicles around and most of the ones he came across were tractors or army Land-Rovers. Farmers and soldiers both gave him curious looks but neither seemed to regard him as a threat. He could see, though, that they read the signs on the side of his van and he knew that an Oriental landscape gardener would not be easily forgotten. He dismissed the idea of leaving the Renault in one of the nearby villages or towns because being so near the border any strange parked vehicle was bound to attract attention. He needed a place a good distance from the farm, but close enough that he could get to and fro within a few hours. Five or six miles or so would be about right, and ideally with a route that offered some cover from the army patrols and the helicopters which occasionally buzzed overhead. Looking at the map, it seemed as if Tollymore Forest Park offered the best prospects. He drove east along the B8 and then turned left on to the B180 which cut the woods neatly in half on the way to the village of Maghera. He eased the van along the road looking left and right for places to turn off and spotted several possibilities. When he emerged from the forest he clunked the gears through a three-point turn and headed back towards Haltown. He ignored the first three tracks as being too obvious from the road. The first path he'd identified as being suitable went deep into the trees but the Land-Rover tracks in the mud were too fresh and there were too many of them, suggesting that it was used regularly by foresters or possibly by the army. He turned the van round and drove back to the main road. The second track was more what he'd hoped for, a single pathway that was overgrown by ferns and brambles. He drove the van far enough into the trees so that he couldn't be seen from the road and then got out of the car and checked the ground and the over-hanging vegetation. The tyre prints in the dried mud were old and flaking and there were fresh green shoots growing through them. The ferns that had encroached on to the track were unbroken and there were no smears of dirt or grease. No one had driven a vehicle down the path for at least a week, and probably much longer, and there were no footprints, none that were human, anyway. He saw where foxes had crossed the path, and rabbits, but that was all.

Satisfied, he got back into the van and slowly drove it down the track, gripping the steering wheel tightly as it jerked like a wild thing. When he'd gone a hundred yards or so further, he turned off the track and guided the van carefully between the trees. When he was sure that anyone driving down the track would not be able to see the van he switched off the engine.

Nguyen spent an hour going back along the route to the path, covering over his tracks as best he could. It wouldn't fool anyone who was searching for him, but a casual observer would be unlikely to spot where he had driven off the track. He gathered armfuls of ferns and dead wood from the forest floor and spread them across the roof of the van. He'd seen enough helicopters flying overhead to know that there was a risk of being spotted from above, albeit a slim one. He picked up handfuls of damp soil and rubbed them over the sides of the van, and the front and back, transforming the white paintwork into muddy smears, and then took more branches and draped them all around it.

He looked at his watch. There were hours to go before dusk so he climbed into the driver's seat and took a portion of rice and another of pork from the take-away carrier bag. He ate slowly, chewing each mouthful thoroughly before swallowing, not tasting or enjoying the food but knowing that it would provide the energy he needed. When he'd finished he settled back in the seat and tried to sleep, saving his strength for the night ahead. In the distance he heard the whup-whup of a single-rotor helicopter, flying low and fast. He slipped into sleep.

The air was filled with the throbbing of helicopters. It was 1975. Nguyen was with his wife and daughters running through the crowded streets of Saigon, sweating from fear and the heat. The roads were packed tight with panicking faces, young and old, families and individuals, all heading towards the US Embassy and the helicopters. Almost everybody was carrying something, a suitcase, a big wicker bag, a bicycle loaded with clothes or electrical appliances. Children barely big enough to walk were clasping bags to their chests, old women were bent double and gasping for breath as they hurried along with bags attached to both ends of bamboo poles. Nguyen had told his wife to pack one bag for the four of them and he carried it while she held the two children. She was crying as they trotted down the street and the faces of the children were drawn and frightened. Nguyen appeared cold and impassive but inside his mind was racing.

He and his family had moved into Saigon because it wasn't safe for them in the country any more. The NVA was walking all over the ARVN and by February Nguyen heard whispers that a helicopter evacuation of Saigon was being planned. Hue fell on March 24 and less than a week later the NVA overran Da Nang and the South Vietnamese were struggling to hold a defensive line north of Saigon. The Defence Attaché Office put together a list of seven thousand or so people it reckoned should be evacuated as the ARVN fought a last-ditch battle at Xuan Loc, just thirty miles east of Saigon. The noise of exploding rockets kept Nguyen's children awake at night. Nguyen went to see his commanding officer and was told that if Saigon fell he would be evacuated along with the American forces.

On April 28 he was told to prepare for evacuation the following day. The NVA attacked Tan Son Nhut airfield on the northern edge of Saigon, preventing commercial aircraft from flying out with evacuees. The plan now was for helicopters to ferry the US forces and their supporters out to ships waiting offshore. Nguyen, along with thousands of other Vietnamese who had served the US forces, was told to wait at home where he would be picked up by a specially marked bus. They waited, but the buses never arrived. Nguyen phoned the US embassy every fifteen minutes but was always given the same answer. Wait. He heard helicopters flying in the direction of the embassy and he waited. He heard the rumble of guns at Bien Hoa and still he waited. When he heard the crackle of small-arms fire he grabbed his wife and children and ran into the street. It was almost 9.30 p.m. and the street-lights were on.

Nguyen dropped the bag in the street and took one of the girls from his wife, scooping her off her feet and letting her sit with her legs around his neck. She giggled and played with his hair. His wife picked up the other girl. Time was running out. There were fewer helicopters hovering over the embassy. The roads were packed with cars, trucks, bicycles and pedestrians, and everyone seemed to be heading towards the embassy. The crowds were moving faster now, and they had to be careful not to trip over abandoned luggage as they pushed down Thong Nhat Avenue. In the distance they could see the squarish block of whitewashed cement that was the American embassy. More helicopters flew overhead. The crowds were so thick that Nguyen and his family couldn't get any closer than fifty yards or so to the nine-foot wall that surrounded the embassy. The top of the wall was wreathed in barbed wire and protected by Marines with machine guns. The only way in was through the gate, and that was only opened when refugees could produce the correct paperwork and identifying codeword. Nguyen's daughters were crying. Midnight passed and with it came an end to the distant thudding explosions at the airport and still the helicopters came and left after picking up the lucky ones from the landing pads on top of the embassy building. Dawn broke and they had made almost no progress, the solid mass of anxious humanity locked solid. Nguyen's wife almost collapsed from exhaustion but was held up by the pressure of the people around her until he managed to slip his arm around her waist and support her. She looked at him with pleading in her eyes but there was nothing he could do. The papers that guaranteed sanctuary were in his breast pocket but they were useless unless he could get to the embassy gates. It was hopeless. The crowd roared and screamed and Nguyen looked up to see a helicopter lift off from the roof and head out towards the sea where the Seventh Fleet waited. The chopper was alone in the sky and Nguyen realised it was the last one. There were no more guards around the wall, none on the embassy roof. The Americans had gone. Xuan Phoung cried softly. The crowds dispersed quickly, knowing that the T-54 tanks of the North Vietnamese Army would soon arrive. The streets were littered with abandoned ARVN uniforms and equipment.

Nguyen took his family back to their small flat and helped Xuan Phoung put the exhausted children to bed. He held her tightly and kissed her, and she led him by the hand to their tiny bedroom and he made love to her, urgently and with more passion than he'd shown in a long time. It was the night that Kieu Trinh was conceived.

Nguyen jerked awake, his face drenched with sweat. It was dark outside and he sat for a while, forcing himself to relax. He filled his mind with images of the Buddhist shrine at his home – his former home, he reminded himself. He climbed over the back of the seats into the rear of the van and placed the three pipe bombs into the rucksack. He also packed the filled water-bottles and the remainder of the take-away food, along with six coils of plastic-coated wire, two clockwork alarm clocks and a few tools that he reckoned he would need. The batteries which he planned to use to detonate the bombs were zipped into the pockets of the camouflage jacket so that there could be no possibility of them accidentally going off. He also packed the binoculars and the map.

He stripped off all his clothes except for his underpants and socks and then slipped on the camouflage trousers and jacket. He pulled on a pair of thick wool socks and his old, comfortable boots. He rolled up the right leg of his pants and tied the scabbard of one of the throwing knives to his calf. The other knife he tied to one of the straps of the rucksack so that it hung upside down, the handle lowermost where it was accessible in an emergency. He did the same with the big hunting knife.

When he'd finished his preparations he climbed into the front of the van and left by the driver's door. He kept his eyes firmly closed while he opened and shut the door because he didn't want the internal light ruining his night vision. There was no point in locking the door because if the van was discovered it would all be over anyway, but he buried the keys near the roots of a tree he'd be sure to recognise later.

He covered the door with tree branches and stood for a minute taking a bearing from his compass. There was a thin sliver of moon in the cloudless sky and enough starlight to see by. He headed west through the trees, parallel to the B180. He moved at a brisk pace but even so the constant weaving to and fro to avoid trees meant that it took the best part of two hours to cover three miles and emerge from the forest. He kept going due west for another two and a half miles, travelling across fields, sticking close to hedgerows wherever possible, until he reached the B8. After crossing it he took another bearing from the compass and began walking north-west. He changed direction twice to avoid farms and several times he dropped to the ground when helicopters buzzed overhead. Eventually he reached Hennessy's farm. Behind the buildings loomed the empty blackness of the hill which he'd climbed the previous day.

He lay in the sweet-smelling grass for a full thirty minutes before he was satisfied that everyone inside was asleep, then he began to crawl silently towards the farmhouse. He didn't want to risk crossing the road leading to the farm, even in the near-darkness, so he circled around the stables and the manager's cottage and behind the barns until he arrived at the outbuildings. He crept up against the stone wall and slowly got to his feet. He moved on tiptoe through the gap between the wall and the barn, placing his feet carefully so that he made no sound.

When he reached the courtyard and its collection of cars he slowly scanned every inch, his eyes wide to pull in as much reflected light as possible. Only when he was sure that no guards had been posted did he turn right and slip along the rough wall towards the farmhouse. He drew level with a large window made up of four dirty panes of glass in a wooden frame and he peered inside. He could see metal barrels stacked on top of each other, thick wooden benches and a collection of farm tools. He eased himself past the window and reached a wooden door with ornate metal hinges. There was an ancient keyhole and two bolts, one high up and one near the ground. He gingerly pushed back the upper bolt and was relieved that it moved silently and smoothly. Though the door was old and battered, it was obviously regularly opened. The second bolt was similarly quiet. He held his breath, seized the metal door handle and turned it slowly. It grated a little but not enough for the sound to carry and then he pushed the door inwards. It hadn't been locked and it opened with a mild creak. Nguyen slid inside and closed the door behind him.

The room smelt of dust and decay and there was a bitter chemical taste to the air. Nguyen went over to the barrels. Most of them were full and according to the labels they contained weedkillers of various kinds. He was glad that they weren't fuel drums because at this stage he wasn't planning to burn down the house, he simply wanted to prove to Hennessy how serious he was.

He knelt down on the concrete floor and took off his rucksack. He took out one of the pipe bombs, an alarm clock and two of the shortest coils of wire. The glass had already been removed from the clock leaving the hands exposed. Nguyen fastened one end of one of the coils of the wire to the hour hand of the clock, twisting the wire around three times and then spreading the copper strands out into a fan shape. He did the same with the other piece of wire and the minute hand. He cut the length of wire in half with his knife and bared the cut ends. He took one of the batteries from his pocket and connected the wire from the minute hand to one of its terminals, and the loose piece of wire to the other, before setting the clock to twenty-five minutes to five and checking that it was fully wound. He now had about fifty minutes before the two wires came together. He put the pipe next to the wall under the windows and then connected the two wires protruding from it to the timing circuit by twisting the ends together. When the minute hand had crawled round to meet the hour hand and the two bare wire ends touched they would complete the circuit between the battery and the flash-bulb detonator which would in turn explode the bomb.

He repacked his rucksack and put it on before he gently rolled four of the full barrels of weedkiller over and ranged them around the bomb in a semicircle which would have the effect of concentrating the blast against the wall where it would do the most damage. The hands of the clock were forty minutes apart when he edged silently through the doorway and bolted the door.

Nguyen retraced his steps, but he didn't begin crawling when he left the courtyard, instead he ran around the barns in a low crouch, dropping down only when he came within earshot of the cottage. When past the cottage he rose up again and jogged by the stables. The horses were locked inside and he heard snorts and whinnies but no panic. He reached a point in the field where he could see the entire front of the farmhouse and he dropped down into the grass. He took his binoculars out of the rucksack, put them on the grass in front of him, and looked at his watch. Eight minutes to go.

He lay listening to the night sounds: the hoot of a hunting owl, the bark of a faraway fox, the whup-whup of army helicopters. In his mind, Nguyen pictured the clock ticking away the seconds, and his concentration was so intense that it was almost as if he could hear the metallic clicks emanating from the storeroom, getting louder and louder until the air resonated with the beat and he was sure it would wake everyone for miles around.

The blast, when it came, shocked him, even though he was expecting it. From where he was he couldn't see the explosion but the farmhouse was silhouetted by the flash and a fraction of a second later he felt a trembling vibration along his body and a thundering roar filled the night.

He clamped the binoculars to his eyes and scanned the farmhouse. Within seconds a light went on in one of the upstairs rooms and a figure appeared at the window. Nguyen recognised the man as being one of those who had searched him at Hennessy's office. No other lights came on upstairs so Nguyen got to his feet and, keeping low, scurried back along behind the stables. He moved carefully but he was sure that all eyes would be on the shattered outbuilding which was now burning fiercely. He heard the horses neighing in their stalls and the thuds as they kicked out with their hooves. He dropped down and crawled because he realised that someone would probably go in to calm them down. He made his way past the cottage and didn't stop until he was in the orchard. He crouched behind an apple tree and examined the upstairs rooms of the farmhouse. The door of the cottage burst open and a middle-aged man in a striped dressing-gown came running out, shouting, followed by three bare-chested young men. Nguyen checked them out through the binoculars. They were holding guns.

A light had gone on in the window on the right-hand side of the building, the end nearest the outbuildings, and there were lights in the two rooms on the left. As Nguyen watched, a woman came to the window and opened it. She was middle-aged and dark-haired. A light came on downstairs and then the door opened and two figures appeared. One of them was the man he'd seen at the far side of the building, the other was Hennessy. They ran towards the flames. A young woman ran out of the cottage and the middle-aged man shouted something at her. She changed direction and headed for the stables.

From the farmhouse four more men emerged, none of whom Nguyen had seen before. One of them was carrying a fire extinguisher and the rest had shotguns at the ready. The flames were flickering out of a jagged hole in the wall where the door and window had been. Most of the roof tiles had been blown off and were scattered around the courtyard and on the cars. The fire extinguisher spluttered into life and the man played foam around the hole. The girl ran out of the stables carrying another fire extinguisher and she gave it to the man in the dressing-gown. He joined in the fire-fighting. The woman shouted down and Hennessy waved at her and yelled something back. Probably his wife, thought Nguyen. One of the men went back into the farmhouse and reappeared with another fire extinguisher and before long the three columns of foam had the blaze under control. Nguyen decided he had seen enough. He crawled on his belly, away from the farm and into the darkness. There was a wedge-shaped copse of trees about a mile away that he'd earlier identified as a suitable place to lie up during the day and which would allow him to keep the farm under observation.

Murphy and Hennessy stepped gingerly over the broken brickwork and peered into the smoking wreckage of the outhouse. Steel barrels had been torn apart in the explosion and they were careful not to tread on any of the twisted shards. The blast had shredded the tough, wooden benches and chunks of wood were scattered around misshapen tools, what was left of them.

A slate from the shattered roof crashed down on to the floor and Murphy pulled Hennessy back. 'Careful, Liam,' he said. 'We'd better wait until daylight before we go messing in there.'

Hennessy nodded and followed Murphy back out into the courtyard.

'Jesus, Mary and Joseph, what in heaven's name is going on?' said Joe Ryan, standing with an empty extinguisher in his hand, his dressing-gown flapping around his legs. Ryan had been the manager of Hennessy's farm for more than twenty years. He'd been a little surprised when Hennessy and Mary had arrived with McMahon, Murphy

167

and seven men from Belfast who were now standing around the courtyard carrying various weapons that obviously weren't for shooting rabbits, but Hennessy hadn't offered an explanation and Ryan hadn't asked for one.

Hennessy went over to his manager and put a reassuring arm around his shoulder. 'My fault, Joe, I should have told you earlier. But I had no idea he'd follow me here.' As they walked to the kitchen door of the farmhouse he explained about The Chinaman.

Mary was waiting for them in the kitchen in a green silk dressing-gown and slippers. She'd made a huge pot of coffee and had placed a bottle of Irish whiskey and a dozen glasses on the table for the men. She poured a generous measure into one of the glasses and gave it to her husband. She told Murphy to fill the rest of the glasses for the men who were filing in behind him. 'Are you all right?' she asked Hennessy, touching his shoulder as she spoke, her concern obvious and genuine.

'I'm fine, right enough,' he said.

'Another warning?' she said, and he wasn't sure if she was being sarcastic or not.

'He wasn't trying to kill anyone, if that's what you mean, Mary,' he said, and took a mouthful of the smooth whiskey.

He turned to Murphy. 'Get Kavanagh down here straightaway,' he said. 'Tell him there's no point in looking for The Chinaman in Belfast. And tell him to bring a dozen or so of his men here. Including Willie O'Hara.' Murphy grunted and went out to use the phone in the hall.

Ryan pulled a chair out and sat down, helping himself to a mug of coffee. 'Has this Chinaman got hand grenades or what, Liam?' he asked.

'Nitroglycerine,' said Hennessy. 'He made his own

nitroglycerine in Belfast.' The kitchen was full now, men standing or sitting, some of them still coughing to clear the smoke from their lungs. Ryan's daughter, Sarah, stood behind her father, smoothing down his hair, more to calm her own shaking hands than anything.

Hennessy stood with his back to the sink and cleared his throat loudly to attract everybody's attention. 'We're all going to have to be on our guard,' he said. 'I've under-estimated The Chinaman up until now, and that's not a mistake I intend to repeat. For the rest of tonight I want six of you on guard outside.' He nodded or pointed to the six men to indicate those he'd chosen. 'Jimmy McMahon can sleep in the kitchen and I'll have Christy Murphy stay by the front door. Joe, you and Sarah should lock yourself in the cottage, and keep Tommy with you. Everyone else try to grab some sleep. By tomorrow I'll have worked out what we're going to do.'

The men assigned to guard duty finished their whiskey, checked their guns and went outside. Ryan and his daughter went back to their cottage with Tommy O'Donoghue in tow.

Murphy came back into the kitchen. 'Jim's on his way.'

'Good,' said Hennessy. 'Mary and I are going to bed. Jimmy'll sleep here tonight. Can you stay in the hall? We'll get a proper rota fixed up tomorrow after Jim gets here.'

'Fine by me,' said Murphy.

Hennessy and Mary went up the stairs together. She carried a bright-yellow mug of coffee cupped in both hands. To Hennessy, though, it appeared that she was more annoyed than upset by the disturbance. In the bedroom, she put the mug down on her bedside table and brushed her hair with short, attacking strokes.

169

'I don't think you should stay here, not with all this going on,' said Hennessy, taking off his dressing-gown and hanging it on the back of the door.

'I was thinking the same myself,' she answered, watching him through the dressing-table mirror as she brushed her hair. He walked over to the open window and looked down at the courtyard. There were two of his men there, one with a shotgun. They waved and he waved back before shutting the window to keep out the smell of smoke. He drew the curtains with a flourish.

'The house in town isn't safe, even while The Chinaman's here,' he said. 'Abroad would be best, just until we've solved this problem.'

'This problem!' she said, and laughed, her voice loaded with irony. 'This problem, as you call it, Liam, is stalking around our farm with nitroglycerine bombs intent on God knows what and you call it a problem. You can be so pompous at times!' She shook her head, sadly, while Hennessy stood confused, not sure what to say. She made the decision for him. 'I thought I'd go and stay with Marie.' Marie, their daughter, was studying sociology at university in London and there were still some weeks to go before summer holidays. They'd rented her a one-bedroom flat in Earl's Court and Mary had been to stay on several occasions.

'I'd prefer it if you went well away, to America or the Caribbean, London is still a bit close to home,' he pressed.

She turned to look at him, still brushing her hair. 'Liam, I'll be perfectly safe in London,' she said frostily. 'In the first place, he's hardly likely to know about Marie's rented flat, and in the second, it's you he's after, not me.'

Hennessy couldn't argue with that, so he reluctantly agreed.

170

'Besides, I'll fly over and I'll make sure I take a very close look at everyone else who gets on the plane. If I see anyone who looks vaguely Chinese, I'll call you,' she said. She put down the brush and switched off the light. He heard the rustle of silk against her skin and then she slipped under the quilt. He got into his side of the bed.

'Good night,' she said. He felt a light kiss on the cheek and then she turned her back on him, drawing her legs up against her stomach. Liam lay on his back, his eyes closed tight.

The French window was wide open allowing the fresh river air to stream in along with the early morning sunshine. Denis Fisher sat on the white plastic chair, a stack of Sunday newspapers on the circular white table. He was wearing a white T-shirt and faded blue Levis and a pair of black plastic sunglasses. His feet were up on another chair, he had a cup of strong coffee at his elbow, and he appeared to be at peace with the world. He ran his fingers through his blond hair and stretched his arms above his head.

'How's it going?' he called into the lounge.

MacDermott, the one they called The Bombmaker, was sitting at the dining-table in front of a collection of electrical equipment, wiring, batteries and timers, and peering into the innards of a laptop computer.

'Fine. There's acres of space here. More than enough. What I'm trying to do is to use the computer's internal clock as a timer and to connect the detonator to its internal battery. If I can it'll save a hell of a lot of weight. All I'll be adding will be the explosive, the detonator and a few inches of wire.'

By the side of the computer was an oblong slab of what appeared to be bright-yellow marzipan, covered in a thick film of plastic. It was less than one inch thick but almost nine inches wide and twelve inches long. On top of the block, under the plastic, was a white paper label with a black border containing the words EXPLOSIVE PLASTIC SEMTEX-H.

The explosive had come a long way. It had been manufactured years earlier in the Semtex factory deep in the woods in western Czechoslovakia in the days when it had been behind the Iron Curtain. Production of the high-performance military explosive stopped in 1980, but between 1975 and 1981 the Czechs sold 960 tons to Libya for six million US dollars through the Omnipol trade agency and several tons of that had found its way to the IRA. The Libyan leader Colonel Gaddafi had filled six brick and sandstone warehouses a few miles outside Tripoli with boxes of the high explosive. The Libyan leader had been a staunch supporter of the IRA throughout the early seventies, but it was after the siege of his embassy in London in the summer of 1985 that he began to help them with a vengeance, as a way of getting back at the British Government.

In October 1986, six months after President Reagan ordered a US bomber strike on Tripoli, a converted oil industry safety ship sailed into Libyan waters and over two nights took on board eighty tons of weapons, including a ton of Semtex. The Semtex was unloaded at a small beach in south-east Ireland and over the next year or so much of it was secretly transferred to caches in Britain. The two packages on the table were from the 1986 consignment.

Fisher put down his *Independent on Sunday* and walked

back into the flat. He watched over The Bombmaker's shoulder.

'It looks hellishly complicated,' said Fisher.

'I've never done anything like this before,' said MacDermott. 'I'm testing it with this torch bulb here until I'm sure it'll work. The timing is the crucial thing. The amount of explosive we'll be using is so small that it won't do much damage if it goes off in the wrong place. And there's no room for booby traps or secondary circuits.'

'How much will you use?' asked Fisher.

'Two hundred grams is more than enough to blow a hole in the fuselage and cause decompression. It was three hundred grams that brought down the Pan Am jet at Lockerbie. Mind you, it's the Lockerbie fiasco that's making it so hard now.'

'What do you mean?'

'You remember that doctor whose daughter died on the flight, the one that took a fake bomb on a BA jet to New York to show how lax security was? He filled a radio with marzipan and a battery but he proved his point and now the airlines routinely check all electrical equipment.'

'Does that mean they'll take it apart?' said Fisher, frowning.

'They won't take it apart, but they will ask to see it working, and they'll peer through the grilles and any gaps. And they'll X-ray it. Before the summer of 1990 they'd let you take them on board without putting them through the X-ray machine, but the Secretary of State for Transport changed the rules.'

'Won't the explosive show up?'

'It's supposed to on the new models, but I'm hollowing out the transformer and taking out the modem circuit and packing most of it in there. It'll look OK, no matter how good their equipment is, don't worry. Anyway, this is the sort of thing they expect people to take on planes, so if it works OK and the right person is carrying it they won't suspect anything. And it will work, I'll make sure of that.'

Fisher put his hand on MacDermott's shoulder and squeezed. 'If anyone can do it, you can. How's the Ascot bomb coming on?'

The Bombmaker nodded at a metal camera case on the floor. 'That's child's play in comparison. I'll finish it tonight.'

Fisher smiled, satisfied.

'Have you any idea which plane yet?' asked The Bombmaker.

Fisher shook his head. 'We're going to have to be careful, bloody careful,' he said. 'We can't hit a flight where there could be Irish on board, or Americans, or kids. What I'm really after is a plane in the Queen's Flight, or one carrying the Prime Minister or any of the Government bastards. Or maybe an RAF plane. I just want to have the bomb ready so that we can use it immediately we get an opportunity. And a mule. We need a mule to carry it on board. Someone with access. A pilot, a journalist, a policeman, someone who can get close without raising suspicion.'

'It's risky, mixing with people like that when we're trying to keep a low profile.'

Fisher grinned. 'I know it's risky, but think of the rewards. Just think about it. It'd be like another Brighton bombing, another Mountbatten.'

The phone rang and O'Reilly put down the gun he was cleaning, a Smith & Wesson 9-millimetre automatic

174

pistol, on the coffee-table. 'Shall I get it?' he asked, but Fisher already had it in his hand.

'Yes, yes, understood. Yes,' he said to the voice at the other end and hung up.

'Interesting,' he said, rubbing his chin. O'Reilly and The Bombmaker looked at him expectantly. 'The code-word has been changed,' he explained. 'As of tonight.'

'Good of them to let us know,' smiled O'Reilly as he picked up the automatic and began stripping it down. 'They might not have taken us seriously.'

Hennessy was alone in the large pine bed when he awoke. He bathed and dressed and went downstairs to find his wife in front of their stove frying eggs and bacon and grilling toast. Jim Kavanagh, Willie O'Hara, Christy Murphy and Jimmy McMahon were sitting around the table drinking coffee.

Despite the bomb shattering their sleep, Mary looked radiant and seemed to be relishing her role as a short-order cook.

'Right Christy, here's yours,' she sang, and plopped down a plate of bacon and eggs in front of him. Willie O'Hara was already halfway through his breakfast, mopping up egg yolk with a piece of fried bread. Kavanagh had finished and was buttering a slice of toast. Liam had heard him arrive in the early hours and he didn't look as if he'd had any sleep, either. Mary broke another two eggs into the pan and put them on the burner, took four more slices of toast from under the grill and slotted them into the toast rack on the table.

'Good morning, Liam,' she said cheerfully, and poured him a glass of orange juice. 'What would you like?'

'Just toast,' he said. He had never been a big eater, and considering the stress he was under just now he doubted if he'd be able to force down much toast. 'Thanks for getting here so quickly, Jim,' he said to Kavanagh.

'I'm just mad at myself for not getting him in Belfast, then none of this would've happened.'

'Where are the men who came down with you?'

'They've relieved the guys who were on duty during the night, and they're over in the cottage having breakfast. We didn't think it fair to all impose on yez good lady wife.'

'Nonsense,' said Mary, walking over with another plate of food. 'Jimmy, here's your breakfast.'

Hennessy pulled out a chair and sat down. 'How many men are here at the moment?' he asked Kavanagh.

'There's the six that came down with me, plus the seven who came down with ye and Christy. And there's three farmworkers who we can use if necessary. And Mr Ryan and his daughter have offered to help. I think they're a bit reluctant to be out working the farm with this Chinaman on the loose.'

Hennessy nodded thoughtfully and sipped his juice. 'We can't use the farmworkers, or the Ryans, not for this. If we need more men we'll bring them in from Belfast. So we're talking about thirteen men, plus you four.' He saw a look of panic pass over O'Hara's egg-streaked face. 'Don't worry, Willie, I won't be asking you to carry a gun.' Willie O'Hara was notoriously afraid of firearms, despite being one of the organisation's foremost explosives experts. 'And Christy, I want you to take Mary to London later today.'

'Och Liam, he doesn't have to go all the way to London

with me,' chided Mary over her shoulder as she fried more eggs.

'To London,' insisted Liam. Murphy nodded. 'Jimmy, you'll be driving them to the airport.' McMahon grunted through a mouthful of food.

Hennessy asked Kavanagh how many men it would take to make the farm secure.

'Nothing can ever be secure, ye know that,' he answered. 'Yez could put a hundred men on guard but a determined man could still get through.' He could see that Hennessy was not pleased with his answer so quickly added: 'Three guards could secure the courtyard, but there's a risk then that he could throw something in through one of the windows of the outside of the building, or get to the barns. Yez'll need a man guarding the barns, two by the stables, one in the courtyard, and three covering the front of the farm.'

'So seven men in all?'

'That's at night. During the day four should do it because this place is surrounded by fields and yer'll see him coming for miles.'

'That's still eleven men and that doesn't include sleeping time.'

'That's right enough. Yer'll need at least twenty-two, and if it goes on for any length of time, Liam, yer'll need as many again because they're going to get tired and careless.'

Hennessy slammed his hand down on the table, rattling the breakfast plates. 'Damn this man, damn him,' he cursed.

Mary put a filled plate in front of Kavanagh and he thanked her. 'Are you sure you don't want anything else, Liam?' she asked, and when he said no she took off her apron and put it over the back of a chair. She was wearing tight ski pants and a blue sweater and Hennessy could see O'Hara and McMahon watch her backside twitch as she walked to the door. Did she know that men took such pleasure from watching her move? Hennessy was pretty sure that she did. While he took pride in having such an attractive wife, many were the times that he wished she'd age just a little faster, that she'd look a little less attractive so that men would stop looking at her with lust in their eyes. He wished she'd join him in middle-age and not keep acting like a teenager. Maybe she'd give him more of herself then.

'Christy, get on the plane with her and see her all the way to my daughter's flat. If at any time you even remotely suspect that The Chinaman is anywhere near, get to a safe place and call for help. Don't take any risks. This bastard is out to get me and he might just decide to hurt me through my family.'

Murphy put his knife and fork together on his plate. 'She'll be safe with me, Liam, I promise you.'

McMahon drained his coffee cup and stood up. 'I think I'll take the car to the garage in the village and fill her up so that we don't have to stop on the way. Are they open on a Sunday?'

'The sign'll say closed, sure enough, but sound your horn and old man Hanratty will come out and serve you,' said Hennessy.

McMahon wiped his hands on his trousers and went out into the courtyard. They heard the car start up and drive out of the courtyard.

'Willie, I want you to go through what's left of the outbuilding and find out what caused it, whether or not it was one of the home-made bombs you described. Then I think we ought to arrange a . . .'

His words were cut short by the echoing thud of an explosion in the distance, as if a huge pile of earth had been dropped from a great height. Kavanagh got to his feet first and he led the way as they rushed through the hall and out of the front door.

The Jaguar was lying on its side in the field next to the track about fifty yards before it joined the road. There were clouds of steam coming from under the bonnet which had burst open and the engine was racing. Three of the IRA guards were already running down the track to the car and two more came running from the stables, guns at the ready. One of them reached through the side window and switched off the engine.

'Oh God, Jimmy,' said Hennessy under his breath as he began jogging towards the Jaguar. By the time he arrived there, with O'Hara in tow, they'd pulled McMahon out of the car and lain him on the grass. His face was cut in a dozen places, there was blood on his shirt and he was mumbling incoherently. Hennessy knelt down by McMahon and held his hand. It was covered in blood.

'Get a car here, we'll have to take him to hospital,' he said to Michael O'Faolain, the gangly, red-haired youth who'd come down from Belfast. 'We don't have time to wait for an ambulance.' O'Faolain ran back down the track towards the farmhouse. 'Willie, find out what the hell happened,' he said to O'Hara. O'Hara went to look at the car, but Hennessy had already seen the crater in the track and knew what it meant. 'The fucking Chinaman,' he hissed.

McMahon groaned but didn't open his eyes. His

trousers were burnt and ripped and through the slashed material Hennessy could see blood pouring from the injured legs.

O'Hara appeared at his shoulder. 'Nitroglycerine bomb by the look of it, Liam, buried a couple of feet down in the track. Detonated by wire.'

'That means he was close by.'

'Still is, I reckon. Depends how long his wires were.' He pointed across the field towards a distant copse. 'The wires run in that direction. If you move fast . . .'

'Christ, what was I thinking of!' Hennessy blurted. 'We should be after him now.' He called Kavanagh over and told him to take all but three of the men and follow the wires and to go after The Chinaman. As an afterthought he told Murphy to stay behind because after what had happened he was even more keen to get Mary out of the way.

O'Faolain arrived in the Range Rover and Hennessy, Murphy and O'Hara helped lift McMahon on to the back seat. There was a large tartan blanket there and they used it to wrap him up in. Hennessy delegated another of the young men to sit in the back and make sure that McMahon wasn't tossed around too much on the drive to the hospital. The Range Rover roared off as Hennessy shielded his eyes and looked at the group of men running across the fields, fanning out the further away they got from the track. Of The Chinaman there was no sign, but he had to be out there somewhere.

Nguyen had begun to crawl through the grass as soon as he had detonated the pipe bomb. The wires had been about fifty yards long which put him about halfway across the field, but he could move quickly on his stomach and by the time the front door of the farm had opened he had reached the relative safety of a hedgerow that cut it off from the neighbouring field where a flock of sheep and lambs grazed and played.

He'd set the bomb in the early hours of the morning before the sky had streaked with red and the sun had made its first appearance. He'd planned to dig down into the track but as it turned out there had been no need. It cut across the field with a narrow ditch on either side to keep the rain running off it during the wet weather. In places, the earth by the side of the track had begun to crumble into the ditch and Nguyen found a spot where he could pull out handfuls of soil with a minimum of effort. He scooped out enough to hide one of the pipe bombs, and he carefully ran the wires down into the ditch and through the grass as far as they would go. The grass was barely tall enough to conceal him but the ground was uneven and towards the road it sloped steeply away from the farm so Nguyen knew that, so long as he kept low, he'd be able to reach the hedgerow without being spotted. He'd lain flat on the ground for about six hours, not moving. He'd seen the sun come up and heard the birds begin their dawn chorus and counted half a dozen helicopters flying overhead before the Jaguar had come down the track.

After he detonated the bomb he rolled under the hedge and found a gap big enough to squeeze through and then began crawling away from the road, back towards the farm. After he'd travelled two hundred yards he peeked through the hedge. He could see Hennessy kneeling on the ground cradling the driver. Nguyen doubted that he would be badly hurt, the bomb had been too far underground to do too much damage. He'd been careful to detonate it just under the front bumper, not so far ahead that the blast would send the windscreen glass spinning into the driver's face, but not so far back that the petrol tank would be ignited. Nguyen didn't want to kill unless it was absolutely necessary, he still hoped to get what he wanted by pressurising and intimidating Hennessy. If that didn't work then he'd rethink his strategy.

A small, thin-faced man was bending over the crater in the track. He knelt down and picked up something and looked at it and then went over to look at the blasted car. He examined the damage to the underside of the car and then walked back to the crater. He looked into the ditch and then jumped over it and began searching the grass. Nguyen knew that he was looking for the wires and that before long he'd find them. He cut away from the hedgerow and ran with his back to the farm-buildings, his rucksack banging on his shoulders. He tramped across a small stream and vaulted over a five-bar gate into a field containing a dozen or so brown and white cattle, breathing heavily because he wasn't used to running. He reached the edge of the copse where he'd hidden the previous evening and slipped into the cool undergrowth before looking behind him. The field was clear, and so was the one behind that, but it was only a matter of time before they came after him. Not that Nguyen was worried. He'd only seen ten men in the courtyard dealing with the fire last night and he doubted that Hennessy would allow them all to go tramping through the fields and woods, leaving the cottage unprotected. Five, or maybe six, that would be all, and Nguyen knew he was more than capable of handling that many because they'd have to spread out.

The copse covered several acres and was on land which was obviously too wet for grazing sheep or cattle. He'd spent several hours getting to know his way around and could move confidently through it, knowing where the best hiding places and vantage points were. The trees were a mixture of oak, horse chestnut and beech, all of them old and draped in moss and surrounded by bushes and brambles. The canopy of branches overhead blocked out much of the sunlight and the air was filled with the chatter of birds jostling for territory. Nguyen made his way towards the middle of the copse, being careful not to break branches or leave obvious signs of his passage. In the distance he heard shouts. They'd be able to follow the wires to the place where he'd lain in the grass and then they'd be able to see where he'd crawled to the hedgerow, but unless they were expert trackers they wouldn't be able to see where he'd gone from there. They'd see the trees but they wouldn't be sure if he'd gone to ground there, or if he'd run through or passed by, so they'd probably split up. Two, maybe three. It would be easy.

A rustling sound to his left made him drop into a crouch, senses alert. A grey squirrel sprinted out from underneath a bush, its tail streaming behind it like a banner, and it ran headlong up a tree with something held in its jaws. Nguyen relaxed and as he did he heard more shouts, heading in his direction. A meandering trail roughly bisected the wood, it was nothing more than a flattening of the soil where countless generations of feet had used it as a shortcut through the trees. By the side of the trail was a huge oak, a centuries-old tree which was gnarled and misshapen with age. It was a good twelve feet across at the base and its roots were as thick as a man's waist before they dived down into the earth. Behind the tree, on the side furthest away from the path, was a deep split where the wood had cracked, half covered with a rambling bramble bush with sharp thorns. Nguyen had marked it out as a good place to hide because anyone searching the copse would probably take the easy way and follow the path. Some fifteen feet or so either side of the tree he'd tossed small, dry twigs along the path which were sure to crackle and break when stepped on so he'd be able to hear them coming no matter how careful they were. He'd prepared traps along the trail in places where it narrowed. Nothing elaborate because he hadn't had the time, just holes dug in the earth, a foot or so deep, with sharpened sticks, smeared with his own excrement, pointing upward. The holes had been covered with a mesh of fine twigs and leaves and overlain with soil, and overnight they had blended in perfectly with the rest of the trail. Even Nguyen himself could see no traces of the traps.

He slipped by the brambles and edged into the hole in the tree, first removing his rucksack so that it wouldn't snag. He unclipped his knife and held it by his side, breathing slowly and evenly. There were more shouts to his left, outside the wood, and then a yelling voice to his right. There were more voices, closer, whispering. He heard someone forcing his way through the undergrowth, but moving away from him, and then a similar noise to his left, also moving away. Two men at least, then. They had entered the copse together and had split up either side of the trail and were moving through the trees. The shouting continued in the distance so he had been right, some of the men had gone by the copse and were probably even now running across the fields and checking the hedgerows.

Nguyen let his mind totally relax so that he could concentrate on listening for his pursuers. They moved like large animals through the trees, pushing branches out of the way, not caring where they trod, and he had no problem in pinpointing their positions. He closed his eyes and let his mind roam the woods. He heard the dry crack of a twig and homed in on the sound, twenty, perhaps twenty-five feet away, someone moving slowly and carefully, somebody who cared how and where he walked. There was a pause of perhaps ten seconds then a second sound, the rustle of a leaf being disturbed.

Nguyen blanked out his mind, wiping away all thoughts and concentrating only on the approaching man. He tried to make himself invisible. Nguyen had once tried explaining it to the instructors from the 5th Special Forces Group at Recondo School outside Saigon, how his sixth sense worked and how he would shield his own thoughts from pursuers so that he could blend into the jungle and not be seen or felt. They'd laughed, thinking he was talking about magic or voodoo, but Nguyen was serious. His talent had saved his life, and the lives of his men, many, many times. It wasn't a case of hearing, or smelling, it was sensing, but even Nguyen didn't know exactly what it was that he sensed. It was as if he could tune into the electrical field given off by a human being or an animal, as if he could detect their auras from a distance. And he believed that the reverse was true, that other animals and humans could detect his aura and home in on it unless he dampened it down.

He heard a small movement and knew that the man

185

was now level with the tree, heading down the trail. Nguyen's mind was empty now, like a placid pool with not a single ripple disturbing its surface. He was no longer aware of the heavy knife in his hand or the pressure of the ground against his left knee as he knelt inside the tree trunk. He was invisible. He flowed out of the tree as gentle as a soft wind, brushing the brambles silently aside. His steps were small and only the balls of his feet made contact with the ground, his legs bent at the knees. The man on the trail was slightly taller than Nguyen. He stood with his back to him, wearing jeans and a dark-blue bomber jacket. In his right hand he carried a gun. Nguyen had planned to silence the man with his left hand and stun him by driving the handle of his knife against his temple but he couldn't risk it now because the man's finger would tighten involuntarily and the gun would go off. Still moving, he slipped the knife into one of the pockets of his jacket and moved behind the man, both hands out. Only at the last minute did the man sense his presence and begin to turn his head, but by then Nguyen was in position. His right hand moved down swiftly and clamped over the gun, fingers splayed so that he caught the hammer and prevented it from being released. His left hand simultaneously clamped over the man's mouth and nose. He pulled the nose between his thumb and the first joint of the opposing index finger while gripping the jaws between the heel of the hand and the remaining finger tips. The man tried to lash out with his left hand but Nguyen twisted away, out of reach. From experience Nguyen knew that it could take up to two minutes for the man to lose consciousness and he gripped tightly until the man sagged and the gun dropped from his nerveless hand. Nguyen put the gun into his jacket pocket and took out the knife. He let the man's dead-weight carry him to the ground. Killing him would have been easy; a quick slash across the subclavian artery would take just three seconds, cutting the carotid artery and jugular vein would kill within twelve. But Nguyen knew that killing the enemy wasn't always the best way, not when you were up against more than one. A dead comrade could be abandoned while the fight continued, but an injured one became a drain on the enemy's resources. He had to be cared for and transported out of danger, with the added psychological damage that a wounded man could do to the able-bodied. Time and time again Nguyen had seen it happen in the jungle. A group of Americans on a mission, the man on point would run into a booby trap, his leg blown off or a poisoned stick through his foot, and his screams and blood would terrify the rest. Not only that but the mission would be suspended while a helicopter was called in or the man was stretchered back to base. And next time a patrol moved down the trail they'd do so with twice the care at half the speed.

He heard a shout far to his right and an answer over to his left. He knelt down by the unconscious man and stabbed him twice in the upper thigh, not deep enough to cut an artery but enough to cause a considerable flow of blood.

The shouting was getting closer and Nguyen ducked behind the tree to pick up his rucksack and began to run down the track, keeping low. A gunshot behind him made him duck and he ran faster. Twice he jumped over places in the track where he'd earlier set spike traps. The man he'd ambushed must have come round because he heard frantic screaming. His screams and the gunshot would bring the rest of the men running to the copse, but Nguyen was still perfectly calm because he had many other hiding-places prepared. It would take a dozen men many days to search the copse thoroughly and they had no way of knowing whether he'd gone to ground or if he'd left the woods. They'd be sure to follow his tracks down the trail but there was a good chance that one of them would fall into one of the foot traps and that would slow them up even more. Everything was going to plan.

It seemed to Hennessy as if his life had been turned upside down. Mary had left with Christy Murphy in one of the Land-Rovers, driving over the fields for a mile or so before turning on to the road just in case The Chinaman had set other bombs. In a few hours she'd be in London where at least she'd be safe. Jimmy McMahon was in hospital where his condition, the doctors said, was as well as could be expected. They'd been told that a faulty generator had exploded because Hennessy didn't want the RUC sniffing around. The man who'd been stabbed in the wood had turned out to have superficial wounds despite all his screaming and they'd patched him up and he was being driven up to Belfast for treatment along with a teenager who'd put his foot through six wooden spikes smeared with what looked like shit. He could barely walk and he'd need antibiotics if the wound wasn't going to go septic.

In the space of an hour, three of his men had been injured and all they had to show for it was a description of a small Oriental man in camouflage gear carrying a rucksack. And if he wasn't armed before, now he had a gun.

Hennessy had posted four guards around the farm and everyone else was now indoors. Joe Ryan and Sarah were staying in their own cottage. With three men injured, one driving the car to Belfast, and Murphy on his way to London with Mary, it left Hennessy with just Jim Kavanagh and Willie O'Hara sitting at the kitchen table. He poured O'Hara and himself measures of whiskey and asked Kavanagh what he wanted.

'I'll make myself a brew, if that's OK with yez,' Kavanagh said. He pushed back his chair and put the kettle on the stove.

'We're going to need more men,' Hennessy said to his back. Kavanagh shrugged but didn't turn round as he busied himself washing the teapot and preparing a cup and saucer. 'Can you arrange for half a dozen good men from Belfast?'

'I'm not sure if that's such a good idea, Liam,' said Kavanagh quietly.

'What do you mean?' O'Hara emptied his glass and mumbled something about checking the bombed outhouse and let himself out of the back door. 'What do you mean, Jim?' Hennessy repeated.

Kavanagh turned round, drying his cup with a big, white tea-towel. 'I'm just not sure that we're going to be able to solve this just by bringing in more people, that's all. There were a dozen here last night and they didn't stop him.'

'They weren't prepared,' said Hennessy.

'They were prepared when they went into the wood,' said Kavanagh. He put the cup and the cloth on the draining-board and sat down, looking earnestly at Hennessy. 'Look, Liam, yer know that I'd do anything to protect ye, anything.

189

But this isn't a question of numbers, it's quality not quantity. Yez could bring in a hundred men but they're used to the city, not the country. They're used to fighting in the streets not in the hills.'

'So we bring in men from the farms. Come on Jim, that's not what's worrying you. Spit it out.'

Kavanagh looked uneasy, as if knowing that what he would say would offend Hennessy. Hennessy found his reluctance to speak embarrassing, he'd always thought that they trusted each other implicitly.

'What's wrong, Jim?' he pressed.

Kavanagh leant back in his chair, as if trying to put as much distance as possible between the two of them. 'This man, this Chinaman, has made it personal. It's ye he wants, right enough. Not the organisation. Ye. I just think that if ye use too many of the organisation's resources, it could backfire on yez.'

Hennessy nodded. Kavanagh had a point. There were men in Belfast and Dublin who were looking for an excuse to discredit him. They were unhappy at the move away from violence and blamed Hennessy for the switch in policy.

'And the thing of it is, I don't reckon that bringing in more men is going to help. Look at it this way, he could travel ten miles or so in a few hours with no trouble at all. And a ten-mile radius from here will cover about three hundred square miles – that includes Newry, Castlewellan, and Warrenpoint, and most of the Mourne Mountains. There aren't enough men in the whole of Belfast to cover an area that large.'

'So we don't search for him. OK. But I have to have guards here. I can't just sit here defenceless and wait for him to attack again.'

'But how long do ye keep the guards here, Liam? A week? A month? A year? Round-the-clock protection from one man – think what a drain that would be on the organisation's resources. Think how it would look. I'm telling ye this as yer friend, yer understand? Playing devil's advocate, yer know?'

Hennessy nodded. 'I know, Jim. I don't doubt your loyalty, you know that.' He reached over and squeezed Kavanagh's arm. 'I already owe you my life, you don't have to prove anything to me. And I know you have my best interests at heart. But what am I supposed to do? He obviously means business.'

'If ye want my opinion, it was a mistake coming here. It's too open, there are too many places to hide.'

'It sounds like you've had a change of heart, Jim. I seem to remember that it was your idea to get me out of Belfast in the first place.' He said it softly, not meaning to criticise.

'That was then,' admitted Kavanagh. 'I thought it was a good idea because I didn't think he'd know about the farm. But now that he does know I think we should go back to Belfast. All yez need there is me and Christy, maybe a couple of others. Now that we know who he is he won't be able to get close to ye. He'll stick out like a sore thumb in Belfast.' He held up his hands. 'I know what yez going to say, that he managed to blow up yez office while we were there, but yer've got to remember that when he did that we didn't know what a threat he was then. It won't happen again.'

Hennessy took a long, thoughtful swig from his glass.

'I don't know, Jim. He got to the car, didn't he? And he's obviously a patient bastard. He'll just wait until he gets another chance, sure enough.'

'Yeah, but he'll be waiting in Belfast, not hiding in a wood. In the city we can search for him without worrying where we're stepping all the time.'

The two men sat in silence for a while as Hennessy considered his options. He knew that Kavanagh was talking sense, but he knew too that there were advantages in keeping The Chinaman away from Belfast. God knows what it would do to his reputation if it became known that he was being stalked by a maniac with home-made bombs. The Press would have a field day. And so would his enemies within the organisation. Damn The Chinaman. Damn him for ever.

'There is something else yez should think about,' said Kavanagh, interrupting Hennessy's thoughts. Hennessy raised his eyebrows quizzically. 'The reason he's after yez,' Kavanagh continued. 'He wants the names of the team who're planting the bombs in London.'

'We don't know who they are.'

'No, but yer trying to find out. And yer'll find out eventually, they can't keep going for ever. Either we'll find out who they are or they'll make a mistake and the fucking Brits will get them. Either way that'll be the end of yez problem. All we have to do is to keep him off yez back until then. Liam, I know you're handling this yezself, but how close are ye to identifying them?'

Hennessy looked levelly at Kavanagh. He trusted the man sitting in front of him, but it was crucial that only Sean Morrison knew what he had planned. 'At the moment we're no closer than we were a week ago,' he said. 'But if everything works out it shouldn't be much longer. Days rather than weeks. That's all I can say.'

'That's good enough for me, Liam,' said Kavanagh.

The kettle began to shriek and he stood up and poured boiling water into the teapot. 'Until then, we'll stick to yez like glue. When is Christy back?'

'I told him to take Mary all the way to London and to hang around for a while to make sure that she isn't followed. He should be back tomorrow night.'

There was a scrabbling at the door and Jackie bounded in, her tongue lolling and her coat damp. She careered over to Hennessy and put her head in his lap; he stroked her absent-mindedly.

'I hear what you're saying,' Hennessy said to Kavanagh. 'Let's wait until Christy gets back until we decide what to do.'

'It's yer call, Liam. But if I were ye I'd get a few more men around – not from Belfast but locals, workers from nearby farms maybe, fellahs yez can trust. They'll be used to dealing with poachers and the like and at least they'll be careful where they put their feet.'

'That's a good idea, Jim. I'll make a few calls. It shouldn't be a problem.'

Jackie growled softly, seeking attention.

Woody had the mother and father of all hangovers. His head felt twice its normal size, his mouth was dry and bitter and every time he moved his stomach lurched and only an intense effort of will kept him from throwing up. It was a normal Sunday morning. Saturday was always the paper's busiest day and once the presses started running and they'd checked that the opposition papers didn't have any earth-shattering exclusives then all the paper's journalists headed for the pub. The Saturday-night sessions in the King's Head were legendary, but Woody didn't just go for the alcohol and the company, he went because he had to keep in with the news desk and the paper's executives. The paper, along with most of Fleet Street, was cutting back all round, slashing a red pen through expense claims and reducing the number of casual shifts. It was like a game of musical chairs and Woody was fighting like hell to ensure that when the music stopped he'd be one of those left sitting at a desk. The hangover was a small price to pay.

He heard the phone ring on the floor below and one of the other tenants answered it and then he heard his name being called.

Woody groaned and pulled a pillow over his head. Footsteps clattered up the stairs and a hand hammered on his door and the student who lived in the bedsit directly below his yelled that the office was on the phone. If it had been anyone else Woody wouldn't have bothered answering, but a call from the paper probably meant there was a shift going so he coughed and forced himself to sit up, feeling waves of nausea ripple through his stomach. He breathed deeply and groped for a pair of jeans before padding slowly down the stairs, holding his head in his hands.

The phone was hanging down by the wall and he pulled it up and put it against his ear. His head swam and he closed his eyes.

'Ian Wood,' he said, flinching as the words echoed around his skull.

'Woody?' said a voice. It was a man, but Woody couldn't place it.

'Yes?'

'Woody, it's Pat. Pat Quigley. I didn't get you out of bed, did I?'

Woody moaned and leant against the wall. 'What the fuck do you want, Pat?'

'Jesus, Woody, you sound terrible. Are you sick or something?'

'Pat, you have exactly ten seconds before I go back to my pit. It's Sunday morning, you should be in church and I should be in bed.'

'Got you, Woody. OK, listen. Do you remember those Sinn Fein guys you were asking me about a while back?' Woody grunted, but said nothing, so Quigley continued. 'Well, there's something funny going on here. I've been told that someone has started some sort of vendetta against one of the men I told you about, Liam Hennessy. He's one of Sinn Fein's top advisers, and a leading lawyer here.'

'A vendetta? What the fuck are you talking about?'

'Someone set off a bomb in his office. Just a small one, a chemical bomb I'm told, not high explosive. A warning, maybe. No one was hurt. It seems like a coincidence, you know, happening so soon after we spoke. That's all.'

'I still don't see what you want from me, Pat.' Actually Woody had a pretty good idea what was going on. As well as stringing for the *Sunday World*, Quigley filed copy for one of the daily heavies and they were probably pushing him for a Sunday for Monday story, what with it being a quiet news week and all.

'I was thinking that perhaps you passed Hennessy's name on to someone, someone who might want to, I don't know, put pressure on him, maybe. I mean, I'm told the attack wasn't sectarian, it was too amateurish for that. Come on Woody, what's going on?'

'Fucked if I know, Pat. Honest. Anyway, my notebooks are all in the office, I can't do anything now. But I'm sure you're barking up the wrong tree, mate. It was just a reader who wanted to contact someone in Sinn Fein, that was all.'

'OK, Woody. I thought it was worth a try. Maybe I'll call you in the office during the week.' He sounded disappointed, but Woody felt no urge to help him, not in his present weakened state. Besides, Woody could smell a possible story. What was The Chinaman's name? He couldn't remember so he stopped trying and instead concentrated on getting back to his room without throwing up over the threadbare carpet.

The taxi dropped Morrison close to the South African embassy in Trafalgar Square. A group of half a dozen demonstrators were outside, standing on the pavement close to the road. They were dressed like students, pale-faced girls with straggly hair and men with beards and John Lennon glasses. One of the women had a megaphone and she harangued two policemen who stood either side of the door to the building. 'End Apartheid now!' she yelled, the electronically amplified shriek echoing off the stone walls of the embassy. Morrison wondered why they bothered. You didn't change things by standing on street corners with faded banners and shouting slogans. You changed things by taking action, by hurting those in power, and then by negotiating from strength. And by being committed to change. The anti-Apartheid movement in the UK had never really learnt that lesson, mainly because they had never experienced the discrimination they were protesting about. The vast bulk of them were from comfortable middleclass backgrounds or were working-class kids with chips on their shoulders. Most of them weren't even black. They'd be a hell of a lot more effective if they couldn't get work because they followed the wrong religion, if they didn't have a fair say in the running of their own lives, and if they and their friends and family could be beaten and tortured by the soldiers of an oppressive regime in a country that didn't even belong to them. The IRA was effective because its members cared and because they all stood to benefit if they were ultimately successful and the British pulled out of Ireland.

He crossed over the road and walked by one of the huge, majestic lions. It was surrounded by a group of Asian tourists laden with designer shoulder-bags and expensive camera equipment. A crocodile of Scandinavian sightseers were following a tour guide and Morrison stopped to let them go by. There were pigeons everywhere, fluttering through the air, sitting around the fountains and waddling along the floor. They had grown fat and lazy and had no fear of humans. On the contrary, they gathered in noisy flocks around the tourists who had paid for little tubs of bird seed and sat on arms and wrists while they fed.

Morrison looked around the square. He normally had a nose for plain-clothes policemen or off-duty soldiers, a sixth sense honed by years of surviving in Belfast. He tagged a man in his forties in a brown leather bomber jacket as one possibility, and he paid close attention to a balding man in a fawn overcoat, but both left the square eventually. Bromley got to within a dozen paces before Morrison realised he was the man he was there to see. Tallish with horn-rimmed spectacles and a well-trimmed black beard, Bromley looked more like a history professor than a Detective Chief Inspector with the Anti-Terrorist

Branch. He was wearing a greenish jacket of some inde-
terminate material with baggy corduroy trousers and a
brown wool tie. He was smoking a pipe. Morrison thought
the pipe could be cover because it looked brand new, but
the man appeared to have no problems inhaling and blew
out a cloud of bluish smoke as he drew near.

'Detective Chief Inspector Bromley, I presume,' said
Morrison. He made no move to shake hands, and neither
did the inspector. Each was highly suspicious of the other.
Both knew that they could be under observation and
whereas a clandestine meeting could possibly be explained,
a handshake or any other sign of friendliness would be
damning. And in Morrison's case, possibly fatal.

'How can I help you, Mr Morrison?' said Bromley with
exaggerated politeness.

Morrison began walking slowly around the perimeter
of the square. 'It's about the bombs, the bombs on the
mainland,' he said. 'We're not responsible.'

'By we, who do you mean?'

'The organisation.'

'Well, Mr Morrison, there appears to be some confusion here. The forensic evidence we have suggests that the
devices are standard IRA type, and each time responsibility has been claimed they've given the correct codeword.
Can you explain that?' Bromley shook his head and puffed
on his pipe.

'We think there's a renegade unit behind it. We don't
know who.'

'Are you trying to tell me there's an active service unit
on the loose and you don't even know who it is? Where
are they getting their explosives from?'

'They've managed to gain access to several arms dumps

in and around London. They have explosives, detonators and firearms. But they haven't been sanctioned by us. We're as keen as you are to see them stopped.'

'And the codewords?'

Morrison nodded. 'We think they're being helped by someone high up in Belfast or Dublin. But again, we don't know who.'

Bromley thrust his hands deep into the pockets of his corduroy trousers and studied the ground as he walked. 'You know they've taken explosives, but you don't know who they are?'

'We've checked out all our caches. Some ordnance was missing.' Morrison chose his words carefully because he couldn't afford to give away any more information than was absolutely necessary. The IRA was still at war with the British Government, when all was said and done.

'Can't you just identify which IRA members are unaccounted for?'

'It's a big organisation. We're working on it.'

'It's a big organisation but I doubt if you've that many bombmakers.'

'You'd be surprised,' said Morrison. 'But with the organisation structured the way it is, it's harder than it used to be to get in touch with people. You of all people should know that.'

Bromley grunted around the stem of his pipe. He knew what Morrison meant. Following several much publicised coups by the intelligence services in the late seventies and early eighties, the IRA had undergone a transformation, doing away with the old brigade command structure in favour of a more complex network of cells, each with different but often overlapping functions. Most of the units in Northern Ireland reported to the high command in Belfast, but in the countryside the chain of command was a great deal more flexible, harder to pin down. The cells were graded into four levels. The most important were active service units responsible for fund-raising robberies, assassinations, bombings and weaponry, numbering about one hundred of the organisation's most trusted members. At any one time at least half of them could be found in the H-blocks of Long Kesh.

The second level consisted of about three hundred and fifty men and women divided into small cells, all of them trained and ready to go into action but held in reserve until needed. They were generally less well-known to the security forces and it was members of the second level who were often sent into active service on the mainland or the Continent.

The third level comprised a small number of cells, mainly Dublin-based terrorists who were active during the sixties but who had effectively disappeared from the political scene and who did not appear on any current intelligence files.

The fourth level was made up of what Morrison thought of as the enthusiastic amateurs, usually Belfast teenagers who'd graduated from street fighting or youngsters from Catholic farming families helping with the organisation's smuggling operations. They were useful as couriers or lookouts, or for causing disturbances, but not sufficiently trained for anything more sophisticated. Most were expendable and would rise no higher in the organisation.

The structure had been set up so that if any one cell were exposed, its links with the rest of the organisation would be minimal. The system made the IRA much more secure, but it also made it difficult to run checks on who was doing what. Each cell had to be contacted individually, and that would take a great deal of time. And that wasn't allowing for the IRA members like Morrison who weren't even members of a cell but who worked alone.

'So what are you saying, Mr Morrison?'

'We have a plan,' said Morrison quietly.

'We?'

That, realised Morrison, was the problem. 'We' meant Hennessy and Morrison and nobody else, so he was going to have an uphill struggle to persuade Bromley to help. And it was made even more difficult by virtue of the fact that the policeman would also have to be sworn to secrecy. It was, whichever way you looked at it, an unholy alliance.

'The Provisional IRA is not responsible for the bombings, that I can promise you. They're using our ordnance and our codewords, but they are acting without official sanction. We plan to change the codeword, but different codes will be given to each member of the high command. When they claim responsibility for the next bombing, we should know who their link is.'

Bromley bit down on the pipe, his brow furrowed. 'You mean you want the police to tell you which codeword we get?'

Morrison nodded. 'That's all you have to do. Give us the word, we'll do the rest.'

'That's all I have to do!' exclaimed the policeman. 'All I have to do is to co-operate with the IRA! Can you imagine what would happen if that ever got out?'

Morrison stopped walking and confronted Bromley, putting his face close up to the policeman's. 'And can you imagine, Detective Chief Inspector Bromley, how long I'd have to live if anyone in the organisation knew what I was proposing? My life is on the line here, so don't give me any crap about your reputation being at risk.'

'You're asking me to co-operate with you in a bombing campaign. You're asking me to give you confidential information on an investigation.' A pigeon fluttered noisily over Bromley's head, saw he had no seed and flapped away.

'The bomb will go off anyway, whether or not you decide to help, Bromley. I don't know when, I don't know where, but there will be another bomb and people will probably die. There's nothing we can do to stop it, but maybe, just maybe, we'll be able to stop the one after that.'

Bromley returned Morrison's gaze with steady, hard eyes.

'Who else, Mr Morrison? Who else is involved?'

Morrison swallowed. He had hoped to persuade the policeman without bringing Hennessy's name into it, but he could see that it would not be possible. Bromley wouldn't believe this was a serious operation unless he knew who was running it. 'Liam Hennessy,' he said slowly. He was rewarded by the sight of Bromley's eyes widening with surprise.

Bromley turned away and Morrison walked with him. They passed a line of tourists queuing up to buy seed to feed the pigeons and neither of the men spoke. Two uniformed policewomen walked by, a blonde and a brunette, and Morrison wondered how they'd react if they knew that a member of the IRA and a Detective Chief Inspector from the Anti-Terrorist Branch were considering working together. Bromley waited until they were some distance from the policewomen before speaking again.

'When do you plan to change the codeword?' he asked.

'It's already done,' replied Morrison. 'Hennessy did it yesterday. Himself. Only he knows who was given which word. Even I don't know.'

Bromley knew of Hennessy, and of his role as Sinn Fein adviser to the Belfast IRA council. He was one of the most powerful men in the organisation, just one step away from the seven-man Dublin-based army council. He was listened to by the council in Belfast but held equal sway over the headquarters staff in Ireland, the men who ran the active service units across Europe.

What Bromley really wanted was the list of men in the high command and the codewords they'd been given, but he knew Morrison would not hand out information like that. He would have to play by the rules Morrison was laying down or not play at all. Could he risk it? Could he afford not to? Morrison hadn't asked him how close the authorities were to catching the bombers. He hadn't needed to. They were no nearer identifying the active service unit behind the bombs now than they were when the campaign started. And it wasn't as if enough resources weren't being put into the investigation. Joining in the hunt for what was in all probability a small, self-contained unit, were the combined resources of Bromley's own Anti-Terrorist Branch, MI5, the Metropolitan Police, Special Branch, the Secret Intelligence Service, the SAS and the Defence Intelligence Service, not to mention the RUC in Northern Ireland. Actually, mused Bromley, combined resources wasn't the correct phrase because all the various anti-terrorist operations tended to work alone and to jealously guard whatever intelligence they collected.

'When I give you the codeword, what happens then?' asked Bromley.

Morrison noticed how the Detective Chief Inspector had said 'when' and not 'if'. The decision had been made. 'We'll track down the leak and interrogate him,' he answered.

'Which will lead you to the bombers?'

'If Hennessy is right, yes.'

'And then?'

'Then?' Morrison was confused.

'I don't think you've thought this through. How are you going to eliminate the unit that is setting these bombs? You can't send another IRA active service unit into London to knock out the first, can you? Or maybe you think you can.' Bromley thought for a while. 'How do I know that this is Hennessy's idea?' he said.

Morrison shrugged. 'You're going to have to trust me on that,' he said. 'There's no way on God's earth that he can be seen with you. He'd never be trusted again. And that's assuming they didn't just kill him.'

Bromley went quiet again and puffed on his pipe. 'Very well. I agree. I'll tell you which codeword is given after the next explosion. But on two conditions. And they're not negotiable.'

Morrison raised his eyebrows quizzically.

'When you find out where the bombers are, you tell me. You let the authorities handle it.'

'The authorities?'

'Whoever it takes. Police. SAS. Whoever. It has to be that way. You can't handle it, not in London.'

Morrison nodded. Hennessy had intended from the start that the Brits would clear up the mess, because if it was ever discovered that the IRA had betrayed its own, the organisation would be fragmented beyond belief. It had taken years of diplomacy and compromise to weld the various factions together and Hennessy did not want to undo it all because of a handful of lunatics. 'And the second condition?' he asked.

'You give me a telephone number where I can call Hennessy. I'll only give the codeword to him. We'll share the risk.'

They walked in silence again until Morrison reached his decision. 'OK,' he said. He gave him the number of Hennessy's farm and Bromley wrote it down in a small leather-bound notebook.

'I hope I never have to make the call,' said Bromley.

'So do I,' said Morrison. 'But you will.'

They parted without a handshake.

Woody didn't usually go into the office on Monday, most of the freelance shifts were towards the end of the week, the paper's busy period, but Quigley's phone call had intrigued him. The security guard on duty nodded good morning over the top of his copy of the *Sun*, he was used to journalists coming and going at all hours.

Woody helped himself to a plastic cup of machine coffee and then began rummaging through the drawer of the filing cabinet where he stored his old notebooks. He found the one he'd used the week The Chinaman had called and flicked through the pages. Among his spidery shorthand he saw 'Chinaman' and a telephone number. He couldn't find an address, nor any note of the man's name. There was one name there among the hieroglyphics: S.J. Brown. Or Browning. Woody couldn't make it out.

He racked his memory while he dialled the telephone number. After ten or so rings a sleepy voice answered.

'Double Happiness Take-Away,' a man said. Woody scribbled down the name.

'My name is Ian Wood,' he said. 'Are you the gentleman who came to the *Sunday World* about the reward?'

'No,' the voice said, and hung up.

'Terrific,' said Woody to himself. He picked up a telephone directory and went through it. There was only one Double Happiness Take-Away, it was in Clapham and the number matched. What he needed now was The Chinaman's name. He rang down to the cuttings library but there was no one there so he went himself and pulled the file on the Knightsbridge bombing. There were two foreign names among the dead: Nguyen Xuan Phoung and Nguyen Kieu Trinh. Woody wrote them down in his notebook and underlined Nguyen.

The knock on the door startled Morrison because he hadn't ordered anything from room service and he wasn't expecting any visitors. He was lying on his bed in a white towelling bathrobe, his hands clasped behind his neck. He sat up and looked at his watch. Ten o'clock. He'd been in no rush to get dressed because he was still waiting for instructions from Hennessy. Morrison had phoned him twice the previous day. The first time there had been no answer, and the second time he'd sounded strained and it was obvious that there were others in the room with him. Hennessy had told him to stay put and that he'd call on Monday. Something was wrong but Morrison realised he'd simply have to wait to find out what it was. The knock on the door was repeated, but harder and faster as if the caller was losing his patience. He felt a sudden rush of fear, thinking it might be the police or even a UDA hit-squad, but realised just as quickly that it was irrational, nobody knew where he was except for Liam Hennessy. Even so, he slid silently off the bed and padded to the door. He placed his hands flat against the wall either side of the door and eased his eye to the peep-hole. Even through the distorting lens he recognised her. She knocked again and he pulled the door open but kept his arm across the doorway as if blocking her way.

'Sean Morrison,' she said, grinning.

'Mary Hennessy,' he said. Morrison wasn't sure what emotions he felt as she stood in front of him. Pleased, for sure, but worried, too. Worried about what she was doing here. And guilt. Lots of guilt. And desire. Always desire. He'd never been able to look at Mary Hennessy without getting aroused, without wanting to possess her. There were other feelings too, regret, fear, sadness, all mixed up.

'Aren't you going to let me in?' she said.

He stepped to one side to let her pass and then closed the door behind her. She was carrying a white trench coat and she dropped it over the back of a chair before turning to look at him, hands on hips. She was wearing a white blouse with the collar turned up at the back and a soft skirt, patterned with large yellow flowers, and there was a small black bow in her brown hair. She was looking at him with a mischievous smile, her head on one side. Two years, he thought. They'd gone so quickly, so quickly that she hadn't changed one bit. He didn't know how old she was because he'd never cared enough to ask. He knew she was at least a decade older than he was but it hadn't shown two years ago and it didn't show now. Part of him had hoped that if he went away for a few years he wouldn't find her so attractive when he came back, that age would take away the desire, the lust. Her brown eyes sparkled as if she'd read his mind. She walked up to him, slowly, her hands still on her hips. Even with her high heels she had to tilt her head up to look in his eyes. She stood close to him, so close that he could smell her hair, clean and sweet.

'It's been a long time, Sean,' she said softly. She reached up and rested her hands on his shoulders.

'I don't think you should be here,' he said. The voice didn't sound like his own, it sounded thick and hesitant.

She raised her eyebrows. 'Don't you?' she said. She stood up on her toes and put her lips up close to his. Their lips didn't touch but he could feel her warm breath. He swallowed. Even up close her skin was smooth and clear. The only signs of age were the laughter lines around her eyes and they just added to her attractiveness. 'Don't you?' she repeated. She moved her head forward, just enough so that their lips touched. She opened hers slightly, but that was all. There was no pressure, no urging. She wanted him to prove how much he wanted her, to take the initiative. Part of him, the guilty voice in the back of his mind that had told him to go to New York, wanted to resist, but he already knew that he was lost. His lips parted too and his hands seemed to take on a will of their own, moving forward to link around her narrow waist. Still she stood on tip-toe waiting for him to make up his mind. He kissed her, once, a quick press of the lips, then he moved his head back and looked at her and then in a rush grabbed her and pulled her tightly to him, kissing her hard, forcing his tongue into her soft, moist mouth. For a few seconds she remained passive, allowing him to invade her, and then she began to kiss him back, returning his passion. He grunted as she kissed him and he closed his eyes as the urge to possess her washed over him again. She slowly put her heels on the ground so that he had to bend his neck to kiss her and she tried to pull away but he put his right hand behind her neck and pushed her head against his.

She used both her hands to push his shoulders away. A strand of hair had come loose, curling over her left eye, but she ignored it. She held him away, bending backwards slightly and pushing her groin against him. He felt as if he was on fire between his legs. Her eyes flashed. 'Tell me you want me,' she said.

'You know I do,' he answered, and tried to kiss her, but she moved her head out of the way, pressing her thighs even harder against him.

'Tell me you want me,' she said again. She moved her right hand slowly down from his shoulder and traced her fingernails across the hairs on his chest. He gasped as the sharp nails scratched against his flesh, parting his robe as they moved down between his ribs. She moved her hand lightly across his stomach and then down to his groin. 'Tell me,' she urged and at the same time took him in her hand. She squeezed him gently and he groaned and surrendered.

'I want you, Mary,' he said. She pushed the robe off his shoulders so that he was standing naked in front of her and pulled his head down to hers, grabbing his hair so tightly that it hurt, forcing her body fully against his. He lifted her up and she raised her legs, gripping him around the waist and locking her ankles together. Now there was only one thought in his head. Her.

Nguyen lay motionless and listened to the birds singing in the treetops overhead. He'd made his way back to

Tollymore Forest under cover of darkness and found the van exactly as he'd left it. There were a few things he wanted from the back of the van which he loaded into his rucksack, and he took a red can of petrol. He rejected the idea of sleeping by the van in case Hennessy should send a search party to the forest. It was an outside chance but not one worth taking because if they surprised him there would be no escape.

He found a safe place a hundred yards or so away and rested until mid-morning. He sat up and leant against a towering pine tree, the air thick with the smell of pine needles. He was surrounded by thousands of bluebells, shifting listlessly in the wind. He spent an hour or so cutting off the heads of three boxfuls of matches and crushing them into red powder which he carefully poured into one of the boxes. He cut a three-foot length of plastic-coated wire and then stripped off an inch of the plastic midway along it. With the point of his knife he made a hole at either end of the matchbox and threaded the wire through, knotting it so that the bared portion was in the middle, in contact with the powdered match heads. He stripped the ends of the wire clean of plastic and then coiled it up, wrapping it around the box. Nguyen removed the glass front from one of the plastic alarm clocks he'd brought with him and put it into the rucksack with the wired-up matchbox. Connecting the clock, the matchbox and a battery in a simple circuit would give him a basic timed fuse which would be more than sufficient to ignite the can of petrol.

The gun he'd taken from the man in the copse was a Browning HiPower automatic pistol which weighed about two pounds. Nguyen ejected the magazine and counted the bullets. Thirteen. An unlucky number for the Westerners, but not for a Vietnamese. He stripped the gun apart and cleaned it, checking that the mechanism worked. It was fine. The gun had two safeties, one worked by the thumb and one by the magazine, so that it couldn't be fired accidentally. It was a serious weapon. It was too heavy to carry around in his pocket for long so he put it in his rucksack. The smell of roast pork reminded him how long it had been since he had last eaten so he took out a carton of meat and one of rice and ate with his fingers. It had been a long time since he had eaten outside. What was it the Westerners called it? He'd seen the word in one of Kieu Trinh's English story books. Picnic, that was it.

As he ate he worked out what he was going to do next. One thing was for sure, he had to confront Hennessy one last time before he took things a stage further and that meant going back to the farm. Now that Hennessy had seen how much damage he could do, surely he would be more co-operative? Put anyone under enough pressure and they would bend. Not break, perhaps, but certainly bend.

Nguyen sighed and lay back in the pine needles. He took no pleasure in what he was doing. When he'd left Vietnam he'd thought that his days of fighting and killing were over, that he'd be allowed to raise his family in peace. When he saw the last helicopter leave the American embassy in Saigon he still had hopes of escaping from the North Vietnamese and eventually living in the United States. He'd fought alongside the Americans and had seen hundreds of American teenagers die in the fight for a free Vietnam so he didn't regard being left behind as an act of betrayal. He could see what a difficult logistical exercise it was for the Americans to pull out, and he knew that he wasn't the only one to have been left behind. It was only later, when Thi Manh and Mai Phoung died, that the resentment burst like a septic boil and he vowed never to seek sanctuary in the United States. They'd been surprised at the refugee camp in Hong Kong when he'd told them that he would go anywhere in the world but not to America. Officials from the United Nations High Commission for Refugees had interviewed him many times and had explained that because of his war record he would be welcomed with open arms in the United States but he had steadfastly refused and had been equally insistent that he would not explain his reasons. He had told them that two of his daughters had died on the voyage across the South China Sea but never detailed the circumstances. In Nguyen's mind, they had no right to know. They were so beautiful, Thi Manh and Mai Phoung, and even now, after more than ten years had passed, he could picture them clearly in his mind, jet-black hair, high cheekbones, bright eyes and ready smiles, as pretty as their mother had been before the tough years had taken their toll. They had been such well-behaved children and it had been thoughts of them that had kept him going throughout his three years in the so-called 're-education' camps, working fifteen hours a day on a near-starvation diet, until the North Vietnamese were satisfied that he was a good Communist again.

There had been no doubt in his mind that he would be punished by the North Vietnamese but he had no idea of how severe that punishment would be. On the morning of April 30, 1975, he had slipped out of bed, leaving Xuan Phoung asleep clutching a pillow, and stood in the doorway leading to the alcove where his daughters slept together in a single bed, heads touching like Siamese twins. He stood there for more than an hour trying to imprint the scene on his mind, certain that it would be the last time he would see his daughters. The street noises had changed, there were no more helicopters whirring overhead, instead there was the far-off rumble of trucks carrying North Vietnamese troops and supplies into Saigon and the sound of cheering as the bo doi – the soldiers of the people – were welcomed by crowds of onlookers. In the early morning, while he was making love to his wife, Nguyen had heard tanks driving through the streets and the occasional rattle of machine-guns, but whether it was the North Vietnamese mopping up pockets of resistance or simply high spirits on the part of the victorious forces, he had no way of telling.

He dressed casually in washed-out cotton trousers, a faded checked shirt and an old pair of sandals. He'd dropped his army uniform in the street and he'd cleared all evidence of involvement with the US forces from their flat. They had made their plans long before the Americans pulled out, when it had first become obvious that there was no way the South could win the war. They had closed their bank account and transferred all their money into gold, knowing that when Saigon fell paper money would be virtually worthless. They had kept the gold in a safety-deposit box, along with several gold Rolex watches and pieces of jewellery that they had been able to buy on the black market with Nguyen's wages, and two weeks before the NVA arrived at the outskirts of Saigon they had taken everything out of the bank vault. They had already decided that Nguyen should go. It was the only chance the family had of surviving.

Xuan Phoung had friends who would help her to get a job as a kitchen worker and she would hide their savings under the floorboards until Nguyen was allowed to return, or until she got the opportunity to escape with the children. Before he left, Nguyen took a photograph from his wallet, a picture of Xuan Phoung and the two girls, and put it on the bed. He had carried it with him throughout the war but it would be dangerous for them to be caught with it now. He took all identification from the wallet, leaving only a small amount of paper money. It would not be long before a thirty-one-year-old man walking alone would be picked up for interrogation and anything in his pockets would be taken from him, so he left his wedding ring and his watch and his Special Forces cigarette lighter on the bed next to the photograph before kissing his wife once, on the cheek, and then dashing downstairs before he could have a change of heart.

The streets of Saigon were every bit as packed as they had been the previous night, but whereas the rush then had been to escape with the Americans, now the crowds were there to welcome the NVA. Children were waving NVA flags – red and blue with a gold star – and it seemed as if every shop in the city had managed to get a photograph of an unsmiling Ho Chi Minh in its window. Battered lorries covered with thick red mud rattled along loaded with troops, young men with baggy olive-green uniforms and rubber sandals, cheering and lapping up the attention.

He was picked up around lunchtime by a group of five teenage soldiers who prodded him with their guns and demanded his papers. He told them he'd been robbed two days earlier and they slapped him around the face and accused him of lying. They made him kneel on the ground, blindfolded him, handcuffed his hands behind his back and then dragged him roughly and threw him into the back of a truck. Throughout the day more men were thrown into the vehicle. All were blindfolded and manacled and told that if they spoke to each other they would be killed. When the truck was full they were driven for three days with just a handful of foul-smelling rice which they were forced to eat like animals, pushing their faces on to the floor to lick the grains up because their captors refused to unlock the handcuffs. Nguyen assumed they were being taken North and wondered why they bothered because the Communists now controlled the whole country. For a wild moment he thought that perhaps the NVA feared that the Americans would be back but in his heart he knew that could not be true. The evacuation of the embassy was not the action of an army planning to return.

He never discovered the name of the place he was taken to but there was no doubt that it was a prison, and had been for many years. He was thrown into a small cell, two paces by four paces, containing only a wooden bench and a bucket. They took off his blindfold and he saw that the bench was rubbed smooth from the bodies that had slept there over the years. It looked ages old and had obviously been used by the French to hold Vietnamese captives. The bench sloped so that any liquids would run off and there was a small drain hole at the bottom of one of the walls. There was no window in the cell, the only light came from the corridor through the open door and whenever it opened cockroaches ran for the dark corners. Nguyen was forced to lie on the bench and his feet were locked into a set of leg-irons which were fixed to the wall. They put the bucket within reach and took off his handcuffs and left without a word, locking the door behind them. They left him there for two weeks, opening the door only once a day to put down a handful of rice on a banana leaf along with a piece of stale bread. It was stifling hot in the cell and he was always thirsty but he was only given one earthenware jug of water to drink with his food. The cell stank of urine and sweat and decay. The cockroaches did not worry him, even when they ran over his body, but there were mosquitoes and he was covered in itching bites that made him want to scream. His legs were in pain too, rubbed raw by the metal leg-irons.

After two weeks of solitary confinement they dragged him out of his cell and into a room where he saw his first glimpse of the sun through a murky skylight. To the left of the skylight, set into the ceiling, was a large, rusty meat hook. Two NVA officers questioned him for an hour and then he was returned to the leg-irons and the darkness. A week later he was taken out and interrogated again. There was no violence, no threats, just a series of questions, almost identical to the ones he'd been asked on the first occasion, and he was sure that he gave the same answers. The same lies. He was a mechanic, he had never been in the army. He had no family. He had lost his papers. It was impossible to tell from the blank faces of his interrogators whether or not they believed him, and most of the time he could only look through squinting eyes because after the enforced darkness he found even the weak sunlight which managed to get through the dirt-encrusted glass blindingly bright.

They took him back to his cell and left him there for just three days before hauling him back to the interrogation room. By that stage he could barely walk and his gums were bleeding from malnutrition. He had diarrhoea and the backs of his legs and backside were a mass of sores. The older of his two interrogators, a kindly looking major with white hair, told him that they did not believe his story and that they would be grateful if he would tell them the truth this time. He insisted that he was not lying and they nodded, almost sadly. Four NVA soldiers came into the room, holding bamboo canes, and they beat him senseless. Then they threw a bucket of water over him to bring him round before beating him unconscious again and dragging him back to his cell.

For six days the process was repeated. They would ask him for the truth, he would stick to his story, the soldiers would beat him up.

On the seventh day, by which time he'd lost three of his teeth and they had broken four of his ribs, they changed their tactics. They took a long piece of rope and bound his wrists behind him and then wound it excruciatingly tightly around his arms before hauling him up on the meat hook. It was strange, but he could not remember much about the days they tortured him. He could remember that he had never in his life felt so much pain and he knew that at one point it had been so bad that he'd pleaded with them to kill him, but now, as he lay on the pine needles and looked up through the branches to the clear blue sky above, it seemed as if it had all happened to someone else and that they were borrowed memories. Only one thing had got him through – the images of his wife as he left and his two daughters, asleep with their heads touching. Of all the images that stuck in his mind, they were the strongest, because throughout the torture he'd concentrated on them. They were the reason they could not break him.

He never knew whether or not they believed him, or whether they simply gave up trying to break him, but eventually the torture stopped and he was transferred to a re-education camp where he worked in the fields for fifteen hours a day but where at least there was food. He was forced to write endless self-criticisms which were duly filed away and he spent two hours each day sitting cross-legged on the floor with other prisoners being lectured to on the merits and ideals of Communism and being beaten with sticks if they nodded off. There were other punishments, meted out for the most trivial of offences. Men were shackled upside down and left hanging for days until their legs were weeping with gangrene, locked into cramped steel boxes in the sun or buried up to their necks in the ground. Nguyen was there for three years. Three years of living a lie. Three wasted years.

When he was finally judged to be a good Communist he was released on probation and was assigned to work on an irrigation project to the west of Hanoi. He had to report to a political officer three times a week for further indoctrination. He was lucky, he knew that, because tens of thousands of South Vietnamese were kept in the camps for much longer.

He fled one night and managed to get to Hanoi where he stole identification papers and money and journeyed south to Saigon. He lived rough in the city for several weeks before he dared approach Xuan Phoung and when he did it was at night. He knocked timidly on her door and when she opened it it was clear from her bewildered face that she did not recognise him. It was hardly surprising because he had lost so much weight and appeared to have aged ten years, but she took him in her arms and cried softly. She ushered him into the room and sat him down, knelt in front of him and held him around his waist, crying all the time and whispering his name. He realised then that however badly he had suffered it could have been nothing compared with what his wife had been through. At least he had been able to look forward to returning to her and the children. She had had no way of knowing if he was even alive.

She made him green tea and while he was drinking it she went into the bedroom and brought out a tiny child. A girl. The daughter he had never seen, conceived on the night that the Americans abandoned Saigon and now almost three years old.

'Kieu Trinh is her name,' said Xuan Phoung. 'But we can change it if you don't like it.'

'It's perfect,' said Nguyen. He held her in his arms and then his wife woke Thi Manh and Mai Phoung and brought them in to meet the father they barely remembered. He had been away for almost a quarter of their lives. Nguyen was so filled with happiness that he could barely speak, he just held all four of them. His family.

Before he could ask, Xuan Phoung said, 'The gold is still here, and I know someone who can get us out.'

'We must go soon,' he said, his voice thick with emotion.

'I know,' she said. 'We were only waiting for you.'

Nguyen and his wife and children travelled by night to a fishing port in Kien Giang province, all their valuables and papers in two canvas bags. They'd paid a deposit in gold to a middleman in Saigon and were told when and where they were to pay the rest.

They had to spend the night in a dirty hut that stank of fish, sleeping on small cots with another two families who were also waiting for the boat. During the night little Kieu Trinh developed a hacking cough and when Xuan Phoung put her hand on the child's forehead it was hot and wet. She got worse through the night and kept them all awake. Nguyen stayed by her side, wiping her forehead with a cloth dipped in water and wafting her with a piece of cardboard. She got worse during the day. It was Xuan Phoung who said it first, even though Nguyen had already reached the same conclusion: the child was in no condition for a sea voyage, especially in an unhygienic boat crammed to the gills with refugees. Xuan Phoung suggested they wait in the village until the child was well enough to travel, but Nguyen pointed out that if they did they'd lose their deposit. And it represented a big chunk of their hard-earned savings.

'You must go ahead, with Thi Manh and Mai Phoung,' she said. 'We will join you in Hong Kong.'

He'd refused at first, but eventually realised that what she said made sense. If he went with the two teenage girls, he was sure the captain could be persuaded to accept the deposits of all five of them towards the cost of the trip, leaving more than enough money for Xuan Phoung and Kieu Trinh to buy their passage when the child was well again. When the captain came for them later that evening, Nguyen explained what had happened and eventually he agreed that the five deposits could go towards the three fares, albeit with an extra ounce of gold thrown in. For another ounce he agreed to bring in a doctor to tend to the child.

When Nguyen saw the vessel that was supposed to take them across the South China Sea to Hong Kong, he almost had second thoughts. The boat was about fifteen metres long, its hull rotting and repaired in many places. There were already thirty or so refugees sitting or squatting on its deck and Nguyen and his two children and the two families that had shared the hut had to squeeze between them to find space. The boat was worryingly low in the water.

The captain was joined by a crew of three, men barely out of their teens in ragged T-shirts and cut-off trousers. It took half an hour of patient coaxing to get the engine started and it chugged uneasily out to sea as the huge orange sun sat low in the sky.

There was a hatchway in the deck leading to a hold containing a dozen camp beds where the refugees took it in turns to sleep. There was a small stove there and the women cooked what little food the crew had brought with them: some rice, strips of dried fish and a sack of green vegetables. Some of the men rigged up fishing lines and from time to time pulled in fresh fish to supplement the meagre rations, but mainly they fished to fight the boredom. Most of the days were spent cross-legged on the deck, watching the horizon and hoping that the boat would stay afloat.

Water was rationed and they were each given just a cupful every four hours, carefully meted out by a crewman using stained tin mugs. A blanket had been stretched out from a mast and tied down with ropes to provide some shade during the day and shelter from the occasional rain storm. Conditions were so grim that Nguyen was glad that Kieu Trinh had stayed behind.

They were three days out from Vietnam when they met the fishing boats. There were three of them painted in identical colours as if part of the same fleet. The decks were painted red and piled high with plastic barrels and coils of rope, and the wheel-houses were white. The hulls were pale green and there were lines of white Thai writing on the bows. The crews seemed friendly enough, smiling and waving as they drew close, and they shouted to the captain that they had water and ice to sell. The captain waved them away but a few of the refugees shouted to him that they would pay for it. Nguyen could see that the captain was uneasy and he whispered to the refugees to keep quiet, that the Thais could be trouble, but they ignored him and began calling over to the fishermen. The captain shouted at the man who was on the wheel and the old boat started to turn away but even Nguyen who had little sailing experience knew that there was no way they could outrun the fishing boats if they gave chase. He stood up and as he did he saw one of the Thais produce a rifle and put it to his shoulder. Nguyen yelled a warning but he was too late, there was a loud bang and the captain took the bullet in his chest. More rifles were produced and the wheel-house was riddled with bullets, killing the two crewmen inside. The refugees began to scream as the boat drifted aimlessly. Nguyen frantically looked around for a weapon, but there was nothing at hand. One of the Thai boats drew up alongside and the fishermen used poles with hooks on the end to secure the boats together.

The refugees moved away to the opposite side like cattle shying away from a snake and the boat tilted alarmingly. Women and children were crying, the men shouting, wanting to put up a fight but not knowing how to, not when all they had were their fists and the Thais had guns and hatchets and hammers. Nguyen found himself separated from his daughters, unable to move closer to them because of the crush.

A second boat cut across their bow and half a dozen menacing Thais jumped across, stocky men toughened by years at sea, their faces and bodies darkened by the sun and scarred from fights and accidents with the nets and ropes.

They moved through the refugees, separating the men from the women and the children, killing anyone who protested or tried to stop them. One of the Thais, a swarthy, thickset man with a huge tiger tattoo across his chest, looked down into the hatch. He shouted down in bad Vietnamese that all the women and children were to come up. There were screams and sobs from down below but no one appeared so a fisherman with a rifle jumped over from the boat alongside and fired twice into the hold. There were more screams and shouting and then three women and a young girl came up. One of the women was in her sixties and the fisherman cursed her in Vietnamese and stabbed her in the stomach, twisting the knife right and left before kicking her back down into the hold.

There was an uproar among the refugees and they began to surge forward but a volley of shots rang out and four of the men fell to the deck, screaming in pain. The Thais began searching the men, taking from them their watches, jewellery and any other valuables they had before throwing them down into the hold. Those that put up a fight were killed and thrown over the side. Some of the younger women were grabbed and carried screaming on to the Thai boats where more fishermen were waiting with their arms outstretched to take them. Nguyen watched in horror as the men began tearing the clothes off the women, slapping and hitting them if they struggled too much, before throwing them down on to the deck and raping them. He saw one girl who couldn't have been more than fifteen years old held down by two men while a third climbed on top of her. Her screams chilled him, and then he heard his own daughter, Mai Phoung, screaming for him. Two Thais had her and were taking her to the bow of the boat where more fishermen waited, lust in their eyes.

'She's only thirteen!' Nguyen cried.

'The youngest fruit is the sweetest,' said one of the Thais in rough Vietnamese and slammed the butt of his rifle into Nguyen's sternum so that he collapsed to the deck, gasping for breath. Through a red haze he saw Thi Manh dash over to claw at the men in an attempt to save her sister. The men laughed and one of them grabbed her. He seized her shirt and pulled it savagely, the buttons popping off like small gunshots, revealing her small breasts and smooth skin. He was joined by two other men who used large fishing knives to cut away the rest of her clothes. She was screaming hysterically, begging Nguyen to rescue her. He staggered to his feet and pushed his way through the refugees who were still on the deck. Mai Phoung had been thrown across to the Thai boat and was being stripped and beaten by a group of three Thais who were snarling and growling like wild dogs. She too was calling for her father. Nguyen stepped forward towards the men holding Thi Manh but as he moved one of the Thai fishermen appeared in front of him holding a rifle. It was pointed at Nguyen's chest and the man was laughing, his finger tightening on the trigger. Nguyen leapt as the man fired, he felt the blast and a searing stripe of pain across the side of his head and then he was under water, choking

224

and coughing, his head a mass of pain and the taste of blood in his mouth. He surfaced, spitting out salt water and when his eyes cleared he saw the Thais setting fire to the boat and rushing back to their own vessels.

Nguyen trod water, fighting to stay conscious. He would never forget the horrified screams from the hold, and the howls from the women on the Thai boats. He never saw his daughters again. Part of him wished that he could die too, but his survival instincts took over. There were many bodies floating in the waves and Nguyen used his belt to tie two of them together. He clung to the macabre raft for more than fifteen hours before he was picked up by a British freighter on its way to Hong Kong.

He was told that he was lucky to have been spotted, but Nguyen didn't feel lucky. He felt ashamed, he felt that he'd betrayed his daughters, that he should have saved them or died trying. The guilt of that day had lived with him forevermore. He'd reacted instinctively, without thinking, and not a day went by, not an hour, when the events of the last few minutes on board the refugee boat didn't flash through his mind.

He opened his eyes and looked up through the branches above his head. His arms were shaking and his breath was coming in ragged gasps. He wanted his time over again, he wanted to be back on the boat, because he knew this time he would make the right choice, that he would die trying to save his daughters rather than leaping over the side to save his own life.

He would not fail this time.

Mary Hennessy lay with her head on Morrison's shoulder and made small circles on his chest with her index finger.

He kissed her on the top of her head and she smiled up at him.

'It's been a long time, Sean Morrison,' she said.

'It has that, Mary Hennessy,' he said lazily. He looked at his watch. Eleven o'clock.

'My time's not up, is it?' she said. She ran her hand slowly down through the hairs on his chest. 'I bet I could change your mind . . .'

Morrison laughed and reached down and intercepted her wandering hand. 'Mary, even you can't raise the dead.'

She giggled. 'Not dead, just resting,' she said, but she put her hand back on his chest. 'You're not going to throw me out, are you?'

'I'm waiting for somebody to call me,' he said.

'A girl?'

'There's no girl, Mary Hennessy.'

They lay together in silence for a while, enjoying each other's warmth.

'You shouldn't have left me, Sean,' Mary said eventually, so quietly that at first Morrison thought that she was talking in her sleep. 'There was no need for you to have gone.'

He sighed. 'There was every need.'

'Because of Liam?'

'Because of us. Because it was wrong.'

She laughed harshly. 'The way the world is and you worry about the right and wrong of what goes on between a man and a woman. You amaze me sometimes.'

'And you, Mary Hennessy, are a constant source of wonder to me.'

'I didn't even know how to get hold of you in New York.'

'That was the idea,' he said. 'Out of sight, out of mind.'

226

She shook her head. 'Absence makes the heart grow fonder.'

'You were the one who wouldn't leave her husband,' said Morrison. 'You were the one who said that an affair was fine but that it couldn't go any further.'

'I've been married for a long time, Sean. A long time.'

'I know. I know that.'

She sighed and he felt her warm breath on his chest. 'If I was free, you know that I'd be with you like a shot. If you wanted me.'

'If!' he exclaimed.

'I'm so much older than you, Sean.'

He squeezed her and stroked her hair. 'It never mattered in the past, and it doesn't matter now.'

'But it might in the future. It might.'

Morrison closed his eyes. This discussion was a repeat of thousands they'd had before. Sometimes, before he'd left New York, it seemed to him that they'd spent more time discussing the relationship than living it.

'I wish Liam was more like you,' whispered Mary.

'What do you mean?'

'Stronger. Harder.'

He laughed and she slapped his chest. 'That's not what I meant, idiot. He's changed, he's gone soft. Soft on the Cause. I used to be so proud of him, he had power and he wasn't afraid to use it. Now he'd rather talk, negotiate. He acts like an old man, trying to make his peace with the world.' Her voice was becoming increasingly bitter and she spat out the last few words like an angry cat. Morrison didn't know what to say so he lay in silence and concentrated on smoothing her hair, trying to calm her down physically rather than by talking to her.

'I've never forgiven him for Gerry, you know,' she said. Her brother had been shot and killed by a Protestant death squad three years earlier. Four men in balaclava masks had forced their way into his house and shot him in front of his wife and three children on Christmas Eve. Mary had been there delivering Christmas presents and she'd been splattered with his blood. Morrison had seen her in the City Hospital several hours later, standing with Liam in the white-tiled corridor with flecks of blood over her dress, a red smear across one cheek, her eyes puffy from crying. That's when he'd fallen in love with her, he realised now.

'He found out who did it, you know?' she said.

'Yes. I know.'

'They killed a farmer on the border a month later and got caught, stupid bastards. I begged Liam to have them killed before they got to court. He said no. They're in Long Kesh now, all four of them, and still he won't do anything. One of them is studying sociology with the Open University, Sean, can you believe that? Gerry's dead and buried and he's getting a fucking degree. And Liam says that justice has been done and that the time for revenge is past, or some such philosophical crap. He's lost his fire, and he lost it when I needed it most.'

Morrison could feel her heart pounding against his chest and he kissed her softly on the top of her head.

'That's why I'm here, you know. In London. Because he's running away from a bloody Chinaman. One man and he's hiding like a frightened child. And he wants me to hide, too.'

'What do you mean?' Morrison asked.

Mary sat up. 'Of course, you don't know. He followed

us to the farm. He blew up one of the outbuildings and the car. Jimmy's in hospital.'

'Is he OK?'

'I don't know, I left right after he blew up the car. Liam thought it would be safer if I came to London. I didn't argue because I knew it would give me the chance to see you.' She straddled him and kissed him and then rolled off the bed and skipped into the bathroom. He heard the shower kick into life.

The phone rang and Morrison jumped involuntarily. Guilt? Probably. He reached for the receiver. It was Hennessy.

He told him about the car bombing and the attempt to flush The Chinaman out of the woods and how it had ended in disaster. Morrison expressed surprise and asked who had been hurt even though he'd already been told by Mary.

As he talked, Mary came out of the bathroom wearing a towelling robe that was far too big for her. She was rubbing a towel through her hair. Morrison felt a sudden rush of guilt and he turned to one side so that he didn't have to look at her.

'We're obviously after a man who is used to fighting, some sort of terrorist maybe. Maybe he has jungle warfare experience, you know. Malaysia maybe,' said Morrison. Mary had finished drying her hair and she began to brush it slowly, watching Morrison in the dressing-table mirror.

'The area around the farm is hardly a jungle,' said Hennessy.

'It's not a jungle, I agree, but there's acres of woodland and a million and one places to hide. A man who knew what he was doing could stay put for weeks, living off the land, hiding during the day and making a nuisance of himself at night. And the more men you send in looking for him, the more damage he'll do.'

'That's pretty much what Jim Kavanagh's been telling me. He says we should go back to Belfast. He says it'll be easier to protect me there.'

'That's true, but at least you know where he is now. If you can deal with him in the countryside you should be able to keep a lid on it. In Belfast it could turn into a blood-bath.' Mary stopped brushing her hair and sat looking at Morrison.

'You have a suggestion?'

'Set a thief to catch a thief. We send in one man, a man who's an expert at tracking, and we let him get on with it. No manhunt, just sit tight and let our man winkle him out.'

'Come on, Sean. Where are we going to find such a man?'

'What about Micky Geraghty?'

'Retired,' said Hennessy.

'Well un-retire him, Liam,' said Morrison, exasperated. 'He's the perfect choice. He was a gamekeeper as a kid, his father was one of the best in Ireland.' Gamekeeping wasn't the only talent Geraghty had, but his skill as an IRA assassin wasn't the sort of thing to be discussed on an open telephone line. Morrison knew of at least three kills he'd been responsible for, two long distance with a rifle and one close up, a senior RUC officer who'd blinded a young Catholic during a particularly nasty interrogation. The boy had been a second cousin to Geraghty and he'd asked for the assignment. It had been personal, but professional. If he had truly retired, it was one hell of a loss to the Cause. 'Doesn't he work as a deer tracker or something in Scotland now?'

'He's retired,' Hennessy repeated. Mary stood up and walked over to where Morrison was sitting on the bed. He looked up at her and smiled and she shrugged off the robe so that she was standing naked in front of him. His mind whirled and he fought to keep his voice steady, certain that Hennessy would be able to sense that something was wrong.

'The sort of skills he's got you don't forget.' Morrison wasn't just referring to gamekeeping, and Hennessy knew it.

'I don't mean retired from work, Sean, I mean he retired from the Cause.'

'Nobody retires from the Cause,' said Morrison. Mary pushed Morrison back on to the bed and pulled his robe apart. He closed his eyes and almost gasped when he felt her take him in her mouth. Her soft hair brushed his groin and as she caressed him with her mouth she ran her hands up and down his chest, gently scratching him. She was making small groaning noises and he was sure Hennessy would be able to hear her.

'He was a special case,' said Hennessy. 'His wife died five years ago. Cancer. It was very, very bad. He lost heart after that. He was no more use to us.'

'So who decided he could retire?'

Hennessy didn't reply, which gave Morrison the answer. 'It was you, wasn't it, Liam?' Still Hennessy said nothing. 'If it was you, he owes you a favour. All you have to do is to make it personal. And let's face it, this is as personal as you can get.' Mary began moving her head up and down, running her tongue along the whole length of him.

231

He wanted her to stop but at the same time he didn't, and his confusion was compounded by the overwhelming guilt of it all, talking to Hennessy while his wife knelt naked in front of him.

'He might agree to help track this man down, but that's all. He wouldn't take it any further.'

'OK, but that's a start. At least let me talk to him. He might jump at the chance of helping his old friend.' A thought suddenly occurred to Morrison. A solution. 'In fact, I'll ask him to take me with him. He can find him, I'll do the rest.'

Hennessy thought about it for just a few seconds and then agreed. He told Morrison to wait while he rummaged through his desk and dug out an old address book. Morrison could feel himself about to come and reached down with his free hand to stroke Mary's hair and to gently push her away. She slid him out of her mouth and moved over him, licking her lips like a satisfied cat, her eyes flashing. He knew what she was going to do and he shook his head and tried to roll away but she pushed him down and continued to move over his body until her thighs were either side of his hips. She seemed to be revelling in his discomfort, knowing that he couldn't resist too much while he was on the phone, and knowing too that deep down he didn't want to resist, that he wanted her as much as she wanted him. She held him with one hand and positioned herself above him, rubbing him against herself, allowing him inside but only an inch or so and then easing herself away, teasing him and watching his face all the while. Hennessy came back on the line.

'He still does some deer tracking, mainly for Japanese

tourists, but he also runs a survival school for executives, based near Thurso,' he said.

'Thurso?' replied Morrison and as he spoke Mary pushed herself down so that he was completely inside her. He gasped involuntarily. She moved slowly up and down, grinding her pelvis against him, her eyes half closed, her mouth open and panting.

'It's in the far north of Scotland, about as far north as you can go before you hit the sea.' He gave Morrison the address and a telephone number. Morrison told him he had to get a pen and paper. Mary stopped moving and, with him still inside her, leant over to the bedside table and gave him a black ballpoint pen and a sheet of hotel notepaper. He asked Hennessy to repeat the details and he wrote them down, thankful that Mary had at last stopped moving. He felt as if his groin was about to explode.

'And Sean, don't push him, OK? If he doesn't want to do it, forget it.'

'OK, Liam,' said Morrison. Mary squeezed him with her internal muscles and began to ride him again, throwing her head back and gripping him tightly with her thighs.

'How did the meeting with Bromley go?' asked Hennessy.

'Fine,' answered Morrison, closing his eyes and concentrating on his breathing and trying with all his might not to come. 'But when he gets the codeword he'll call you direct. He insisted.'

'That's OK.'

'Everything ready at your end?'

'Yes. I've given out the words. All we can do now is to wait for the next bomb. See you soon, Sean.'

233

'Will do, Liam. Take care.' He threw the phone to one side and reached up to caress Mary's breasts. She took one of his hands and placed two of his fingers in her mouth, sucking and licking them as she rode him.

'You, Mary Hennessy, are a bitch. A teasing, dangerous, gorgeous bitch.' She laughed throatily and rode him all the harder.

Afterwards, she lay curled up with her back against him, her skin moist with a thin film of sweat. Morrison licked her back, enjoying the salty taste of her.

'That's nice,' she whispered.

'I wish you'd come to New York with me,' he said.

She sighed, and pushed herself back against him. 'Don't start, Sean,' she chided. 'Just enjoy the time we have together. You already have more of me than anyone else in the world.'

'Except your husband.'

'You wouldn't want to swap places with him, believe me.'

Morrison knew that they were going over old ground, replaying the same arguments they'd had before he left for the United States, but he couldn't help himself. It was like picking the scab of an old wound.

'How did Liam sound?' she asked, changing the subject.

'Worried. Very worried.'

'About The Chinaman?'

'Yeah, and the London bombings. I'm not sure which worries him the most.'

'Do you think he'll be able to find out who has been setting off the bombs?' She reached behind herself and began stroking his thighs with the back of her hand.

234

'It's the only chance we've got,' he said.

'That's what Liam says, too. But do you really think his plan will work?'

'If there is another bomb, and if the bombers give the codeword when they claim responsibility, it'll lead us straight to whoever's behind it. With a bit of luck, it'll work.'

'I hope so,' she sighed.

Her hand became more insistent but he pulled himself away from her. 'I'm going to have to go,' he said.

'Where?'

'Scotland. To talk to a man who might be able to track down The Chinaman for us. What will you do?'

'I'm to stay in London until Liam says it's safe to go back. So if you're not here I'll just have to amuse myself.'

Morrison went to the bathroom where he shaved and showered and when he came out Mary had dressed and was brushing her hair. She stood up on tiptoe and kissed him full on the mouth. 'It's good to have you back,' she said. 'Don't stay away so long next time.' She turned and picked up her trench coat and blew him a kiss before closing the door behind her.

Morrison shook his head, trying to clear her from his mind. Two years, and it seemed as if he had never been away. If anything he wanted her more now than before. He forced himself to concentrate on the job at hand. He wondered why the normally confident Hennessy was so touchy on the subject of Geraghty and if it really had been the painful death of his wife that had led to his exile in Scotland. He looked at his watch. Two o'clock. He hadn't a clue how to get to Thurso, or how long it would take, but he knew he had to speak to Geraghty in person, it would be too easy for him to decline on the phone. He rang down to reception and told them he'd be checking out and also asked if they'd find out the quickest way to get to Thurso.

'Is that in Cornwall?' the girl had asked. She said she'd phone back once she'd checked with a travel agent and Morrison began to pack his suitcase. He'd just about finished when the girl rang to say that he could go by train but that he wouldn't get there until the following day. The best way would be to fly up to Inverness and go the rest of the way by train or hire a car and drive. Morrison said he'd fly and asked her to arrange for a car to take him to the airport and have it put on the bill.

Woody was, as usual, short of cash, so he took the Tube to Clapham.

An unsmiling middle-aged Oriental woman was serving behind the counter of the Double Happiness Take-Away, and when it was Woody's turn he asked her for sweet and sour pork and chips. 'Is the owner here?' asked Woody.

'Huh?' she said, her mouth dropping open.

'The owner. Can I see the owner?'

'In kitchen,' she said.

'Yes . . . right . . . OK . . . could you ask him to come out? Tell him it's Ian Wood, from the newspaper.'

'Ian Wood. Newspaper,' she repeated. She stuck her head through the serving hatch and shouted. There was an equally raucous reply and she turned to Woody again.

'He busy,' she said.

'I know, he's cooking my food,' said Woody. 'Look, he knows me.'

236

'He say he not know you,' she said emphatically and folded her arms across her chest.

Woody waited until his order arrived and she plonked the carrier bag on the counter in front of him. He paid for it and then asked to see the owner again. She glared at him before yelling through the hatch once more. This time a bald, Oriental giant came out carrying a huge carving knife. He stood next to the woman and barked: 'I here. What you want?'

Woody looked at the couple, confused. 'I'm sorry, you're not the man I wanted to see. I wanted Mr Nguyen.' He had assumed that The Chinaman owned the restaurant because of all the cash he had, but perhaps he was an employee. 'Does Mr Nguyen work here?' Woody asked.

'No,' said the man.

'Do you know where he is?'

'No.'

Woody was taken aback. He took his notebook from his pocket and looked at the telephone number that Nguyen had given him. He picked up one of the printed menus off the counter and compared the telephone number there. They were the same. He held the notebook out to the man. 'Look, I spoke to Mr Nguyen at this number. Here.'

The man didn't look at the notebook. 'I own Double Happiness now,' he said.

'So Mr Nguyen was the previous owner?'

'He own Double Happiness before. He sell to me.'

At last Woody understood. 'But you don't know where he went?'

The man shook his head.

'He was very upset about what happened to his family,' said Woody. 'Do you know if that was why he left?'

'No.'

'No you don't know why, or no that's not why he left?'

'No,' the man repeated. 'I busy, you go now.' He made to go back to the kitchen.

'Do you have a photograph of him?' Woody asked.

The man's eyes screwed up. 'What do you mean?'

Woody drew a square in the air with his hands. 'Photograph. A picture. Click, click!' He mimed using a camera.

The man nodded enthusiastically. 'Ah! Picture!' he said.

'You have?' Woody asked eagerly.

'No,' he answered, shaking his head.

Woody saw the doorway that led off from behind the counter. 'He lived upstairs?' he asked, and pointed.

'My house now,' said the man emphatically.

'Can I look?' Woody asked.

'No.'

'I'll pay,' said Woody, reaching across to lift up the counter.

The man raised the knife and it glinted under the shop's fluorescent lighting. 'This my house now. My restaurant. My house. You go now.'

Woody held up his hands, admitting defeat. He left the shop, thought about eating the sweet and sour pork but decided against it and dropped it into a rubbish bin before walking back to the Tube.

Hennessy sat at the kitchen table with Jackie sprawled at his feet and a pile of typewritten sheets in front of him. Except for the dog he was alone. Jim Kavanagh was in the next room, while Willie O'Hara had gone upstairs for a few hours' sleep after volunteering to be on guard duty overnight.

238

The papers Hennessy was studying were the lists of the munitions supplies that had been secreted in mainland Britain. There were sixteen lists in all. Most had arrived at his office before they'd left Belfast and he'd requested that the few remaining lists be delivered to the farm. Of the sixteen, five had been raided with about thirty-five pounds of Semtex in all unaccounted for. Detonators had been taken, and some ammunition, but no guns or rifles were missing. What worried Hennessy was that there appeared to be no common thread linking the arms dumps that had been tampered with, either geographically or in terms of people who knew about them. Hennessy was starting to think that perhaps more than one person was involved, or that security among the high-ranking IRA officials wasn't as secure as it should have been. And there was the added complication that whoever was behind the bombings could have lied when compiling the list of the contents of his own caches. He slammed the table in frustration and Jackie jerked awake, ears back. To have gone to all that trouble for nothing, cursed Hennessy. Jackie got to her feet and put her head in his lap, whining for attention, and he stroked her flanks.

Kavanagh popped his head around the door. 'There's somebody coming,' he said.

Hennessy gathered the papers together and put them into one of the drawers of the Welsh dresser. 'It looks like Hugh McGrath. It's his car, anyway.'

Hennessy went with Kavanagh through the hall to the front door. Two of the guards had already stopped the blue Volvo some fifty yards or so from the house. There were four men in it, including the driver. Hennessy used his hand to shield his eyes from the afternoon sun and recognised the grey, slicked-back hair and angular features of Hugh McGrath, wearing the tinted glasses that gave him what Mary always mockingly referred to as his Clint Eastwood look. McGrath owned a farm to the south-west, several hundred acres but little in the way of crops or livestock. Instead he earned a small fortune taking advantage of the price differentials between the North and South. That's how McGrath would have explained it. Hennessy called it by its true name – smuggling.

Price anomalies between the two parts of the divided Ireland meant that McGrath could always make a turn somewhere, be it on wheat, pigs, milk or petrol, or by smuggling things like contraceptives to the south or antibiotics to the north.

Hennessy had always been unhappy at McGrath's smuggling operations but he was a powerful man within the organisation and had many supporters. His role as liaison officer with the Libyans was also vital to the IRA, and he was one of the few men from the organisation who had actually met with Gaddafi. McGrath knew his value and capitalised on it.

The Volvo pulled up in front of the farmhouse and McGrath unwound his angular frame from the back seat. He was a good head taller than Hennessy, even with his slight stoop. He held out his hand and his grip was strong and confident.

'Liam,' he said. 'How are you this fine afternoon?'

'Fine,' said Hennessy. 'Come on in.' McGrath's driver and his two bodyguards stayed in the car as Hennessy led him into the lounge. Hennessy waved him towards the floral-patterned sofa in front of the unlit fireplace.

'Drink?' he asked, and McGrath asked for a whiskey.

Hennessy half filled two crystal tumblers before settling down into a leather wing-tipped chair opposite the sofa. Jackie butted the door open with her head and lay down at Hennessy's feet after first sniffing at McGrath's legs and accepting a pat on the back.

'How goes it?' asked McGrath.

'It's going OK.'

'You checked out my arms dumps?' McGrath had been responsible for three arms caches, all close to London, and according to the reports Hennessy had received one of them was missing two packages of Semtex.

Hennessy nodded and told McGrath what his searchers had found. Or rather, what they hadn't found.

'I can't believe that one of mine has been touched. Do you have any idea yet who's behind this, Liam?'

'Not yet, no.'

'It makes a mockery of our security, right enough. I know we don't see eye to eye on the question of main-land bombing campaigns, but this looting of our supplies is something else. We have to know who we can trust, Liam. Our organisation depends on it.'

Trust and fear, thought Hennessy. In equal amounts usually, though in McGrath's case it was mainly fear. He came from a long line of Catholic landowners. His father was one of the driving forces behind the removal of many Protestant farmers from the border country. His method had been simple and brutal. He had targeted all the farms in the area where there was only one son and he had had them systematically murdered. When the parents became too old to work the farm and they were put up for sale, he made sure that there were no Protestant offers. Those farms where there were several children waiting to claim their inheritance were forced out of business by arson and poisoning campaigns and they, too, were sold to Catholic buyers. McGrath's own farm had once belonged to a Protestant family until their only son was shot through the back of the head as he sat on a tractor eating his lunch one day. The farm was put up for auction a year later and the sealed bid from McGrath's father was the highest, just as he knew it would be. Ironically, McGrath was an only son himself, with three sisters as siblings, but in his case it had been an advantage – not a death sentence.

'I gather you're having a wee spot of bother,' said McGrath, stretching out his long legs.

'It's nothing I can't handle,' said Hennessy.

'An explosion in your office, your farm and car bombed, Mary whisked off to London, and now Jim Kavanagh is trawling around the farms looking for men to guard you at night. I don't doubt that you can handle it, whatever it is, but I thought I might be able to help.'

'I'm working on it,' said Hennessy. He was worried about showing weakness in front of McGrath. He was one of the most political, and ruthless, men in the organisation, and always called in his debts. Accepting favours from Hugh McGrath was like doing a deal with the devil himself.

'Do you want to tell me about it?' McGrath asked.

Hennessy knew there was nothing to gain by not telling McGrath, because the man's intelligence network was second to none. He'd find out everything anyway. Hennessy explained about Nguyen and how his questions had turned into threats and how his threats had become reality. McGrath listened, occasionally grunting.

'Would it help if I seconded a few of my men?' McGrath asked once Hennessy had finished.

Hennessy shook his head. 'No thanks, Hugh. Jim Kavanagh is getting a few of the local lads in. And I'm hoping to bring Micky Geraghty over. He should be able to track the bastard down, sure enough.'

'Geraghty? Will he come back?'

'I hope so. I reckon he'll stand more chance than a group of townies trampling over the fields.'

'I hope it works out. But let me know if you need help, OK?'

'I will, Hugh. I will.'

McGrath drank his whiskey. It seemed to Hennessy that he had something on his mind.

'Is there something else, Hugh?'

'I don't know, Liam. It's this whole business of bombing on the mainland. Maybe we're going about this the wrong way. Maybe now is the time we should be applying pressure, not pulling back. Now is just the time to show our strength. To show that we're serious. And to give the British public a taste of their own medicine.'

Hennessy raised his eyebrows. 'What do you mean?'

'Let them have roadblocks on their roads, armed troops in their towns, body searches before they go into shops. Let them feel what life is like under an oppressive regime.'

'I don't doubt that the bombs on the mainland will result in an over-reaction from the Government, and I know that'll probably result in a backlash of public opinion, but what about the damage the bombs are doing to our image? They're killing civilians, Hugh. With no warnings. They're not legitimate targets. You know as well as I do what we say in the *Green Book* that we give to volunteers. The only civilian targets that are legitimate are the Establishment, those who have a vested interest in maintaining the present status quo in Ireland: politicians, media, judiciary, business elements and the British war machine. That's virtually a direct quote.'

McGrath shook his head. 'There are no soft targets, no hard targets. Just targets. The Brits elected their Government, so they're responsible for it. They are all legitimate targets, every bit as legitimate as those in Ulster.'

'And no warnings?'

'That's what makes them so effective. You should be embracing these bombers, Liam. You should be grateful to them, for the way they're raising the profile of the Cause around the world.'

Liam looked incredulous. 'By killing civilians?' he said. 'What do you think that does for our reputation?'

McGrath held up his hand as if to calm an impatient child. 'It doesn't matter. It never has. That's the big mistake everyone makes, Liam, they assume that when we kill what you call a soft target everyone turns against us. It doesn't happen. We kill a couple of tourists by mistake, we blow up a child, we shoot an old woman, it has no effect. It doesn't affect the votes we get at election time, it doesn't make a blind bit of difference to the amount of money we raise. In fact, you know as well as I do that a big bomb on the mainland, aimed at civilians or the army, often results in more money flooding in from the States, not less. It proves to them that we're serious, that we're prepared to fight for what we believe in.'

McGrath shook his head, almost sadly. 'Liam, I can't believe we're having this conversation, I really can't. It used to be you who had the drive, the energy. It was you who put the fire into the boys. Have you forgotten? Aldershot 1972? The M62 bombing in 1974? The Guildford pub bombings the same year? The Hilton bomb in 1975? You were with us then, Liam, you were the one who was calling for an escalation of the campaign, right enough.'

'That was then, things have changed,' said Hennessy. 'There's a time for violence and there's a time for negotiation.' He sounded tired.

'The Regent's Park bandstand bomb in 1982? The Brighton bombing in 1984? Have you forgotten that you were involved, that you pushed for them? What was it you said then, when Thatcher escaped? They were lucky. They'll always have to be lucky, but we only have to be lucky once. Christ, Liam, you knew what you were talking about then. And it holds true now.'

Hennessy said nothing and McGrath continued. 'Look what the ANC achieved in South Africa, through violence, look at Israel, founded on bloodshed.'

Hennessy stood up and went over to the window. McGrath's bodyguards and driver were sitting patiently in the Volvo. One of them looked up when he saw the movement at the window.

'You've not forgotten what we're fighting for, have you, Liam?' said McGrath quietly.

Hennessy whirled round and jabbed his finger at McGrath. 'That's not bloody fair!' he shouted. 'I won't have you questioning my loyalty. Not now, not ever. There's no one who's done more for the Cause than me and my family. It's not three years ago that I buried my own brother-in-law, and before that my father and two cousins. My family has shed more than its fair share of blood.' He stepped towards McGrath as if about to attack him. 'And, I might add, my family hasn't been profiting from the border. We've given our lives in the struggle for a united Ireland, not set out to make fucking money from it. So don't you ever, ever, ask me if I've forgotten what we're fighting for!' He loomed over McGrath, his cheeks red and spittle spraying from his mouth. His fists were bunched and his shoulders quivered with tension.

McGrath looked stunned. He opened his mouth to speak but then seemed to think better of it.

'God damn you, McGrath!' shouted Hennessy. 'Get out of my fucking house. Now!' He stood glaring at the man sitting in front of him and then turned and stormed out of the room. He waited in the kitchen until he heard McGrath leave the house and the Volvo start up and drive down the track. Hennessy stood over the sink, gripping the edge of the draining board with his shaking hands. He felt the acidic taste of vomit in the back of his throat and he retched several times but nothing came up from his stomach. He poured himself a glass of water and was drinking it when Kavanagh came into the kitchen.

'Are ye all right?' he asked Hennessy.

'A wee exchange of words with Mr McGrath,' said Hennessy. 'I lost my temper with him.' Hennessy tried to get his thinking straight. What had upset him so much? Part of it was McGrath's total unwillingness to even consider his point of view, and his almost inhuman eagerness to see innocent bystanders murdered. There was also the bitter memory of the friends and relatives who'd died, deaths that Hennessy had never really gotten over, like Mary's brother, Gerry. That was another reason for the burning anger coursing through his system, Hennessy realised. Mary.

'Jim, did anyone speak to McGrath on the way in?'

'Just one of the men on guard. He recognised him straightaway and let him through.'

'No one else? Did you say anything to him?'

Kavanagh looked mystified. 'I didn't, Liam. I'll ask the others. What's wrong? What d'ye think might've been said?'

Hennessy took another mouthful of water and swilled it round his gums before spitting it into the sink. The sour taste was still there, washing wouldn't get rid of it.

'He knew Mary was in London,' he said quietly. 'I want to know how he knew.'

Even with the address Hennessy had given him, Morrison had a hell of a time finding Geraghty's house. The village it was supposed to be near was just a sprinkling of stone cottages in a valley sheltered from the biting winds of the North Sea and none of the roads seemed to have names. Geraghty was supposed to be living at Garryowen Farm but there was nothing even remotely like that on the map Morrison had bought in Inverness. It was dark and there were spots of rain flecking the windshield. Morrison decided to try the local pub, a weathered stone building with leaded windows that glowed yellow like the eyes of a wild animal. He parked his hired Rover next to a collection of mud-spattered farmer's vehicles and didn't bother locking his door. Above him the pub's sign – a fox with a dead chicken in its jaws – creaked in the wind. He pushed open the gnarled oak door and more of the yellow light oozed out, bringing with it the hubbub of pub conversation, predominantly gruff, masculine voices discussing sheep prices and football. It all stopped when he stepped over the threshold. It was, Morrison realised, like the scene

247

in a vampire film when the stranger asks for directions to Dracula's castle. At a table near a shoulder-high hearth four old men in tweeds had been playing cards, but they had all stopped and were looking at him, wondering who he was. Under the table lay a black and white sheepdog, its ears up as it sniffed in his direction. A line of four younger men standing at the bar with pints of beer in front of them turned as one to look at him and even the barmaid, blonde haired and rosy cheeked, checked him over as she pulled a pint.

Morrison smiled at no one in particular and closed the door behind him. There was a thick mat just inside the door and Morrison carefully wiped his feet on it.

The card game began again and the dog settled its head down on to its paws with a sigh. Morrison walked over to the bar and put down the map.

'Good evening,' said the barmaid. She finished pulling the pint and handed it to an old man wearing a grubby tartan cap. 'Here you are, Archie,' she said.

The pub was similar to those in farming communities all over Scotland and Ireland, the sort of pub where everyone knows everyone else and strangers are regarded with suspicion bordering on hostility. It was one large room, a handful of wooden tables worn smooth with age ranged against the outer wall and a bench seat either side of the fireplace which was unlit but contained a couple of roughly hewn logs on a blackened metal grate. The bar ran parallel to the wall, the full length of the room, and behind it was a door that obviously led to the landlord's private quarters. The walls of the room had once been painted white but had been stained a deep yellow by years of cigarette and pipe smoke and fumes from the fire. The floor was stone-flagged with a large, rectangular carpet of some long-faded red and blue pattern under the tables. On the gantry behind the bar was an impressive collection of malt whiskies, many bearing simple black labels with white lettering identifying the distillery that had produced them.

'What can I be getting you?' the barmaid asked, and Morrison indicated one of the Islay malts.

He savoured the bouquet of the deep-amber liquid before sipping it.

'Good?' asked the barmaid. She began drying glasses with a white cloth.

'Magic,' he said. 'Could you help me? I'm trying to find Micky Geraghty's house. Do you have any idea where it is?'

'To be sure,' she said. She put down the cloth and reached for the map. She looked at it carefully, frowned, and then giggled. 'I can't make head nor tail of this,' she said. She held it out to one of the men standing at the bar. 'Here Scott, can you show me Micky Geraghty's house?'

The man took the map, studied it and nodded. He put it down on the bar and pointed. Morrison looked over as the man ran his finger along a thin black line.

'Follow the road outside for about half a mile until you get to this crossroad here. Go left and then left again where the road forks, here. About two hundred yards later there's a single track to the right, you'll see a white post each side of the entrance. Micky's about half a mile down the track.'

'It's no wonder I couldn't find it,' said Morrison, taking another pull of the whisky. He offered to buy the man a drink and quickly extended it into a general offer for his three companions.

'You know Micky?' Morrison asked the man who'd given him directions.

'Sure, he's usually in here a couple of times a week. And every now and then his escapees will find their way here.'

'Escapees?'

The man laughed. 'He runs one of them Outward Bound places but for middle-aged executives. Teaches them survival stuff, rock-climbing, sailing, things like that. Sometimes he makes them spend a couple of nights on one of the islands, or dumps them miles away with just a compass and a pack of Kendal mint cake. The lucky ones manage to stagger in here to beg Tess for a drink.'

The barmaid giggled. 'They don't have any money, but we always give them credit. And they always come back and settle up. They're so grateful, bless 'em.'

Morrison finished his whisky and said his goodbyes. He followed the man's instructions and ten minutes later he was outside a two-storey grey stone building with a steeply sloping slate roof. There were four cars parked outside the house and Morrison drove slowly past them. The track curved around the house, leading to a large, stone barn which had been converted into flats, and a short row of cottages. There were more cars parked there, all new models, so Morrison reckoned that Geraghty had a group of executives under his wing.

He found a parking space next to a white BMW and walked back to the front door of the house and pressed the bell.

The door was opened by a chestnut-haired girl in tight

jeans and a green and white checked shirt. She looked at him with clear blue eyes and raised eyebrows.

'Is Mr Geraghty at home?' Morrison asked.

'Yep, come in,' she said, and moved to let him into the hall. She closed the door and led him down a wood-panelled corridor. 'My dad's in the study,' she said over her shoulder. 'Who shall I say is here?' Her accent was north Belfast, as far as Morrison could tell, but soft and with a gentle lilt.

'Morrison. Sean Morrison.'

'From Belfast?' she asked.

'That's right.' He wondered how come she was so willing to let a stranger into her house, especially a stranger from over the water. Surely she must know of her father's past and that he'd always be at risk from Protestant extremists? They reached a door and she pushed it open. A grey-haired man with a weather-beaten face was sitting behind a desk talking into a phone. The girl showed Morrison in.

'I'll leave you here,' she said. She left the door open and went back down the corridor. Somewhere in the distance he could hear a television set.

Geraghty waved at Morrison with his free hand, indicating a leather chair to the side of the desk, and Morrison sat in it.

'I'm booked pretty much solid now until the end of August,' Geraghty said into the phone. He listened, frowned, and looked at a large book on the desk in front of him. 'What, the twenty-eighth? Yes, we could do that. Until the eleventh? OK, I'll pencil your group in for that. Can you drop me a letter confirming it? Yes, yes, I'll look forward to it. Take care.' He replaced the receiver.

251

'You'll be Sean Morrison?' he said, taking Morrison by surprise. Geraghty laughed at his discomfort. 'Liam was on the phone to me earlier, said he didn't want me worrying overmuch when a stranger arrived on my doorstep. More likely didn't want me taking your head off with a twelve-bore. Good to see you, anyway, Sean. There's a bottle by the table next to you, pour yourself a drink, and one for me, too.'

Morrison poured two measures of Irish whiskey. 'I'm surprised we never met in Belfast,' he said as he poured.

'I was what you might describe as low profile,' laughed Geraghty. 'I was always kept pretty much in the background.'

'I know of the work you did, of course. You were one of my heroes.'

'I'm sure you don't know half of it,' said Geraghty, raising his glass. 'But thanks anyway.'

They drank. The study was very much a man's room. Floor-to-ceiling bookshelves lined one wall, every inch filled with a mixture of paperback novels, leather-bound classics and wildlife reference books. The other three walls were wood panelled, much the same as the hall outside, with several framed prints of hunting dogs. The furniture was sturdy, well-worn leather and wood that had long since lost its shine, comfortable chairs, a spacious desk with a brass reading lamp and three small circular tables. It was a room in which Morrison felt secure. To the right of the desk was a small window over-looking the line of cottages. A light winked out and Morrison could imagine an exhausted executive collapsing on to his bed.

If the study inspired a feeling of security, the man

himself suggested a quiet confidence, that Micky Geraghty was a man who kept his word, a good guy to have at your back in a fight. He looked to be in his early fifties, broad shoulders and strong hands. His hair was grey but it was thick and healthy and his skin was wrinkled from exposure to the elements rather than age. His blue eyes were set aside a nose that had been broken several times. It was a strong, good-looking face, one that Morrison was sure would go down well with Japanese tourists wanting a set of antlers to take back home.

'Did Liam tell you why I was coming to see you?' Morrison asked, and Geraghty nodded.

Morrison continued: 'The idea is for you to go in with me. You find him, I'll do the rest.' From the look of it Hennessy's reservations were groundless, Geraghty appeared to be enthusiastic about the idea. Morrison relaxed, settling back in the chair and sipping his whiskey.

Geraghty laughed, his eyes sparkling. 'I'd love to help, Sean, God knows I owe Liam a favour or two, but you're going to have to count me out.'

Morrison frowned. 'I don't understand, what's the problem?'

Geraghty leant back in his chair and swung his left leg up on to the desk. It was covered in greying plaster from his toes to just above his knee. He slapped the cast and pulled a face. 'This is my problem,' he said ruefully. 'I broke it two weeks ago. The Doc says it'll be a couple of months yet before the cast can come off. Until then . . .' He shrugged.

Morrison's heart fell. For a wild moment he thought that perhaps Geraghty was making it up, that the cast was fake and he was just using it as an excuse to back out, but his disappointment seemed genuine, and so did the cast. It had been autographed in several places and the plaster was crumbling a little around his toes.

'How did it happen?' he asked.

'Teaching a group of sales reps to climb. I went up a rock-face to knock in a bit of protection and the guy who was paying out the rope lost concentration. I slipped and he let me fall about thirty feet further than he should have done. Problem was, I was only twenty-five feet above the ground. He was very upset about it.'

'I bet,' said Morrison. 'Who's running things while you're out of action?'

'The admin and the lectures I can handle myself, and I've a couple of instructors working with me. And my daughter, Kerry, the girl who let you in, knows as much as I do.'

Geraghty saw the look on Morrison's face and he smiled. 'I hope that wasn't a chauvinistic comment I saw forming on your lips,' he said. 'Kerry knows as much about tracking as I do, and she's been teaching survival courses with me for five years or more. And if the truth be known, she's a darn sight fitter than I am, even without the cast.'

'Why, Dad, you've never said that to my face,' said a voice from behind Morrison, and he turned to see the girl, standing in the doorway with her hands on her hips and her eyebrows arched.

'How long have you been there, girl?' asked Geraghty. He didn't appear annoyed and Morrison knew that from where he was sitting he could see the length of the corridor leading away from the study so there was no way she could have crept up on them without him seeing her. In fact, the chances were that Geraghty had paid her the compliment knowing that she was within earshot. Morrison wondered how much she knew about Geraghty's past.

'I just came to see if you and Mr Morrison wanted a cup of tea, or something. God forbid I should eavesdrop.' She shook her hair back from her face and swept it behind her ears. She had her father's eyes, and the same confident way of holding her head with the chin slightly raised. Her skin was healthy and bronzed and she was wearing hardly any make-up, just a touch of blue eye-shadow and mascara. Morrison put her age at about twenty-five. Geraghty was right, she looked fit. She caught him looking at her and she grinned at him. He looked away.

Geraghty held up his whiskey glass. 'We're doing just fine,' he said.

'And I,' said Morrison, getting to his feet and putting his glass on the table, 'must be going.'

'I'll show you out,' said Kerry. Morrison shook hands with Geraghty, who wished him well, and then followed Kerry back down the hall. She wasn't wearing shoes and her bare feet brushed against the carpet. 'Uncle Liam wanted my dad to do something for him, is that right?' she asked.

'Something like that,' said Morrison.

She turned to look at him, stopping so suddenly that he almost bumped into her. Her clear blue eyes bored into his. 'What did you want him to do?' she asked. 'It must have been important for you to have come all this way. Important for the Cause.'

Morrison looked at her, unsure how to react. She had

255

called Hennessy 'Uncle' and she was undoubtedly her father's daughter, but he didn't know her well enough to discuss IRA business with her. 'We needed his help, but his leg puts paid to that,' he said.

Her eyes sparkled and she reached forward, touching his arm. 'Don't go yet,' she whispered. 'Come with me.' She took him past the front door and into a comfortably furnished lounge. The television was on but the room was empty. She nodded towards an overstuffed sofa. 'Wait there for a while,' she said. 'Let me talk to my dad. OK?'

'OK,' Morrison replied, bemused. He sat down and crossed his legs and wondered what the hell she was up to.

Kerry walked back to the study where her father still had his leg on the desk. He had a knitting needle in one hand and was wiggling it down inside the cast trying to get at an itchy place. He grinned at her apologetically. She was forever warning him that scratching would only make it worse.

She leant against the door jamb and folded her arms across her chest.

'Uncle Liam needs our help, yes?' Liam Hennessy wasn't a blood relative, but he was just as close. He was her godfather and when they'd lived in Ireland barely a month went by when she didn't see him. He'd taught her to ride on his farm, had given her the run of his rambling library and spent hours just talking with her when her mother was in hospital and dying bit by bit. Kerry loved Liam Hennessy fiercely and would do anything to protect him.

'He needs my help,' said Geraghty.

'It's been five years since we were in Ireland, so I guess

it's something they think only you can do, something that you can't do with a broken leg? Something to do with tracking, is that it?'

Geraghty sighed. 'Why don't you just ask me what it is they want, Kerry? It would save us both a lot of time.'

'You'll tell me?' she said, surprised.

'Try me,' he answered.

'What is it Uncle Liam wants?'

To her surprise her father explained about The Chinaman and how Hennessy was stuck in his farm. 'He wanted me to go with Morrison, to go into the country-side and flush him out.'

'And then what?'

Geraghty fixed his daughter with his eyes, suddenly cold and harder than she'd seen them for a long time. 'If he's lucky, Liam will hand him over to the police. If he's unlucky, well, you know that some of Liam's friends can play pretty rough, Kerry. It could get nasty.'

'But the man's trying to kill Uncle Liam, that's what you said. So he's only got himself to blame.'

'Whatever. But it's all immaterial anyway, Kerry. I can't do it, they'll just have to find someone else.'

She leapt to her feet and leant over the desk, her hair swinging from side to side.

'No!' said Geraghty before she could speak.

'But I'm perfect for it,' she said, exasperated. 'You've taught me everything there is to know about tracking, and yet you never let me prove how good I am. You never let me take the hunting parties out on my own.'

'You know why that is. The Germans and the Japs pay top whack to be taken out by a traditional Highland gamekeeper, tweeds and flat cap and all. It's part of the enjoyment for them, it'd spoil it if their tracker was a pretty girl young enough to be their daughter.'

Kerry ignored the compliment, realising she'd been sidetracked into an old argument.

'I know about tracking, and I know the area around Uncle Liam's farm, probably better than you do. I've ridden and walked over every inch, I know every hiding place.'

'It's several hundred acres, my girl, I doubt if you know every inch.'

'It's three hundred and twenty-four acres, Dad, and I know it like the back of my hand.'

'It'll be dangerous,' he warned, and she knew then that she'd won the argument about whether or not she had the ability.

'Dad, which of us is the best shot?'

'I can't fault your marksmanship Kerry, but I'm not having you trekking around the Irish countryside with a hunting rifle. It's practically a war zone.'

'All right then, I won't take my gun. But it's Uncle Liam this man is after, not me,' she pressed. 'He'll be focused on him, not me.' She waved her hand at the books lining the wall to her left. 'I've read every book on trapping and tracking on those shelves, and I read most of them before I even went to school.'

It was true, Geraghty acknowledged. Even as a child she'd had a fascination for the books, and she'd taught herself to make snares and simple traps and learnt to recognise spoors and tracks from the diagrams they contained. There were other books, too, manuals on warfare and booby traps and explosives, some that he'd bought out of curiosity and others that he'd acquired in connection with his work for the IRA, and she'd read them just as avidly. But unlike Geraghty, almost all her knowledge of booby traps was theoretical and not practical.

Kerry could see that her father was wavering so she decided to raise the stakes.

'It's not just a question of helping Uncle Liam,' she said. 'I want to do something to help the Cause. I didn't stop you when you said you wanted to leave Ireland after Mum died, but you know that deep down I wanted to stay in Belfast and help in any way I could. I feel as strongly as you do about getting the British out of Ireland. You know that.' Geraghty could feel the intensity of her conviction burning across the desk, and he remembered how, years before, he had felt the same desire to see a united Ireland. 'Let me do this, for the Cause if not for Uncle Liam. This is something I can do, something that's a hell of a lot more constructive than throwing petrol bombs at troops or harassing the RUC.'

Geraghty closed his eyes and rubbed them with the backs of his hands. He sighed deeply and Kerry knew that she'd almost won. One more push and he'd agree. It was time to play her trump card. She sat back down in the chair, pulled it closer to the desk, and leant her elbows on it so that her head was on a level with her father's. 'And,' she said thoughtfully, 'it would get me away from here for a while.' She paused, for emphasis. 'From him,' she added, just in case he didn't get the message.

'You're not still seeing him, are you?' Geraghty asked.

'I'm trying not to,' she answered. For almost a year she'd been having an on-off affair with a British Telecom engineer who lived nearby. He was married but couldn't make his mind up whether to leave his wife or stop seeing Kerry. He'd sworn that he hadn't touched his wife in years, but midway through the affair he'd confessed that she was pregnant and that he couldn't abandon her. 'I suppose it'll be a fucking virgin birth,' she'd screamed, and thrown an ashtray at his head, but the following week she'd phoned him and their lovemaking had been better than ever.

Geraghty had made his disapproval plain, but had also refused to interfere, knowing that his daughter was old enough to make her own mistakes. He figured that she'd realise what a hopeless situation she'd gotten herself into and that she'd come to her senses. He was right. It had been almost two months since she had seen him, though she was still at the stage where she had to keep fighting the urge to call him and jumped whenever the phone rang. She knew that if she saw him again she'd end up in bed with him. Geraghty sensed the pressure she was under and thought that perhaps she was right, a spell in Ireland might be just what she needed to get the man out of her system once and for all.

'If you go, you're going to have to be careful,' he said.

'I will be,' she said earnestly.

'I mean very careful,' he said. 'It's not a game there, you know. It's not too far from the border. It's a war zone. You don't carry a gun, under any circumstances. You track him, and that's all. You don't take any risks, understand?'

She nodded furiously. 'I promise. Can I go?'

Geraghty smiled, but it was an uncertain smile. 'Yes,' he said. 'You can go.'

She whooped, and grinned, and reached over the desk to hug him and kiss him on the cheek.

'Go and get Morrison for me,' he told her. 'I want a word with him.'

Geraghty watched her rush down the corridor. He wasn't surprised at her keenness to return to Ireland, or to help the Provos. She'd put up a hell of a fight when he'd first decided to leave Ireland, and she'd come close to staying behind. Kerry had a stubborn streak, and he guessed that she'd got it from him. She had a hard side, too, a tendency to viciousness which went beyond simple devotion to the Cause. There had been times in Belfast when he'd felt she was actually enjoying taking on the army and the RUC, that she was getting some sort of kick out of the Troubles. Despite his apparent change of heart he was still reluctant to allow her to go back to Belfast and its violent influences, but he owed Liam Hennessy. He owed him a great deal. Besides, he knew that if she really set her mind on going back, he wouldn't be able to stop her. He knew his daughter, and he knew that she wasn't above telephoning Hennessy herself and offering her services. And if things were as bad as they sounded, he doubted if Hennessy would turn her down. And if Hennessy asked him if it was OK for Kerry to go back, could he refuse? Could he refuse any request of the man who held his life in his hands? No, he could not. And she knew that, his darling daughter. She knew that full well.

Kerry found Morrison still watching television. 'Dad wants to talk to you,' she said. 'He says I can come with you.'

'You?' said Morrison, surprised.

'To help you track down the man who's trying to hurt Uncle Liam.'

A bemused Morrison followed her back down the corridor and into Geraghty's study.

'Leave us alone, Kerry, and shut the door this time,' Geraghty told her. He waited until she'd gone before speaking. 'She wants to help you, Sean,' he said.

'Can she do it?' asked Morrison.

'Oh yes, she's a first-class tracker, I've taught her everything I know. She often comes with me out on to the moors after deer. She's a good shot, too. That's what I want to talk to you about. I don't want her carrying a gun out there. Under any circumstances. I don't want her put in any danger.'

'I'll take care of her. I promise.'

'There's something else.' Geraghty scratched his chin and scrutinised Morrison. 'I'm not sure how to put this, Sean. Kerry can be a bit, er, overenthusiastic sometimes. Do you know what I mean?'

Morrison shook his head, mystified.

'She's always idolised Liam, and me, and ever since she was a kid she was on the fringes of the Organisation, running errands, taking messages, the sort of stuff we all went through, you know? Throwing stones at the troops, giving the RUC a hard time. But I never wanted her to get drawn into the real rough stuff, the sort of things I was involved in. I mean, she has a pretty good idea of what I did, and I think she wishes she could be more like me.'

Morrison laughed. 'Jesus, Micky, it's hardly a secret, is it? There's barely a pub in Derry where they don't sing songs about you on a Saturday night when the beer's flowing.'

'Aye, Sean, that's right enough. And I'm not ashamed

of what I did, far from it. We're at war with the fucking British and I'd do it all over again, the killing and everything. But my family has given enough. I don't want Kerry to get any more involved. I didn't then and I don't now. I promised my wife, God rest her soul, I promised her before she died that I'd take Kerry away from Belfast before she got in too deep. I don't want her to go back.'

'You're going to stop her?' said Morrison, frowning.

'No. No, I can't stop her. But you must make sure she realises that this is a one-off. Don't romanticise it for her, don't pull her back. Just use her this one time, then send her back to me.'

'I understand,' said Morrison.

'Then good luck, and God bless. And take care of her. She's all the family I've got left.' He swung his plaster cast off the desk and it thudded on to the floor. 'It's late. You should stay here tonight and make an early start tomorrow. I'll get Kerry to cook us a meal. You might want to telephone Liam and let him know what's happening, if Kerry hasn't done so already.' He reached for a set of metal crutches leaning against the wall and used them to clump out of the room.

Maggie linked her arm through Woody's as they stepped out of the cinema.

'Good film,' she said. 'Bit violent, but fun.'

'Yeah, I've always liked a bit of mindless violence,' laughed Woody. 'You hungry?'

'Mmmm. Sure.'

'Italian?'

'Italian would be great.'

Woody suggested a place in Covent Garden and they

walked together out of Leicester Square and down Long Acre. Maggie asked him how he was getting on at work and he told her about the stories he was working on. She was always interested in what he was doing at the paper and seemed to hang on every word. He told her about the phone call from Pat Quigley and the mysterious Chinaman. She raised her eyebrows when she heard about the money in the carrier bag.

'What do you think's going on?' she asked.

Woody shrugged. 'I was thinking that maybe this Chinaman had paid someone to go after Liam Hennessy, some sort of hit-man.'

'Wow!' she said.

'Yeah, wow is right. It'd be one hell of a story, if only I can nail it down.'

They stood at the roadside and waited for a gap in the traffic before crossing.

'So what's the problem?' she asked.

'He's gone. Vanished. I went round to where he lives and he'd moved. No forwarding address. I don't even have his full name.'

'You don't think that perhaps he's gone to Ireland himself?'

'Seems unlikely, doesn't it? I mean, a Chinaman in Belfast on the trail of an IRA leader. It's a bit unbeliev-able, even for our paper.'

'I suppose so.'

They walked in silence through the evening crowds, and then stopped to watch a man in a clown's suit juggling five flaming torches.

'Do you get to write much about the IRA?' she asked.

'Depends,' said Woody. 'I covered the Knightsbridge

bombing, remember? The night I met you. Depends when it happens, you know.'

'The *Sunday World* usually takes the Government line, doesn't it?' she said.

Woody nodded. 'Slightly to the right of Attila the Hun, we are.'

'What about you? What do you think?'

'Hell, Maggie, I don't know. I'm a reporter, not a politician.' The juggler put down three of his torches to scattered applause and then began fire-eating. 'I guess I take the view that we should just pull the troops out and let the Irish sort it out themselves. You know the troops went to Northern Ireland in the first place to look after the Catholics. To protect them from the Protestants. And now it's the IRA who want them out. It doesn't make sense. It isn't something the British Government can sort out, that much I'm sure. It's an Irish problem. What about you?'

'I suppose you're right. At the end of the day what-ever the MPs in Westminster say isn't going to make the slightest difference. Maybe your paper should say that.'

Woody laughed. 'I don't think many MPs would take any notice of what appears in the *Sunday World*. *The Times* maybe, or the *Telegraph*.' Something tingled at the back of Woody's mind. Something to do with an MP. He watched the clown blow flaming liquid up into the night sky, a glistening bluish stream which flared into orange and yellow. Of course, thought Woody. S. J. Brownlow, the name in the notebook. Sir John Brownlow. The Chinaman's MP. He'd said he'd written to his Member of Parliament and been to see him. With any luck he'd have The Chinaman's letter on file.

'What are you smiling at?' Maggie asked.

'Nothing,' he said. 'Come on, let's go eat. I'm starving.'

As the darkness crept through the forest, Nguyen opened one of the containers of chicken and ate it slowly, along with a container of boiled rice. When he'd finished he scraped leaves away from the forest floor and buried the remains in the soil. He drank from one of his canteens and put it in the rucksack alongside the components of his firebomb detonator and the stolen gun. The can of petrol was too bulky to fit into the rucksack so he was forced to carry it. He waited until the sun had gone down before moving through the forest. The can slowed him, not because it was heavy but because it was awkward and forever catching in the undergrowth, but once he left the trees and was out in open fields he picked up speed.

He varied his route slightly this time, cutting through different fields and crossing the B8 further north than he'd crossed the previous night. Once he almost stumbled into an army patrol, half a dozen teenage soldiers walking along a narrow country lane, their faces blackened and their rubber-soled boots making almost no noise. They were strung out over fifty feet, walking in two lines. Nguyen was heading in the opposite direction, on the other side of a hedgerow looking for a gap so that he could cut across the track, when he heard one of the men sniff. Nguyen froze and as he did the petrol slapped against the side of the can. The field he was in had recently been ploughed and offered little in the way of cover but there was nowhere else for him to go so he dropped and rolled into a deep furrow and flattened himself down. He was invisible. He heard them go by, and heard the man sniff again. He stayed where he was for a full thirty minutes just in case they retraced their steps.

It was after midnight when he eventually reached the hill overlooking Hennessy's farm. He lay down close to the summit, careful that he didn't break the skyline, and studied the farm buildings through his binoculars for more than an hour until he was satisfied that he had spotted all the guards. The starlight wasn't strong enough to illuminate their faces but he could see that they were carrying shotguns. There was one in front of the cottage, another close by in the gap between the barns and the stables and three standing guard close to the farmhouse. One of them was smoking a cigarette, he could see the small red dot hovering in the air. He sniffed but could smell nothing. There had been times, Nguyen remembered, when he could smell a campfire two days' march away in the jungle, or smell the toothpaste or chewing gum or tobacco of an American who had passed by three hours before, but he was younger then and his senses were more acute.

During the hour he watched, the men walked up and down, occasionally talking to each other, but they did not bother patrolling the perimeter of the farm. Static sentries, thought Nguyen. The easiest to deal with.

He moved slowly down the hill and then crawled across the fields towards the barns, giving a wide berth to the stables and the cottage. He lay in the grass about a hundred yards from the barns and concentrated on them, checking that he hadn't missed a guard, and then began to crawl towards them. He moved only one limb at a time, left arm, right leg, right arm, left leg, keeping his body an inch off the ground to minimise noise while at the same time reducing his silhouette. It took him half an hour to

267

cover the hundred yards to the nearest barn. He hugged the wall and slipped inside among the tractors and farm equipment. The barn was the furthest away from the farm but it would have been his first choice anyway because the other contained nothing but hay and the idea was to cause a diversion not to start a huge blaze that would have fire engines rushing over from the nearest town.

He put the can of petrol under a blue tractor and took off his rucksack. He knelt down and carefully removed the clock, the matchbox and its wire, and from his pocket he took out a fresh battery. He connected short lengths of wire to the hands of the clock and set them at quarter to and quarter past and then connected the battery and the matchbox and its match heads into a continuous circuit. He unscrewed the cap of the petrol can and poured half of it on the floor around the tractor then stood it under the cab. He lowered the matchbox into the can so that it was suspended above the liquid. It was important that the match heads were ignited in the vapour and not swamped with petrol or there would be no explosion. He wound the wire around the handle of the can so that the matchbox couldn't accidentally slip lower. He had thirty minutes to get into position. Plenty of time. He put his rucksack back on and eased himself out of the barn and slithered slowly along the ground, back the way he'd come, and then he crawled clockwise around the barns until he could see the side of the farmhouse and the gap that led to the courtyard.

He waited. The petrol bomb exploded with a whooshing noise followed by the crackle and hiss of the tractor burning. There were shouts and yells and the men at the front of the farmhouse ran towards the barn. Lights went on in the farmhouse and the door to the cottage flew open. When the guards had run through into the court-yard Nguyen made his way to the outbuildings and lay down in the shadows. Hennessy came out of the back door along with two other men, he in his dressing-gown, they in pullovers and jeans and holding handguns. Nguyen had planned to climb the drainpipe and get in through the bathroom window but he saw that Hennessy had left the back door open. The kitchen light hadn't been switched on so the doorway was in darkness. He waited until he was sure that no one else was coming out of the farm-house and he moved along the wall, hugging the shadows like a cockroach, and then slipped through the door into the kitchen, listening carefully.

He moved on the balls of his feet, knees slightly bent, ready to move quickly if he had to, but it was all clear and he crept into the hall and up the stairs. The stairs turned to the left and he reorientated the map of the farm-house that he held in his head and when the stairs opened into the first-floor hallway he knew immediately which way to move so that he would pass the bathroom and find Hennessy's bedroom. He unclipped the hunting knife from its scabbard on the strap of the rucksack and held it blade up as he put his hand on the bedroom door and pressed his ear to the warm wood. He hadn't seen the woman leave the house. She might have left during the day but there was a chance she was still in the room. He turned the doorknob slowly and smoothly and eased the door open. The light was on and the bed was empty. He pushed the door and stepped into the room. At the foot of the bed was a wicker dog basket and a brown dog growled at him and then began to bark. Nguyen closed the door as the dog got to its feet and moved towards him, barking and snapping, its tail down between its legs and the fur standing up along the back of its neck.

'Good dog,' said Nguyen, holding the knife to his side.

Hennessy stood with his hands on his hips as he watched two of his men spray the burning tractor with fire extinguishers, the foam hissing and bubbling on the hot metal. Joe Ryan had run a hosepipe from the stables and he yelled over his shoulder for his daughter to turn the water on. The hosepipe squirmed and kicked and then water burst from the nozzle and he played it over the walls of the barn.

The rest of the men were busy moving equipment away from the fire, either to the far side of the barn or out into the courtyard. Kavanagh stood at Hennessy's shoulder. In the distance Hennessy heard Jackie bark. 'Still think I've got enough guards, Jim?' he asked. Kavanagh remained silent, not sure if Hennessy was getting at him or not. 'Any idea what caused it?' Hennessy asked.

'There's a can under the tractor and some melted plastic. It's The Chinaman, right enough. We were lucky that the can didn't explode, it could've been a lot worse. By the look of it the flames came shooting out of the top of the can like a jet engine, spraying fire across the wall and setting light to the tractor's tyres. It's a lot worse than it looks.'

'He cocked it up?'

'Looks like it.'

'Thank God he didn't set fire to the other barn. If the hay had gone up we'd have never got it under control.'

The men with the fire extinguishers put out the burning

tractor and moved to help Ryan douse the burning side of the barn. The tractor's tyres had melted and warped and the tractor was blackened and burnt and smeared with bubbly white foam. The smell of burnt rubber was choking and Hennessy and Kavanagh moved back into the courtyard. Hennessy looked up at his bedroom window. Jackie had stopped barking. 'Still think we should go back to Belfast?' asked Hennessy.

'No question about it, Liam.'

'And if he sets fire to my house? Could you stop him doing that?'

Kavanagh realised that whatever he said he'd be in the wrong, so he said nothing. They stood together and watched the men douse the final flames.

'Morrison should be back tomorrow,' said Hennessy eventually. 'He's bringing someone with him who might be able to help. Kerry Geraghty.'

'Micky Geraghty's girl?'

'Yeah. She's going to try to track down The Chinaman. Micky was going to do it but he's got a broken leg, though from what Sean tells me she's every bit as good. We'll give her a go. While she's trying I'll have to stay here otherwise The Chinaman will just disappear, but if it doesn't work then we'll go back to Belfast and we'll handle it in the city. OK?'

'It's your call, Liam,' said Kavanagh.

'You mean it's me he's after,' said Hennessy. He smiled ruefully. 'And you're right, of course. Look, there's nothing we can do here. I'm going back to bed and I suggest you do the same. I doubt if he's going to do anything else tonight and there's nothing we can do in the dark.'

'I'll wait here until the men've finished,' said Kavanagh.

Hennessy began walking back to the farmhouse. Kavanagh called after him and Liam turned round. 'I'm sorry about all this,' said Kavanagh.

'Not your fault, Jim,' said Hennessy. 'And I didn't mean to imply that it was. I'm just a bit tense, that's all. This Chinaman is getting under my skin. I'll talk to you tomorrow.'

He went into the kitchen and switched the light on. He poured himself a double whiskey and carried it upstairs to his bedroom. He hung his dressing-gown on the back of the bedroom door and placed the tumbler of whiskey on his bedside table. Jackie lay on the floor at the side of the bed. Hennessy was disappointed that she hadn't welcomed him back with her normal tail-wagging and frantic licks. She was probably sulking because he'd kept her in the room. 'Come on, Jackie,' he said softly, and patted the bed. Mary didn't allow the dog into the bedroom, least of all on the bed, but when she was away Hennessy reckoned that he should be allowed to give Jackie a treat. He patted the bed again and clicked his tongue, but still she ignored him. He went over to her and knelt down. 'Come on, Jackie, old girl,' he said, and stroked her neck. There was no reaction and Hennessy began to panic. He stood up and switched on the bedroom light and immediately saw that there was blood pooling around the dog's neck. 'Oh God, no,' he groaned. He bent down to pick up the dog but as he did he realised that he was not alone in the room. In the gap between the large oak wardrobe and the wall he saw a pair of legs in baggy camouflage trousers and he looked up sharply.

'You!' he said.

Nguyen stepped forward out of the shadows. In his

left hand he carried a gun which he pointed at the head of the kneeling man. In his right he held two wires between his fingers and around his neck was hanging what appeared to be a length of grey tubing. He'd used a length of insulation tape to suspend the tube so that it lay against his stomach. Various nails and screws had been stuck to the tube with more tape. To Hennessy it appeared that Nguyen had undergone a complete trans-formation. It wasn't just the outfit, though the camouflage and the gun gave him a military appearance that was a far cry from the down-trodden Oriental who had turned up at his office, it was more a question of bearing, the way he carried himself. There was a new air of confi-dence about the man and for the first time Hennessy felt afraid. He looked down at Jackie and ran his hand along her fur.

'You didn't have to kill my dog,' he said, shaking his head sadly.

'He was barking.'

'She. Not he. And you didn't have to kill her.'

'I am sorry,' said Nguyen. He walked behind Hennessy and bolted the bedroom door. 'Please sit in the chair.' He pointed with the gun at a pink armchair in a corner away from the window. The curtains were closed but Nguyen didn't want shadows to be seen by the men in the court-yard below. Hennessy stood up and slowly lowered himself into the chair. From where he was sitting he could see Jackie's head, her eyes nothing more than milky orbs, her tongue hanging grotesquely from the side of her mouth.

'Can I cover her?' he asked Nguyen. Nguyen took the dressing-gown from the hook on the back of the door and draped it over the dog's body.

'What is it you want?' asked Hennessy. He felt naked sitting in the chair wearing only his pyjamas.

'You must talk quietly,' said Nguyen. He nodded down at the tube on his chest and held up the hand which was holding the wires. 'This is a bomb, the same type I used to destroy the car. If anyone comes into this room all I do is put the wires together. Then we all die.' He held up the gun. 'And I have this. If we talk quietly nobody will hear us. Do you understand.'

'Yes,' sighed Hennessy. 'I understand. But what do you want to talk about?'

'The names. I want the names.'

'I cannot help you.'

'You know that I am serious. You have seen what I can do.'

'Yes.' Hennessy looked down at the dead dog. 'Yes, I know now what you can do.'

'So you know that I can kill you? That I will kill you?'

'Killing me will make no difference, no difference at all. You see, I have absolutely no idea who is behind the London bombings.'

Nguyen looked confused. 'They are in the IRA?'

'Maybe.'

'I do not understand.'

Hennessy sighed because deep down he didn't understand either. 'I'll try to explain,' he said. 'They're saying that they are in the IRA, but I don't know who they are. Nobody in the official IRA knows who they are. You must believe me, we don't want to kill innocent citizens. I'm doing everything I can to find out who's responsible.'

Nguyen walked from the wardrobe to the end of the bed and sat down, facing Hennessy. Hennessy could see light glistening on the sweat that covered the man's hands. The wires that would set off the lethal package were less than two inches apart. Nguyen saw him looking at the wires and smiled. 'Do not worry,' he said. 'It will only explode if I want it to explode.'

'Killing me won't get your family back,' said Hennessy quietly.

'I do not want to kill you, Mr Hennessy. But I cannot allow the men to be unpunished.'

'This is getting us nowhere,' sighed Hennessy.

'The explosives the men use. Do they make their own?'

Hennessy shook his head. 'They've been using our explosives. We have it stored in several places in Britain. It looks as if they've been stealing it.'

'Semtex?'

'Yes.'

'Which sort? Semtex-H?'

'Yes.'

'It would be,' said Nguyen. 'Everything moves in circles.'

'You know about Semtex?'

Nguyen smiled tightly. 'I know about Semtex-H,' he said. 'Hexagen is added, that is where the H comes from. Very stable explosive, but very powerful, more powerful than TNT.'

Hennessy's mouth dropped open. 'How come you know so much about Semtex-H?'

'I use many times in Vietnam.'

'In Vietnam?'

'You do not know your history, Mr Hennessy. Semtex-H was made for the Vietnamese during the war. It is our explosive. They made it for us, the Chax.'

'Czechs, you mean. It was made in Czechoslovakia.'

'Yes. The Czechs. They made it. Before, when the French were in Vietnam, then we used a French plastic explosive. When the French left we asked the Czechs to make same style for us. They made Semtex-H. Very good for making bombs and for traps. Many Americans were killed by Semtex-H. Now the IRA uses it to kill my family. That is, how do you say, ionic.'

'Ironic,' said Hennessy. 'The word is ironic.'

'Yes, it is ironic. Vietnamese explosive kills Vietnamese family.'

'I am sorry about what happened to your family. But it is not my fault.'

Nguyen pointed the gun at Hennessy's throat. 'You will tell me who killed my family. You will tell me or you will die. And when you are dead I will go and ask someone else. I will find out eventually.' He said the words in a cold, flat voice and Hennessy knew that he meant it. The gun was cocked and ready to fire and he saw Nguyen's finger tighten on the trigger. Hennessy held up his hands as if trying to ward off the bullet.

'No!' he said.

'Then tell me,' hissed Nguyen.

'I don't know,' said Hennessy.

'Then die,' said Nguyen.

Hennessy turned his head away, his eyes tightly shut. 'I don't know but I'm trying to find out,' he said, his voice shaking with fear.

'What do you mean?'

'I've set a trap for them. If it works I'll know who they are.'

'When will you know?'

Hennessy stopped flinching from the gun, sensing that

Nguyen was taking him seriously. Perhaps he had a chance after all. 'When the next bomb goes off.'

'What is your plan?'

'When they claim responsibility for the bomb they give a codeword that tells the police that they are with the IRA. I have changed the codeword and the one that they use will tell me who has been helping them.'

'And then what?'

'We'll give their names to the police. And they will end it.'

Nguyen thought about what Hennessy had told him, but the gun never wavered. Eventually he nodded to himself as if he had come to a decision.

'Very well,' he said. 'I will give you three days. In three days I will come back. But if you do not have the names by then, I will kill you.'

'But what if they haven't set off a bomb by then?' protested Hennessy.

'That is your problem,' said Nguyen.

'That's not fair!' protested Hennessy.

'Fair? Nothing that has happened so far has been fair, Mr Hennessy.' Nguyen stood up and backed to the door. He reached for the light switch and plunged the room into darkness.

'Why are you doing this?' Hennessy asked quietly.

'You killed my family.'

'There's something else. Something you're not telling me.'

Nguyen moved silently to the window and pulled back one of the curtains. There were only two men in the court-yard below. One was carrying two fire extinguishers, the other was rolling up a hosepipe. He heard the back door

277

of the farmhouse slam shut. The two men in the court-yard walked over to the cottage and Nguyen let the curtain swing back into place.

'I mean, I've lost relatives in the Troubles, my own brother-in-law was killed not so long ago. Almost everyone I know has had someone they know killed or maimed, but I've never met anyone who has taken it so . . . so personally . . . as you have.'

'Perhaps if you did take it personally, the war in Ireland would not have dragged on for so long.'

'What do you mean?'

'What are you fighting for?'

'To get the British out of Ireland. To be allowed to live our own lives without prejudice or persecution.'

'So why do your people not take up arms against the British and drive them from the country?'

'Many do.'

'But not enough. Not enough people care. Not enough take it personally. The Vietnamese fought the French until they left the country. And the Communists fought the Americans and the army of the South until the Americans left. They won because the desire to be one country was stronger than anything else. It seems to me that you will never force the British to leave Ireland. Not enough people care. You play at war.'

'And you? Why are you doing this?'

Nguyen ignored him. He put his ear to the door and listened. He heard nothing. He turned to Hennessy. 'I will go now. Do not shout, I still have the bomb and I will kill anyone who comes after me. I will be back in three days.' He slipped the bolt back and opened the door, looked left and right down the corridor before easing himself out of the bedroom, keeping close to the wall. He went silently to the bathroom and put the gun in the rucksack and disconnected the wires before he stepped on to the toilet and climbed out of the window. He held the drainpipe and shinned down, taking care not to scrape his feet against the wall. When he reached the ground he pressed himself against the wall and checked out his surroundings. There was a lingering smell of burnt wood and scorched metal in the courtyard but there was no sound. He crept between the cars, keeping low, and made his way to the stables. Inside he heard the horses snorting and he wondered if they could sense that he was there. He heard footsteps by the cottage so he moved in the opposite direction and left the courtyard between the stables and the far end of the farmhouse.

Hennessy sat in the bedroom, slumped forward with his head in his hands. Part of him wanted to sound the alarm immediately but he knew that The Chinaman had meant what he'd said. He would use the gun and if that failed he would set off the bomb killing God knows how many. He gave him five minutes then switched on the light and went down to get Kavanagh who was stretched out on a sofa in the lounge. By the time Kavanagh had gone out to warn the men on guard duty Nguyen was long gone, slithering through the grass as silently as a snake.

O'Reilly caught the 10.33 a.m. train from Waterloo station and found himself a seat towards the front in a carriage full of men in morning suits and women in long dresses and expensive hats. Two of the couples in his compartment were obviously travelling together and one of the men had produced a bottle of champagne and four glasses and made a big show of opening it. Champagne sprayed out and as the man held it to one side it splashed over O'Reilly's aluminium camera case.

'Sorry old man,' said the racegoer.

'No problem,' said O'Reilly. He looked out of the window as the train pulled out of the station. Ascot was forty minutes away so he settled back in his seat and let his mind drift. In the inside pocket of his blazer was a badge to get him into the Members' Enclosure, which he'd bought from a ticket agency a week earlier. He'd wanted to get in on Ladies Day but hadn't been able to get a ticket for Thursday and had settled for Tuesday instead. Tuesday or Thursday, it didn't really matter, because a successful bombing at Royal Ascot would be news around the world.

The camera case at his feet was the sort professionals used to carry their equipment, about two-feet long, a foot wide and eighteen-inches deep, with a thick nylon carrying strap. The Bombmaker had stripped out the lining of the case and fitted slabs of Semtex, ten pounds in all, around the sides and the bottom. There were two detonators, each connected to a single timer made from a small electronic travel alarm. The alarm had been set for 2 p.m. and the bomb was armed. O'Reilly was tense but not over-anxious. He'd carried live bombs before and he had complete faith in The Bombmaker. The lining had been replaced over the explosive with alterations made where necessary, and it now contained two camera bodies, a selection of lenses, a light meter and boxes of film. Around his neck was a Nikon with a telephoto lens and a pair of binoculars in a leather case. Attached to the binoculars were a dozen or so badges from earlier race meetings and that, and the trilby hat, marked O'Reilly out as a regular racegoer and not just a social butterfly hoping for a glimpse of a famous face at Royal Ascot.

The train arrived at Ascot station at 11.15 a.m. and O'Reilly joined the crowds flocking to the racecourse. There were plenty of police around but most of them were wearing yellow reflective jackets and were directing traffic with bored faces and aching arms. O'Reilly stood with a group waiting to cross the road. A middle-aged man in a morning suit saw a gap in the traffic and started to cross but a young constable in the middle of the road shouted at him to get back. 'Bollocks,' muttered the man in the morning suit. He looked to be twice as old as the constable, a roughly hewn face and shoulders that strained at his jacket.

The policeman motioned at the traffic to keep moving and walked over to the man. 'Have you got a problem?' he asked, jutting his head forward, his cheeks reddening. He had a thin moustache and the manner of an adolescent with something to prove.

'I think I'm old enough to cross the road on my own,' said the man with barely restrained anger. He looked like a man more than capable of looking after himself in a fight and O'Reilly knew he'd be able to handle the copper with one hand.

'That's not what I asked you. I want to know what you said.' He was glaring at the man, his teeth clenched together and a vein was pulsing on the side of his forehead. O'Reilly wondered what his problem was because his reaction was out of all proportion to what the man had said.

'Nothing,' said the man through tight lips. 'I didn't say anything.'

The policeman stared hard at the man for several seconds and then nodded slowly as if satisfied. 'Good,' he said, then walked back into the road and continued directing traffic. The racegoer got a few sympathetic glances from pedestrians around him and he shook his head, exasperated. The Great British Bobby, thought O'Reilly. An angry young man with authority he couldn't handle. It was something he'd grown up with in Ireland, where the Protestant police and the teenage British soldiers would exercise the power of their uniform just for the hell of it, just to feel good. He was used to being stopped on the street and given a hard time from RUC officers who didn't say 'sir' and didn't bother to keep their contempt out of their voices, and even as a schoolboy he'd been thrown against walls and roughly searched by gum-chewing soldiers in camouflage jackets. The abuse of authority was nothing new to O'Reilly, and it was with no small feeling of satisfaction that he now saw it spilling over to Britain.

Eventually the policeman held up his hand to stop the traffic and allowed them to cross. He seemed to be glaring at them all, as if blaming them for having to stand in the road.

Despite the strong police presence – there seemed to be hundreds organising the flow of coaches and cars into the carparks around the racecourse – O'Reilly saw no sniffer dogs at the entrance. There were two policemen there but they seemed to be more concerned about eyeing up two pretty blondes in white, figure-hugging dresses and floppy hats. The girls were twins, barely in their twenties, tanned and draped in gold. One of the policemen smiled and touched his helmet in salute. The girls smiled and giggled, and one of them looked back over her shoulder as they walked towards the grandstand.

A steward in a bowler hat squinted at O'Reilly's badge and waved him through the gate and then another steward who looked about seventy years old asked if he'd mind opening up his case. The police stood watching the twins, their long, lithe legs moving with the grace of thoroughbred racehorses.

'Security, you understand,' said the old man apologetically.

A couple of middle-aged women in tweed suits were looking into handbags but the checks were nothing more than a cursory glance. O'Reilly wondered what the hell they expected to find – a black ball with 'BOMB' written on it and a burning fuse maybe. The steward in front of O'Reilly rubbed his moustache and smiled and O'Reilly smiled back and put the case on the grass and clicked it open. The old man peered inside.

'Nice equipment,' he said approvingly. He looked up at O'Reilly with watery eyes. 'I do a bit of photography myself.'

'It's a great hobby,' said O'Reilly. He took out one of the camera bodies and showed it to the old man. 'I always use Nikon,' he said. 'What about you?'

The man looked pleased about being asked his opinion. 'Canon,' he said. He handed the Nikon back to O'Reilly. 'Enjoy yourself today,' he said.

'Got any tips?' asked O'Reilly. He stashed the camera body away, and as an afterthought took the other Nikon from around his neck and put that away, too. He grunted as he picked up the case and slung its strap over his shoulder.

283

'You could do worse than back Eddery in the third,' said the steward. Pity, thought O'Reilly, who wasn't planning to be around for the third race. In fact if everything went the way Fisher had planned it, there wouldn't be a third race.

He bought a race card and walked for a while among the crowds, listening to the plummy voices and girlish giggles. The idle rich at play, he thought. Who else could afford to walk around in thousands of pounds' worth of high fashion and jewellery in the middle of the week? Champagne corks were popping everywhere, and everyone he looked at had the glint of gold on their wrist or around their neck. Some of the women were simply stunning, like the coltish blonde twins he'd seen at the gate, but in the main they were overdressed, overweight and wore too much make-up. They stood in groups, eyeing up the competition, reading the price tags on their outfits every bit as easily as they identified the brand names. They looked fearful, thought O'Reilly. Fearful of what they might lose.

He took his place in the grandstand and scanned the crowds through his binoculars. He spotted a couple of minor starlets who were wearing considerably more than they did in their movies, and several captains of industry who presumably had nothing better to do at the office. There was minor royalty around, too, but he couldn't see any of the heavyweights. He wondered what the chances would be of catching one with the blast but knew that the likelihood was remote. Not that it mattered, the fact that a bomb went off at an occasion attended by the Royal family would be more than enough to guarantee worldwide coverage. He checked out the positions of the television cameras, which were there to cover the crowds as much as the horses. They'd have no problems recording the explosion and its aftermath.

He studied the race card for a while, though he didn't plan on placing any bets. The steward had been right, though, Eddery did look a sure thing in the third race. O'Reilly looked at his watch. Half past one. The aluminium case was under his legs, silently counting off the seconds. Part of him wanted to go now, to get as far away as possible from the bomb before the alarm clock completed the circuit, but he knew that if he left it unattended for any length of time there was a risk that it might be discovered. Fisher had been quite specific about the timing, and, besides, McCormick wouldn't be outside until exactly five minutes before two. He re-read the race card and surveyed the crowds again, anything to keep his mind off the bomb. Once or twice he found himself eavesdropping on the chatter going on around him but he stopped himself and blocked out the conversations. His neighbours in the stand would be at the centre of the explosion and he didn't want to know anything about them. He didn't want it to be personal.

The minute hand on his watch gradually crept around to ten to the hour and he stood up, stretched, and lifted his case on to the seat. He took off his hat and placed it on top of the case and then moved himself along the row to the aisle, apologising all the way and looking for all the world as if he was on a pre-race visit to the toilet or the Tote. He walked up the aisle, passed the bar and took an escalator down to the ground floor. He slowed down and ambled across the grass to the pre-arranged exit, some way along from where he'd come in so that he wouldn't be recognised by the stewards. The pavements outside were still thronged with racegoers waiting to get in and he pushed through, smiling apologetically.

The green and white Yamaha 750 purred up to the kerb. McCormick was wearing black leathers and had on a white helmet with a tinted visor. A second helmet was attached to the side of the bike and McCormick unclipped it and handed it to O'Reilly. He put it on and fastened the strap under his chin as he slipped on to the seat and found the foot rests. McCormick clicked the bike into gear and drove off towards London. The roads away from Ascot were clear but he stuck to the speed-limit because there were so many police around. Even so, they were still four miles away from the racecourse when the bomb exploded.

Woody was in the office early so that he could hit the phones before Simpson and the rest of the news desk staff arrived. He wasn't surprised that he couldn't get through to Sir John Brownlow himself because the *Sunday World* didn't usually get to the top of the lists of calls to be returned by Members of Parliament. Woody's luck was in, though, because he did get to speak to Sir John's assistant, a pleasant-sounding girl called Ellen. She remembered The Chinaman coming to see her boss, but like Woody couldn't remember his name. He told her that the family name was probably Nguyen and she went off to check the MP's correspondence files. A few minutes later she was back on the line.

'His name's Nguyen Ngoc Minh,' she said. 'I've got his letter here.' She read out the address on the letter and Woody checked it against the address of the Double Happiness Take-Away. They matched. He asked Ellen to spell out Nguyen's full name and he wrote it down in his notebook and then he asked her to read the letter out to him. It was pretty much the same story that he'd told when he visited the *Sunday World*'s office, and there didn't appear to be any information in the letter that would help Woody track him down.

'Can you remember anything else about this Chinaman?' Woody asked. 'Anything at all?'

'Well for a start, he isn't Chinese,' said Ellen. 'He was Vietnamese, that's what he told Sir John. I can't remember if he said he was from the north or the south, but I certainly got the impression he was a refugee. You know, one of the boat people. He has full British citizenship.'

'Anything else?'

'I'm sorry, that's all I can remember,' she said. 'Wait a minute, I've just had a thought. Why don't you try the Home Office?'

'The Home Office?'

'Sure. If he was a refugee then they'd have to have a file on him. It wouldn't matter if he was Chinese or Vietnamese or whatever. There's a hell of a lot of paperwork to go through to get citizenship.'

Woody thanked her gratefully and flicked through his contacts book. He'd met a Government Information Officer who worked in the Home Office some years earlier when he'd been chasing up a story on immigration and he'd taken her for a couple of boozy lunches afterwards to thank her. He couldn't recall her name but he'd filed her under 'Home Office' in his book. Annie Byrne. She wasn't there when he called but he left a message and he passed the time reading the morning papers and drinking coffee until she called back.

'Woody, long time no hear,' she said. She seemed genuinely pleased to hear from him and Woody tried to remember why he hadn't kept in touch with her. He explained that he was trying to get information on a refugee but skipped over the IRA connection. Was there any way that he could get to see the man's file?

'Certainly not officially, no,' she said. But she suggested that Woody came round to her office at lunchtime anyway, which Woody took as a good sign.

While Woody was on the phone the news desk drifted in one by one and when he hung up Simpson waved him over.

'You're in early, Woody,' he said. 'Got much on?'

'A couple of things. I'll let you know when they harden up.'

'OK, I've got something here that needs knocking out, something worthy of your talents.'

Woody sensed a trap.

'Don't look so nervous, Woody. You're gonna love it. I want you to give me fifty places where you can take the kids over the summer holidays. You know, a guide for the little horrors that the parents can cut out and keep.'

'Thanks, mate.'

'Come on, Woody, cheer up. A shift is a shift, it's all money in the end.'

'Yeah, yeah, yeah,' said Woody, and slouched back to his desk.

He left the office just before noon and took the Tube to St James's Park. He'd assumed that Annie was just after a lunchtime drink and a chance to catch up on Fleet Street gossip so he was pleasantly surprised to be shown into her office. She was a short, bouncy girl and she shook him firmly by the hand. She spoke like a head girl and laughed a lot and Woody wondered how long it would be before she was snapped up by one of the Civil Service high-flyers and installed in a country house where she'd breed children and horses. She was a very attractive girl but Woody remembered why he'd never tried to see more of her. She was, he realised ruefully, totally out of his league.

There was a blue cardboard file on her desk and she tapped it with her left hand. An engagement ring glinted under the lights. It was a big diamond. The girl had done well. 'Nguyen Ngoc Minh,' she said. 'I tell you, Woody, this is one damned interesting file. It's just a pity that I can't let you see it. Home Office regulations, you understand. It'd be more than my job's worth. And you know how much my job means to me.' She grinned and then looked at her watch. 'Golly, is that the time. Look, Woody, I've got a meeting to go to. Can you amuse yourself for a while? I'll be gone for about half an hour. OK?'

'OK. Do you want me to wait outside?'

Annie walked around her desk and patted him on the shoulder as she headed for the door. 'No, Woody, you stay where you are. I'll be back.'

She closed the door behind her and Woody leant over and picked up the file. It wasn't the first time a civil servant or a police officer had shared information by leaving an open file on a desk, and Woody was sure it wouldn't be the last. At some point in the future he knew Annie would call in the favour. Besides, she'd already read through the file to check that it contained nothing secret or damaging to the Government. He opened it and began leafing through a sheaf of forms and written reports with a growing sense of wonder.

There were reports from the United Nations High Commissioner for Refugees in Hong Kong and from the Hong Kong Government's Security Branch, documents from the US Consulate, photocopies of service records and signed statements from senior American army officers detailing Nguyen's time with the US forces. One of the sheets was a photocopy of the inside of a British passport with Nguyen's photograph and there were photocopies of two awards made to his unit in Vietnam. There was a Meritorious Unit Commendation and a Republic of Vietnam Gallantry Cross Unit Citation, along with a memo from a US colonel recording the fact that Nguyen's unit had the highest body count in Vietnam during the first half of 1973. By the time he'd finished reading the file he was shaking his head in amazement. The man was a bloody war hero, a trained assassin and an expert in jungle warfare.

He went back through the papers, filling his notebook with dates and copying down quotes from the reports. God, it was good stuff. Amazing. The story in the file was award-winning copy in itself. If Nguyen really was after the IRA, it would be dynamite.

It was a very thick file, sheet after sheet. Even in the early eighties, when Nguyen was in a refugee camp in Hong Kong, all incoming Vietnamese boat people were given a thorough grilling to check that they weren't Communist spies or simply criminals on the run. Nguyen Ngoc Minh's story was so complicated, and, Woody had to admit, so frankly unbelievable, that he was interviewed many times. Officials from the UNHCR and the Hong Kong Government's Security Branch had gone over his story again and again, cross-checking and cross-referencing in an attempt to catch him out, until eventually they believed him.

Woody flicked through the file, taking down details of Nguyen's switch to the South Vietnamese and his time with the Long Range Reconnaissance Patrols. The fact that Nguyen had been left behind by the Americans and his time in prison and the re-education camp were detailed in the matter-of-fact reports. Woody could only imagine the horrors the man had endured before he'd finally managed to escape. There were few details of the actual journey to Hong Kong, though it was clear that two of his daughters had died. Nguyen had refused to expand on what had happened and the psychiatrist reckoned that Nguyen was trying to block out painful memories.

Woody wrote quickly. By the time Annie returned to the office the file was back on her desk and Woody was sitting reading through his notes.

'Sorry about that,' she said.

'No problem,' he smiled.

'I hope you weren't too bored. Right, come on, you can buy me lunch.'

Morrison and Kerry arrived at Belfast airport late in the afternoon. Willie O'Hara was there to meet them with the Range Rover. Morrison got in the front passenger seat while Kerry climbed in the back. She noticed a large black stain on the seat and O'Hara explained that they'd used the car to take Jimmy McMahon to the hospital.

'How is he?' Morrison asked.

'On the mend, thank God. If the bomb had gone off a second later it would've taken his legs off. But it looks as if he's going to be OK. This focking Chinaman is bad news, I can tell you. He was at it again last night.'

'He was?'

'Yeah, he set fire to one of the barns. And killed Hennessy's dog.'

Kerry leant over the seat. 'Jackie? He killed Jackie?'

O'Hara nodded. 'Slit its throat.'

Kerry slumped back into the seat, her hand over her mouth. To Morrison it seemed that she was more upset about the dead dog than about the man in hospital. They drove in silence down the M2 towards the city. When they passed the ferry terminal Kerry leant forward again. 'I'm going to need some things. Can we drive into the city?'

'Yeah, good thinking,' said Morrison. O'Hara turned off the motorway and guided the car through central Belfast. They had to pull to one side when a fire engine came up behind, lights flashing and siren blaring. In its wake followed two armoured RUC Land-Rovers. They parked the car and walked to a shopping centre, a pedestrian road sealed off with a metal fence at either end. To get in they had to pass through a turnstile and two surly RUC officers checked through Kerry's handbag and body-searched Morrison and O'Hara. Kerry had said she wanted to go to a sports shop, the sort that sold skiing equipment, and O'Hara took her to one that he knew of.

'I've got to be honest, Kerry, but you're not likely to see much in the way of snow in County Down at this time of the year,' said Morrison as she examined a selection of ski-poles. She took one from the rack and held it, feeling its weight. She wasn't satisfied and replaced it with another, slightly longer, version.

'We'll need tracking sticks,' she explained. 'Walking

sticks will do but ski-poles are the best. You can use them for moving vegetation, and they stop you getting tired. Choose one for yourself, pick one that feels sturdy but not too heavy. This one's fine for me.'

Morrison followed her advice while she went over to a display of American baseball caps. When he caught up with her she was looking at herself in the mirror, a blue cap on her head.

'Cute,' he said.

'You'll need a hat to shade your eyes from the sun. It makes it easier to follow tracks in bright sunlight. You should get one.'

'Whatever you say, Tonto.'

By the time he'd found a cap that fitted she was looking at a black squash racket. 'Don't tell me,' he said, 'you use it for filtering soil looking for clues.'

She laughed and shook her head. She put the racket back on its stand. 'Come on. That's all we need from here. Unless you want to stock up on ski masks for the boys.'

Morrison paid for the purchases and followed her out of the shop. 'Anything else?' he asked.

She nodded. 'Elastic bands, a tape measure, couple of notebooks and pens. And torches.'

'I won't ask,' he said.

When they'd bought everything that Kerry wanted they went back to the car and continued their journey south.

Fisher and McCormick sat on the leather Chesterfield watching the television. O'Reilly was on the balcony, sunbathing. They each had a can of Guinness and McCormick was smoking. The news came on and the Ascot bombing was the first item. Eight people died, the

293

newsreader said, and fifteen were injured, six of them seriously. McCormick whooped and O'Reilly came inside to watch. There were shots of the dead and injured being carried to ambulances and a shot taken from a helicopter giving a bird's eye view of the damage to the grandstand. Fisher and McCormick clunked their cans together and then both did the same with O'Reilly.

'Great crack,' said Fisher. 'Those pictures will go around the world.'

A senior policeman with a suitably dour expression was being interviewed. The IRA had not claimed responsibility, he said, but there were similarities between this bombing and the previous attacks.

'Yeah,' said O'Reilly. 'When do we make the call?'

'You can do it now,' said Fisher. 'But this time don't give a codeword. Just tell them that it was an active service unit of the Provisional IRA, and tell them where and when the bomb was planted. You can also say how much explosive it contained.'

'Ten pounds,' said The Bombmaker, who was sitting at the dining-table, probing into the laptop computer with a voltmeter.

'Tell them ten pounds of Semtex,' said Fisher. 'And tell them there will be more bombings until the British Government withdraws its armed forces from Ulster. They'll believe you.'

O'Reilly frowned. 'Why aren't we using the codeword?'

Fisher waved his can of Guinness in the air. 'Change of strategy,' he said. 'I had a phone call from Ireland while you were out. No codewords from now on.'

'Did they say why?'

'Does it matter?' asked Fisher.

O'Reilly grinned. 'Not really.' He picked up the London street atlas. 'Where shall I make the call from this time? How about Barking? I've never been to Barking.'

Fisher shook his head. 'There are times, O'Reilly, when I wonder if you're quite right in the head.'

Hennessy heard the Range Rover crunching down the track and went to the front door to meet it. He was too late, the car had gone round the back to park in the court-yard so he went back through the house and out of the kitchen door. By the time he reached the car Kerry had already got out. She rushed up to him and hugged him.

'Uncle Liam,' she said, holding him tightly.

'Kerry, thanks for coming.' Over her shoulder he greeted Morrison. 'Was your flight OK?' he asked Kerry.

She released him from the hug and stood back, still holding his shoulders. 'Uncle Liam, I'm so sorry about Jackie. She was a lovely dog.'

'She was that,' agreed Hennessy. He'd buried Jackie himself in a patch of rough ground just beyond the vegetable garden. He helped Kerry in with her bag while Morrison carried his own and O'Hara held the ski-poles. Morrison saw the curious look that Hennessy gave the poles and he shrugged. 'Don't ask,' he said.

Hennessy took Kerry up and showed her the bedroom he'd prepared for her. She'd stayed there many times, especially when she was a teenager. It was a small, pretty room, with pink curtains and pine furniture. She put her case at the foot of the bed and looked out of the tiny window. 'Is Auntie Mary here?' she asked.

'No, she's gone to visit Marie in London.'

'That's a pity,' she said.

'We thought it best. Why don't you freshen up and join Sean and me downstairs,' said Hennessy. 'I've put some clean towels in the bathroom for you. And you know where everything is.'

He went downstairs. Morrison had put his bag in the lounge. 'There's a bedroom upstairs ready for you, Sean,' Hennessy told him. 'Second on the left at the head of the stairs, when you're ready.'

'Great, thanks, Liam.'

'You know there's been another bombing?'

'Yeah, Willie said on the way in. Blew up your barn, he said.'

Hennessy sat down. 'No, I mean another bombing on the mainland. At Ascot. Today. Eight killed.'

'Has Bromley phoned?' Morrison asked, dropping into an easy chair opposite Hennessy.

Hennessy shook his head. 'Not yet.'

'I wonder what he's playing at.'

'He definitely said he'd go for it?'

'No question about it.'

'Then we just have to wait.'

'Yeah. I gather The Chinaman was in the house last night. Willie said he was in your room with a bomb.'

'Unbelievable, isn't it. Got in and out of the house without anyone seeing him.'

'So the fire in the barn was a diversion?'

'I think so, right enough. He said he wanted to talk.'

'And?'

'And he's given me three days to find out who's behind the bombings. Then he's going to kill me.' The dispassionate way Hennessy described the threat belied his true feelings. 'Do you want a drink?'

Morrison shook his head. 'No, Kerry says she wants to have a look around while the light is still good. I'd better keep a clear head.'

Kerry appeared at the door and the two men got to their feet. She'd changed into jeans and a dark-blue sweatshirt. 'You're starting already?' asked Hennessy. 'Are you sure you don't want a bite to eat?'

'It's the light, Uncle Liam. The best times to see tracks are early in the morning and late in the afternoon. It's to do with the angle of the sun and the shadows it casts. We've only got an hour or so. Is there someone who can show me where they saw him?'

'Jim Kavanagh knows where the car bomb was triggered. And he can show you where one of our men was attacked.'

'Right,' she said, rubbing her hands together, 'let's get started. Sean, where are the poles and stuff?'

'Willie put them in the kitchen.'

'Come on then.' She led the way to the kitchen leaving Hennessy and Morrison smiling at each other.

'Looks like she's taken charge,' said Hennessy. 'I think you might have to watch yourself there.'

They walked into the kitchen to find Kerry putting the two poles on the table. She slipped off the discs from the end of each of the poles, the bits that stopped the poles from sinking too deep into the snow. 'I forgot to get some binoculars, do you have some?' she asked Hennessy, and he produced a pair in an old leather case from the hall. She opened the case and slotted in a notebook and pencil and the tape measure. She took one of the torches and handed the other, and a notebook and pencil, to Morrison. 'Right,' she said. 'Let's go.'

Morrison found Kavanagh at the front of the house and he asked him to show them where The Chinaman had been when the bomb had destroyed the Jaguar. Of the Jaguar there was now no sign, Ryan had towed the wreckage away with one of the tractors and put it in one of the barns, away from the prying eyes of army patrols and low-flying helicopters. The crater had been filled in with soil but was still obvious, like a gaping wound.

'Your hat,' said Kerry, holding it out to Morrison as they walked down the track. He took it and put it on.

'Cute,' she said.

'That's not a word we normally use to describe Sean Morrison,' said Kavanagh, grinning. 'But yez right, he does look cute.'

'Thanks guys,' said Morrison dryly. 'Can we just get on with the business at hand.'

Kavanagh took them up to the filled-in crater and then led them through the grass. It was trampled down in many places and even to Morrison's untutored eyes it was obvious that a number of men had been there, presumably chasing The Chinaman. Morrison couldn't stop thinking of Nguyen as The Chinaman, even though he knew he was from Vietnam.

'We found a battery here,' said Kavanagh, indicating a flattened-down area. 'And it's where the wires ended. He lay here until he saw that the car was over the bomb, detonated it, and then ran that way.' He pointed towards the hedgerow.

'Ran?' asked Kerry. 'You saw him?'

'Well, crawled, I suppose. We didn't see him, not then, but we were too busy trying to get Jimmy out of the wreckage. We saw the wires and guessed that he'd gone that way.'

'Where did you first see him?'

'I didn't. We saw some tracks leading to that copse,' he pointed again, 'but we didn't know if he'd gone into the trees or run by and gone through the fields. We split up, I went that way, three of the men went into the woods. He attacked one of them and stole his gun, the other two saw him running away, then they lost him again.'

'OK, show me which way he went.'

Kavanagh led the way, following the trampled grass to the hedge and showing her where the gap was. She examined the broken twigs and the mud by the hedge's roots. 'It looks like an army went this way,' she said. 'They've obliterated any tracks there might have been.'

'Hey, we were chasing the bastard, not tracking him!' said Kavanagh angrily. 'We'd just seen Jimmy get blown apart, we weren't too concerned about where we were putting our feet.'

Morrison put his hand on Kavanagh's shoulder. 'OK, Jim, cool down. She wasn't getting at you, she's just trying to help.'

'I only meant that it's easier when there's one set of tracks, Jim,' she said.

Kavanagh shrugged off Morrison's hand. 'Yeah, OK, I'm sorry I snapped at yez. We're all under a lot of pressure, and we didn't get a lot of sleep last night.'

'Forget it,' said Morrison. 'Show us which way he went.'

Kavanagh took them through another field, towards the copse he'd pointed at earlier. 'I went that way, but three of the men went in to check out the woods.' He pushed through some waist-high bushes until they were standing on a pathway that wound through the trees. 'The way they tell it, the three of them split up, and one of them, the one that got stabbed, went down the path.'

Kerry knelt down and looked at the ground. It was crisscrossed with a multitude of footprints, but she said nothing.

'Where was he stabbed?' asked Morrison.

'In the leg,' answered Kavanagh.

Morrison laughed sharply. 'I meant where in the woods was he attacked.'

'Oh right, I see what yez mean. This way.' He took them along the path and showed them. The soil had been flattened and there was a rusty discoloration. Dried blood, Morrison realised.

'Right,' said Kerry. 'Can you two gentlemen please get the hell off the path?'

Morrison and Kavanagh stepped to one side while she scrutinised the tracks. She walked back down the path a few paces and then squatted down and squinted, moving her head from side to side as she scrutinised the footprints and the place where the man had lain on the ground. She switched on her torch and shone it along the path, altering its angle as she played the light over the soil.

'Any good?' asked Morrison.

She shook her head and stood up. 'What happened then?' she asked Kavanagh.

He nodded down the path. 'He went that way. One of the others saw him and fired a couple of shots but didn't hear anything. They chased him down the path until one of them got caught in a trap.'

'A trap?'

'A hole in the ground with small stakes in it. Smeared with shit, believe it or not.'

'How far?'

'A hundred yards or so. But be careful, there could be others. Yez wouldn't want to put yez foot in one of them.'

She motioned for them to stay where they were and went down the trail, prodding carefully in front of her with the stick. She came upon the trap and crouched down beside it. There were still too many footprints to be able to tell which belonged to The Chinaman. She continued along the path but found nothing to help her. She did find another trap, though, and she cleared the soil away from it so that nobody would step in it.

She went back to Kavanagh and Morrison and began examining the vegetation either side of the path, using the ski-pole to move brambles aside. 'He must have hidden somewhere to have caught your man by surprise,' she murmured. 'Somewhere where he couldn't be seen but from where he could reach the path quickly – and quietly.'

'What are you looking for?' asked Morrison.

'Bruised stems, broken twigs, pebbles that have been moved. It's hard to say, I'll know it when I see it. Problem is, he was here two days ago which means a lot of the traces will have gone. We're lucky that it hasn't rained, but the wind obliterates a lot of stuff and any soil he kicked up will have dried out long ago.'

She bent down and looked at the brambles. 'Come on, Chinaman, where were you hiding? Where would you feel safe?' She was talking to herself and Morrison could only half hear. She turned round and began searching the opposite side of the path. There was a large spreading oak tree and she scrutinised the brambles at its base.

'Sean, come and look at this.'

He stood next to her and looked down at the tangle of thorny strands.

'What am I looking at?' he asked.

She pointed with the end of her pole. 'See that bit there, see how it's stuck under that thorn?'

'Yes,' he said hesitantly, not sure what she was getting at.

'See how it's under tension,' she continued. 'It's slightly distorted, it's been pushed into that position and the prickles on that bit are holding it down.'

'Which means what?'

She sighed and gave him a withering look. 'It means, Sean, that something, or somebody, pushed it into that position. Watch.' She used the ski-pole to push the bent strand and it sprang free and wavered in the air like the antenna of a huge insect. Kerry began pushing more of the brambles to the side. 'Help me, Sean,' she said.

Together they cleared a section of the undergrowth away from the earth. 'There! See?' she said. There were two smudges in the soil. 'He was walking on the balls of his feet.' She held the torch down and shone the light at an angle to the impressions, the shadows highlighting the marks.

'Yes, I see it now. God, you're right. He must have been hiding behind the tree, and attacked our man from behind.'

'Come on, we'll go round the tree in the opposite direction, see if there are any better footprints there.'

She and Morrison pushed the brambles apart and followed the curve of the tree around. She found the crack in the trunk and moved aside to show Morrison. In the soft earth were clear signs that The Chinaman had waited there, a number of footprints and a circular indentation which Kerry explained was probably made by his knee. She showed him places on the trunk where he had leaned against it and scraped away parts of the lichen on the bark. She pointed at the best example of a print with her pole. 'Now we use our notebooks,' she said, opening the binoculars case. She took out her notebook and pencil and with painstaking concentration made a drawing of the print, using the tape measure to ensure that it was an exact copy. She watched as Morrison did the same, correcting him over the shape of the heel of the boot and the pattern of the sole. 'We do this so that we'll always know from now on if it's his footprint that we're looking at,' she explained. 'And when we've finished this we'll draw a print of him walking on the ball of his foot.'

When they'd finished the drawings to Kerry's satisfaction, she took the two men along the edge of the path, following the prints of running men past the two exposed traps. After a hundred yards or so the trees thinned out and they were standing in a large field, lush, green grass peppered with daisies and dandelions.

'Question now is which way did he go when he left the woods?' she mused. She pulled the peak of her cap down and scanned the horizon. 'Come on, Chinaman, which way would you go? You'd be pretty exposed crossing the field wouldn't you, even if you waited until it was dark. So you'd look for cover, wouldn't you?' She turned to Kavanagh. 'Did your men go after him, across the field?'

'No, we reckoned he went to ground somewhere in the copse, but we couldn't find him. We didn't have enough men.'

'And were there any animals in the field?'

Kavanagh scratched his head. 'I don't think so.'

Kerry dropped down low and scanned the field, moving her head slowly but keeping her eyes fixed ahead.

'What are you doing?' Morrison asked curiously. She kept turning her head left and right as she answered. 'Changes in colour,' she said. 'Easier to spot when your eyes are moving. If he went through the grass he'd alter the way the blades lie. The underside of a blade of grass is a bit lighter than the part that faces the sun. You won't notice one or two but you can spot a trail through long grass. That's one of the ways we track deer. Trouble is the grass reorientates itself fairly quickly, just a few hours if it isn't too badly damaged. It depends how tall it is. This is quite long so it could take a while before it reverts to the way it was. Damn, I can't see anything. Come on, walk over here.'

She took him a few paces to the left and tried again. She slapped her thigh in frustration. 'Damn,' she said. She stood up and arched her back, her hands on her hips. 'The light's starting to go,' she said. 'Let me just check the edge of the wood and then we'll call it a day.'

She began walking slowly along the perimeter of the copse with Kavanagh and Morrison following behind. She scrutinised the ground and the vegetation overhanging the grass. Several times she stopped and bent down to examine a fallen leaf or a twig, causing the two men to pull up short, but she found nothing to give an indication that The Chinaman had passed that way. Then, just as she was about to give up, she saw a large leaf that had been pressed into the ground. She picked it up and held it out to Morrison. 'Yes!' she exclaimed. 'See how it's bruised, how it's been crushed across the middle?' she said. 'That's a sure sign that it's been trodden on.' She turned it over. There were several grains of soil pressed into it. 'See that? You can tell by the state the leaf's in that it happened within the last day or two. See how it's still fairly fresh?'

Morrison nodded. 'But couldn't it have been an animal?'

'It would have had to have been a fairly large animal, I mean the bruising couldn't have been done by a rabbit or a fox. I reckon this is where The Chinaman came out of the wood. Now, did he go across the field, or did he walk along the edge to that hedgerow?' She scanned the field again with her strange fixed stare. 'No, not that way,' she murmured. She continued along the side of the copse, pushing straggling vegetation to the side with her pole.

'Got him!' she cried, and waved the two men to come and stand beside her. She grinned and pointed down. At some point in the past a tree stump had been poisoned to kill its roots and the earth for some distance around it was devoid of grass. There, in the soil, were two prints, a left foot and a right foot, less than a metre apart. She took her notebook out and compared the prints to her drawing. They matched.

She slipped two elastic bands on the ski-pole, twisting them around so that they gripped tightly, then held it above the two footprints, parallel to the ground and an inch or so above the soil. She put the tip of the pole above the back of the heel of the front print and slid one of the bands to mark the position of the tip of the toe of the rear print. Morrison watched her, enthralled. Kerry moved the pole so that it ran through the centre of the rear print and she slid the second elastic band down to mark the position corresponding to the rear of the heel, so marking the length of the stride. She stood up and showed her pole to Morrison. 'Did you follow that?' she asked, and he nodded. 'OK, you have a go then.' She watched over his shoulder as he positioned two elastic bands on his own pole.

When he'd finished he got to his feet. 'Do you want to tell me what we're doing?' he asked.

'Now we've got a record of the length of his stride, and the length of his footprint. And you can use the stick to get an idea of where the next footprint is when you're following a trail. I'll show you tomorrow.'

'You didn't learn that following deer around the Highlands,' said Morrison.

'I got it from a book,' she said. 'A guy called Jack Kearney wrote it. My dad has it in his collection.'

'And where did he learn a trick like that?'

'He was a border guard in southern California. He spent more than twenty years hunting down Mexicans who tried to get into America illegally, and he used to help track down missing kids and the like. Come on, I just want to see which way he went when he got to the hedgerow. My bet is that he turned right and headed east.' She was right. When she reached the hedge she followed it along and eventually discovered a footprint. 'Look, let me show you how to use the stick,' she said. She put the two elastic bands on either end of the print. It was a perfect fit. 'You can see from the way the heel is slightly deeper than the sole that he was walking, rather than running. So if we put the toe marker on the front of the print, and swing the pole around in an arc, we know that the next print should be within the area it covers. There you are. See?'

Morrison looked and saw the rounded mark of a heel

in the ground, not as clear as the first print but definitely there, nevertheless.

Further on the ground sloped sharply down. Kerry held up her hand to stop the two men and she spent a lot of time examining the slope.

'That's interesting,' she said, indicating a bluebell that had been crushed against the grass.

'He went that way?' asked Morrison.

'Look at the way it's been trodden on,' she said. She sat down on the grass next to it and Morrison joined her.

'I don't follow you,' he said.

'The head of the bluebell is higher up the slope than the stalk. That means that whatever squashed it was moving up the slope, not down. If it was The Chinaman, he was coming this way, not going.'

'You mean it would be the other way if he'd been going down the slope?'

'Think about it, Sean, picture a foot coming uphill. It'll push the stalk up. And a foot going down would push the stalk down.'

'Was it definitely him?'

'Can't say for definite. The grass is too thick and springy, there are no marks in the soil. But if it is him, he's going back the same way he came, he's not just running away. He's returning somewhere.' Kerry looked up at the darkening sky. 'We might as well go back,' she said. 'We'll make an early start tomorrow.' Morrison stood up and helped Kerry to her feet.

'Shouldn't we go on?' Kavanagh asked.

'We need a good light,' she explained. 'Otherwise we'll miss something. We know which way he's headed now, we can pick his trail up at first light.'

The three of them walked back to the farmhouse together. Hennessy was waiting for them in the kitchen. Sarah Ryan was there and she rushed over to hug Kerry and kiss her on both cheeks.

'Liam didn't tell me you were coming,' she cried. Sarah was a couple of years younger than Kerry and when they were teenagers they had spent a lot of time together during the school holidays, riding and picnicking in the countryside around the farm.

'God, it's been so long,' Kerry said.

'I've a few more wrinkles,' laughed Sarah.

'Twenty-two years old and you talk about wrinkles, wait until you hit twenty-four!' They hugged each other again.

'Do you want some sandwiches and coffee?' Sarah asked, and Kerry and Morrison both said yes.

O'Hara came in from the hallway as Sarah busied herself with the food. 'Any luck?' he asked.

'More than I would have thought possible,' said Morrison, leaning his pole against the Welsh dresser next to Kerry's. He held out his notebook.

'Very good,' said O'Hara. 'By Sean Morrison, aged four.'

'It's a drawing of his footprint, you prat,' laughed Morrison. He handed it to Hennessy. 'Kerry found the spot where he was hiding in the woods. And we think we know which way he went.' He took off his baseball cap and dropped it on the table.

'Uncle Liam, do you have a map of the area? A large-scale one,' asked Kerry.

'I think so,' he said, and went through to the lounge. He returned with several maps including a large one rolled up in a cardboard tube. He popped it open and pulled it out and she helped him spread it over the kitchen table. Morrison used a cruet set to anchor it down at one side and Sarah gave them two knives to weigh down the other side.

Kerry sat down in front of the map while Morrison and Hennessy looked over her shoulder. She traced out the route they'd taken with her finger, down the track, across the field to the copse, around the edge of the trees and to the hedgerow. 'We got as far as here,' she said, tapping the map. 'But the light was starting to go and I didn't want to make any mistakes. We'll start again first thing in the morning. The interesting thing was, Uncle Liam, there were signs that he was going back the way he'd come. As if he had a base somewhere, you know what I mean?'

'That's a thought,' said Hennessy. 'He must be staying somewhere. I suppose I just assumed that he was living rough.'

'What about the van?' said Kavanagh. 'He'd need somewhere to store the stuff he used to make his explosives. And the landlady in Belfast said he drove away in his van.'

Kerry took one of the small-scale maps and spread it out on top of the first map. She drew a line on it in pencil. 'This is the way he was heading,' she said. The line cut across the B8 and B180 and through Dundrum Bay. 'That's his general direction, so if we assume that wherever he was heading was twenty degrees or so either side of that line, we're left with this,' she said, and drew two more lines either side of the original one, creating two wedge shapes.

'That's still a hell of a lot of countryside,' said Kavanagh, unconvinced.

'Agreed, but he's not likely to be travelling too far, not at night. Let's say two hours, six miles maximum. That would put him in this area.' She made a curving line that cut across the first three lines.

'That includes a good piece of the Mourne Mountains. And a fair smattering of villages,' said Kavanagh.

'He's not likely to leave his van where it would be seen,' said Morrison. 'He's not stupid. He'll know that the army is all over the place and that they don't take kindly to strange vehicles.'

'The van is the key,' agreed Kerry. 'Assuming he has the van, he must have driven it to where he hid it, which means it can't be too far away from a road. I don't think he'd hide it in the mountains, even if he could drive there. I think we should look for a wooded area with a road nearby. I reckon this is the best bet.' She pointed at the Tollymore Forest Park.

Sarah put mugs of coffee on the table and mouthed 'See you tomorrow' to Kerry before slipping out of the kitchen door. Kavanagh looked at the map and scratched his head.

'Yez making a lot of assumptions,' he said. 'The Chinaman could've doubled back, he could've ended up by going west, not east. He might've ditched the van. He could be holed up less than half a mile away, Christ, he could be back in the copse, he could even be watching the house right now.'

'You're so bloody defeatist!' snapped Kerry, surprising them all. She realised her show of temper had shocked them so she smiled in an attempt to defuse the situation. 'You're right, of course,' she said. 'But I don't think west is likely. One, because he headed in the opposite direction, and two, because going west would mean crossing the River Bann, either by bridge, where he'd risk being seen, or through the water, which would be perfectly possible but uncomfortable.'

'And he did say that he'd be back in three days,' said Hennessy.

'Three days?' said Kerry.

'He said I had three days to tell him who's behind the bombings in England,' explained Hennessy. 'He said that if I didn't have the names by then that he'd kill me.'

'Oh God, Uncle Liam. That's terrible.'

Hennessy shrugged. 'It'll be OK, Kerry. Don't think about it. But the fact that he's given me the deadline means there's no need for him to stay close by. And I don't think he'll dump the van. How else is he going to get away when all this is over? I think you're right, Tollymore looks the best bet. Castlewellan Forest Park is another possibility, but that's a mile or so further away.'

'I'm not sure what you're suggesting,' Morrison said to Kerry. 'I thought the idea was to track down The Chinaman.'

She nodded quickly. 'Yeah, yeah, but a two-pronged attack doubles our chances. You and I go after him, following his trail as best we can. But at the same time I think you should send some men to check out the forest and come at him from behind.'

'But the forest is several square miles,' O'Hara protested. 'It would take for ever.'

Kerry shook her head. 'You're forgetting the van,' she said. 'If we're right and he's hidden the van among the trees, then he must have driven it off the road. All you'll have to do is drive along slowly looking for places where he could have turned off. You've got to think like your quarry, put yourself in his place. It might come to nothing, but it's worth a try. And what's the alternative?'

'She's right,' said Hennessy. 'Jim, can you take three of the guys tomorrow morning? Use two of the cars and take a run through the forest. No guns, just in case you come across the army. Just the shotguns, we've got licences for them.'

'Sure, Liam. Whatever ye says.' Kavanagh still sounded decidedly unconvinced.

Kerry sipped her coffee. 'Right, that's all I can do tonight,' she said. 'I'm going to get an early night.'

Hennessy raised his eyebrows. 'It's only nine o'clock, Kerry.'

'When I said we'll make an early start, I meant it,' said Kerry. 'We'll be up at five.'

'Five!' snorted Morrison.

Kerry stood up and grinned at him. 'Say goodnight, Sean,' she said and leant over to kiss Hennessy on the forehead. 'Goodnight, Uncle Liam.'

Hennessy reached over and held her hand. 'Goodnight, Kerry. And thanks. For everything.'

'I haven't done anything yet,' she said. 'But it's going to be all right, I promise.'

The four men watched her go.

'She's one hell of a girl,' said Morrison.

'She's her father's daughter, all right,' agreed Hennessy. 'It must be in the genes.'

'Oh yes,' said Kavanagh, watching Kerry's hips swing. 'It's definitely in her jeans.'

'You, Jim, are a sexist pig.'

'We all have our faults, Sean.'

'If you two children are going to squabble all night I'll

leave you to it,' said Hennessy, getting up from the table and gathering the maps together. He left the three of them sitting together, drinking coffee and reminiscing about the old days.

Morrison woke to the smell of freshly made coffee. He screwed up his eyes and squinted at Kerry, who was sitting on the edge of his bed holding a steaming mug.

'Rise and shine,' she said, and waited until he hauled himself up into a sitting position before handing him the mug. She pulled the curtains open but the sky was just a smudgy grey.

'What time is it?' he asked.

'Four thirty,' she said.

Morrison groaned. He gulped down his coffee and gave her back the empty mug. 'How come you look so wide awake?' he asked.

'I'm used to it. When we run the executive courses, Dad always gets me to do the night-time marches and stuff like that. It's great fun, we send them to bed at midnight and then wake them up at three in the morning and take them for a six-mile hike. They look like death when they get back.'

Kerry looked nothing like death, just then, Morrison thought. Her blue eyes were bright and clear and she seemed to be bursting with energy, her chestnut hair was still damp from the shower and she'd even put on make-up, a little mascara and a touch of lipstick. He doubted that it was for The Chinaman's benefit and he felt suddenly pleased that she'd made the effort for him.

'What are you thinking?' she asked. 'You've a wistful look about you, Sean Morrison.'

'I was just thinking how dog-tired I am,' he lied. 'Right, get out of my room and let me wash. I'll be downstairs in five minutes.'

'Do you want breakfast?' she asked.

The mere thought of food at that time of the morning made Morrison's stomach lurch and he declined, but said he wouldn't mind another coffee.

When he walked into the kitchen, drying his hair with a blue towel, it was waiting for him. Kavanagh was there, along with three men he'd decided to take with him to the woods: Roy O'Donnell, Tommy O'Donoghue and Michael O'Faolain, all of whom looked totally wrecked. Hennessy was there, too, sitting at the table with a collection of guns and walkie-talkies in front of him. As Morrison sipped his coffee, Hennessy handed him one of the guns, a small automatic. 'Be careful,' warned Hennessy. 'Any sign of the army and dump it fast.'

Morrison nodded, more interested in the two other guns on the table. They had short, wide barrels and looked as if they fired just one cartridge. He realised what they were just as Hennessy began to speak. Flare guns. Hennessy was a keen sailor and they were obviously guns for firing distress flares.

'I want you to take one of these, Sean, and let it off if you get close to The Chinaman and need help. You can call in with the radio, but that won't identify your position, so call us up and then fire the flare. I'll give you half a dozen cartridges.'

'Do we take the other one?' asked Kavanagh.

'No, I've only got the two and I'll need one here to signal to Sean and Kerry.'

'But we'll have the walkie-talkie,' said Morrison.

'Yes, but only to call me, you won't be able to leave it on receive in case you get close to The Chinaman and he hears it. If I want to contact you I'll let off a flare and you can call me up on the radio when you're sure it's safe. You'll only use the walkie-talkie if I signal you with the flare or if you've dealt with The Chinaman.'

'Dealt with?' said Kerry.

'Captured,' said Hennessy. 'Or whatever.' He held out two of the walkie-talkies to Kavanagh. 'You can use these, Jim, keep one in each car. If you catch The Chinaman you call me and I'll contact Kerry and Sean. Does that make sense?'

'It sounds hellish complicated,' said Morrison.

'Uncle Liam's right though,' said Kerry. 'Out there in the countryside sound travels a long way, especially electronic noise.'

'And don't forget the army monitors all radio frequencies so we'll have to keep all transmissions to a minimum anyway,' added Hennessy. He gave a small canvas haversack to Morrison. 'You can use this for the flare gun and the radio,' he said.

Kerry picked up the ski-poles from beside the Welsh dresser and stood by the kitchen door.

'What about food, and water?' Morrison asked.

She patted a small rucksack slung over her shoulder. 'Here,' she said. 'And the maps. And torches. And anything else we might need. Come on, Sean, time to saddle up and move out.'

'Yes, Tonto,' he laughed. He packed the walkie-talkie and the flare gun and slipped the automatic into the inside pocket of his bomber jacket. It was heavy and the jacket bulged.

'This might be more comfortable,' said Kavanagh, and slid a clip-on holster across the table. Morrison slotted the gun in and then clipped the holster to the back of his jeans.

'Better?' asked Kavanagh.

'Much,' said Morrison. 'Good hunting, OK?'

Kavanagh made a gun with his hand and sighted down it at Morrison as he and Kerry went out of the door.

'You lads had better be careful, too,' warned Hennessy. 'We've got licences for those shotguns but don't go waving them around the Brits, for God's sake. The last thing we need right now is trouble with the army.'

'Don't yez worry, Liam, we'll be just fine,' said Kavanagh. 'We'd better be off.' Kavanagh took the three men out into the courtyard and shortly afterwards Hennessy heard the two Land-Rovers start up and drive off. Willie O'Hara, his hair tousled and his eyes bleary, staggered into the kitchen and slumped into a chair.

'What's all the noise, Liam?'

'The lads on the way out after The Chinaman. Do you want coffee?'

'A whiskey'd go down a treat, right enough.'

'Aye, you're right. I'll join you.'

As Hennessy poured the whiskey into two tumblers, Kerry and Morrison walked across the fields towards the copse. The grass was covered with a sheen of morning dew that glistened in the early light. This time there was no need to walk through the trees so Kerry took him around the perimeter of the copse and along the hedgerow. When they arrived at the slope where they'd examined the squashed bluebell the previous evening, Kerry slowed the pace right down and began walking slowly, her eyes scanning the ground left and right like a fighter pilot scrutinising the sky. Morrison followed behind her and slightly to her left.

'What exactly do I look for?' he asked.

'If we're lucky we'll see a clear sign, like the footprints we saw yesterday, or vegetation that's been trampled. But signs like that'll be few and far between. Generally all we can expect to see are slight changes, small things. It's hard to explain. Sometimes it's just a feeling that something isn't right.'

'What sort of changes?'

Kerry prodded the ground with her pole and knelt down to inspect the grass. 'Differences in texture or colour of the vegetation, any regular marks in the ground that aren't natural, flattening of leaves or dirt, twigs or stones that have been moved. Anything that he might have dropped. None of those things in themselves prove that he's gone this way but taken together they all add up to a trail.' She turned round as she crouched and pointed back the way they'd come. 'You can't move across a field without leaving some sort of trace,' she said.

Morrison turned and looked. Two lines of footprints were clearly marked in the damp grass stretching back across the fields as far as he could see.

'The obvious signs will disappear as the sun evaporates the dew over the morning, but you see what I mean.' She began walking again. 'A lot of it is common sense, too,' she said. 'You've got to think like your quarry. If you come to an obstruction, like a hedge or a river, then you've got to be able to guess what he'll do, whether he'll go to the right or the left, whether he'll go through a group of trees or round them, what he'll do if he comes across a cottage or a farm. In some ways it's easier to follow a man than a deer. A man usually has a reason for going somewhere, unless he's lost, and if he's lost then he's pretty keen to be found. A deer is trying to avoid humans and most of the time it's probably just grazing.'

'You've hunted humans before?'

Kerry laughed. 'Not with a gun, no. Even the Germans draw the line at deer, but it's a thought, isn't it? We could even arrange for the ears to be mounted.'

'Yeah, OK, hunted was the wrong word. Tracked, then.'

'From time to time a tourist will get lost in the mountains and the mountain rescue team will call up my dad and ask him for help. I've been with him a couple of times. But like I said, it's one thing to track someone who's hoping to be found, it's quite another to trail a man who wants to hide. And The Chinaman is certainly going to be hiding. At least the weather's going to be good. I suppose you know how the Blackfoot Indians forecast the weather?'

'What?'

'Weather forecasting, Indian-style. Here, I'll show you.' She bent down and picked up a small stone and twisted a piece of grass around it so that it was hanging like a conker on a string.

'That's it?' asked Morrison, intrigued.

'That's it,' she said. 'You hold it in front of you like this, and you watch it. Here, you hold it.'

She handed it to him and Morrison studied the stone. 'Now what?' he asked.

'Well, first you touch it. If it feels dry, the weather is fine. If it feels warm, it's a hot day. If it turns white, it's snowing. And if it's wet, it's raining. Then you look at it. If it's swinging from side to side, it's windy.'

Morrison laughed, realising he'd been taken for a ride.

'And, Sean . . .'

'Yes,' he said warily.

'If you can't see it, it's probably foggy.' They both dissolved into laughter.

The telephone rang in the hallway. 'I'll get it,' said O'Hara, who was sitting closer to the door than Hennessy. He picked up the receiver and then put his hand over the mouthpiece. 'It's for you,' he called. 'Won't give his name.'

Hennessy pushed himself up from the table and took the phone from O'Hara. 'Liam Hennessy,' he said.

'It's Bromley,' said a gruff voice. Hennessy reached behind him and closed the door on O'Hara, not wanting him to hear.

'They called?' Hennessy asked.

'They called, but they didn't give a codeword. What's going on, Hennessy?'

Hennessy was confused and he put his hand to his head. 'Look, Bromley, if they didn't give the codeword, maybe it wasn't them.'

'It was them all right. The Press Association took the call last night. It was a man, Irish accent, and he said there would be no further co-operation with the British security forces and no more use of the codeword system.'

'So how do you know the call was kosher?'

'He knew exactly where the bomb had been placed and how much explosive was in it. And with all the other bombs they claimed responsibility within twenty-four hours. We had the normal hoax calls but that was the only one that had enough details to convince us that it was genuine.'

Hennessy closed his eyes. This wasn't what he had expected at all.

'Somebody talked,' said Bromley.

'That's not possible,' insisted Hennessy. 'Only two people knew what was happening. Me and the man you met in London, Sean Morrison.'

'Well, one of you isn't to be trusted. And only you know which one it is.'

'I brought Morrison back from the United States especially for this. He'd been away for two years, so there's no way at all that he could be involved with the active service unit.'

'Maybe you talk in your sleep,' said Bromley.

'I'll treat that remark with the contempt it deserves,' replied Hennessy, but something cold ran down his spine and settled in the pit of his stomach.

'So what do you think went wrong? Do you think it was just coincidence, that they decided on a whim not to use the codeword so soon after you changed it?'

'No, of course not. We've changed it twice before this year and each time they've picked it up immediately. No, you're right, they've been warned off. But for the life of me I can't think who it might be. Look, give me a number where I can reach you. I've got some thinking to do.'

Bromley read out a number and Hennessy wrote it down. 'I can get you there day or night?' he asked.

'If I'm not there, they'll be able to get hold of me.'

'I'll call you as soon as I find out what's happening.'

'For your sake I hope it's not too late,' said Bromley.

'What do you mean?'

He heard Bromley click his tongue as if thinking, and when he spoke again his voice was hesitant. 'The climate is changing here, Hennessy. These bombings have been so vicious that public opinion is turning against the IRA in a way that I've never seen before. We're not just talking about right-wing MPs calling for the death penalty or sending in the SAS, this is different. Part of it is the lack of warnings, but a lot has got to do with the choice of targets. When the IRA killed MPs like Airey Neave and Ian Gow you might have been able to justify them as political killings, and the Stock Exchange and the Carlton Club could just about be described as establishment targets, but these latest atrocities, I mean, Bank Tube station, for God's sake. And Ascot. I'll tell you, Hennessy, if much more of this goes on you could find the rules changing.'

'What do you mean, rules changing?'

'I mean that, despite what you might think, in the past the IRA has had a relatively easy ride from the British Government.'

Hennessy snorted. 'Bullshit. The Catholics in Northern Ireland have been ridden rough-shod over in a . . .'

'We're not talking about Catholics, we're talking about the IRA. And all I'm saying is that you and your friends in Dublin, if you're serious about not being involved in these bombings, are going to have to pull your fingers out, or you'll feel a backlash the likes of which you've never known before.'

'I hear what you're saying, Bromley. And I've got your number.' The line went dead. Hennessy went back into the kitchen, where O'Hara was sitting at the table spooning cornflakes into his mouth.

'Trouble?' he asked, seeing the worried look on Hennessy's face.

321

'It's OK, Willie. Nothing I can't handle.' Oh really? said a voice in his head that sounded disturbingly like Mary's.

Christy Murphy arrived at the farm just before ten o'clock. Hennessy was making coffee when one of the guards knocked on the kitchen door and announced that somebody was driving down the track towards the farm. A few seconds later a car crunched into the courtyard and Murphy let himself into the kitchen.

'Christy, just in time for coffee,' said Hennessy, waving the large man to a chair. 'Come on, sit down. How's my wife?'

Murphy stood where he was, clenching and unclenching his hands like a prize-fighter about to get into the ring. His big, square face was creased into a frown and for a moment Hennessy feared that something had happened to Mary.

'Mary's all right, isn't she, Christy?'

'She's fine, Liam, but . . .' His voice tailed off.

Hennessy pushed his plate away. 'What's wrong, Christy? Cat got your tongue?'

Murphy seemed to be struggling for his words, and although he was normally a quiet man this was something different. He was acting like a small boy who wanted to confess to breaking a window but who was worried about being punished.

'Can I speak to you, Liam. In private?' he said.

'Of course, of course. Come through to the lounge.' Hennessy got to his feet and took the big man through the hallway.

As the morning sun climbed higher and higher in the sky, Kerry found it progressively harder to follow The

Chinaman's trail. Morrison didn't have to ask why, she'd already explained about the importance the angle of the sun played in defining footprints. Eventually, after it had taken her the best part of an hour to cover a hundred yards, she called a halt.

'I think we should rest for a while,' she said. She indicated a leafy birch tree in the middle of a hedgerow. 'Let's sit in the shade,' she said. They dropped down into the cool grass and she opened her rucksack. She took out a pack of sandwiches and two cans of ginger beer. 'I knew we'd be out here for some time,' she said.

'How long do you think it'll take?' he asked, helping himself to a sandwich.

'The trail is cold,' she admitted. 'He's still heading for the forest, by the look of it, and if he is we've a better chance of finding him among the trees. It's harder to move through woods without leaving signs.'

'Can't we just go straight there?'

Kerry shrugged. 'We could, but we'd be taking a risk. There's still a chance he might turn north or south before we get there, and even if he doesn't we won't know for sure where he went into the trees. You can't take short-cuts, Sean. If we make a wrong call, we might have to spend hours backtracking.' She popped open the can of ginger beer.

'You know best,' he said. He held up his sandwich. 'These are good,' he said. 'You make them?'

'Yeah, I had plenty of time while you were still in the land of Nod.'

They ate together in silence, enjoying the feel of the fresh summer breeze on their faces.

'You live in New York now?' Kerry asked, brushing crumbs from her trousers.

Morrison nodded. 'Yeah, raising funds, flying the flag, telling the Yanks where their money is going.'

'Don't you miss it?'

'Miss what?'

'The crack. The kick from being in Belfast, where it's all happening.' She frowned. 'You know what I mean, surely. The fight is in Northern Ireland, not in the States, and certainly not in Scotland.' The look of intensity was back in her eyes.

'There are different ways of helping the Cause,' he said quietly, aware once again how quickly her temper could flare, how she'd snapped at Kavanagh in the farmhouse.

'Like my dad, you mean. Hiding in Scotland. And keeping me with him.'

'Hey, come on now, Kerry. Your father has heard the rattle of soil on too many coffin lids to deserve that. No one has done more for the IRA than Micky Geraghty, you shouldn't forget that.'

She shook her head. 'I know, that's not what I meant. It's not so much that he's out of it now, it's more that he won't let me get involved. He's so fucking protective.'

Morrison looked at her and immediately felt protective towards her himself. Her cheeks were flushing, her chin was up and her eyes flashed fire. She looked as if she was ready to fight the whole world. She was keen, there was no doubt about that, but he also knew that Long Kesh was full of men who had failed to temper enthusiasm with wisdom. 'You should be glad you're out of it,' he said quietly.

'I'll never be glad until the British are out of Ireland.

324

It's our country, Sean, our country and our religion. You know what I mean, I know you do. You feel the same as I do when you see the black bastards swaggering through the streets in their bowler hats and sashes, their flutes and drums, ramming their religion down our throats. Did it never happen to you, Sean? Being grabbed by the bastard Billy boys and being forced to say "Fuck The Pope" and "All Catholics Are Shit". Tell me that never happened to you. Tell me that your bile doesn't rise when you see an Orange parade.'

Morrison said nothing, because he knew she was right.

'I want this Chinaman,' she said. 'I want to show Uncle Liam what I can do. If I can prove myself just this once, he'll let me do more for the Cause, and it won't matter what my dad thinks.'

In the distance to the west a white star climbed into the sky leaving a greyish-blue trail zig-zagging behind it. The star popped with the sound of a bursting balloon.

'That's Uncle Liam!' she said.

Morrison took the walkie-talkie out of the haversack and switched it on. 'Are you there?' he said. No names were to be used because the army constantly swept the airwaves.

'I want you back here,' said Hennessy's voice. 'Now.'

'OK, we're on our way. Have you found him?'

'No, I just want you back.'

'Understood.' He switched off the receiver.

Kerry had heard and she sat forward. 'I wonder what's happened?'

'No idea,' said Morrison.

'Look, Sean, I think I should stay out here. Uncle Liam said they haven't found The Chinaman yet. And you can see how slowly it's going. I want to keep at it, you can come back here once you've sorted out what he wants.'

'How will I know where you are?' he said. 'You're the tracker, not me.'

'I'm not going to be moving that fast.' She picked up a long twig from the hedgerow. 'I'll leave sticks like this sticking up every hundred yards or so, and I'll drag the pole through any patches of soil I pass. You'll have no problems finding me again. And I'm not likely to stumble across him, am I? This trail is dead cold. It'll save time.'

'I'll have to check with him,' said Sean, and switched the receiver back on. 'Are you there?'

There was a delay before he heard Hennessy reply. 'I'm here.'

'I'll come back alone.'

'Is that wise?'

'It'll save time later and we are quite sure there's no danger out here. Unless there's a problem.'

Hennessy was quiet for a while as he considered Morrison's suggestion. 'Be careful,' he said eventually.

'Yeah!' said Kerry.

'Any doubt at all and you both come in,' Hennessy said to Morrison.

'Understood,' he replied, and switched off the receiver again.

'Like he says, be careful,' Morrison said. He opened the haversack and took out the flare gun and the cartridges. He handed them, and the walkie-talkie, to her. 'You'd better take these,' he said.

'What about the gun?' she asked.

Morrison shook his head emphatically. 'No, no gun,' he said. 'Liam was quite clear on that score. And if you think you're getting close and there's any chance of you finding him, then pull back and call me on that.' He nodded at the walkie-talkie. 'I'll be back once I've found out what it is that he wants.'

'It must be important otherwise he'd have told you on the radio what it was,' she said.

Morrison thought about that as he jogged back to the farmhouse. Though they had been out for more than five hours they had covered just three miles and it only took him forty minutes to get back.

He was in good condition and he'd barely worked up a sweat by the time he walked into the courtyard to find O'Hara there with two men carrying shotguns. The guns were broken, the barrels pointing down to the ground, but Morrison could see the brass ends of cartridges in place.

'Liam's in the lounge,' said O'Hara.

'Everything OK?' asked Morrison, hoping for some clue as to what was going on.

'Fucked if I know,' said O'Hara. The two men with shotguns said goodbye to O'Hara and walked across the courtyard towards the cottage. Morrison felt himself sigh with relief. For a wild moment he had thought that they had been waiting for him. An armed escort.

He wiped his feet carefully on the mat by the kitchen door and walked through to the lounge. The door was half open and he walked in to find Hennessy sitting in one of the armchairs by the unlit fire. He didn't get up as Morrison entered. 'Sit down, Sean,' he said. He seemed distant, almost shocked, and the one thought in Morrison's mind was that there had been another bombing. As he went over to the sofa he realised there was somebody else in the room, standing by the door. It was Christy Murphy.

'Christy!' he said, surprised. 'When did you get back?'

Murphy looked away from Morrison and seemed ill at ease.

'Christy, you can wait outside,' said Hennessy, and Murphy practically ran out of the door so keen was he to get out of Morrison's presence. Hennessy studied Morrison with unsmiling eyes as Murphy closed the door and Morrison began to worry, but the fear was a shapeless, nameless thing, made all the more terrifying by his inability to identify it. He wanted to speak, to ask what was wrong, but felt that to do so would be to imply guilt and that his interests would be best served by keeping quiet. He could feel sweat on the palms of his hands but he resisted the urge to wipe them on his trousers. Liam Hennessy might look like a kindly grandfather but he had the power of life and death and would have no compunction at all about killing somebody who he thought had crossed him. Thoughts of Mary Hennessy flashed into his mind and he felt his cheeks redden.

'The bombers have claimed responsibility for the Ascot bomb,' Hennessy said flatly.

Morrison frowned, because that surely was good news, and yet Hennessy said it as if he was announcing the death of a close relative. 'And?' he said.

'And they didn't use the codeword. In fact, they said they weren't going to co-operate with the authorities any more and that there would be no more use of the codeword system.'

Hennessy looked at Morrison with cold, unblinking eyes and Morrison fought to keep his own steady on the older man's face, trying to stay cool. Eventually he weakened and looked out of the window. The two men with the shotguns were back. He looked at Hennessy again.

'Which means that somebody tipped them off,' said Hennessy. He continued to stare straight at Morrison and again Morrison was forced to avert his gaze. 'The problem is, only two people knew about the reason for the change in the codeword. You. And me.'

Morrison held up his hands. 'I don't know what you're thinking, but I didn't tell anyone, Liam. I knew how important this was. I spoke to Bromley, and that was all. I swear, on my mother's eyes, I swear it.'

Hennessy steepled his fingers underneath his chin and studied Morrison as if he was an undecided juror.

'You must have said something to somebody, Sean. Think very carefully.'

The two men sat in a silence which was disturbed only by the ticking of a grandfather clock in the corner. Morrison was genuinely bewildered, because he knew that he hadn't broken Hennessy's confidence. He was sure of it. And yet Hennessy seemed so convinced.

Morrison shook his head, not knowing what Hennessy expected to hear.

'Would it help if I told you that I had Christy follow Mary in London?'

Morrison felt as if he'd been kicked in the stomach. He would have been able to face it better if Hennessy had shouted or banged his fist or thrown something at him, but he did none of those things, he simply sat in his easy chair and waited for a reply. It was his quiet acceptance of the facts, an acceptance that bordered on apparent indifference, that made the man seem all the more menacing. Morrison wondered if he was about to die, shot in the back of the head because he'd slept with another man's wife. He thought of lying, of claiming that she had just popped round to the hotel as a casual visitor, but he knew that it wouldn't work. Murphy wasn't stupid, he'd have found out that she'd gone to his room and would have known how long she was in there.

'Liam, I'm sorry . . .' he began to say, but Hennessy held up a hand to silence him.

'I don't want apologies, I don't even want to know what happened in your room. We'll leave that for some other time. All I want to do right now is to establish what went wrong, how they found out what we were up to. I know Mary was in your room on Monday morning, what I don't know is what you said to her. What you talked about.'

'You don't suspect Mary, surely?' said Morrison.

'At the moment I don't know who to trust, you've quite clearly demonstrated that I'm no judge of character,' said Hennessy savagely. 'Now don't fuck with me, Sean. Did you or did you not discuss our plan with Mary?'

'No,' said Morrison immediately. 'I mean yes, sort of. She already knew what you were doing.'

'She did not,' said Hennessy emphatically. 'I told no one. And I mean no one.'

'But I'm sure . . .' He lapsed into silence, trying to remember exactly what she'd said as she lay in his arms in the afterglow of their love-making. 'She seemed to know already.'

'Think carefully about what she said. We spoke on the phone, remember? Could she hear what we were saying?'

It all came back to Morrison with a rush, him lying on his back talking to Hennessy on the phone as Mary made love to him. 'Yes, she could hear us,' he said. His voice sounded a million miles away. He wondered if Hennessy could see into his mind, if he knew exactly how he'd been betrayed. 'And you're right, it was afterwards that she mentioned the codeword.'

'She steered the conversation?'

Morrison nodded. 'She made it sound as if you'd already told her what was going on. Most of the time I was just agreeing with what she said.'

'She is good at manipulating people,' said Hennessy, his voice loaded with sadness. Morrison suddenly felt sorry for the man. And guilty. And afraid.

'You think that Mary told the bombers?' asked Morrison. The possibility seemed so remote it was almost laughable.

'Not directly, no. But I think she found out from you what we were planning, and I think that she passed that information on to someone else.'

'Who?'

Hennessy fell silent again. He leant forward in his chair, his elbows on his knees. He took a handkerchief from his top pocket and wiped his brow. 'Do I trust you, Sean? After the way you've betrayed me, can I trust you?'

'My loyalty to the Cause has never been in question, Liam. The thing with Mary, that's different. I never meant to hurt you, I didn't plan for you to know. We were always very careful.'

'You lied to me, you went behind my back. And now I'm supposed to trust you?'

'Liam, I'm sorry. If it makes a difference, it was one of the reasons I went to the States. To put distance between Mary and me. To stop it.'

'You mean she wanted to continue the affair?' Hennessy sounded wounded, hurt.

Morrison realised he was making it worse by talking about it. Maybe Hennessy hadn't even considered that the affair had been going on before he went to New York. 'We decided it was best,' he lied. 'Liam, whatever happened is in the past, what matters now is to get these bastards and to put an end to the bombings. To do what we set out to do. We can deal with our personal problems afterwards.'

Hennessy nodded and settled back in the chair. 'Maybe you're right, Sean. All right, we'll put that to one side. For the moment we'll concentrate on minimising the damage, maybe even turning it to our advantage.'

'What do you mean?'

'I had a visitor before you and Kerry arrived. Hugh McGrath. He knew Mary was in London, but there was no way he could have known that.'

'Unless she told him?'

'Unless she told him,' agreed Hennessy. 'She spoke to you, she tricked the information out of you, and then she called him.' Hennessy let it sink in, and then twisted the knife. 'She used you, Sean.' There was bitterness in his voice, a nasty edge which cut through Morrison. He wondered then whether Hennessy really was prepared to put the affair behind them while they sorted out the bombing business. But he knew that Hennessy was right. Mary had bedded him and used him, barely waiting for him to leave before ringing McGrath. Another thought wormed its way into his mind. Maybe she was also McGrath's lover. Maybe she did to McGrath the same things she did to him, gave him her kisses, her passion, her energy, the things he thought she saved solely for him. He thought of her sitting astride McGrath, his hands on her breasts, her riding him until she came, and he felt the anger burn inside and realised for the first time exactly how bitter and betrayed Hennessy must have felt.

'I know she was angry, but I never thought she'd go that far,' said Hennessy, almost as if he was talking to himself, or unburdening himself at confession. Morrison couldn't think of anything to say, knowing how easy it would be to provoke the man. 'Mary never forgave me for not going after the men who killed her brother.'

'They're all in Long Kesh, aren't they?'

'You know as well as I do that we could get to them, wherever they are, H-blocks or no H-blocks. She knew that, too. She never let me forget it. We've been arguing for months. Years.'

'Arguing?'

'Mary's always been one hundred per cent behind the organisation, much more than most people realise. We used to have the most fierce arguments, she couldn't understand why I was trying to take a more conciliatory line with the Protestants. She was always pushing me to gear up the campaigns, to turn the screw, to drive the British out. And that was before Gerry was killed. His death pushed her over the edge, I guess. I should have realised, I should have talked to her more. But by then I suppose we'd stopped talking. Really talking, you know what I mean?'

Morrison nodded, but he was fearful of being forced into the role of confessor. Hennessy was a man who guarded his secrets jealously.

'McGrath was always a possibility, anyway,' continued Hennessy. 'He makes more money out of the border than anyone else in the organisation, and he has strong links

333

with Gaddafi. It'd also explain why we haven't been able to pin down the active service unit's bombmaker. It could be a complete outsider, someone that McGrath sent to Libya for training without telling us.'

'Is that possible?' said Morrison, eager to turn the conversation away from Mary.

'Perfectly. We've always given him a lot of leeway when it came to dealing with the Libyans.'

'But why would he have to take explosives and equipment from our stocks? Couldn't he just bring in his own supplies?'

'Some, maybe, but not on any large scale. He'd have to use our established routes to get it into the country and he couldn't do that without us knowing. And he'd know that if he was discovered organising secret deliveries that we'd know what he was up to. He wouldn't want to take the risk. Much safer to take what he needed from existing caches.'

'OK, so assuming it is McGrath, what next?'

'He has to tell us where the bombers are,' said Hennessy. 'We get him here and we get the names from him.'

'He's a powerful man, Liam. He carries almost as much influence with Dublin as you do, and he's virtually got his own private army on his farm. We can't just wade in and expect him to open up to us.'

'I know, I know. I'm going to speak to Dublin now. And McGrath is going to come to us. I want you to call him and tell him that I've called an emergency meeting of our top officials here at the farm. Tell him it's about a change in our bombing strategy, that should bring him running. Tell him the boys are coming down from Belfast and the meeting is for noon.'

'Sure,' agreed Morrison. He felt somewhat easier now that Hennessy was concentrating on McGrath but he knew that underneath his neutral exterior the man must be in turmoil. Liam Hennessy was well used to concealing his emotions in the courtroom, and his big advantage had always been that his opponents never knew what he was thinking. He was a difficult man to read, but, no matter how calm he looked, the business over Mary would be gnawing at his insides and at some point it would emerge into the open. Morrison would have to be careful, very careful. One of the men with shotguns was looking into the window and he caught Morrison's eye. The man winked. Morrison didn't feel any better.

Fisher stood on the balcony with half a loaf of stale bread on the table next to him. He picked up a slice and tore it into small pieces and tossed them out into the air. A flock of unruly seagulls sitting on a barge across the river came squawking over and swooped and soared around him. He picked up another slice and ripped it into small bits and threw them one at a time high into the air so that the birds could catch them on the wing.

'You know what I'd like?' said McCormick behind him.

'What's that?' Two of the black-headed gulls collided in mid-air with the sound of a quilt being thumped.

'A twelve-bore shotgun,' said McCormick. 'Then we could have some real fun.'

'You, McCormick, have no beauty in your soul.' Fisher tossed out a handful of bread and birds swooped from all directions, beaks wide and wings flapping. When all the bread had been devoured, he went back into the flat.

'It's done,' said The Bombmaker.

Fisher sat down and looked at the laptop computer. 'It looks so inoffensive, doesn't it?' he said, running his hand along the smooth plastic. 'And it works just as it did before?'

'Sure. There's no way of discovering that it's been modified unless it's taken apart. And they won't do that.'

'Excellent,' said Fisher.

'I've even fixed it so that the time is set by using the keyboard. It's a trick the Libyans taught me, a relatively simple program incorporated into the disk operating system. Once we know when we want it to explode, I call up the program and input the time. The computer does the rest.'

Fisher grinned. 'I'm impressed,' he said. 'And it'll get through the X-ray machines?'

'Even the new models. The only drawback is that there's no room for a barometric device. We can't use altitude to detonate it, so we have to be sure of the timing.'

Fisher nodded. 'I don't see that being a problem, so long as we stick to a scheduled flight. What about the mule?'

'I've narrowed it down to two. A journalist and a cameraman who works for Thames TV. What about you?'

'There's a girl, an investment banker, who says she'll be going to Paris next week. She always flies British Airways, she says. I think we take the first one to confirm a flight, agreed?'

'Fine by me,' said The Bombmaker.

Woody worked flat out to finish the school-holidays feature because he hadn't been told yet whether or not he was working the Saturday shift and the news desk weren't at all happy about his three-hour lunch with Annie. He was determined to keep in their good books, at least until they'd drawn up the weekend rota, but he was suffering. He was all too well aware that he hadn't become a journalist twenty years earlier to end up writing crap like that, but, as usual, he needed the money. He'd cashed two cheques at separate pubs and promised that he'd have enough money in his account to cover them by the end of the following week. He'd been fighting to keep his head above water financially for the last two years but he was getting nowhere. He needed a staff job, but Woody was a realist, his age and his track record were against him. What he needed was a big one, an exclusive story that he could sell for big money and which would restore his tarnished reputation. Yeah, he thought, dream on. Number forty-eight. Take them to the zoo. And feed them to the lions, he typed, and then just as quickly deleted it. It'd be just his luck for something like that to get into the paper.

He finished the feature and as he sent it into the news desk queue the phone on his desk rang. It was Pat Quigley, calling from Belfast.

'Hiya, Woody. I wasn't sure if I'd catch you in, this early in the week, but I remember you didn't like being bothered at home.'

Woody leant back in his swivel chair and put his feet on the desk. 'No need for sarcasm, mate. You caught me at a bad time. Anyway, how's it going?'

'Not so bad, Woody. I'm calling about the Hennessy thing.'

'Yeah?' said Woody, suddenly interested but trying to conceal it.

'His driver's in hospital. Somebody bombed his car.

I'm told by a really good source that it happened on his farm. I started making a few enquiries and it seems that two more of his men are in hospital here in Belfast. One's been stabbed, the other has some sort of strange wounds in his foot. It's bloody curious, Woody, especially after the attack on Hennessy's office. Do you have any idea what's going on?'

'Sounds bloody mysterious to me, Pat. Are you sure it's not the Protestants?'

'Doubtful. There hasn't been much aggro between the guys at the top, not for a while. I suppose it could be starting up again, but it doesn't feel right. There haven't been any other attacks, either on the IRA or the UDA. It looks like a one-off.'

'I don't know what to say, Pat. I don't see how I can help.'

'You said you'd have a look for the name of the reader who was asking about Hennessy.'

'He wasn't asking about Hennessy. He just wanted to write to a few Sinn Fein officials. I really don't think he's your man.'

'OK, fine, but can you at least dig out his name for me?'

'I tried, but I can't find it in any of my notebooks. I did look, Pat, honest. It's just one of those things, you know?'

'OK, Woody. Fair enough. I thought I'd check.' Woody could tell he wasn't convinced, but there was nothing he could do. Like Woody he was a freelance and dependent upon the paper's goodwill, he couldn't afford to offend anyone, even another freelance, especially a freelance who was doing regular shifts at head office. Quigley rang off.

When Woody went over to the news desk, Simpson was leaning back in his chair, his immaculate shoes on the desk.

'Good piece, Woody, a classic!' he shouted, giving Woody the thumbs up.

Woody gave him a mock bow from the waist and pulled his forelock before approaching the desk. 'About that story idea I had,' Woody said.

'Pull up a pew,' said Simpson and kicked over a chair.

Woody sat down. 'Remember that guy who came to the office trying to offer a reward over the Knightsbridge bombing?'

Simpson screwed up his face like a baby about to cry. 'The Chinaman?' he said.

'Yeah, The Chinaman. Only I've found out he's Vietnamese, not Chinese. His wife and daughter were killed in the bombing and he wanted to get the men responsible.'

'Thousands of pounds in a carrier bag, right?'

'Right. He rang back a while later, said he wanted to talk to the IRA direct. He wanted names of people high up in the organisation.'

'And you gave them to him?'

'Right. Not the IRA, because you know what they'd do to him, but I gave him a few names of the top Sinn Fein people. Now someone is running some sort of vendetta against one of the men, Liam Hennessy. His office has been bombed, his car has been hit and three of his men are in hospital. And the man that came to see me has disappeared.'

'Disappeared?'

'He used to own a Chinese take-away in Clapham. He's sold up and vanished.'

'And you think he's in Belfast?'

Woody nodded. 'If he was crazy enough to offer a reward, he might just be crazy enough to take matters into his own hands.'

'But you said Hennessy's office was bombed. You think this Chinaman has got hold of bombs?'

Woody leant forward, his eyes sparkling. 'That's the kicker. He's a Vietcong assassin! The bastard can kill with his bare hands, he can make bombs, booby traps, the works.'

'Woody, someone's been pulling your chain!'

Woody explained about the Home Office file and Nguyen's life story. When he'd finished, Simpson picked up a ballpoint pen and began chewing the end. 'So what are you suggesting, Woody?'

'Let me go to Belfast and sniff around.'

'Expensive,' said Simpson.

'If the paper'll pay for my flight and cover my expenses, I'll take the fee as lineage. No story, no payment.' Simpson agreed. 'But if I get a splash, I want serious money. You'll have the best exclusive this year.'

'If you're right.'

'If I'm right. Is it a deal?' he asked.

'I've got a better idea, a better deal.'

'What?' said Woody, warily.

Simpson reached for a letter on his desk and handed it to Woody.

'We've been invited to a conference in Rome. A security conference. All the top guys are going to be there, including David Tucker, the head of Scotland Yard's Anti-Terrorist Branch and a couple of MPs. Some of Europe's top terrorist experts are going to be speaking. It's supposed

340

to be about computerised intelligence systems, but we've been tipped off that they're going to announce a new international database to help in the hunt for terrorists worldwide.'

'Government tip?' asked Woody.

Simpson grinned. 'Who else? We might show a fair bit of tits and bums but politically we're right behind the Government, and we've got several million readers. The Government wants a big show from this conference, so a few select newspapers have been invited along. They're offering to fly us out on a chartered flight with some of the speakers, all we have to do is cover expenses.'

'And report the Government line.'

'Don't bite the hand that feeds you, Woody,' replied Simpson.

'Perish the thought,' said Woody. He waved the letter. 'You want me to go to this? You know the flight is tonight?'

'Yeah I know. We were sitting on it but in view of what happened at Ascot, we'd be crazy to turn it down. I was thinking about sending Williams but he's gone down with the flu. You'll get a bloody good story out of the conference, and you're sure to pick up some juicy stuff behind the scenes. And while you're there you can pick their brains about what's going on in Belfast. I'd be amazed if they hadn't heard something.'

Woody nodded his head thoughtfully. It made good sense. 'And what about me going to Belfast?'

'Fly straight there from Rome when the conference is over. We'll fix up the ticket for you. Can you fly direct?'

'I dunno, I'll find out. So it's a deal?'

'It's a deal, Woody. Just one thing.'

'What's that?'

341

'Keep off the sauce.'

'You know me,' said Woody, heading back to his desk.

'Yeah,' muttered Simpson. 'Too true I do.'

Woody went back to his desk just in time to answer his phone. It was Maggie. 'Hello, Woody. Do you fancy a drink some time tomorrow?' she asked.

'I can't, I'm afraid. I'm off to Rome tonight. You must be psychic, I've only just been told.'

'What time are you going?'

He looked at the letter. 'Eight thirty, so I'll have to get to the airport about seven, I suppose. And then I'm going to Belfast.'

'Belfast?' she said. Woody explained briefly about the conversation he'd had with Pat Quigley.

'Wow, so you're going after The Chinaman? Hey, if you need any help while you're over there, you should call my cousin, he's a freelance journalist there. God, it's quite a coincidence, he was in London a couple of weeks ago.'

'In Belfast? What's his name?'

'Eamonn McCormick, do you know him?'

'No, but it'd be useful to meet up with him. I'll need some help while I'm there. I should even be able to put some money his way, too.' It would be best to keep out of Pat Quigley's way when he arrived in Belfast so another contact would be useful.

'Great. He left some stuff with me. You could give it to him when you see him. He's a really nice guy, you'll like him. Look, I tell you what, why don't I pop round and give it to you tonight, before you leave?'

'Lunch would be better.' Woody looked at his watch. It was 11.30 a.m.

'I can't, I'm tied up. Why don't I come round to your house? Give me the address.'

Woody gave her the address of his bedsit in Fulham.

'What time did you say the flight was again?'

'Eight thirty. It's a special Government charter, high security and all that. I mustn't be late. I'll have to leave the flat by five thirty, just to be on the safe side.'

'That's OK, I'll come round about four thirty, maybe five.'

'Aren't you working?' he asked.

'I'm supposed to be visiting clients so it's no problem. I might have to sell you an insurance policy, though.'

'With my lifestyle, I don't think I could afford the premiums.' He laughed and they said their goodbyes. Woody smiled as he replaced the receiver. Maggie was great fun and he was looking forward to seeing her again, even though it was likely to be a fleeting visit. He had yet to get beyond the kiss-on-the-cheek stage, but he lived in hope.

Morrison stood by a window in one of the front-facing bedrooms looking down the track that led to the road. It was just before noon. He saw McGrath's Volvo estate with four men in it and he ran to the door. 'He's coming,' he shouted downstairs and then rushed back to his vantage point.

Two of Hennessy's men walked towards the car and flagged it down, checking the occupants. Morrison saw the rear window being wound down and then the glint of sunlight off McGrath's glasses. He felt his heartbeat increase and his mouth went dry and he recognised the signs of his body preparing itself for violence. It had been four years since Morrison had killed a man, and then it had been in the heat of a fire-fight at the border near Crossmaglen, but the deaths he was responsible for caused him not one night's lost sleep and he was quite prepared to kill again. He had made the mental switch many years earlier, suppressed the values he'd been taught by the priests and by his teachers at school in favour of the creed of the political terrorist, that violence was justified in the quest for self-determination. When Morrison finally met his maker he would do so with a clear conscience and an untarnished soul, he was sure of that. The death of McGrath, if Hennessy ordered it, would be an added bonus and would go some way to quenching the jealous fire that burned through his mind. As he watched the Volvo bounce down the track and slow to crawl around the filled-in hole that marked the scene of the earlier bombing, images of McGrath and Mary filled his mind again, the two of them naked, enjoying each other, her arching her back and calling out his name.

'Are you OK?' asked a voice behind him, and he turned to see Murphy standing by the door, a large automatic in his hand.

'I'm fine,' he said. Morrison was no longer sure how to react to Murphy. They had never been especially close. They were about the same age yet Morrison had gone much further in the organisation, taking a great deal of responsibility at an early age, while Murphy had remained as little more than a bodyguard. Morrison often felt that Murphy begrudged Morrison the access he had to Hennessy and to the other top IRA officials, but now he had something on which to pin his envy. He would never forgive Morrison's betrayal of his employer, and Morrison would forever have to watch his back when the man was around.

Murphy looked at Morrison for a second or two with cold eyes and then nodded, just once. 'Liam says he wants us downstairs, in the lounge,' he said.

Morrison followed him down the stairs where Hennessy was waiting for them. He took them into the lounge and showed them where he wanted them to stand, just behind the door. The lights were switched on because he'd drawn the curtains so that no one could look in from the court-yard.

'I'll lead him in, you close the door behind him,' Hennessy said. 'He doesn't normally carry a gun, but I want you to frisk him, and don't be gentle with him. I want him off balance, disorientated, OK?'

The two men nodded.

'If I say hit him, hit him. If I say shoot him in the knee, you do it. No hesitation, no argument. He must know that I am totally serious and that if he doesn't co-operate he will be killed.'

'And will he?' Morrison asked.

'Oh yes, Sean. Quite definitely. But we both know that anybody can be made to talk eventually, don't we? Every man has his breaking point. And McGrath is used to giving pain, not receiving it. I think that the mere threat of violence will be enough, but if it isn't he must have no doubt that I mean what I say.'

They heard the Volvo drive into the courtyard. 'Right, I'll bring him in,' said Hennessy and left them. The two men avoided looking at each other and Morrison wondered if Murphy had already been told what Hennessy had planned for him, and if those plans included a bullet in the back of the neck. He shrugged off the morbid thoughts, knowing that there was no point in dwelling on them. Whatever his fate, there was nowhere he could run, Hennessy would have the full backing of the IRA High Command. Morrison was just one man. That thought brought The Chinaman to mind, one man who was taking on the organisation, and who had so far come out on top. He wondered how Kerry was getting on. There were voices in the corridor and then McGrath entered the room, closely followed by Hennessy.

'This is hellish short notice, Liam. When will the rest be getting here?' McGrath said as Hennessy closed the door.

Morrison stepped up behind McGrath and pressed his gun against the man's neck.

'Don't make a sound, Hugh. Don't say a word,' said Hennessy.

Morrison moved round in front of McGrath, keeping his gun against his throat, pushing hard so that his head was forced back. Murphy went behind McGrath and kicked his legs apart and then roughly searched him, going through all his pockets and then slapping down his legs and his arms.

'He's clean,' said Murphy.

'Now listen to me, Hugh, and listen good. We're going to walk through into the kitchen and we'll stand at the back door. You're going to tell your men that you'll be staying the night and that you'll be going up to Belfast with me tomorrow. Then you and I are going to come back here and have a wee chat. If you try to warn them, they'll be shot. If you try to run we'll shoot you in the legs and then we'll bring you back here and we'll still have a chat, except this time you'll be in a lot of pain. Whatever you do, it's going to end the same way. Do you get my drift?'

'Have you lost your mind?' hissed McGrath.

'No,' said Hennessy levelly. 'I've lost my wife.'

'Is that what this is about? Mary? I don't fucking believe it. I don't know what you're playing at but there'll be all hell to pay when Dublin finds out about this.'

Morrison pushed the gun hard into McGrath's throat and made him wince.

'Once your men have gone you can call Dublin and you can speak to whoever you want. But it should be obvious to you that I wouldn't be doing this without their approval. And I'd better warn you, Hugh, they've given me *carte blanche*. Now, are you ready to speak to your men?'

McGrath glared at Hennessy as if about to refuse but suddenly the fight seemed to go out of him and he agreed.

Morrison slid his gun into the pocket of his bomber jacket, making sure that McGrath saw what he was doing. Hennessy opened the door and led the way. Morrison pushed McGrath ahead of him and Murphy fell in behind, his gun held behind his back. They went through the kitchen in single file and Hennessy unlatched the door. McGrath's driver and two bodyguards were in the car, laughing at something. Beyond the car, McGrath saw two of Hennessy's men carrying broken shotguns.

He and Hennessy walked over to the car while Morrison and Murphy remained in the doorway. The window wound down and McGrath put his hand on the roof of the car and dipped his head.

'I'm going to stay over with Liam, and we'll be going

up to Belfast tomorrow. You lads can go back to the farm, I'll call you when I get back.' His voice sounded to Hennessy as if it was about to break up but his men didn't appear to notice that there was anything amiss. They asked him if he was sure, McGrath insisted, and they started up the car and drove out of the courtyard. Morrison stepped out of the kitchen and around McGrath, shepherding him back inside. Murphy took off McGrath's glasses and threw them on the ground. He stamped on them, grinding the pieces into the ground with his boots, then followed him down the hallway, pushing him roughly in the back.

McGrath tried to talk to Hennessy as the group moved back into the lounge but he was ignored. Morrison recognised the technique of sapping the man's confidence to make him more susceptible to questioning. He took a wooden chair from the kitchen and placed it in front of the fire, facing Hennessy's favourite easy chair. Morrison and Murphy shoved McGrath on to the chair and then stood behind him. He began to turn round but before he did Murphy clipped him a glancing blow with the barrel of his gun. McGrath yelped involuntarily and put his hand to the side of his head. It came away bloody.

'Liam, what the fuck do you want?' He squinted over at Hennessy, trying to focus. The tinted glasses weren't just for show, McGrath was also quite short-sighted.

Hennessy ignored him and went over to the window. He untied two thick cords which were used for holding back the curtains, and he threw them over to Morrison. 'Tie his hands behind him, and tie his legs to the chair,' he said. Morrison did as he was told while Murphy held his gun against the back of McGrath's head. Hennessy sat down in his armchair.

'Is this about Mary?' asked McGrath. 'Is that what that line about losing your wife was about? You're not losing her, Liam. She'll never leave you, she made that clear right from the start.'

Anger flared inside Morrison and he stepped forward and smashed his gun across McGrath's face. It cut deep into his cheek and blood spattered across the carpet as Morrison raised his gun again.

'No!' shouted Hennessy. 'Leave him be.'

Morrison let the gun hang by his side. He was breathing heavily, his heartbeat pounding in his ears.

'We know what you're fucking angry at, don't we, Morrison?' taunted McGrath. Morrison whirled around and slapped him across the face so hard that McGrath keeled over, taking the chair with him and slamming into the floor.

'Sean!' said Hennessy. 'You do that again and there'll be hell to pay. Get him up.'

Morrison pulled McGrath and the chair back upright. McGrath was dazed and he spat blood on to the floor, groaning and shaking his head.

Hennessy waited until McGrath seemed to regain his senses before speaking again. 'This is not about Mary, Hugh. Or at least not in the way you mean. It's about the bombings. The London bombings.'

'I don't know what you mean,' said McGrath.

'Hit him,' Hennessy said to Murphy, and Murphy smacked his gun across McGrath's head.

'This is me asking you nicely,' said Hennessy. 'In a while I'm going to stop asking you nicely and Sean here is going to blow one of your kneecaps off. He's good at that, is Sean. He's done quite a bit of kneecapping in the past, though sometimes I think he's forgotten where his roots lie. But kneecapping is a bit like riding a bike, once you've got the hang of it you never lose it. And I think we both know that Sean might have personal reasons for enjoying putting a bullet or two in you. In fact, I might have trouble persuading him to keep his aim low. You get my drift, Hugh?'

'Yes, Liam. I get your drift,' mumbled McGrath. He seemed to have difficulty moving his lips, and there was blood trickling down his chin. Morrison realised then what a devious, cunning bastard Hennessy was. McGrath was frightened, not just because of the threat of torture, but because he was being put in the hands of the man he'd betrayed most in all the world, the one man who really wanted to kill him with his bare hands, to tear him apart and to eat his raw flesh. McGrath could see the bloodlust in Morrison's eyes and it was infinitely more terrifying than Hennessy's threats. Morrison was being used by Hennessy almost as cynically as he'd been used by Mary. He knew that, but at the same time he didn't care. He just wanted to see McGrath in pain, and he hoped with all his heart that he'd refuse to answer Hennessy's questions.

'What is it you want to know?' McGrath asked quietly.

'You are behind the bombings?'

'Yes.'

'Why?'

'Because I think it's the only way to defeat the British.'

'There's more to it than that. There must be.'

McGrath shook his head.

'Where did you get the people from?'

'A couple from Scotland, two from Southern Ireland. I got to them before they joined the organisation, told them there was more they could do for the Cause by working directly for me. I sent them to Libya for training, then sent them to London to establish cover stories, to blend into the community.'

'Where did the money come from? You couldn't touch IRA funds without it being noticed.'

'I used my own money.'

'Very noble of you. Hit him, Christy.' The gun smashed into the back of McGrath's head again and he moaned and sagged in the chair. Murphy seized him by the hair and pulled his head back. 'Where did the money come from, Hugh?' said Hennessy. 'I'm about to stop asking nicely.'

'Some of it from Libya,' said McGrath. 'But most of it came from the Iraqis. They channelled the money through Libya.'

'You took money from the fucking Iraqis?'

'It's not where the money comes from that counts, it's what we do with it. You know that.'

'How much did they pay you?' asked Hennessy.

'I don't know, it was . . .'

'Shoot him, Sean,' said Hennessy quietly.

'No!' screamed McGrath. 'For the love of God, no. Two million. That's what they paid. Two million pounds.' Morrison squatted down and pressed the barrel of his gun behind McGrath's left kneecap. 'Get him away, for God's sake get him away.' He was screaming and crying and straining against the cords.

'Where's the money?'

'A Swiss bank account. It's yours, Liam, I promise. You can have the fucking lot. Just get him away from me, get him the fuck away from me!'

Hennessy waved Morrison away and he reluctantly took his gun away from McGrath's leg. Hennessy picked up a notepad and a pen. 'I want the number of the account, and I want the names and addresses of the bombers.'

'What then?' asked McGrath. 'I give you the names and then what?'

'I won't kill you,' said Hennessy. 'You give me the names and I'll take you down to Dublin and you can plead your case to the High Command. That's the only deal you're going to get from me. Now do I get the names?'

McGrath swallowed and coughed, and spat out more bloody saliva. 'You get the names,' he said.

Despite the sun being almost directly overhead, Kerry began to find the going easier, helped by the fact that The Chinaman appeared to be heading due east, albeit sticking to the hedgerows wherever possible. It would have been harder to follow him if he'd cut across the fields where the grass was thick and springy. As it was she found several good examples of his footprints in muddy places formed where rainwater ran off into the ditches.

It was just after 12.15 p.m. when she came across the B180 and Tollymore Forest Park beyond. She pulled a twig from the hedge and stuck it into the ground like a miniature bonsai as she'd done every hundred yards or so as a signpost for Sean. She took a plastic bottle of water from her rucksack and drank as she planned her next move. He'd obviously crossed the road but it would take some time to find out where. The better bet would be to cross the road straightaway and check the trees where she was more likely to spot evidence of his passing on the forest floor.

'Sean Morrison, where the hell are you?' she said to herself. She wanted to go into the trees immediately, knowing that he'd be certain to be hiding somewhere in there. She felt the same as she did when she got within shooting distance of a deer that she'd stalked for hours, the adrenalin flowed and the desire to get in close was so strong that she could almost taste it. Only one thing held her back, once in the woods she wouldn't be able to see the flare and she'd have to keep the radio off at all times because she'd have no way of knowing if The Chinaman was within listening distance. She could sit down and wait, but she didn't want to. She took out the walkie-talkie and switched it on and pressed the talk button.

'Can you hear me?' she asked, remembering Sean's instructions not to use any names over the air. There was no answer, just static. 'Is there anybody there?' she asked. When no one replied to her third attempt she took that as a sign that she was on her own and that Sean Morrison had no one to blame but himself if he couldn't find her. She put the walkie-talkie and the bottle of water back into the rucksack, waited until the road was clear and then dashed across, into the cool, enveloping greenness of the woods.

Hennessy left Morrison and Murphy in the lounge as he went to use the phone. He took the notebook because the four names McGrath had given him were new to him. He dialled the number and it was answered by Bromley himself.

'It's Liam Hennessy,' he said.

'Yes,' said Bromley. Hennessy heard the sound of a pipe being tapped against an ashtray. The thought suddenly came to him that Bromley probably recorded all his calls, but he'd gone too far now to worry about that. He read out the list of names and gave Bromley the address of the flat in Wapping where McGrath said they could be found. Bromley repeated the names and the address back to Hennessy and then asked if there was anything else.

'Such as?' asked Hennessy.

'Such as the name of the man in your organisation who planned all this?'

'You'll have to leave that side of it to us, Bromley. We'll be washing our own dirty linen.'

'You won't even give me the satisfaction of knowing who it was?'

Hennessy laughed harshly. 'No, I'm afraid I won't. Just be assured that we'll take care of it.'

'Permanently?'

'You have what you wanted, Bromley. Just do what you have to do.' He replaced the receiver.

He went back into the lounge.

'What are you playing at?' said McGrath, squinting up at Hennessy.

'Gag him,' Hennessy told Murphy.

'Oh for the love of God, Liam, you won't be needing a gag,' said McGrath, panic mounting in his voice.

'Gag him,' Hennessy repeated. Murphy took a large green handkerchief from his pocket and forced it between McGrath's teeth before tying it behind his head. McGrath grunted and strained, but nothing intelligible emerged. His eyes were wide and frightened, but Hennessy ignored his pleas. 'Christy, take him out and shoot him.'

Murphy didn't express surprise or argue, he'd killed on Hennessy's orders before, always without question. He moved to untie McGrath from the chair, but the man went wild, thrashing about like a mad thing and trying to scream through the gag. Murphy calmly clipped the butt of his gun against McGrath's temple, knocking him senseless without so much as a whimper.

'Here, let me help you,' said Morrison as Murphy slung the unconscious man over his broad shoulders.

'No, Sean, you stay with me,' said Hennessy. 'Do it in the barn, Christy. You can bury him in one of the fields tonight.'

Hennessy waited until Murphy had carried McGrath outside before speaking again. 'I want to explain why McGrath is being killed, so that you don't get the wrong idea,' he said quietly.

'Wrong idea?'

'Dublin were quite explicit about what they wanted doing. They wanted the bombings stopped and they wanted the man responsible out of the way. I explained that I thought McGrath was the man, and they said that didn't make a difference.'

'But you told him he'd get a chance to plead his case.'

'That was to encourage him to talk, to give him hope. But they'd already said that if I was one hundred per cent certain then he was to be taken care of here. No appeal, no trial, no publicity. No corpse.'

'Why did he do it?'

Hennessy shrugged. 'I guess the money helped persuade him. Gaddafi and Hussein have their own axes to grind against the British Government, and someone like McGrath would be a godsend. McGrath earns a small fortune from his smuggling operations, he's been playing the border like a bloody one-string fiddle. But most of that disappeared with the European Community's single market, so recently he's had to depend even more on his other sources of income in Belfast, and they in turn depend to a great extent on the Troubles. He's behind a number of protection rackets in the city. Most of the cash goes into IRA funds, but I doubt if he passed it all on. I'd be very surprised if some of it didn't find its way into his Swiss bank account, along with the Libyan and Iraqi money.'

'His men won't be happy.'

'Dublin will take care of that. Anyway, that's not the point. The point I'm trying to make, Sean, is that McGrath is being killed because he was a traitor to the Cause, because he betrayed the IRA, not because of Mary.'

They heard a muffled pistol shot in the distance, but neither of them showed any reaction to the noise.

'I love Mary,' said Hennessy. 'Despite everything. We've been together a long time, and sometimes I think I know her better than she knows herself. I'm the rock over which she breaks, if you understand what I mean. I give her stability, a base, security, but she's always needed more than that, more than I can give her.' His voice began to falter. 'I'm not explaining myself very well,' he added.

Morrison felt embarrassed. It wasn't often that Liam Hennessy was lost for words, his oratory skills were legendary in the courts of Belfast. Morrison didn't know what to say and he looked out of the window, hoping that he would finish and he could get back to Kerry and the hunt for The Chinaman, where at least he'd be out doing something. 'What I'm trying to say is that you don't have to worry. I'm angry, sure enough, but not to the extent that I'd tell Christy to take you out to the barn. I'm angry at Mary, too, but that's something I'm going to have to work out myself. You've hurt me, Sean, but I've been hurt before and I'll get over it. And your loyalty to the Cause has never been in question. Neither has hers, funnily enough. McGrath might have been doing it for the money, but Mary I'm sure was doing it because she felt it was in the best interests of the Cause. And for revenge, maybe. Because of that I'll try to protect her, though God knows it's going to be hard.'

He looked at Morrison, his face unsmiling, but there was no hatred in his eyes, just sadness. In a way, thought Morrison, hatred would have been easier to deal with. Compassion and understanding just made him feel all the more guilty.

'One more thing,' Hennessy added. 'When all this is over, I'd be happier if you went back to New York, but I guess that's what you'd want, anyway.'

Morrison nodded. 'Liam, I'm . . .'

'Don't say it,' interrupted Hennessy. 'I don't want your pity, Sean. Just help me get The Chinaman out of my hair and then go back to the States.'

Morrison realised there was nothing more to be said so he went through to the kitchen. Hennessy's walkie-talkie was lying on the kitchen table and he picked it up. He tried to call Kerry but got no reply and that worried him. Surely she wouldn't have left it switched off, not when she was out there on her own? He retrieved his ski-pole and the canvas haversack, checked his gun and stepped into the courtyard. Murphy walked over from the barn. He appeared to be totally impassive, no sign that he'd just taken a man's life.

'You're off then?' he said to Morrison, his voice cold.

Morrison wondered what Murphy was thinking, and how he would have reacted if he'd been told to take

357

Morrison into the barn and put a bullet in the back of his neck. He wondered too how much he could actually trust Hennessy now and what would happen once The Chinaman had been dealt with. He would have to be very, very careful.

'Yeah, I've got to catch up with the girl.'

'Be careful,' said Murphy. Morrison smiled, but he realised as he did so that he had no way of knowing if Murphy's words were a genuine expression of concern, or a threat.

Roy O'Donnell was driving one of the Land-Rovers while Kavanagh sat in the passenger seat scanning the roadside. The Land-Rover containing Tommy O'Donoghue and Michael O'Faolain was about a quarter of a mile behind them. They drove slowly and on many occasions impatient drivers had sounded their horns and they'd had to wave them on. At one point a convoy of army vehicles had come up behind them and they'd had to speed up so as not to attract attention. A Lynx helicopter flew low above the army patrol, keeping watch. That had cost them half an hour because when they'd eventually found a place where they could turn off they had had to wait until the convoy was well out of sight before they could drive back along the road and restart the search.

Now they had an excuse to dawdle because ahead of them rumbled a large, mud-covered red tractor. Kavanagh was looking for gaps in the yellow-flowered gorse and the trees, anywhere where a van could be driven. They'd stopped at half a dozen possibilities on the right-hand side and gone into the woods as far as they could but found nothing. Kavanagh's plan was to go all the way through the forest and then to drive back, westwards, checking the other side of the road.

'Slow down,' he said to O'Donnell. 'Och, too late. Do a U-turn and go back.' O'Donnell indicated and pulled hard on the steering wheel. The Land-Rover behind them copied the manoeuvre. 'There,' Kavanagh pointed.

'I don't see anything,' said O'Donnell, screwing up his eyes. 'What am I looking for?'

'There's a track there. Look.' They drove by a gap between the trees.

'Could be, I suppose,' said O'Donnell. 'Shall we go down it?'

'Let's give it a go,' said Kavanagh. They did another U-turn and this time when they reached the gap O'Donnell indicated a left turn and drove slowly between the trees. When both Land-Rovers were off the main road Kavanagh told O'Donnell to stop the vehicle and he got out. He waved at O'Donoghue and O'Faolain to come over. The four men stood on the track with their shotguns, like a group of country farmers out on a rabbit shoot. Kavanagh looked down at the muddy ground, but he wasn't sure what he was looking for. There were some tyre tracks but he had no way of knowing how long they had been there or what had made them.

'We'll leave the Land-Rovers here and walk,' he said. 'Spread out and keep your eyes open.'

Nguyen heard them coming from almost a quarter of a mile away. He was sitting next to a thick gorse bush by a patch of bluebells eating rice and chicken with his fingers. The first thing he heard was a group of startled birds flapping out of the trees. He put the cartons of food on the ground and stood up. He listened carefully, moving his head from side to side to get a bearing on where they were coming from. Eventually he heard the crunch of a boot on a twig and a sniff from the direction of the track. He couldn't tell how many there were because he was too far away, but he was sure there were more than one. He put the lids back on the foil cartons and packed them in the rucksack next to the pipe bomb. There was no point in using the bomb, for it to be effective it had to be in a confined space. The gun would be better. He checked the magazine before slipping the rucksack on his back and moving in a crouch through the undergrowth towards the track. There was no point in running blindly away, first he had to see who it was. It might be nothing more sinister than a group of forestry workers.

He moved parallel to the track, placing each foot carefully so as to make no noise, stopping and listening every few steps. He took cover behind a leafy horse chestnut and waited for them to draw level with him. There were four of them, three well-built men and a thin youth, all of them carrying shotguns. He recognised one of the men from Hennessy's farm. They were moving slowly, watching the ground more than the forest, and Nguyen doubted that they would fail to find the van, despite the effort he'd made in covering his tracks. None of the men spoke and they were obviously trying to make an effort to move quietly, but to Nguyen they sounded like water-buffaloes. Feet were crunching on twigs, kicking leaves aside, squelching into damp soil. Nguyen could have followed them with his eyes closed.

He crept from tree to tree, flitting from cover to cover like a shadow. The men came to the point where he'd driven the van off the track, and for a moment he hoped that they'd missed it because they continued on, but then the man who appeared to be the leader of the group held up his hand for them to stop. The man knelt down and studied the ground and then went back along the track. He motioned for them to gather around him and then began to whisper earnestly, making small movements with his hand. Nguyen was too far away to hear what he was saying but it was clear that he was telling them that they were to spread out and move through the trees.

Nguyen knew that he had to make a decision now. He could abandon the van and vanish into the woods until the time came to confront Hennessy again, but that would mean that when it was all over he'd have nowhere to go, no way of getting out of the country. He'd be stuck with only what he was wearing and what he carried in his ruck-sack. And while that was ideal for living rough it would give him a lot of explaining to do when he tried to board a ferry or a plane. But if he killed the men it wouldn't be too long before Hennessy would send more to investigate. And he doubted that he'd be able to conceal four bodies plus whatever transport they had arrived in, not well enough to survive a full-scale search of the woods. He could kill them and then bring his plans forward, go back to Hennessy's farm for the final confrontation. But if he did that then there was a good chance that Hennessy would be none the wiser about the bombings and he'd have to kill him and start all over again with one of the other Sinn Fein names that the London journalist had given him. He'd have to move to a different hiding place, take his van somewhere else. It was possible, he decided. He heard an excited shout and realised that his van had been discovered. He took the safety off the Browning and crept towards them. The leader was standing by the front of the van, pulling away the ferns and branches Nguyen had used to conceal it. He was joined by the red-haired youth and then the two heavyweights came trampling through the undergrowth. They cleared away all the vegetation covering the Renault while Nguyen moved as close as he could without being seen. He hid behind a bush half a dozen steps from the rear doors of the van.

'Open the bonnet, Tommy,' he heard a voice say. 'And, Michael, check what's in the back.'

The gangly youth walked round to the rear of the van. He transferred his shotgun to his left hand and with his right twisted the door handle. It wouldn't move, because Nguyen had locked it. Nguyen put the safety back on and stuck the gun into the waistband of his trousers before slipping the hunting knife out of its scabbard on the rucksack strap. He was reluctant to go in shooting because it was one against four and as soon as they heard a shot they'd all start firing.

He held his left hand up in front of him, his right ready to stab with the knife, because a stab always went deeper than a slash. He took three quick steps, centre of gravity low.

'It's locked,' the youth called.

'Well force it,' the leader shouted. 'Are yez stupid or what?' There was a smash of glass as one of the other men broke the driver's window with the butt of his shotgun.

Nguyen sprang the remaining distance and forced his left wrist across the youth's trachea and simultaneously drove the knife horizontally into the kidney. He twisted the knife to do the maximum amount of damage. The wrist across the windpipe stopped all noise but Nguyen could feel him struggle and tense and then relax and slump as he died. He eased the body on to the ground and put the knife back into its scabbard.

The man who'd smashed the window had opened the door and was looking for the bonnet-release catch. Nguyen took one of his throwing knives and moved to the right-hand side of the van. He risked a quick look and saw that the man had his back to him. Nguyen ducked away, took out the gun and slipped the safety off once more, holding the gun in his left hand.

There was a loud click and the man shouted: 'That should do it.' Nguyen stepped from behind the van, the knife ready. He was holding the blade about two inches from its tip, the handle upwards. The man closed the van door and as he did, Nguyen had a clear view of the side of his head and his neck and he threw hard. The blade thudded into the man's throat and blood gushed down his chest. Nguyen began moving as the man's mouth opened and closed with no sound because the blade had speared his Adam's apple. He transferred the Browning to his right hand, side-stepped across the rear of the van and moved up the left side. The two men at the front had opened the bonnet and had their heads over the engine. 'What do you reckon, pull out the spark-plug leads?' one said.

'Yeah. And let down the tyres. That should fix the bastard.'

There was a thud as the man with the knife in his throat fell to the ground, his shotgun scraping against the side of the van.

'What's up, Tommy?' said one of the men.

Nguyen stepped swiftly up to the front of the van, knowing that the two men would be distracted by the noise of the falling body.

'Tommy?' said the man again, and it was followed by a curse. As Nguyen got to the front the two men had their backs to him as they moved towards their dying friend. Nguyen put the barrel of his gun up against the head of the man nearest to him and fired. The shot was muffled as the bullet smashed through the skull and exploded out of the man's face in a red and pink shower of blood and brains. The other man whirled around but before the shotgun could point at Nguyen he fired the Browning a second time, hitting the man in the dead centre of his chest. He fell backwards, a look of surprise on his face and blood blossoming on his shirt, the shotgun dropping from nerveless fingers.

It had taken less than a minute but all four were dead. Nguyen took no pride in the achievement. When he'd first travelled over to Ireland he'd hoped to get what he wanted without killing anyone. He knew that people would have to be hurt before they'd take him seriously, but he'd taken enough lives during his time in the jungles of Vietnam and he hadn't wanted to add to his body count. They'd forced him into it, he said to himself. It was their fault.

He stood over the body of the last man he'd killed and listened. The forest had gone silent but gradually the bird-song and insect noise returned and when he was satisfied that all was well he turned towards the corpses.

Kerry heard two gunshots, the second louder and more distinct than the first. It sounded as if they came from two different guns. She had gone about eight hundred yards into the forest and was making progress, albeit slowly. She'd found where Nguyen had entered the trees but had lost his trail soon after and had wasted more than an hour doubling back and then searching backwards and forwards in an arc shape until she picked it up again. There was no obvious path for The Chinaman to follow and he had constantly had to change direction to get around large trees or bushes. And her task was made harder by the fact that Nguyen had travelled in both directions. Half the signs that she found were actually made when he had been going west, towards the farm, not into the depths of the forest.

The shots had come from the east, but she had no way of knowing how far away they had been, or even if they had been the result of Nguyen firing a gun or being shot at. If Nguyen was under fire then there was a chance that he'd now be running through the forest in the other direction, putting even more distance between them. If she carried on at her snail's pace she'd never catch up with him. But if she hurried towards the source of the shots and it turned out to be nothing more than poachers or Uncle Liam's men letting off their guns, accidentally or otherwise, then she risked losing the trail.

She tried to think what her father would do. Stick with the tracks or go after the shots? She thought of the tracking expeditions with her father, usually taking rich Germans and Japanese out into the Highlands to kill deer, looking for the spore and the tracks until they were close enough for the kill. Sometimes he'd take shortcuts, ignoring the signs because he felt that he knew instinctively where the deer were. That's how it felt now, she realised. She knew the shots came from Nguyen. She felt it inside. She began to run eastwards, towards where she thought the shots had come from.

Sean Morrison had heard the shots, too. He was almost a mile from the forest, faithfully following the trail Kerry had left for him. He immediately recognised the sounds as coming from a pistol rather than a shotgun or rifle, and guessed that it had been Nguyen. Kavanagh and the boys had taken shotguns and a poacher or farmer wouldn't use a handgun.

He ran for the trees. He saw a twig that Kerry had placed in the gap between two sycamore trees but he ignored it, taking the path of least resistance through the undergrowth. It was never easy to judge how far away a noise like a gunshot was, but Sean didn't reckon it could have been much more than three miles away, possibly closer. He ran for all he was worth because there had only been two shots and whereas Nguyen was armed he knew that Kerry didn't have a gun.

Nguyen dragged the bodies one by one into the under-growth, putting his arms under their shoulders and letting their heels scrape along the ground. There was no point in going to the trouble of digging graves for them because any serious search would see the disturbed soil, so he made do by hiding them inside a large patch of brambles and covering them with ferns. When he'd finished there were eight wavy lines carved in the mud by their feet and he used a leafy branch to wipe them away.

He went back along the track to find out what trans-port Hennessy's men had used and came upon the two Land-Rovers. They were blocking the track so he'd have to move them when he wanted to drive the van out, but it made more sense to take them further into the forest right away.

Luckily both sets of keys had been left in the ignition. He climbed into the first and started the engine. His hands began to shake and he gripped the steering wheel tightly, the tension making the veins stand up on the backs of his hands. He struggled to control himself, not sure what was causing the nervous reaction. It could have been delayed shock, but it had never happened to him before after combat, and he had no remorse for what he'd done. He had no doubt at all that the four men would have taken his life without a second thought. So what was the problem? He closed his eyes and felt the vibrations of the diesel engine through his arms, making the bones shudder. He had to regain control of himself, he owed it to his family.

Kerry heard an engine start up and a few minutes later a vehicle growl through the trees. She headed towards the noise and in the distance she saw a Land-Rover. In the driving seat was a small, Oriental man dressed in a camouflage uniform.

'The Chinaman,' she said under her breath. She crept forward and hid behind a sycamore tree. She watched as Nguyen stopped the Land-Rover under a spreading horse chestnut at the edge of a clearing and got out. He walked off into the woods and a few minutes later returned with an armful of ferns which he spread over the roof, bonnet and wheels. He then placed branches against the sides of the vehicle before standing back to inspect his handiwork. On his back was a small rucksack, similar to the one she was using to carry her equipment. Stuck into the waistband of his trousers was a large gun and the sight of it reminded her that she didn't have a weapon. Damn Sean Morrison, she thought. Damn him for not leaving the gun. One shot and it would all be over.

Nguyen walked off into the trees again and Kerry followed him. She didn't want to get too close because she was aware that her feet were making a noise as she moved through the undergrowth, no matter how much care she took. She lost him but then heard another engine start up and saw him drive a second Land-Rover along the track. She'd seen it before, parked in the courtyard of her uncle's farm, and with a rising sense of fear she wondered what had happened to the men who'd been driving in the vehicles. Surely The Chinaman couldn't have killed them all? Besides, there had only been two shots.

She crept from tree to tree though with less urgency this time because she knew where he was going. She caught up with him as he was stacking more ferns on the Land-Rover's bonnet and knelt down behind a tree to watch. He walked off into the undergrowth again, presumably for more branches, and he was soon out of sight.

She looked at her watch and wondered where the hell Sean Morrison had got to. The thought suddenly came to her that she hadn't left a trail for him to follow. Would he be smart enough to spot where she'd run through the forest? Had she taught him enough in their few hours together? The only way she had of showing her position was to fire the flare gun, and she couldn't do that without alerting The Chinaman. Her breath quickened at the thought of the flare gun. What if she were to bring in The Chinaman herself? The flare gun would be just as

368

threatening as a pistol. She slid the rucksack off her back and undid the cords at the top. As she put her hand in and groped around for the flare gun she heard a click behind her and found herself looking down the barrel of an automatic pistol.

'Stand up, slowly,' said Nguyen. He kept the gun trained on her face as she got to her feet, still holding the rucksack. She clutched it to her chest like a baby. 'Who are you?' he asked.

She thought frantically. 'I'm a . . . I'm a . . . er . . .' she stammered. 'I'm a birdwatcher. Watching birds. My binoculars are in here.' She nodded at her rucksack. 'Let me show you.' Her shaking hand tightened around the handle of the flare gun, but she suddenly realised that it wasn't loaded, the cartridges were loose in the rucksack.

Nguyen held out his hand. 'Give me,' he said. She handed over the rucksack. 'Drop the pole. And move into the clearing,' he said, gesturing with the gun. They walked together out of the shade of the trees and he made her stand by one of the Land-Rovers.

'How old are you?' Nguyen asked, frowning.

'Twenty-four,' she said.

'I had a daughter who would be twenty-four this year,' said Nguyen. He stepped back and put the rucksack on the floor, kneeling down beside it. She wondered if she could rush him, but he never took his eyes off her, using his hands to search the rucksack. He pulled out the case containing the binoculars and opened it.

'Bird-watching,' repeated Kerry, willing The Chinaman to believe her. She was finding it hard to breathe and her mouth had gone dry.

Nguyen nodded, placed the case on the ground, and

continued to rummage inside the rucksack. He took out the walkie-talkie and examined it and put it next to the binoculars. Again his hand went in like a conjuror looking for the white rabbit, though this time he came out with Kerry's notebook.

Kerry began to say that it was for drawing birds she had seen but Nguyen ignored her and slowly turned the pages. He saw the sketch she'd made of his footprint and he nodded to himself. 'Birdwatching,' he mused.

They both heard a crashing noise from the depths of the forest, the sound of a man running. Nguyen looked over his shoulder, then back to the girl, obviously unsure what to do. Kerry knew that The Chinaman was considering shooting her, or maybe using the big hunting knife fastened to the strap of his rucksack. Her stomach turned liquid.

The crashing noise got louder and Nguyen moved away from Kerry, deciding that she was the lesser threat. He ran in a crouch to the edge of the clearing, his gun at the ready. As he ran, Kerry grabbed her rucksack and groped for the flare gun and a cartridge. Her hands were trembling and it took several attempts before she managed to open the gun and force home the cartridge.

She moved to the side so that she could see over The Chinaman's shoulder. He was standing about fifty feet away from her, cocking his head and listening, and then raising the gun as Morrison came into view. Kerry saw him at the same time as Nguyen did, his dark hair waving in the wind and his haversack banging on his hip as he ran. Nguyen ducked behind a tree and Kerry stepped forward, aiming the flare gun with both hands.

Morrison saw her and shouted, and began waving frantically.

'Sean, watch out!' she yelled, as Nguyen moved from behind the tree and pointed his pistol at Morrison.

'Nguyen, it's all right! It's all over!' Morrison yelled, and The Chinaman lowered his gun. As he did, Kerry pulled the trigger.

'Kerry! No! No!' Morrison screamed.

The pistol kicked in her hands but she kept it steady and there was a loud whooshing noise as the flare erupted from the barrel and hurtled through the air leaving behind a trail of white smoke in the still air. It smacked into the rucksack on Nguyen's back. Nguyen whirled round and pointed his gun at Kerry. She flinched, throwing her hands up in front of her face, knowing that he wouldn't miss at that range. Nguyen's finger tightened on the trigger but he couldn't do it, he couldn't bring himself to shoot her. Not a girl. He could smell the burning flare and his ears were filled with the hiss of melting nylon and he knew that she had killed him, that there were only seconds before the heat ignited the bomb in the rucksack. He dropped the Browning and struggled with the straps of the rucksack, yelling at her to get away from him.

Morrison burst into the clearing and saw Kerry kneeling on the ground, her head in her hands. At first he thought that she'd been shot but there was no blood and he hadn't heard The Chinaman fire his gun.

'Go away, go away!' screamed Nguyen. 'Bomb! Bomb!'

Suddenly Morrison realised what was happening, why The Chinaman had thrown his gun on the ground and why he was now frantically fumbling with the nylon rucksack. Morrison rushed forward and grabbed one of the straps, forcing it down off his shoulder. The Chinaman was gasping for breath, twisting and turning to get the deadly package off his back. The heat from the flare seared Morrison's hands and he saw the hairs on his wrists shrivel and blacken, then he was hit by a wave of pain that made him cry out. The white light was blinding and he closed his eyes as the rucksack pulled away from The Chinaman's shoulders and he slumped to the ground. Morrison swung the burning mass as hard as he could and let it fly up into the air, hissing and spluttering into the trees, and then he dived over to shield Kerry, falling against her and knocking her to the ground, then lying across her and shouting at her to keep her eyes closed and her face covered.

The explosion came within seconds, the blast deafening and vibrating the ground like a small earthquake, followed by a barrage of twigs and chunks of wood that fell like a tropical rain shower and then stopped just as suddenly. The forest was silent, as if the bomb had killed every living thing for miles. Morrison rolled off Kerry and helped her to her feet. In the distance a bird whistled and was answered by another. Short, nervous calls as if they were testing the silence. Satisfied that Kerry hadn't been hurt, Morrison went over to The Chinaman, who was rubbing his eyes with the knuckles of his hand, coughing and retching.

'Thank you,' he said, surprising Morrison with his politeness.

Morrison heard a metallic click and he turned to see Kerry, her hands dwarfed by the big Browning.

'Move away, Sean,' she said quietly. 'I've got the bastard covered.'

'Easy, Kerry,' said Morrison. 'Put the gun down. He's not going to hurt anyone.' The Chinaman showed no fear. He looked at Kerry, his face expressionless.

'I'm going to kill him,' she said, her voice oddly flat. Morrison wondered if maybe she was in shock. Her eyes were cold, almost blank, as if she was sleep-walking, but she seemed to have no trouble in keeping the gun pointed at the centre of The Chinaman's chest.

'It's over,' said Morrison, holding his hand out for the gun. 'We've found out who the bombers are. We know who was backing them. It's finished. We can all go home.'

'It's not over!' she hissed. 'It won't be over until he's dead.'

Morrison looked at The Chinaman. He was standing with his hands loose at his side, his head slightly bowed but his eyes fixed on Kerry's face as if willing her to shoot, as if he wanted her to end it. There was, Morrison thought, a sadness in his eyes, a look that said that there was nothing else they could do to him. Morrison looked back at Kerry, his hand still outstretched.

'Kerry, he could have shot you. He didn't. You can't kill him. He's not armed, he's not a threat.' He stepped forward and she took half a step back. 'He had a deal with Liam, and we're going to stick to it. It's over. Give me the gun and we can go home.'

Her finger began to squeeze the trigger and Morrison knew that she was about to fire. Still The Chinaman stayed rooted to the spot. 'Kerry, if you do this you're doing it for the wrong reason. You're not doing it for Liam Hennessy, or for your father, or for the IRA,' Morrison said. He took another step forward. 'You're doing it for yourself.' Another step. The gun was almost within reach. 'It'd be on your conscience for ever. It's not worth it. Trust me, I know. It's not worth it.' He moved quickly, bringing down his right hand and forcing the gun to the side, away

373

from The Chinaman, and then he grabbed it and twisted it out of her grasp. She tried to get the gun back but he held it out of her reach. She yelled in frustration, then drew back her hand and slapped him across the face, hard, and began to sob. He stepped forward and took her in his arms, holding her close but being careful to keep the gun where she couldn't grab it, just in case. She put her head against his shoulder and he could feel her body shudder as she cried. He turned with her slowly, as if they were dancing to a slow song, until he was facing The Chinaman.

'Go,' said Morrison.

'You said you had the names?'

Morrison told him the names of the bombers, and the address of the flat in Wapping where they were based, and Nguyen repeated them to himself, imprinting the information on his memory.

'Thank you,' Nguyen said.

'Don't thank me. Just go.'

Nguyen turned and walked into the undergrowth, leaving Morrison and Kerry alone in the clearing. She had stopped crying and he could feel her chest rising and falling in time with her breathing. 'I'm sorry, Sean,' she whispered. 'I'm so sorry.'

He smoothed her hair and kissed her on the top of her head.

'It's OK,' he said. 'Sometimes it gets you like that. The violence. It gets a grip on you without you realising it. It's like a drug, it pulls you along . . .'

She turned her head up and pushed her lips against his, kissing him hard, reaching around his neck with her arms. Her baseball cap fell off and her hair swung free. Her tears wet his cheeks as they kissed and she pressed herself against him. He threw the gun away and then held her with both hands, touching and caressing as her tongue found its way into his mouth, probing, teasing, exciting him until all thoughts of The Chinaman evaporated and he concentrated on her, the feel of her, the smell of her, the taste of her. She pulled him down on to the ground, her hands groping for his belt, her breath coming in small gasps as she said his name over and over again. He made love to her quickly but gently, in the grass, under the trees, next to The Chinaman's gun.

Nguyen couldn't believe that the man would let him go. He was sure that he planned to shoot him as he left the clearing, but there was no gunshot, no thump in the back, he just kept on walking. Once he was sure they really were releasing him he began to run through the forest towards the van. It would only be a matter of time before the four bodies were discovered and when that happened he doubted that Liam Hennessy would be as generous. Nguyen wasn't surprised at how easy it had been to kill the men, he'd always been good at it, all that was required was the mental switch. He'd fought against it when he first started out, but now that he'd killed he knew that he would follow it through to the end. He would avenge his family, he knew that with a diamond-hard certainty. He would do whatever it took, and there would be no remorse, no guilt. Afterwards, when he'd finished, then he'd worry about his own future, but at the moment he could look no further than the flat in Wapping and the IRA bombers.

He opened the back door of the van and quickly threw out all the supplies inside. He stripped off his camouflage gear and changed back into jeans and a pullover, checked that his money was still under the front seat with his pass-port, and then he drove the van back down the track and on to the main road and headed for the airport.

They travelled in three Range Rovers with a police motor-cycle escort, roaring down the outside lane of the M40 at more than ninety miles per hour. The flashing blue lights and the howling sirens forced a clear path through the early afternoon traffic on the motorway, though there were plenty of resentful looks from the company reps in their Sierras and Escorts as the men in the unmarked Range Rovers went by. Pulling over for fire engines and ambulances was second nature, but nobody liked to move out of the fast lane without knowing why, and there was nothing about the vehicles that identified the men inside as belonging to the SAS.

There were four men in each vehicle, tough-looking men with broad shoulders, but as they hurtled towards London they were laughing and smiling and looked no more threatening than a group of miners on a coach trip to the coast. Mike 'Joker' Cramer was in the front passenger seat of the first Range Rover, laughing at a particularly foul joke that the driver, Pete Jackson, had spun out over the last two miles. The men were tense as they always were when going into action, but they used humour to keep themselves from worrying.

In the back seat were Sam 'Bunny' Warren and Rob 'Ginge' Macdonald. Bunny was tapping the back of his hand against the window and he wasn't as quick to laugh at Jacko's joke as the rest were.

Joker, the assault-team leader, was the leanest of the four men, well over six-foot tall, with a thin face that

376

always appeared haggard no matter how much sleep he got. He looked over his shoulder at Bunny, a swarthy, stocky man with piercing green eyes. 'Is that Morse code, or what, Bunny?' he said.

Bunny stopped tapping. 'Sorry, Joker. Habit.'

'You want some gum?' Joker asked, holding out the packet of Wrigley's which he always carried with him now that he'd given up smoking.

'Cheers,' said Bunny, taking a piece. 'We nearly at the RV?'

'Not far,' said Joker. He leant forward and picked up the A to Z map of London. The Colonel had called from London and given them an address in Rotherhithe Street, alongside the Thames, where they were to meet. The convoy left the A40 and they motored along Marylebone Road, along Euston Road past King's Cross and then they followed City Road to the Thames. The motorcycle riders worked in teams, rushing ahead to hold up the traffic whenever the lights weren't in their favour, then remounting and following up behind like pilot fish busily swimming around prowling sharks. When they reached the river the motorbikes peeled off by arrangement, leaving the three Range Rovers to make their own way across London Bridge to Bermondsey and then left along Jamaica Road to Rotherhithe.

They drove by new wharf-style blocks of riverside flats and then came to the building where the Colonel said they were to meet.

'This is it,' said Joker. The three vehicles pulled up at the pavement. Joker climbed out and looked up and down the road. There were no signs that an operation was under way, no police cars, no ambulances, no nothing, just the sound of the Thames lapping against the banks.

The men got out of the cars and stood on the pavement. They were, Joker had to admit to himself, a motley crew. The one thing they had in common was that they were all in the peak of condition and trained to kill. I don't know what they'll do to the enemy, thought Joker, but they scare the shit out of me. He tried to remember who'd said that first, whether it had been Wellington or Napoleon, because he was sure he'd heard it somewhere. Whatever, that's exactly how he felt about the eleven men who began pulling their kit-bags out of the back of the cars.

'Where do we go?' asked Reg Lawrence, another assault-team leader.

'Fifteen B,' said Joker. 'This one here.'

He pushed the button by Fifteen B and a light clicked on. There was a television camera behind a glass panel and a red light came on above it and then he heard the Colonel's voice tell him to come up. The door buzzed and Joker pushed it and the men filed through and followed him upstairs to the third-floor flat.

An intelligence officer in his distinctive green beret had the door open for them.

'The green slime gets here first for a change,' jeered a voice from the back, but when Joker looked to see who it was he was met with blank, innocent faces.

The flat was spacious, white-painted walls and ceilings and polished wood floors, a fully fitted kitchen but no furniture, and there was a 'For Sale' sign in one of the bedroom windows overlooking the street.

The Colonel was in the lounge looking through a powerful pair of binoculars mounted on a tripod. A large blackboard was leaning against one wall and, as the men stood around, the intelligence officer began drawing a map of the flat under surveillance in white chalk. The Colonel looked up and nodded at Joker. 'Fancy a look?' he asked.

The binoculars were trained on a modern wharf on the north side of the river and when Joker looked through them he saw a large french window and a lounge beyond it, a rectangular room with three men sitting around. The television was switched on but Joker couldn't see what was on the screen. In front of the window was a balcony, twelve-feet square, with a couple of white chairs and a circular table. Joker moved the binoculars sideways. The building was mainly featureless brick wall and double-glazed windows, but two-thirds of the way along the architect had obviously decided to introduce a little variety and he'd staggered the flats so that the one to the left of the flat under observation was about twelve feet further back and the one to the right was an equal distance closer to the river. While it made the building easier on the eye it made it impossible to enter the balcony from either side. There was no flat above the one under observation, but the architect had built a penthouse flat at the right-hand side of the building and its extra-large balcony overlooked it. It was immediately apparent to Joker that the penthouse was the way in. It would be a simple matter to jump down to the balcony below, they wouldn't even have to abseil.

The buzzer sounded from the hallway and the intelligence officer went to open the front door and let in two men from D11, the Metropolitan Police firearms team. They stood at the back of the group of the SAS men, their rifles slung over their shoulders. The Colonel nodded a welcome and went over to the blackboard, chalk in hand.

★ ★ ★

Woody panicked a little when he opened the door to his bedsit. Clothes were strewn all over the floor, a week's worth of newspapers were piled up under the room's one window, and there was a collection of empty lager cans and a three-quarters empty bottle of Bells by the side of the bed. It looked as if a burglar had wreaked vengeance on the place after finding there was nothing worth stealing, but Woody knew it had been in exactly the same state when he left that morning. He rushed around picking up the rubbish, putting the cans and the papers into an old carrier bag, and was just about to carry them downstairs to the dustbin when there was a knock on the door. He cursed and shoved the bag under his bed and smoothed down the quilt. The knock was repeated as he popped into the alcove where there was a mirror above a small wash-basin. He gave his hair a quick comb and then opened the door. It was Maggie in a dark-green suit, her red hair tied back in a ponytail. She was carrying a black leather briefcase and could indeed have been there to sell him insurance, except the smile she gave him wasn't the professional 'have I got the policy for you' type, it was warm and genuine.

He stepped to the side and waved her in. 'It's not much,' he apologised.

She looked round and nodded. 'You're right,' she said.

'It's temporary.'

'It would have to be,' she laughed. 'Does it have a bar?'

Woody laughed with her. 'Yeah, there's some whisky. Let me wash a couple of glasses.' He picked up a glass from off his dressing-table and went back into the alcove. There was another glass on the shelf under the mirror containing his toothbrush and a tube of toothpaste. He tipped them out and washed both glasses, carried them back, and poured them both a drink.

They clinked glasses. 'Sit down,' said Woody.

Maggie looked around the tiny bedsit. 'Where?' she said. There was only one chair and that was covered with a pair of jeans and a couple of shirts that looked the worse for wear. She put her briefcase on the floor by the door.

'It'll have to be the bed, I'm afraid,' said Woody.

She smiled and sat down and Woody joined her.

'So, Rome, then Belfast. You get around.'

'Yeah, I'm sorry it's such short notice.'

'A security conference, you said?'

'Yeah, lots of top guys. And with any luck there'll be a big story, too.'

'I'm pleased, you deserve it. Why is it so hot in here?'

'I told you,' he said. He tapped the wall behind them. 'It's the immersion heater. It's really cosy in the winter.'

'I bet, but this is the middle of summer, Woody.'

'Let me take your jacket,' he said, and helped her slip it off. She opened the top button of her blouse and waved the material back and forth to cool herself. She looked up and caught Woody watching her. She didn't say anything and Woody leaned over and kissed her on her left cheek, close to her mouth.

'Woody, no,' she said softly, but she didn't move away so Woody kissed her again, closer to her lips. He reached up and cupped her breast and tried to kiss her on the mouth but she moved her head and his lips brushed her hair.

'Woody, don't,' she said, but her hand fell into his lap and stayed there and he could hear her breathing heavily.

He massaged her full breast through the soft material of the blouse and he felt her nipple stiffen and when he tried to kiss her again this time their lips met.

He unbuttoned her blouse as they kissed. Her bra fastened at the front and after a couple of attempts he undid that, too. Her breasts fell free and he leant forward and kissed them as she cradled his head in her hands.

'Woody, we don't have time,' she said, running her fingers through his hair and kissing the back of his head.

He pressed his fingers against her lips. 'Shhh,' he said, and kissed her again as he slipped her blouse off her shoulders. She wriggled her arms out of her sleeves and then she helped him off with his shirt and they lay down next to each other, kissing and caressing. Woody broke free and took off his shoes, socks and trousers and then lay down on top of her.

'Woody, we can't,' whispered Maggie as he began to push her skirt down her hips. She lifted her backside to make it easier for him and he used his foot to push it the rest of the way down her legs.

'It's all right,' he said, kissing her again and running his hands down her legs. She was wearing stockings and they rasped against his fingers. He slipped his hand into the top of her briefs.

'No, it's not,' she said. 'We can't make love.'

He removed his hand and raised himself up on one elbow. 'You're not a virgin are you?' he asked.

She collapsed into giggles. 'That's very flattering, Woody, but no I'm not.' She reached up and linked her arms round his neck and pulled him down on top of her. 'It's the wrong time of the month,' she whispered into his ear. 'I'm sorry.'

Not half as sorry as I am, thought Woody. 'That's OK,' he said, but his voice was heavy with disappointment.

Maggie wrapped her legs around him and held him. She kissed him hard, her tongue probing deep into his mouth and then whispered into his ear again. 'Lie on your back,' she said. He did as he was told and she lay next to him, her hand moving gently between his legs. He groaned and she moved up the bed slightly so that her breasts were level with his mouth. 'Kiss them,' she said, while her hand became more insistent, moving faster and harder. 'Kiss them while I make you come.'

The British Airways stewardess stood to one side to allow the passengers to disembark, a flurry of briefcases and forced smiles. She smiled and said goodbye to an Oriental man in a duffel coat, but he looked right through her. He wasn't carrying any luggage and he was scruffily dressed, jeans and a pullover under the coat. There were streaks of dirt across his face as if he'd washed in a hurry and, not to put too fine a point on it, he stank to high heavens. One of the passengers who had been sitting on the same row had asked to be moved and the stewardess had had to agree. The smell turned her stomach, the bitter aroma of skin that hadn't seen soap and water in a long time. The man had been hungry and had wolfed down the tray of cake and sandwiches put in front of him, keeping his coat firmly buttoned up throughout the flight. She'd pointed the man out to the chief steward but he'd told her not to worry, security checks on the flights between Belfast and London were second to none and he looked more like a man taking his first flight than a potential hijacker. The smell? Well, that was a nuisance, but what could you expect, she was told. Nguyen left the plane at a brisk walk. He had to get to central London before the shops closed.

Woody stretched and looked at his watch. 'Christ, is that the time?' he said.

'What time is that?' asked Maggie. She was lying with her back to Woody, her head in the crook of his right arm.

'It's six o'clock. I'm going to have to run.' He slid his arm out from under her neck and kissed her shoulder. She turned and kissed him on the lips and his hand went to her breasts again and he moved on top of her. 'I wish I could make love to you,' he sighed.

'You will,' she said. She hadn't allowed him to remove her briefs or stockings but she had made him scream with pleasure with her hands, extending his pleasure until he was exhausted. He'd asked if he could make her come but she refused, saying that she'd rather wait until they could make love properly and fully. 'When you get back from Belfast,' she'd promised.

Woody sat up and pulled on his underpants, then his socks, then his trousers. Maggie sat up while he went to his wardrobe and took out a clean shirt. She made no attempt to cover herself and Woody turned to admire her breasts while he buttoned his shirt up and put on a tie. She laughed and leant over to pick up her briefcase and swung it on to the bed. She clicked open the case and took out a piece of paper. 'Here's the address and phone number of my cousin. I rang him this afternoon and said you'd be coming over and that you'd call him some time.'

Woody walked over to take the sheet of paper but as he reached for it she moved it away, catching him off

384

balance. 'Ask nicely,' she teased. He leant forward and kissed her and she put her arms around his neck, pulling him down on the bed. Woody pulled away and this time she gave him the paper. 'And can you give him this?' she said, reaching into the case. She took out a laptop computer and put it on the bed beside her. 'He asked me to get it repaired. He bought it in London last year and couldn't get it fixed in Belfast. It's OK now. Do you mind? I know it'll mean taking it all the way to Rome and then back to Belfast, but I don't trust the Post Office.'

Woody shook his head. 'Of course I don't mind.' He picked it up and put it in his overnight bag along with a change of clothes and his washing kit. Maggie made no move to get out of bed so Woody asked her what she planned to do.

'Can I stay here for a while?' she asked. 'I'll let myself out.'

'Sure,' said Woody, looking at his watch again. 'Christ, I'm going to have to dash. I'll call you from Rome. What's your home number?'

She grimaced. 'My phone's out of order. I'll call you from a call box. What hotel will you be staying at?'

'Hell, I don't know. Call the office, they'll tell you.' He picked up his bag and kissed her. He blew her another kiss from the door and closed it behind him.

She lay back in the bed and put her hands over her eyes. She felt sticky and dirty being with the grubby man in his grubby room, relieving him with her hands and pretending to love it. She shuddered. 'The things I do for you, Denis Fisher,' she said to herself.

She slid out from under the quilt and padded over to the sink, washing herself as best she could. She caught sight of herself in the mirror and pulled her tongue out. 'Whore,' she said to herself, and then laughed. She dried herself and put her clothes back on but she still didn't feel clean.

She took the towel and carefully rubbed it everywhere she'd touched, removing all trace of her fingerprints. Only when she was totally satisfied did she pick up her brief-case and let herself out of the room, not forgetting to wipe the door handle.

Woody made it to the airport with time to spare. He could barely keep his eyes open. He'd had a rough drinking session the night before, but it was Maggie who'd sapped his strength. He had no idea as he sat on the bed and tried to kiss her just how enthusiastic she'd turn out to be. He was quite surprised, and pleased. And knack-ered.

He was met by a Home Office press officer, a colleague of Annie's, a young guy who used to work for the *Daily Telegraph* and who Woody vaguely remembered meeting several years earlier.

'I'm sorry, Woody, there's been a change of plan. The jet we've chartered has had engine problems so we're putting everyone on scheduled flights. I've got you a seat on a plane leaving in forty-five minutes.' He handed Woody a ticket. 'It's Economy I'm afraid.'

'No sweat,' said Woody. 'Are you going on the same flight?'

The man nodded. 'Yeah, and I'll be around to look after you at Rome airport.'

'We're not sitting together?'

At least the guy had the grace to look shamefaced as

he admitted that he was flying Business Class. They joined the queue to have their overnight bags X-rayed. Woody filled his mind with images of Maggie as he waited.

His turn came and he handed his bag to a uniformed guard who put it on the conveyor and watched it disappear as he stepped through the metal detector. His bag was pulled out by a squat, middle-aged woman with a pointed face and a flat chest and put on one side with half a dozen others. It seemed that they were pulling out one in three bags for hand inspection, which Woody guessed was a result of the bombing campaign. It wasn't so long ago when it was a rarity to have one of the guards go through your luggage and then it was usually because they'd seen something they didn't recognise on the scanner.

A short youth with a pencil-thin moustache and side-burns gave him a crooked smile and asked him if the bag was his. When Woody said it was, the guard put it down on the counter and asked him to open it. Woody did and the boy thrust his hands into it as if he was about to deliver a baby. He pulled out Woody's wash bag, unzipped it and examined his can of shaving foam and toothpaste. He carefully pushed aside Woody's underwear and shirts and then his hands appeared with the computer. He looked at it front and back, peered inside the ventilation grille, and shook it.

'Can you switch this on for me, sir?' he asked.

Woody opened the machine, revealing the screen and the keyboard, and groped at the back where he knew the on-off switch would be. The screen flickered into life. Woody had used portables many times so he had no difficulty getting the computer to flash up a directory. The guard peered at it, and pressed a few keys at random.

'That's fine, sir,' he said, allowing Woody to switch it off and put it back in his bag. Woody picked it up and slung it over his shoulder. 'Have we got time for a drink before we board?' Woody asked the press officer.

'Probably several.'

'You're talking my language,' laughed Woody.

Joker stood by the French window and looked over the river towards where he knew the Colonel would be. He couldn't tell which of the many windows the Colonel was behind, but that was to be expected. He'd be well back from the window with the rest of his team. If Joker could see him, the IRA would be able to spot him, too.

As he waited for instructions he hummed to himself quietly. There was nothing else to do. He'd stripped and cleaned his Heckler & Koch MP5, the German-made 9-millimetre machine gun that the SAS favoured, reassembled it and replaced the magazine with its thirty rounds. He adjusted his assault waistcoat, more from habit than because of need, and flicked the safety catch off. Ginge stood by his side, while Bunny and Jacko waited behind. There was only enough space for two of them to jump down on the balcony at the same time so they'd agreed that Joker and Ginge would go first. Bunny and Jacko would follow as back-up.

During the briefing, the Colonel had made it clear that only one four-man team would actually be going into the flat and Joker had held his breath, fearing that he'd be going back to Hereford without seeing action. He needn't have worried, because the Colonel knew that Joker's team had been pulling the best scores in the killing house. The other two assault teams had groaned but knew better than to complain. One four-man team was sitting in a Range Rover in nearby Wapping Lane, parked up and listening on the radio to the Colonel's instructions, ready to give chase just in case something went wrong. The remaining four were in plain clothes, two in Wapping High Street and two down by the river in front of the target flat, but well out of sight.

'Stand by,' said the Colonel's voice in Joker's earpiece. 'We think we have a clear shot.' The two D11 marksmen were the only police representatives Joker had seen, and at first he'd assumed it was because the Colonel wanted to keep the operation low-key and not risk having the terrorists tipped off by too much woodentop activity. During the briefing, however, it became clear that there was another reason for the minimum police presence. The Colonel had stressed that they were not planning to take any prisoners. The operation was to be a hit and run, leaving no martyrs alive in mainland prisons as a focus for future terrorist actions, though the Colonel had stressed that one of the terrorists had to be interrogated to discover if there were any devices already planted that hadn't gone off yet. The Colonel suggested that The Bombmaker should be left alive, but that it was Joker's call. Obviously if she was armed she'd have to be taken out immediately.

'They've just switched the lights on. There are three men in the lounge area,' said the Colonel in Joker's ear. 'One sitting at the table, one on the couch, one standing in the hallway. There's still no sign of the girl.'

Another voice in Joker's ear, this time one of the men in the Range Rover, cut in. 'She's coming. A taxi just pulled up in front of the building. It's her. She's going in.'

There was silence for a minute and then the Colonel's voice spoke again. 'One of the men is opening the door. Yes, it's her. The two of them are going into one of the bedrooms. OK, stand down. We can't move while two of them are out of sight.'

Joker and Ginge went back into the flat to wait.

Fisher took MacDermott in his arms and held her. 'Did it go OK?' he whispered.

'It was horrible, horrible. I don't ever want to have to do anything like that again. He was all over me, Denis, like some sort of slobbering animal.'

He kissed her ear. 'Come on, kid. It had to be done, you know that. And think of the prize. If what he told you is right, that plane is going to be the biggest coup we've ever had. And we get to take out some of our worst enemies. Anyway, it's not as if he was grotesque or anything. He was a good-looking guy.'

She pulled away and glared at him. 'That's not the fucking point, Denis. I had to spend weeks around him, fending him off, toying with him, waiting for the opportunity to use him. I feel dirty, really dirty.'

Fisher held up his hands to calm her down. 'OK, OK, I'm sorry. Don't take me the wrong way. We're all proud of you, really proud. And we know what you went through.'

'Do you Denis? Do you really?' She shook her head and there were tears in her eyes. 'I'm going to shower,' she said, pushing past him.

'Stand by,' said the Colonel. 'We see the girl, coming out of the bedroom. She's going into the bathroom. The man is out of the bedroom, too, he's walking towards the lounge.

OK, we have all three men in view. We'll wait for the girl to come out. Get ready, Joker.'

Another voice broke in, this time one of the SAS men on foot. 'There's somebody walking along Wapping High Street,' he said. 'A man. Anyone else see him?'

'We see him,' said the watcher in the Range Rover. 'He's heading towards the block. No, it's OK, it's a delivery. He's carrying a box. He's a Chink, by the look of it. Yeah, I can see Chinese writing on the box. Somebody's ordered a Chinese take-away by the look of it. Nothing to worry about.'

'It can't be for our targets, we saw them eating earlier on,' said the Colonel. 'Keep an eye on him, just in case.'

'He's outside the block,' said the man in the Range Rover. 'He's going in.'

Nguyen hefted the box in his left hand and reached for the doorbells with his right. There were more than twenty individual buttons and he was about to press a few at random to see if anyone would let him in through the security door when he saw movement in the hallway and a second later the door pushed open and a middle-aged man carrying a small terrier went by him. Nguyen caught the door before it swung shut and slipped inside. At the end of the hallway was a lift with its doors open and to the left was a stairway. He headed up the stairs, carrying the box in both hands. He was after Flat 19 but had no way of knowing which floor it was on, so as he reached each landing he quietly eased open the door and checked the numbers of the flats. On the fourth floor he saw a door with 19 on it and he jerked back out of sight. He was almost there. It was almost over.

★ ★ ★

'Get ready, Joker. The girl is coming out of the bathroom. She's wearing a bathrobe, a white bathrobe, and she's heading for the lounge. This could be it. Where's the guy with the dog?'

'He's well away,' said the watcher in the Range Rover.

'No sign of the delivery man?'

'Still inside.'

'OK. She's sitting down on the left in the armchair by the television. Hang on, the man at the table appears to have a gun, an automatic, but he's not holding it. It's on the table.'

The four soldiers looked to their right at a large drawing of the flat below. The Colonel had copied it from the diagram on the blackboard, including details of where the furniture was. It was pretty much a copy of the flat they were in, though smaller. Joker used the barrel of his gun to indicate where the four terrorists would be. Ginge nodded.

'I'll take the man at the table, and the guy on the couch,' said Joker. 'The one in the hallway is yours. Don't forget, we try to take the girl alive. We've got some questions for her.'

'We think we have a clear shot at the man in the hallway. Stand by,' said the Colonel.

'Mine is the couch, yours is the table,' corrected Joker.

'Right ho,' said Ginge.

'Move out on to the balcony,' said the Colonel.

Joker felt the adrenalin surge as he prepared for action. He and Ginge stood side by side waiting for the word. They both cocked the actions of their MP5s, slotting home live rounds into the chamber. They both had their safeties off and their fingers on the trigger guards so that there was no way the guns could go off accidentally when they jumped.

There were live rounds in the chambers of their holstered Brownings but they'd kept the safeties on. They were wearing assault waistcoats loaded with stun grenades over black overalls. They had both chosen to wear light body armour and had discarded the high velocity body armour with its tough ceramic plates that they'd brought with them, partly because there was no sign of anything bigger than a handgun in the flat below and because they didn't want to be burdened down with too much weight when they jumped.

'Prepare to jump,' said the Colonel. The two SAS men eased themselves over the blue-painted metal railings, facing forward and holding on with one hand. The drop was about twelve feet which was easy enough, but they had to twist through ninety degrees to the right as they jumped so balance would be a problem. Joker would be able to land by the side of the white plastic table and chairs but Ginge would drop behind them so he wouldn't be able to move inside as quickly, he'd have to go round. Bunny and Jacko moved up behind them to stand on the balcony.

Nguyen placed the box on the floor and squatted next to it. He took out the cartons of food, long since gone cold, and stacked them against the wall. At the bottom of the box, in pieces, was a replica of a Kalashnikov AK-47. He'd arrived at the shop minutes before it was due to close, out of breath because he'd run down the Strand, and paid in cash. It was realistic down to the last detail, a perfect copy of the Russian-designed 7.62-millimetre automatic rifle that he'd used in the jungles of Vietnam. He assembled it with an efficiency born of familiarity, screwing home the wooden stock and slotting in the magazine. The weight felt slightly wrong but it looked real

393

enough, and the men he was up against were professionals, they would assume that anyone who moved against them would be using the real thing. He'd have preferred to have used the Browning but he'd left that behind in the forest, and besides, there was no way he could have got any weapons at all through the airport security. Anyway, there was a certain irony in using the AK-47, which is why he'd chosen it over the rest of the range of replica guns the shop had in stock. That and the fact that it was the gun he felt most comfortable with. So long as he kept moving, so long as he didn't give them time to think, they wouldn't realise that it was a replica, they wouldn't notice that the barrel was solid metal and that the gun could never in a million years be used to fire bullets. They'd be off-guard, defensive, and scared, and he'd be able to use their confusion to take their own weapons from them. They'd be sure to have guns, and once he'd taken them from them he'd have no further need of a replica. And if he was wrong, if there were no guns in the flat, then he'd use the knives he'd also bought at the shop.

Nguyen no longer gave any thought to his own future, to what would happen if he should succeed. He didn't care any more. He'd given up any hope of justice being done, all he wanted now was revenge. He wanted nothing less than the death of the four bombers and he had no interest in what lay beyond that. His life was over.

When the weapon was ready he put the cartons back in the box and stood up. He slid the rifle inside his coat, barrel down, and held it in place with his right arm and then picked up the box with his left. It felt awkward, but it wouldn't be for long.

★   ★   ★

394

MacDermott ran a towel through her red hair. The shower had helped, she was more relaxed now and the hot water had made her feel a little cleaner, on the outside anyway. She jumped as the doorbell buzzed. Fisher frowned. It wasn't the bell at the entrance to the main security door, it was the doorbell, which meant that whoever was ringing was already inside the building, outside the flat. He motioned to McCormick to pick up the gun as he moved towards the door. McCormick took the automatic in his hand, clicked off the safety and held it under the table.

Fisher walked down the hallway on tiptoe. He put his eye to the security viewer and a distorted Oriental face looked back, grinning. Fisher saw the man press the doorbell again and it buzzed. The man was holding a box with what looked to be cartons of Chinese food.

'What do you want?' Fisher shouted through the door.

'You order Chinese food?' said the man.

'No, you must have the wrong flat,' Fisher shouted back.

'I not hear you,' the man said.

'Wrong flat,' Fisher repeated, his eye still pressed to the peep-hole.

He could see the Oriental shake his head and step back, looking confused. 'I not hear you,' he said.

Fisher reached for the lock and turned it. 'It's OK,' he called to the others. 'Some guy trying to deliver a Chinese take-away. He's got the wrong flat, that's all.' He unlocked the door and turned the handle, stepping to the side as he did. In the lounge, McCormick relaxed and took his finger off the trigger of his gun. O'Reilly grinned and patted his chest with the flat of his hand.

MacDermott began drying her hair again and then

suddenly stopped, her heart pounding as realisation hit her like a kick in the chest. She gasped for breath, her mind whirling as if she was falling from a great height, full of images of Woody's Chinaman, the man on the trail of the IRA, knowing that he was the man outside the door but unable to form the words that she could shout as a warning. All she could think to yell was 'No! No! No!' and her screams echoed around the flat, startling them all. McCormick flinched and began to get out of his chair as Nguyen kicked the door open, sending Fisher sprawling across the hallway.

Nguyen threw down his box and grabbed for the Kalashnikov, swinging the barrel up at waist level. He stepped into the hallway and kicked Fisher, knocking him away from the door, keeping him off balance so he wouldn't be able to get a good look at the gun. Over Fisher's shoulder he saw a man at a table, pushing himself to his feet and pointing a handgun towards him. 'Drop the gun!' shouted Nguyen, aiming his useless replica at the man's chest and stepping forward. The man looked confused and began to lower the weapon.

'We have another target in the flat,' said the Colonel's voice in Joker's ear, calmly and controlled. 'I repeat, there are now five in the flat. Three in the lounge, two in the hall.' There was a pause, and then he spoke again. 'One of the targets in the hallway has an assault rifle. OK, Joker, we have a clear shot at the men in the hall. We'll take them both out from here. Jump on my command.' Another pause, enough for three heartbeats. 'Go!' said the Colonel. 'Go, go, go!'

Joker and Ginge dropped together, and a fraction of a

second after they let go of the rail they heard the double crack of two high velocity rounds splitting the air.

To Joker it seemed that time slowed right down as they pushed themselves out and twisted in the air, knees slightly bent to absorb the shock. They hit the ground together and slipped their fingers over the triggers of their MP5s. It took a fraction of a second for Joker's brain to register the scene in the room. There were three of them, two men and a girl, and they all had their backs to the window. The man on the couch was halfway up, the woman was holding a towel over her mouth. The man at the table had a gun in his hand. All were looking at the hallway where a blond-haired man was slumped against the wall, his hand clutched to his blood-smeared chest, obviously just seconds from death. Another man, an Oriental, stood in the hallway with what looked like a Kalashnikov in his hands and blood pouring from a wound in his shoulder. The man's mouth was opening and closing and he had a look of amazement on his face. He saw Joker, saw the MP5 and then looked down at his own gun as if seeing it for the first time. Joker fired instinctively and put three bullets into the man, two in the chest and one in the head, sending him slamming backwards.

The man at the table began to turn but before he could bring his gun up Ginge hit him with four rounds. Joker took out the man on the couch before he even turned round and he died without knowing what had hit him.

Joker stepped into the room first, followed by Ginge, and Jacko and Bunny dropped down behind them. The girl began to stand up but Ginge pushed her back down. 'You fucking Brit bastard!' she screamed, and Ginge slapped her so hard that she was almost knocked out of the chair. A thin dribble of blood ran down her chin. Her eyes blazed and she stood up, her hands hooked like claws, and she lashed out at Ginge's eyes. He swayed backwards, easily avoiding her attack, and prodded her in the stomach with the barrel of his gun. She doubled up, gasping for breath and retching, and Ginge threw her back into the chair.

'Stay where you are you fucking bitch or you're dead!' he warned. He kept the gun trained on her while Joker moved along the hall, stepping over the bodies of the two men, checking the kitchen, bathroom and three bedrooms. Jacko and Bunny moved behind him. They were a well co-ordinated team, they'd spent hundreds of hours training together in the killing house at Hereford, breathing in lead fumes and smoke as they pumped round after round into cardboard cut-outs of Russian storm-troopers. Compared with the killing house, this was a breeze.

'Clear,' said Joker when he was satisfied.

'You have the girl?' the Colonel's voice asked.

'Secured,' said Ginge.

The Oriental groaned, murmured something in a language none of the men could understand, and then went still, blood seeping from between his lips, his chest a mess of mangled flesh and pieces of ribcage.

The three SAS men joined Ginge in the lounge. Jacko and Bunny checked the bodies while Joker began to search the room, quickly and efficiently. He found the Semtex in a cupboard below a bookcase in the lounge, along with some detonators and several electric clocks. In a walk-in cupboard in the hall, by the front door, he found an empty box that once contained a laptop computer. Inside the box was an instruction manual, still sealed in its polythene wrapping, and pieces of plastic-coated wire. He took it into the lounge and threw it at the girl's feet.

'What's this?' he shouted. 'Is this the next bomb, you Irish whore?' His words came out in short, staccato bursts like bullets from his MP5.

The Bombmaker wiped the back of her hand across her mouth, smearing the blood across her lips like a manic clown's make-up. 'Fuck off,' she said. 'And I'm Scottish you ignorant bastard.' Joker stamped on her instep and she screamed in pain. As she bent down to rub her foot Joker slammed his fist into her face and she hurtled back into the chair. Tears streamed down her cheeks and she covered her face with her hands. Ginge grabbed her hair and yanked her head back.

Joker put his face up close so that she could smell his breath. 'Listen you bitch. We've killed your friends and unless you talk to me you can join them.'

He nodded at Ginge and he dragged her by the hair over to where Fisher lay face down in a pool of his own blood. Ginge threw her on top of the body and rubbed her face in the blood. Joker walked over and kicked her in the back, over her kidney where he knew the pain would be excruciating.

'Get her on her knees,' Joker said, and Ginge hoisted her up by her hair. Joker stood in front of her and levelled the gun at her mouth.

She shook her head from side to side. 'You're too late,' she whispered.

'Stand to the side,' Joker said to Ginge. 'I'm going to blow her fucking head off.' Ginge moved from behind her and Bunny and Jacko went to stand by the window.

'There's nobody who'll know that you didn't die when

we stormed the flat,' he told her menacingly. 'There are no witnesses. This isn't going to be another Gibraltar.'

'You're too late,' she said. 'It's set to go off in less than five minutes. They won't be able to land in time.'

'A plane?'

'No shit, Sherlock.' She cleared her throat and spat down on the floor, not to insult him but because her mouth was filling up with blood and saliva.

'Which plane?'

She was talking now, because she figured that whatever she told him it wouldn't make a difference. She wanted him to know, and to know that there was nothing he could do to stop it. She told him it was a special flight to Rome, that a journalist called Ian Wood was carrying the bomb, and that everybody on board the flight was as good as dead. She began to laugh sourly until Joker hit her on the side of her head with his gun as Ginge began relaying the information to the Colonel.

Woody was on his fourth whisky when the 'fasten seat-belt' light went on and the front of the plane dipped down.

'Ladies and gentlemen, this is the captain speaking. There is some turbulence ahead and we are descending to avoid it. Please make sure your seat is upright and your seat-belt is fastened.'

Woody frowned. He'd flown often enough to know that the normal procedure was to fly over bad weather, not under it. He fastened his seat-belt and sipped his whisky. Better to drink it rather than to take the risk of spilling it, he decided.

'Would passenger Ian Wood please make himself known to the cabin crew,' said the captain. Woody didn't realise at first that it was his name that had been called, but he heard it when the message was repeated. The plane had gone into a steep descent and the stewardesses were briskly moving down the aisles checking that seats were upright and passengers strapped in. Woody could also see that they were scanning the passengers to see if anyone was reacting to the final announcement. He waved to a pretty blonde stewardess. She came over, eyebrows raised.

'I'm Ian Wood,' he said. The woman in the seat next to him was openly listening, curious to know what he'd done.

'Mr Wood, do you have any baggage in the hold?' the stewardess asked briskly. Woody could tell from her tone that something was very badly wrong, so he answered immediately, suppressing his first instinct to make a joke.

'No,' he said. There was a cold feeling of dread in his stomach.

'Could you give me all the cabin baggage you have, please,' she said. She was smiling but he could tell that it was an act to put him at his ease and get his co-operation, the girl was frightened shitless. So was Woody.

'Oh God,' he moaned, and reached between his legs to pick up his bag.

The bomb exploded.

Joker and Ginge kept Maggie covered as they waited for instructions from the Colonel. They had made her lie face down on the bloodstained carpet next to Fisher, with her hands clasped behind her neck. She had a good body, thought Joker. Good legs, firm arse, just the way he liked a woman to be. He looked at his watch.

The Colonel's voice spoke in his left ear. 'The plane

has gone down. We assume with all lives lost. Operation is discontinued. No loose ends. I repeat, no loose ends.'

Joker looked across at Ginge to see if he had heard. Ginge nodded and made a small motion with his MP5, his way of saying that Joker could do the honours. Joker fired once into her back, just over where her heart was.

She didn't die straightaway, they never did. In books they often said that people who were shot died before they hit the ground. It never happened that way, Joker knew. Joker had killed people in Belfast, in the Falklands, in the Middle East, and once in Spain, and he'd yet to see anyone die straightaway, no matter where they were shot. If the bullet went through the heart or the lungs then the brain kept sending out messages for up to a minute or so before their eyes glazed over and they finally died. If they were shot in the head and the brains were splattered over the floor, then the heart continued to pump and the limbs twitch for a while until they realised that it was all over. That's what it was like in real life. Not many people knew the difference between death in books and movies and death in real life. But Joker knew.

When the bullet tore through her back and punched a ragged hole in her chest, her arms flailed out and she grunted. Some time after that she died in a pool of blood, her arms and legs drumming against the floor, saliva dripping from her mouth and panic in her eyes. Joker didn't stand over her and watch while she died, he stood with his back to her, looking out over the river as he waited for the banging and wheezing to stop. Slow deaths always embarrassed him.

Jon Simpson stayed late in his office so that he could see the second editions before going home. His own paper wasn't printed for another seventy-two hours but he wanted to see how the dailies treated the bombing of the jet and the SAS operation against the IRA bombers. News of the bombings had broken too late for the papers to do much in their first editions, though most had managed to get in a few pars.

A copy boy came through the double doors with a stack of papers under his arm and dropped them on to the desk. Simpson separated the tabloids from the broadsheets and went through them first: the *Sun*, the *Daily Mirror*, the *Daily Mail*, the *Daily Express*, the *Daily Star* and *Today*. They all had pictures of the wreckage in the sea, and the head-shots of the active service unit. They had all used the girl Bombmaker's photograph big on their front pages because that was the obvious one to go for, and both the *Express* and the *Mail* had used Woody's picture on the front along with the story of how he'd been duped into carrying the bomb.

Yeah, Simpson thought, that's how he'd do it. The bombing, the betrayal, the SAS operation on the front, along with the girl's picture. Inside, backgrounders on the bombing campaign and the SAS, biogs of the bombers and lots of political reaction. A great story, just a pity that it hadn't happened on a Saturday night. The two pictures of Woody looked up at Simpson. Simpson shook his head sadly. 'Well, Woody, you finally made the front page,' he said to himself. He gathered the papers up and took them home to read in detail.

The call to attend the meeting in Whitehall came as Bromley was reading the morning papers at his breakfast table. The bombing of the jet was on the front of every paper, along with a graphic account of the SAS operation against the bombers in Wapping. From the amount of detail in the reports it was obvious that Ministry of Defence press officers had been hard at work pushing the Government line. There was no mention of The Chinaman in any of the stories. His life, and death, would remain a secret for ever. Another basic fact missing from all of the stories was how the authorities had managed to locate the active service unit. Intelligence, was the nearest thing to an explanation. The press officers knew exactly how to handle the Press, to spoonfeed them with more information than they could handle so that they'd forget to ask the basic questions.

He put his jacket on, kissed his wife on the cheek and went out to the garage to check the underside of his car. He peered through the driver's window to check that the onboard detection device showed that his car hadn't been tampered with and when he was satisfied he took several steps backwards and clicked a small remote-control device that started the car automatically. Only when he was satisfied that his car was safe did he unlock the door and get in. The safety precautions were second nature to him, and had been long before the car-bomb deaths of Airey Neave and Ian Gow.

The early morning phone call meant that he'd have to completely reschedule his day, but a call from the Co-ordinator of Intelligence and Security took precedence over everything else. The Co-ordinator answered to only two higher authorities – the Prime Minister and the Permanent Secretaries Committee on the Intelligence Services. His main role in life was to ensure that all the different intelligence agencies worked together, an uphill struggle at the best of times.

Bromley was one of the last to arrive at the conference room and he eased himself into an empty chair. The room was almost filled by a long, oval table of highly polished mahogany around which sat many familiar faces, several of whom nodded to Bromley. The room itself was typical Whitehall, an ornate fireplace, a smattering of respectable oil paintings in gilded frames and fussy patterned carpets. The man who stood at the head of the table was also typical Whitehall, pin-stripe suit, crisp white shirt, dark-blue tie, neatly combed hair that was greying at the temples, ramrod-straight back behind which were clasped hands with immaculately manicured nails. The Co-ordinator was a career civil servant for whom the fight against terrorism was merely a stepping stone to the knighthood that he regarded as his birthright, but he was every bit as committed to the task as the men who sat waiting for him to speak. They represented, Bromley knew, the cream of the country's anti-terrorism agencies, though he was some-what surprised to see that there were no heads present, they were all number twos or personal assistants to the chiefs. They were all grim-faced, most had lost colleagues or friends on the doomed flight. He recognised represen-tatives from MI5 and MI6, the Defence Intelligence Staff, several members of his own Anti-Terrorist Branch, and there were men he didn't know. Some were high-ranking police officers, others were men with military haircuts and bearing who he guessed were SAS or SBS.

There were no name-cards identifying those present, nor was there any writing equipment on the table – just a few crystal jugs of water and upturned glasses. There were, he noticed ruefully, no ashtrays.

One or two latecomers filed through the double doors

leading to the room, smiling apologies at the Co-ordinator. As they took their places two men in dark suits went out, closing the doors behind them.

'Gentlemen,' said the Co-ordinator, 'thank you for coming. Let me say first that no notes are to be taken of this meeting, and it must not be the subject of any memos or written reports. You should also not record this meeting in your diaries. This meeting never took place. Is that understood?'

He waited for all the men to nod acceptance.

'Thank you. This is by way of a briefing for the various security and intelligence services, and for those police authorities which will be affected by what I am about to tell you. You are free to verbally brief your superiors on the nature of this meeting, but there is to be no down-the-line transfer of the information. This, as you will appreciate when I have finished, is on a need-to-know basis. And those with a need to know are a very, very select group.'

He had the undivided attention of every man in the room now. There was no fidgeting, no coughing, no one looked anywhere except at the face of the Co-ordinator.

'You will all have heard about the horrifying events of yesterday evening. Tragic, absolutely tragic. It did, however, bring about the demise of the active service unit which has been behind the recent atrocities, and for that we are all grateful to Special Branch and to the SAS.' He nodded to representatives of both organisations, including Bromley.

'As you know, one hundred and thirty-six people died in yesterday's plane crash. That includes twelve children and three nuns, as well as the Members of Parliament and civil servants who were on the flight. The public backlash against the IRA has already started. Not just in the Press, though obviously all the newspapers are clamouring for something to be done, including the normal misguided calls for the return of the death penalty. It goes beyond that. This time there is a groundswell of public opinion against the IRA, a feeling that something should be done, that something must be done.'

He paused again, looking round the table at the men who were hanging on his every word. 'Gentlemen, we have here a window of opportunity. Our experts tell us that the reaction against the terrorists will be at fever pitch for the next ten days, possibly two weeks. When the IRA hits a soft target, or kills innocent bystanders, they normally follow quickly with a highly visible attack on a legitimate target. It restores their credibility, as it were. Public opinion is notoriously fickle, but this time they have gone too far. Now, we around this table know that it was a rogue IRA active service unit responsible for the bombing campaign, that in fact it had not been sanctioned by Belfast or Dublin. That information has been kept from the Press. So far as the public is concerned it was an official IRA operation.

'The decision was taken late last night, at the highest level, to take positive action against senior members of the IRA and Sinn Fein. Over the next seven days the top echelons of the organisation will be eliminated, at a time when public opinion will be totally, one hundred per cent, against them. That is the window of opportunity I spoke about. Anything we do now, right now, will have the unqualified backing of the public. This is not, I repeat not, a shoot-to-kill policy. It is a shoot-to-kill operation. A one-off. We have drawn up a list of the twenty-five men, and women, who we see as being the key members of the IRA, without whom we feel the organisation would no longer be a viable terrorist force. A combined, and highly secret, task-force of SAS and SBS operatives will move against them. Wherever possible it will be made to seem like an accident, a car crash, a drugs overdose, a fall downstairs, but if it cannot be done tidily it will be a straight-forward assassination made to look as if it is the work of Protestant extremists. Once the operation is over, the IRA will no longer be an effective threat. Then we can take them on using more legitimate methods, including the formation of a new Anti-Terrorist Task-Force, a single national task-force to counter terrorism. That, however, will be the subject of further meetings later this month. Now, are there any questions?'

Most of the men sitting around the table seemed stunned, though Bromley knew that they would all wholeheartedly support the plan put forward by the Co-ordinator. Most of them had privately been pushing for such a policy for many years, determined that the only way to defeat the IRA was to match their ferocity.

'I would appreciate it if you would confine your comments to questions,' the Co-ordinator continued. 'This is not a discussion forum, there is nothing to be voted on, no consensus is needed. The decision has already been taken at a much higher level. The highest level.'

One of the uniformed police officers coughed and raised his hand. 'When does the operation start?' he asked.

The Co-ordinator looked at a slim gold watch on his wrist. 'It started ten minutes ago,' he said quietly.

Another hand went up. One of the MI6 representatives. 'Can we be told who is on the list?' he asked.